KUTRI

Blake Rudman

A HellBound Books Publishing LLC Book

A HellBound Books LLC
Publication
Copyright © 2023 by HellBound Books Publishing LLC
All Rights Reserved

Cover and art design by Tee N Art
For HellBound Books Publishing LLC

No part of this book may be reproduced, stored in a retrieval system, or transmitted by any means, electronic, mechanical, photocopying, recording or otherwise without written permission from the author
This book is a work of fiction. Names, characters, places and incidents are entirely fictitious or are used fictitiously and any resemblance to actual persons, living or dead, events or locales is purely coincidental.

www.hellboundbooks.com

Dedicated to my beautiful daughter, Selah, as this book was written during COVID-19 when you were a magical hopeful thought soon to be a reality. You're a supreme blessing, and the world is your oyster.
Love, Dad

KUTRI

Chapter One: The Big Event

Beneath a sheet of transparent glass, the swimming pool of the historic mansion had been stocked with bioluminescent jellyfish, forming a living, moving stage at the center of a small amphitheater. Sparks of rainbow light danced beneath the feet of the wedding party, who stood in the heart of the stage, the chief of bliss (a purely ceremonial position) speaking in hushed tones to the bride and groom. Overhead lighting was provided by glowing metallic spheres that hovered high above the stage within a magnetic field. Pairs of spheres orbited one another like binary stars, their movements synchronous but isolated; the pairs of spheres never touched.

Jakob Freeman wasn't sure this was the right message to send the broadcast audience. He had spoken with the director, voicing his concerns on behalf of his employer, the Los Angeles Office of Bliss. The director had promised to pass on his observations to the Studio show runners. That had gone nowhere; either the director had failed to follow through or the Studio had disagreed. Whatever the reason, the spheres had been left to whirl in inharmonious isolation, keeping their distance.

Aside from the psycho-sexual implications of the spheres, Jakob was charmed with the scene. He tried to relax and set aside his misgivings, if not for his own sake, then for his colleague and mentor, Sven Thomson, who had been instrumental in arranging this night's climactic episode of *Good Breeding*. Like Jakob, Sven was a matchmaker. He had been instrumental in selecting the bride from the seven on offer, then shepherded her as she whittled down her selection of suitors to one perfect groom. The wedding's setting, decorations, and supporting cast had all been arranged by the Studio, but it had been Sven who ensured the stars of the show were the best they could be.

The bride was exquisite. Precisely standard height for her racial derivation, which actually made her taller than most men, Miss Aluel Garang's hair had been woven with invisible supports to form a peaked halo above her cherubic face, like the pip on an ace of spades . . . or an inverted heart. (Jakob made a mental note of that inversion to go with his observation about the solitary spheres of light.) Her neck, a long, muscular marvel unique to her phenotype, had been left bare by the production designers, apart from a pair of slender golden bands. This was an excellent choice, in Jakob's opinion, as was the gold netting that barely covered her breasts.

Jakob couldn't remember seeing perkier nipples. Some of their excellence was due to the contracting compound the production designer had applied, but useful as the chemical was for warding off droop on the warm Beverly Hills night, it was genetics and Aluel's fitness that deserved most of the credit for the opulent brown spheres. They were wonderful, and Jakob reluctantly focused away from them to take in the rest of her ensemble: a wide golden belt, cream-colored skirt, and gladiator sandals that completed the outfit.

The outfit had been handed down from the last bride of North African ancestry, but Aluel wore it more gracefully. She was a gem of a bride, and her pearlescent smile shone like a jewel in a splendid crown.

The groom, Kirimi Teng, was equally good looking. He wore a suit of European style and cut. Jakob was always disappointed when the production designers based their fashion choices on convenience instead of ethnicity. Though the young man had been born in a Pan-Sylvanian commune, never setting foot on African soil, Sven had championed Kirimi specifically because of his 97 percent hereditary match with Aluel. It seemed a shame not to highlight the advantage and dress him in something that matched his bride's costume.

At least the designers had put thought into the suit's color. The pale blue evoked the prewar sky. Every man in the audience, from the officemen present in person to the ditch diggers watching the wedding at home, had dreamed of a sky like that since they'd first seen a depiction of it in school. It hardly mattered—a complimentary color was all a groom needed. No one cared what he looked like, so long as his skin was the same shade as his betrothed's.

How little the common man knew of the difficulties matchmakers like Sven and Jakob faced season after season! All the more reason for them to stick together. Jakob caught sight of Sven in the back row of the small live audience section and moved to sit next to the older man.

"A triumph," he said as he folded his lanky frame into the seat between Sven and Dr. Clyde Staley, the director of the LA Office of Bliss. "Well done, Sven."

Sven gave a seated bow. "My dear Freeman, one does what one can. When it works, like tonight, praise Big Dad in the Sky."

Jakob said, "Amen."

Dr. Staley clasped his artificial right hand in his natural left in a pretense of prayer. "Amen. Praise be. Amen."

The director of LA Bliss was Jakob and Sven's superior in rank, if not in intellect. Normally, he would have been seated next to Sven, in order to honor him as man of the hour, but the doctor had a reputation for "loosening his tie" on social occasions, and Jakob had agreed to keep an eye on him while Sven enjoyed his moment.

"Look," said Dr. Staley, nodding. "I do believe that bridesmaid is giving me the eye."

Jakob followed the gesture to the group of wedding attendants gathered at the edge of the pool. The "maid" in question was a handsome youth, one of four beardless boys wearing ankle-length dresses styled to match the bride's. They had naturally been selected for their soft, adolescent features, but Clyde's favorite looked particularly androgynous. An ethnic Yamato, his painted face and fan-shaped hair identified him as an apprentice geisha. Typical of the old pervert to pick out the sole professional in a host of amateurs.

Sven said, "He's not looking at *you*, Clyde. Sorry, but you'll have to get your fun in the usual way—by paying for it. I do believe he's looking at our handsome young friend."

Jakob flushed.

Clyde faked astonishment. "You're so cynical, Sven. You speak as if love and lust were indistinguishable."

This got a chuckle from Sven. "My dear doctor," he said, "it was my understanding love died in the Slow Plague."

"It wounds me to hear you say so," said Clyde. "Look around you. The whole point of this ceremony is to pay homage to love. Doesn't the romance set fire to your soul?"

"I burn for a bright future."

"Hear, hear," Jakob said. "It's a splendid match, Sven."

"It is," Sven agreed. "Gives me hope to see the fruits of a long labor."

The three men watched as the chief of bliss herded the wedding party from the central stage up a fan-shaped ramp to the veranda of the old mansion—the backstage area as it were. The moment they disappeared from sight, electric motors whirred as three camera drones stirred to life, rising into the air above the audience. An amplified voice said, "Everyone face front. Quiet on set. We're going live in three . . . two . . . one! Cue music!"

Music swelled into the evening air, and the light from the floating spheres intensified. The rightmost of a pair of ten-foot-wide video displays, hanging on a scaffold above the swimming pool, flashed the word APPLAUSE! The crowd obeyed. On cue, wedding attendants appeared to line up along the edge of the ramp. The chief of bliss appeared at the top of the ramp and strode to the center of the pool, his deep blue ceremonial robe flowing about him, a beatific smile on his face.

Standing on the giant, gleaming bowl of jellyfish, camera drone all but in his face, he gave his opening spiel over the music, waxing poetic about the bride and groom as the wedding attendants moved through the steps of their choreography, finishing their dance arranged along the edge of the pool, frozen in graceful positions.

The chief beamed and announced that it was his great pleasure to introduce the bride and groom for this season finale. "Here," he announced grandly, "are Kirimi Teng Bol Teng and Aluel Garang!"

The bride and groom appeared side by side and, like the spheres of light above, not touching. The crowd exploded, unprompted, with applause and cheering as the couple moved with unearthly grace to stand before the chief. The three stood, acknowledging the approval, for a full twenty seconds before the applause waned. Jakob was the last to stop clapping.

The chief raised his robed arms and intoned, "The Office of Bliss, may their heads be proudly raised, has certified this couple to be in a state of utmost perfection. This bride, Aluel Garang, is of unrivaled and unimpeachable ancestry. So witness all."

Every man in the audience repeated, "So witness all." With a chill, Jakob imagined the millions of other men, from all over the inhabitable world, raising their voices in agreement.

The chief bowed to the young woman before turning to the groom and saying, "This groom, Kirimi Teng Bol Teng, likewise, is of a lineage of impeccable quality. Kirimi Teng, do you swear to protect the integrity of this woman, to father her many children, and to embody the essence of true stewardship as is owed by a husband to his wife, in obedience to the Office of State, and in full recognition of the penalties that will be assigned to you should you fail?"

At this point, most men would have expressed their excitement with a hearty, "I do!" But Kirimi Teng was silent. The picture being relayed from the camera to the left monitor showed a close-up of the young face. Kirimi wore a closed, almost cold expression—one that Jakob had never seen in private conversation and which was at odds with the young man's usually meek and humble manner. There was nothing humble about him now; he seemed confident and poised.

As Jakob fretted through the slow seconds of delay, he was sure he saw the finely cut, youthful jaw tighten briefly.

The chief cleared his throat. "Mr. Teng, do you swear—"

"Yes," said Kirimi. "Of course. I swear."

The prompter prompted. The audience applauded. The moment of odd hesitation was past.

"Good!" said the chief with perhaps a bit more relief than necessary. "Good." He faced the bride. "And do you, Aluel Garang, swear that you will be faithful to your husband, loyal to your race, and appreciative of the privileges conferred on you by the Offices of Bliss and State? Will you bear as many children as the Great Dad Above shall grant, being sure to notify the Office of State at the first sign of pregnancy, and do you promise to surrender the children freely as the State requires?"

"I do," said Aluel at once. This prompted a spontaneous cheer that Jakob was sure echoed in every country that had signed ISMA—the International Standard for Marriage Administration—the only countries, in fact, to which the wedding was being broadcast.

"So witness all," said the chief.

The audience rumbled, "So witness all."

The chief made a grand gesture, and two of the attendants moved from their static poses to wheel the marque machine down the ramp to the center of the stage. A tapering column of gleaming white plastic, it stood as tall as Kirimi's shoulder and had a transparent horizontal tube at the top. Inside the tube, along the top and bottom surfaces, were a series of laser emitters that would place on the wrists of bride and groom the marque that would join the existing genobrand tattoos that cataloged their DNA.

The chief stared into one of the cameras and announced, "We will now witness the inscribing of the ring."

Aluel appeared on the monitor. She smiled into the camera, her joy at fulfilling her destiny warm enough to melt any chilly heart. Swelling her chest so the nipples trembled, she positioned her arm within the tube and turned her palm up.

Kirimi Teng would now place his arm above hers and grasp her forearm, pressing their wrists together. The upper laser would burn half the brand into the back of his wrist while the lower laser burnt half into hers. From then on, when they joined hands, an unbroken band—a ring— would be seen, to symbolize their union.

But Kirimi didn't move. He held his arm rigidly at his side.

Jakob frowned. Well-concealed stage fright? He had seen nervous grooms before but never one who took reluctance so far. He wondered if the young man's passivity was the result of a drug. Had he been so nervous that someone had seen fit to sedate him?

"What's that blankshooter waiting for?" murmured Dr. Staley. "I would have her skirt off by now."

A man behind them said, "I'd be wearing it for a hat."

A few in the audience emitted a rumble of discontent and some jeers. Jakob glanced at Sven. The Swiss-Canadian's blue eyes remained fixed intently on Kirimi.

"What is it?" said Jakob.

"I'm not sure," said Sven. He got to his feet.

"Are you mad?" Clyde growled.

He reached across Jakob to snag Sven's sleeve, nodding in the direction of the pale adobe walls ringing the swimming pool. The gesture drew Jakob's attention to several figures in glossy black uniforms lingering in the shadows. The featureless, chrome helmets of the Studio hatchetmen made it impossible to tell where they were looking, but as soon as Clyde pointed them out, Sven seemed to feel their gaze. Pretending to straighten his trousers, he resumed his seat.

The chief shifted uneasily, tightened his on-screen smile, and said, "Mr. Teng, clearly you feel the overwhelming awe of this occasion. Will you proceed?"

A hush fell over the audience. Kirimi turned his regal head in the direction of the chief. The camera was at a high angle, but the groom's facial expression was clear: he was puzzled. In a single slow blink, his confusion vanished. Turning from the chief, he addressed the viewers, both present and remote.

"I'm sorry, friends, brother-men. I hesitate only because I am so moved. Such a beautiful woman is my bride. I can't help but be overcome by what she represents. This is a special time. My bride, Aluel, is special to us all."

The camera panned to show Aluel shift demurely, raising her free hand to her heart.

"Isn't she wonderful? A glimpse of coming glory. She can't deny it. You're special, Aluel Garang. You have no idea how special you are."

A sigh went up from the wedding party. The tension that had built during Kirimi's hesitation departed with the sigh. Jakob felt profound relief. How right Kirimi was! Fifty years ago, the architects of the New Society had rescued the seeds of civilization from the dead earth of the Slow Plague and the Twelve Years' War.

Now, Jakob and his fellow men were witnessing a further resurrection of society in the seeds of a glorious future being planted this very night. Kirimi Teng's children, born from the womb of the goddess who delighted them all, would be yet more blossoms on the tree of their pure family lineage. In the children, the work of the past three generations would flower.

As Kirimi reached for the wrist of his betrothed, Jakob held his breath. He felt his brotherhood with every man in the known world—through Kirimi Teng. The feeling was so palpable that Jakob, along with many in the audience, imitated the stretching of Kirimi's hand toward Aluel's arm.

But as his hand hovered over Aluel's forearm, Kirimi's fingers spasmed, and a spatter of blood erupted from the palm of his hand.

Jakob frowned. He had never seen that before. What could it mean? He turned his head, his mouth open to say something to Sven, but the older man surged to his feet, fairly leaping over Jakob and Clyde Staley in his attempt to reach the aisle. Jakob had barely enough time to consider stopping him when a jolt of electric agony froze his muscles. All around him, men stiffened, their eyes going wide with stunned recognition that they were victims of the Civil Obedience Protocol.

Hatchetmen emerged from the shadows, wielding batons with which they were prepared to subdue any man who hadn't been paralyzed when they switched on the COP. They found no targets. Every man born in the last fifty years had been fitted with the Carter-Schnee brain implant that made him subject to COP control. Aside from the hatchetmen, no man should have been able to move or talk in the middle of a lockdown, but Kirimi, visible now from the corner of Jakob's eye, set his bleeding palm on the forearm Aluel had exposed to the machine.

"Do you know why you're special?" he said. "You're a teacher. You're here to teach these fools a lesson." Squeezing his eyes shut, he dragged his palm from the inside of Aluel's elbow to her wrist.

Her scream, caught on the many microphones, was so loud it blurred into white noise. The audience was powerless to react, though the assault on their ears was sharp enough for Jakob to feel it through the fog of Carter-Schnee agony. The image on the monitor, the image broadcast around the world, showed Aluel lunging away from Kirimi. A long, jagged cut had been carved in her smooth skin. Blood gushed from the cut like a split pipe spilling rusty water. If Jakob's stomach muscles had been under his control, he would have gagged.

But the assault was not over. Even as ribbons of scarlet stained Aluel's skirt, Kirimi leapt after the poor girl and flayed her with his bleeding palm.

Jakob couldn't move, couldn't breathe, couldn't close his eyes against the horror. He was powerless against the growing desire to do violence to Kirimi Teng. If he could not kill the man, he would surely explode.

There, in the midst of this new nightmare, his memory assaulted him with another, older one. His young wife on her deathbed. He, standing by her side. He, tucking a strand of lusterless raven hair behind her ear with trembling fingers. Her face, which had been so beautiful, with skin so like rose petals that he had begun to call her that—Rose—had been reduced to a skeletal mask by the disease that was killing her. Her once-sparkling eyes, so like chips of black jet, were sunken and dulled by pain.

He cast the memory out. Why? Why was he remembering this? These were memories he had purposely forgotten, right?

A flash of bright motion caught Jakob's eye. He refocused his eyes on the screen in time to see the apprentice geisha Dr. Staley had noticed fly at Kirimi like a rabid animal. (How was he not frozen?) But the boy was too slight to knock the villain off his feet. Kirimi brushed him away as if he were a fly. Ignoring the boy's attack, Kirimi went at his bride Aluel again, flicking her chin upward with one hand, raising his other bloody hand as if to slash her throat with his invisible weapon. But as he drew back his arm, the audience was released from paralysis. Men surged over the covered swimming pool, the stampede of feet making the jellyfish roil in a mad rush of rainbow colors.

The first men to reach Kirimi threw him to the glass, kicking at and stomping on him in mindless rage.

Knocking the flimsy white folding chairs every which way, Jakob leapt for the stage, eager to join in the mayhem. He knew that in every part of the world, men were shouting, screaming, roaring at their screens. He could imagine their voices so clearly, as if he could hear them from across the Pacific and over the heights of the city's eastern wall. He pushed and shouldered his way through the teeming crowd until finally, at his feet, the former groom Kirimi Teng lay bleeding. Jakob aimed a kick at his thigh. It connected. He then wound up to target Kirimi's torso but was blocked when another of Aluel's avengers dropped on the man's chest and pummeled him, bellowing like a subway train.

Someone else pushed that man aside and took his place. Men traded places to thrash Kirimi again and again until, by the time Jakob had a clear view of Kirimi again, he was an empty sack, unrecognizable as having once been human.

The Civil Obedience Protocol was activated anew, men lost their ability to move, and hatchetmen dragged Jakob away from the wreck that had been a man. He heard a woman moaning and knew that Aluel, the only woman present, was alive. At the moment he registered this, nothing else mattered, but as the hatchetmen maneuvered him through the maze of fallen chairs, he caught sight of Sven sitting rigid in one of the few seats that remained upright.

Tears shone on Sven's cheeks. His shoulders were slumped, his palms turned up on his knees. He was the image of defeat, a building on the verge of collapse. Jakob longed to speak to him, to wrap his arms around him and tell him the horror was not his fault. But that was impossible.

Jakob's escorts dumped him on the mansion grounds in the middle of a vast, sloping lawn whose verdant green was reduced to charcoal gray in the moonlight. As he lay there in the cool grass he could see a bit of the mansion's front portico, a bit of the cobbled, circular driveway and a swath of lawn and plantings, lit tastefully by solar lanterns. All this had been restored and maintained by Little Angel Studio, the juggernaut of broadcasting that had produced *Good Breeding*, operated the Civil Obedience Corps, and administered the city of Los Angeles itself.

Beyond the carefully trimmed grass, behind a row of palm trees that followed the sweep of the drive to the public road, was ruin; jumbles of cracked masonry that had once been mansions every bit as fine as this one lined both sides of the road, which the Studio also maintained. In many of those overgrown driveways sat the rusted-out shells of vehicles that hadn't moved in decades. He could not see the city's perimeter wall.

For the next twenty minutes, all Jakob could do was lie in stiff agony, contemplating the moonlit view. Finally, his COP implant was switched off. He was collected from the lawn and herded, along with a dozen others, into a Studio transport van. He had no idea where they were going but only hoped they might drop him at home to let him sleep off the effects of the COP.

He wondered, as he slumped into his seat in the van, why the hatchetmen had released the audience from the protocols earlier. Why had they allowed the mob to savage Kirimi Teng? He supposed that like most questions he had about life under the New System, they were destined to remain unanswered.

Chapter Two: Miss Chandigarh

The corridors of the Office of Justice were painted a matte dove gray, stingy in its reflection of light. This was for the best, thought the young woman waiting outside the workroom of the first interlocutor of justice. If the corridor had been brighter, it would have been impossible to pretend she couldn't tell what her two brawny guards were thinking.

Though their faces were partly covered by jauntily tilted black berets, clearly they were both assessing her, perhaps fantasizing about what they would do with or to her if they had the opportunity. Possibly they were even picturing themselves on the set of *Good Breeding*, smiling into the lights, reciting the vows, winning the prize.

For her part, Kutri Chandigarh imagined the silent conversation between the two.

The guard to her right—Morris, his badge said—tilted his head. *Want a go?* his face silently spoke.

The guard to her left—Morales—shrugged. *Who wouldn't?*

Morris pursed his lips. *Can we get away with it?*

Morales smirked. *Oh, sure. Who's gonna know?* His eyes made a quick circuit of the several surveillance cameras outside the O of J.

Morris's gaze made the same circuit as he tapped his belt buckle. *I got a buddy in the Security Office . . .*

Kutri Chandigarh wondered how close her imaginary conversation was to reality. She distracted herself from the possible answer by pondering the likelihood of a Morris and a Morales being assigned to escort her to her interview. Perhaps they assigned guards alphabetically.

She feigned a yawn, pretending at a composure that existed only on the surface. The guards made her nervous. Her father had taught her that "man" was just another name for a sentient variety of wolf. As far as her father had been concerned, there had never been and would never be a time she was not some wolf's prey. As a future wife and mother, she was precious, officially protected from harm by every law in the masculine world. But that world was large, her father said, and the men varied in their attention to laws. Laws were pointless if they could not be enforced. It was a mistake to put trust in them.

"The only thing you can trust is yourself," her *pita jee* had told her, which was why she had hidden a selection of hair pins, not only in her hair, but in the folds of her sari. The refugees from her cosmetics kit ranged from the length of her middle finger to the length of her hand from heel to fingertip. They were made of hardwood, metal, even glass. She had filled hours on her voyage across the Pacific jabbing the pins into balls of fabric shaped to resemble men's eyes. In a pinch, she knew of other soft spots on a man's body that her pins could reach. If either man in the corridor tried something, she was ready to blind him before he could catch her wrist. Her bunk on the freighter *Scotus* had been narrow, but not so narrow she couldn't practice jabbing eyeballs. She found that if she held two pins in each fist, poking from between her fingers, she was quite formidable.

She thought *pita jee* would be proud of her if he knew where she was today. She hadn't seen him, or her mother, since she was ten.

The guard on the left tapped two fingers together. The other guard made a scrubbing motion. *One hand washes the other?* The young woman's fingers found a pin in the fabric over her left hip. She twirled the shank to spin it loose.

"The first interlocutor will see you now," said a voice from above. It had come from a speaker over the office door, which belonged to the first interlocutor's assistant, a Mr. Torell. This functionary had lectured her briefly before putting her in the charge of her guards. A bit of an oaf, he had given no indication of appreciating her danger, though she had done her best to hint at it with glances.

"Thank you," she called to the ceiling. Probably there was no microphone on this end of the public address, but it made little difference to her if Torell could hear or not.

The guard on her left opened the door. His thwarted conspirator waved her inside. As she passed beyond their reach, she held her head high, but she also kept her fingers wrapped around the shank of the pin until the door closed firmly behind.

Unlike the paint in the corridor, the paint on the workroom walls had a sheen. As she had speculated, light reflecting off the shiny surface made the room brighter, though not any less gray. The first interlocutor of justice, Alec Simmons, had worked his way up from junior clerk to his current exalted position, according to the oaf Torell. Perhaps he considered color an extravagance, having spent so long roving the gravelly halls.

In addition to the walls, the floor and ceiling and the desk and chair at the far end of the workroom were all gray. From a distance of four meters, the suit the first interlocutor was wearing appeared to be of a slightly lighter gray than its surroundings. The contrast made her think of a storm cloud at twilight, or a dingy vein of quartz cutting across granite. Simmons himself was bald, pale, and angular, with eyes like flakes of lead bracketing a narrow nose. He was not the sort of man she would have approached at a whim, much less one she would have entrusted with the key to her future, if she had had any choice, which of course, she did not.

But he did appear intelligent—fiercely so. Torell had waxed poetic about his superior during their brief exchange.

"An exceptional man. Practically the only man for the job," he had said.

He had gone on to explain that most men were psychologically unfit to handle the responsibility that was the first interlocutor's meat and bread. With a stroke of a pen, Alec Simmons could elevate a window washer to eminence or reduce a conapt engineer to a subsistence wage. Naturally, he never abused his power.

"No man lives in a vacuum," Torell had continued. "There's not an officeman who can gainsay an interlocutor's judgment, but there are some who could make our lives less pleasant. The Office of Finance controls the purse strings, you know, and the Office of State handles security." He had glanced warily at her guards then, and added, "Naturally, we're pleased with the arrangement."

Now, as she stood waiting for the esteemed Simmons to speak, she wondered if he would endorse his assistant's statement. The leaden eyes seemed incapable of being pleased with anything. Sitting with elbows on the arms of the gray chair, fingers steepled and chin hovering above the fingers, Simmons was like a judge about to call for an execution. She wondered what had brought on his murderous mood.

In a voice she was sure was higher than he liked, he said, "You are Kutri Chandigarh?"

With a slight bow, she answered, "No."

The first interlocutor was taken back. He riffled through some papers, the only items on the desk apart from a lamp and the intercom speaker that presumably connected him to the outside world.

"You can't be anyone else," he said. "I was told to expect Miss Chandigarh."

She said, "I am called Chandigarh, but that is not my name. My name is Kutri. It is my only name. Chandigarh is the city where I was . . . found." And perhaps abandoned. She knew her family name, of course, but hadn't spoken it since she'd wandered, lost and tearful, around a marketplace desperately seeking her *pita jee*. He'd had business there, he said, and told her she should wait for him by a fountain. But he never came back for her, and she was unsure to this day whether he was alive or dead. The people who found her seemed kind and promised to search for her father, but she long suspected they never had.

"Irregular," said Simmons. He shuffled the papers before setting them aside in a heap. "I am attempting to confirm my papers. Do you deny you are the person called in my papers Miss Chandigarh?"

"I do not."

"Good. Then you are Miss Chandigarh." He attempted to dismiss the comment with a wave of his hand.

"I would prefer to be called Kutri."

Bending forward over clasped hands, he arched an eyebrow. "Young lady, I am unlikely to call you anything once we have concluded this interview. Can you accept that your preference is noted, whether I honor it or not?"

The sari Kutri wore was made of silk. Its color was honey gold, with a trim of carnelian red. A thousand glistening pearls orbited the breasts and hips in a style Kutri herself had patterned to be provocative. She was sure the first interlocutor was not immune to her charms. Few men were, and a catch in the high-pitched voice made her sure its owner was no exception. Simmons wanted to appear indifferent and was perhaps fighting to make appearance a reality, but he had no special defense against her assault.

Fixing him with a smile, she decided to attack head-on. Her headscarf came off at a tug, and she shook free the jet black braid that swirled to her bare midriff. With an upward tilt of her head and a flash of white teeth, she compelled him to meet her eyes, which were amber, and which she could shut slowly and let flutter open, lifting and enlivening them with a knowing smile.

"Please," she said, "call me Kutri."

Simmons cleared his throat. "Fine. I will. That's fine. Miss Kutri it is. Do you know who I am?"

"Of course. You are the first interlocutor of the Office of Justice. Mr Torell tells me your name is Alec Simmons." She bobbed a curtsy. "Is my pronunciation correct?"

"It's fine, fine."

"Thank you. I am an educated woman, First Interlocutor, but it is difficult for me to tell, since I have not traveled, if I have been well instructed."

He cleared his throat again. "Do you know why you have been sent to me?"

Kutri placed a hand on her hip, simply to see him fidget. "As I understand, you are to approve or disapprove of me as a candidate for *Good Breeding*."

Simmons smiled at the chance to correct her, which she had given on purpose. "That's not quite right. I am empowered to approve or disapprove your stay in Los Angeles. Since you are here to be a candidate on *Good Breeding*, I suppose it amounts to the same thing."

She laughed, almost a giggle. "So it does. Please, I am determined to stay. Tell me what I must do to ensure I may."

The gray man cleared his throat. "Your papers are in order. There are only a few questions I must have you answer. Do please answer truthfully."

"Of course, First Interlocutor. I always do."

After Simmons had riffled through his papers, they got started. He said, "According to this report, your standard genobrand registers you as 98.785 percent pure Punjabi. Is that correct?"

"So I am told," she replied.

He rapped the papers on the desk. The impact made a surprising clatter in the quiet room. "Kutri, we will make slow progress if you give less than definite answers."

"I'm sorry. I was trying to be truthful, as you said."

"Perhaps I was unclear. By truth, I meant the truth I wish to hear. Nothing else is relevant."

His display of yellow teeth made Kutri wish she could turn away. She suppressed the impulse to shudder. "Excuse my confusion. Yes. 98.785 percent."

The rest of the interview was as bland as the porridge she had been served on the *Scotus* for breakfast. Kutri could barely stifle real yawns by the time the questioning was over. Simmons offered her neither a chair nor refreshment but pestered her with questions about details of her life she was sure were written down. They were likely attested in triplicate and each copy signed by her parents! Simmons seemed to enjoy making her squirm, which was normal enough. Most men did.

He asked if she had been found in the Women's Market of Chandigarh at about the age of nine or ten. She had. He asked if her birth date was unknown because she had come from the Hindustan outlands, where not every marriage included a vow of loyalty to New Society rules. That was the case. The Hindustan Bliss Center had inducted her into their Genesis Program when they found her to be of exceptionally rare genetic stock. For the seven years since that day, she had been privately tutored by the Center's director of bliss.

"He insisted I learn at his knee," Kutri told the first interlocutor. She couldn't but twist her mouth as she said it.

"Well, he would have," said Simmons, missing her tell.

It did not serve Kutri's purpose to educate him in the ways of the world, if he did not already know, so she said no more on the subject. The first step in being selected as the next star of *Good Breeding* was going brilliantly. If all the influential men she had to deal with proved as malleable as Simmons, she was all but assured a spot on *Good Breeding*.

Aboard the *Scotus*, she had watched the terrible events of the final night of Aluel Garang's tenure as *Good Breeding*'s match bride. How she had shivered when Aluel bled! Blood appalled her in general, and blood spilled by violence in particular. Long before the brutes in the audience finished dealing with Kirimi Teng, she had retreated from the ship's lounge, pressing a palm over her mouth.

The dreadful crime of that night did not stop her wanting to be Aluel's successor, however. From the first time she had seen an episode of Little Angel Studio's number one broadcast program, which happened to be her first night at the Hindustan Bliss Center, she had fashioned herself after the confident women onscreen. She loved their proud bearing and their expensive clothes. She was unsure how many liters of blood it would take to wash that love away, but it was more than she had seen from Aluel.

For twenty minutes, Simmons asked her question after question. At long last, he cleared his throat before saying, "Fine. That's all, or nearly all." Slowly, he pushed back from the desk. As he rose, Kutri was careful to avert her eyes from his trousers. It wouldn't do to call attention to prominence in that area, or any lack thereof.

"You are slated to speak with the second interlocutor in eleven minutes," said Simmons. Folding his hands behind his back, he stepped around the desk. "In the time we have left, you may remove your clothes."

Kutri took a step back. "I'm sorry. Did you say—" There was no need to complete the question. His straight back and thin mouth showed he meant what he said. She had misread the rigid paper shuffler. He was no cold-blooded creature but a man hiding his fire. Only the hiding made him different from the rest.

"Go on," he said.

She toyed with the fringe of her sari, wondering if he would look without touching. She was content to flatter the first interlocutor. She was even willing to put on a show. But having put an ocean between her and men who had already abused her, she was firm in her conviction that flattery and show were as far as she would go.

She said, "I refuse."

The first interlocutor was unfazed. "You misunderstand. It's merely procedure. I am expected to examine you, physically, and report my observations."

"The doctors at the Center gave me a thorough going-over, I assure you. Director Paquette, I dare say, noted every imperfection he ever found." Kutri held out her forearm, indicating the coded lines of the genobrand above her wrist. "Here is all you need to know."

"I will decide my own needs, thank you."

"Mr. Simmons, I have answered your questions truthfully. I tell you the truth now. You will not see me remove my garments. This I swear by Vishnu—by God."

He appeared to consider his options, weighing the pressure he could bring to bear against the trouble she might cause. "Be careful, Miss Chandigarh, what divinities you invoke. Do you know what happens to women who are not selected for pairing by the Los Angeles Office of Bliss?"

"A private marriage, you mean? *With one girl in ten, every daughter's a gem.*" This last was the popular motto that had been pared down from the Canton Doctrine. It referred to the birthrate of one live girl for every nine live boys, the imbalance that had destroyed the World Before, and remained the most bitter legacy of the Slow Plague. Fertile woman were precious. Not one could go to waste.

"No," said Simmons. "You're thinking too narrowly. I'm not talking about your fellow candidates in *Good Breeding*. I mean the mongs, the mixed-breed women whose genetic legacy is of no interest to blissmen. Some of them are sent to the countryside to the men who run the farms that feed our city. Some are not that fortunate. My own mother was such a woman, it pains me to say. Do you know what her life was like? I could tell you. It's a story I know well."

He advanced a step. Kutri would have liked to stand her ground, but his intensity compelled her to retreat.

"I was born in an LA House of Care. Do you know the term? Think of it as a factory, a factory for turning out people. The girls kept in Houses, girls like my mother, are kept pregnant. With the help of modern science, they can be made to carry twins, even triplets. The survival rate is tolerable, though there are limits to what doctors can do."

He advanced again. Again, Kutri retreated.

"When their test detects a female child, they put the mother to bed immediately and make every effort to save the fetus. Once in a blue moon, they're successful. It's convenient when a girl is born in a House, since she never needs to leave. My mother was born there, one of the precious few. She was nursed in the preschool annex, as I was. The difference between us is that I was sent away. Mother stayed, for thirty-six years, in a building that occupies four city blocks. She died of diabetes. So far as I know, she never saw the open sky. Not that it is much of a sight, even now.

"Life for a woman who is of no interest to the Office of Bliss is dull, cramped, and brief. It's not a life you would like. Naturally, it's not a life you could ever have. You're a wonderful genetic specimen. You could never be forgotten by Bliss, unless somehow the record of your existence in this city were somehow lost. And that could, of course, never happen."

For several seconds, he held her eyes in a leaden stare. She would have been intimidated, if not for the faint gleam of moisture visible in the light reflecting off the walls. He was straining to make her believe she was forgettable and that he was the man who could make her forgotten. She didn't believe it. She didn't believe him.

She said, "It would be a sad fate. I am glad it will not be mine."

As he studied her, she kept her back straight. She held herself like a soldier, ready for battle. Years of watching *Good Breeding* had taught her that candidates chosen as match brides tended toward boldness. They were women of influence, of power, and she was going to be one of them. The first interlocutor would have to be a fool to think he could stop her. She did not think he was a fool, but she did slide her hand into a fold of her sari, searching for a pin, in case she was wrong.

Simmons glared a moment longer. At last, he walked back behind his desk. As if nothing at all had happened between them, he asked, "Were you given lunch?"

"I—lunch?"

"It is past noon. You should have been given a box lunch to carry in."

"I have brought nothing but what you see."

"Unacceptable. I'll lodge a complaint with the Office of Transportation. You're scheduled to meet the nutritionist tomorrow, after your meeting with Bliss. I'll see you're fed until then."

"Thank you. Very kind."

"Not at all. Only a fool would squander the good you can do your race by letting you starve, Miss Kutri. I'm not a fool."

Kutri released her pin. "Clearly not."

Having seated himself, the first interlocutor steepled his fingers. "You are quite rare. Quite precious, if I may say so. The Punjabi people are nearly extinct. Very few men exist to perpetuate the line, to say nothing of women. As I understand it, one of your purity has never been found. When I read the report from the Office of Bliss, I was skeptical. There have been false claims of race saviors before. Now that I have met you, I believe you are what everyone hopes you are—the last, best hope for your people."

He summoned her forward by crooking a finger. Leaning across the desk as though his next words were a secret and someone might be listening, he said, "I feel I must warn you. The Los Angeles blissmen have a history of going from strength to strength. But this Teng-Garang business . . . You are slated to work with a matchmaker named Jakob Freeman. I know him personally, and to be honest, I'm sure he's not up to the job."

Kutri pretended to be alarmed, though she could see Simmons was not being honest, despite what he said. "And is there anything you can do about that, First Interlocutor?"

He answered obliquely. "Bliss and Justice are separate offices. But there is a strategy we might try. Are you familiar with chess?"

At the Hindustan Bliss Center, her mastery of the game was nothing short of legendary.

"I've played a bit."

Leaning back, Simmons produced a key from his pocket. He used it to unlock a drawer in his desk. After moving an assortment of items to one side, he produced a pair of rectangular devices that, as far as Kutri was concerned, could not have been more beautiful if they were carved from jade.

"I bought these from a reputable dealer in Rarities Row. An associate at the Office of Records confirmed their authenticity. Have you ever seen a mobile phone?"

"God above, no. Whoever has?"

Doing nothing to disguise his smugness, Simmons said, "It cost me dearly to bring in a technician from the Studio. I closed the book on many favors to get it done, but the end result is worth it, as I'm sure you'll agree."

He pressed a button on what Kutri supposed was the top of the practically mythical device. The screen sparked, warming instantly from black to dark charcoal. Miraculously, it began to shine bright yellow next, displaying text and a trademark, or some such item.

"Can I touch it?" she said without thinking.

"Carefully," he said. He waited while she slowed her breathing.

The warmth of the phone as it touched her fingers made her draw back. He clucked his tongue and waited until she was able to extend a steady hand. He lifted the other phone and switched it on as well.

"That unit and this one," he said, "are adapted to access the repeater system used by the Studio. In the old days, mobile phone signals used to be bounced off the atmosphere. Some were even shot through it to satellites. The dust in the sky makes such a scheme unworkable now. With the repeaters, these units can broadcast and receive from all over LA."

Kutri turned the phone over in her hands, unable to believe she was holding the technological equivalent of the Holy Grail. It took all her reserve to place the phone gently back on the first interlocutor's desk.

"I've seen pictures," she said, "but I never imagined . . . Why do you show me this?"

"I don't merely show, Kutri. I give. Go ahead. Pick it up. The phone is yours, if you want it."

She couldn't stop herself. Scooping up the rectangle, she tilted its glass face to examine the interface from different angles. The tiny icons glowing under glass looked like squares of candy in a shop display, something she had never seen personally but had read about in books.

"Calm down," said Simmons. "If you drop it, it will shatter."

"I could never drop something so wonderful."

"I'm sure you think so. We have a few minutes left. Would you like to know how to place a call?"

She had spoken over a landline a few times, but this was different. Imagining her own voice speaking from the wireless device gave her such a thrill, there was no need for an audible answer.

Simmons said, "You must promise me, first, that if you see any incompetence from Mr. Freeman, or any deviance, any unorthodox behavior that could put you in harm's way, you'll call immediately to let me know. Do you promise?"

Kutri tapped on an icon and laughed at the chirrup from a tiny, animated bird. "Why are you so worried about this Freeman?"

Simmons scowled. "Because he is outside the bounds of my authority, as you will be, once you leave this room. Trust me, I know Freeman. You must keep an eye out. Alert me at the first hint of dangerous behavior from him. Then, and only then, will I have the power to intervene."

"I understand," said Kutri.

"Good. But do you promise?"

The gift of the phone was wonderfully extravagant. Kutri stared at it longingly, dearly wanting to accept. And why not? She didn't know Jakob Freeman, and the first interlocutor seemed content to help her become *Good Breeding*'s next star. That was all that really mattered, in the end; it was her dream. The phone made the dream seem more solid, somehow. Merely holding it seemed to elevate her status in the New Society, though she could naturally never show anyone the priceless treasure.

She said, "Yes. I promise. If Mr. Freeman proves a threat to me in any way, I'll call."

Simmons gave her a smile. He seemed almost friendly. "Excellent. You're an intelligent woman. All your tests proclaim it. If you make good decisions, you'll go far."

Kutri allowed herself a smirk. "Excuse me, but that is what I will not do."

"Eh?"

"I will not go far, Mr. Simmons. I will stay. First as a candidate in *Good Breeding*, then as a match bride. I will stay in the heights to which stars ascend. I will take a husband and my place among the celebrated women of the age. Any help you can render will be appreciated, but please understand, with your help or without, I am here to stay."

Chapter Three: Under a Cloud

The krows were out in force on Wednesday morning. Jakob was used to seeing four or five of the seven-foot-tall, vaguely avian metal frames hovering above Pershing Square as he crossed from the subway station to Bliss HQ. Generally speaking, they didn't haunt the nicer parts of town like they did skid row or the toy district, but only displayed their dangling cargo of mummified corpses to the few parkgoers who picked their way across the litter-strewn concrete by the light of dawn. It was considered unnecessary to remind law-abiding men what deviancy could cost them by dangling the carcasses of sinners in front of them, so the hundred or so krows carrying their grim burdens north along Fifth Street and West along Olive were unusual, to say the least.

The fifth story of every building in LA was dedicated to generating the magnetic field that protected pedestrians from the nuclear fallout that blew over the A-Rad Wall from what had been the state of Nevada. It was along the lofty, invisible corridors of the field that the krows drifted, inviting every man who passed underneath to take stock of his soul.

A resident of the municipality of Los Angeles all his life, Jakob had long ago adjusted to the krows' presence. They didn't make him uncomfortable, only concerned when they massed in large numbers.

He approached a park vendor, who was placing a plastic lid over a fresh rack of bread and asked, "Why so many? Do you know?"

"Don't you watch the news?" asked the vendor. "The president himself is going to read the verdict in the Garang case. We'll need a krow after that."

Jakob frowned. Officially, there was no Garang case. The Office of State had declined to address the tragedy, though a Studio investigation had been underway. If it showed somebody other than Kirimi Teng shared responsibility for Aluel's assault, there could be only one sentence for the crime.

"A public execution," he said to the vendor.

"Of course. You expected a garden party?"

Jakob had never cared for running as a sport, but long legs gave him a natural advantage. Propelled by the conclusion he leapt to, he bounded over the broken concrete, holding his briefcase under his arm. Who could be up for execution on the corner of Fifth and Olive, at the Los Angeles Office of Bliss HQ?

All Monday and Tuesday he had loitered in a drunken fog. The fog had not totally cleared away, even now, so he couldn't tell if the horrible suspicion driving his feet was reasonable or not. If it wasn't, there was no time to waste.

Sven Thomson was the most conscientious matchmaker Jakob had ever known. His credentials as a psychologist were beyond reproof. It beggared belief that any failure on Sven's part could have contributed to Kirimi Teng's violence. Jakob had said as much when the Studio investigators visited his home. Or had he? He cast his memory back, trying to pierce the veil of obliterating booze. The exact words he had used were gone. So were the reactions of the investigators. For all Jakob knew, he had hemmed and hawed through the interview, convincing the Studiomen of Sven's guilt instead of his innocence.

By the time Jakob passed fully into the artificial dusk created by the massing krows, he was panting for breath. A crowd had assembled in front of Gas Company Tower, the home of Bliss HQ. Thrusting his elbows between pairs of gawkers, Jakob said, "Excuse me. Blissman coming through!"

It was his suit, with the double-helix badge of the Office of Bliss emblazoned on the breast pocket, more than his words, that stirred the gawkers to movement. They sneered and grumbled, but they did step aside. In less than a minute, Jakob elbowed his way to the front row of the crowd. He stood ten feet in front of the tower's main entrance, at the foot of a platform that had been constructed atop a sturdy scaffold.

A screen of Studio hatchetmen protected the platform. One said, "Keep back, you mongs" as the crowd shifted to accommodate Jakob. He and the men around him pressed back immediately, opening as much space as they could between themselves and the bullies with blank, helmeted heads. On the chest of every hatchetman was the rectangular device with its array of buttons that Jakob knew all too well. His bones still ached from Sunday's COP freeze. Despite his concern for Sven, he had no wish to revisit the pain.

So he waited, cowed by the hatchetmen, until a metallic whine erupted from a set of speakers attached to either end of the platform signaling the doors of Gas Company Tower to open. A man in a gleaming silver business suit and white kid gloves stepped out. He mounted the stairs to the platform, waving to the crowd the whole way.

Jakob knew his face. Every man did. They had seen President Gerard Flynn smiling down from countless billboards around the city. They had dutifully tuned in every time he made an address on General Station News. Jakob had actually met the celebrated head of Little Angel at an interdepartmental mixer years ago, though he had been too nervous to shake hands.

Flynn raised his arms, beaming at the crowd with his perfect teeth. He didn't settle on any man in particular but gazed across the street at a TV camera mounted in the back of a decades-old Ford pickup. Only one lane of West Fifth was kept clear for wheeled traffic. The other was strewn with brickwork from a derelict hotel. As Jakob pondered the work that had gone into cleaning up the truck's parking spot, a gaffer switched on a spotlight fitted next to the camera. It illuminated Flynn, lengthening the shadow he cast on the wall.

"Friends," said the president, "thanks for coming out."

His voice was not amplified by microphone. It was sent to the cochlea of every man present. This was another benefit of the Carter-Schnee implant. Men equipped with one could listen to official announcements (in fact, they could not help but listen) from up to a city block distant. All eyes locked on Flynn as he spoke. No other sound could be heard, apart from the clank of krows bumping into each other as they bobbed along.

"You know me, friends," said President Flynn. "You know I don't lie. Truth is good for business. You can take what I say to the Office of Finance. The events of last Sunday were shocking. Were you shocked? I was shocked. Every man in the world was shocked. I know, because the last few minutes of last Sunday's broadcast is the most requested clip on the General Station Playback Service. For two days running, we've fielded nonstop calls up at broadcasting, asking for the replay on GSPS. It's so shocking to watch, the mind can't take it in. You've got to watch again and again.

"Personally, it made me sick the first time I saw that girl marked, her husband-to-be stomped into creamed beef. I had to watch it a few times before my stomach untwisted. I get it, friends, that's what I'm telling you. I get it, and that's why I've commissioned a new channel, Playback Silver Seven, to broadcast the attack on Aluel Garang and the justice done to Kirimi Teng in a continual loop, starting tonight at eight. Tune in, won't you? Make sure you tune in."

Jakob chewed his lip as applause greeted Flynn's announcement. Where was Sven? At all the executions Jakob had attended, the victim had been shown to the crowd while the Studio representative made his speech. Did that mean Sven was off the hook? The thrill that ran through Jakob was so faint, it took him a moment to recognize it as hope.

Flynn took something light colored from a pocket, difficult to make out against the gloves. When he held it up, the object sparkled in the spotlight.

"Do you know what this is, friends?" Flynn paused, giving the camera a moment to zoom in. "It's a shard of razor-edged crystal, found in the right hand of Kirimi Teng. Our experts figure it was surgically inserted. Looking at the tapes, you can see Kirimi opened doors with his left hand, ate meals with his left, even though his genobrand had him down as right-handed. When he struck Miss Garang, it was the first time he had done anything with his right hand in weeks. Do you know what that means, friends?"

Jakob thought he did, and dreaded the answer.

"This was a plan! Kirimi Teng *planned* to kill Aluel Garang from the start. Planned to kill the woman who would have mothered the next generation of their race, saving it from eventual extinction. It's monstrous. Despicable. The question we've got to ask, friends, is did the monster make plans on his own?"

Jakob stared at his feet. He was wearing dress boots. The blood-drenched Oxfords he had worn to the wedding were back at his sleeping chamber, wrapped in a plastic bag. He would have liked to bury them but hadn't found the time. The rest of his clothes from Sunday he had tossed in the fire. Sure, Kirimi was a monster. But what were the men who kicked him to death?

Puffing out his chest, Flynn said, "Friends, Kirimi Teng didn't get to finish his plan. Miss Garang will recover. The doctors are hopeful they can rescue her face. So, is justice done? I ask, but I don't need you to answer. We all know the meaning of the krows up there. Most days, they're a witness to death. But today—today, friends, they're a witness to healing."

He made an expansive gesture, encompassing Gas Company Tower and the block it filled. Hope had sped away from Jakob, but now it sped back. He wasn't sure if he should believe the hope. It mostly returned because he didn't understand Flynn's words.

"The building behind me is the headquarters of the Los Angeles Office of Bliss," the president continued. "Today, it's under a cloud. We all know it. We all see it. I'm here today to tell you that the men inside, the men who work in here, they don't deserve our suspicion." There was hesitation, a catch in Flynn's throat. "They deserve . . . our praise. The blissmen of LA have done a fantastic job matching brides and grooms from the candidates of every race I don't need to tell you that *Good Breeding* is Little Angel Studio's runaway hit. We couldn't put it together without our matchmaker partners."

The krows were dense, denser than Jakob had ever seen. Every krow in the city seemed to be packed into an acre of sky.

Flynn said, "There's a cloud hanging over Bliss. Let's clear it away. What do you say, friends? Let's blow it away."

If a krow had fallen from the sky and landed on Jakob, it would have stunned him less than the president's words and actions. Taking a deep breath, he blew, like a carpenter clearing sawdust from a windowsill. The skeletal krows reacted as though they'd been buffeted by a high wind. They had not quite blackened the sky but had brought on an artificial twilight. At the president's blow, the gaps between krows opened. Sunlight, bright as it ever was, poured in.

Shielding his eyes, Jakob watched the krows retreat, their mummified burdens bobbing on the breeze. Intellectually, he knew the krows were following the magnetic currents, but Flynn's performance had been so convincing, the display seemed supernatural. A chill washed over Jakob, like being dipped in a cool bath.

"Friends," said the president, "it fills me with pride to be so close to heroes. Every blissman is a hero, I tell you. The service they give the New Society is nothing short of heroic. Let there be no doubt, from this moment on, they are innocent in this business. Kirimi Teng acted on his own. The investigation into his crime is finished. Justice is done."

He swept his hand in an arc, indicating the clear, copper sky. Trumpets pealed. There was a surge of applause. Jakob did not see any clapping around him. Embarrassed at having missed their cue, men began to put their hands together, following the lead of the implant soundtrack. Before Flynn left the platform, every man present was applauding.

***

When at last Jakob reached Sven's workroom, two men stood in the hall outside the door. One was Dr. Staley. The other, a stranger to Jakob, was wearing a charcoal suit and holding a clipboard. As Jakob approached, the stranger made a few marks with an exceptionally long pen.

It was Dr. Staley who said, "Best stop there, Jakob. Something unpleasant has happened."

The stranger said, "Is this man with your office? I would like a corroborating signature."

Clyde stroked his chin. Reluctantly, he said, "Yes, he is. Matchmaker Freeman, Office of Bliss, this is Mr. Vique, a morgue attendant attached to Municipal Hospital."

"Pardon me," Vique said, "but I'm the *senior* morgue attendant." He tapped his absurd pen on the clipboard. "If you could step over here, Mr. Freeman, I'll show you where to sign."

A hulking figure appeared in the doorway to the workroom. The doctor and the senior morgue attendant were obliged to step aside. A behemoth in a white coat wheeled a gurney over the threshold. Jakob stumbled sideways, struck by a sudden weakness in the knees.

"Who—" he said, and couldn't finish the question. Moving forward, he stretched out a hand. He had no clear idea what he meant to do.

Vique caught his arm. "No contact, please." Gesturing for Jakob to step back, he unzipped the body bag.

Sven's face appeared shrunken with no pulse to swell it. Otherwise, he was peaceful. He might have been sleeping. Jakob fought an impulse to fall over the body, offering his colleague his own warmth and breath. In public, Sven had always been decorous at the best and worst of times. He hated hysterical displays.

"Do you recognize this?" asked Vique, holding a pill bottle to the light.

Jakob stared, uncomprehending. The bottled contained a small number of octagonal pills.

Dr. Staley explained, "They're Aremoden. Mind wipers."

"From the residue on his desk," said Vique, "it appears that he popped a few at a time until there was no turning back."

"We're blissmen," said Jakob. "He wouldn't. He—"

Vique held up a hand. "I understand. It's hard to find out someone you work with is capable of . . ." He gestured at Sven's body. "If you don't mind, I do need those signatures. There's a triple homicide in Glendale I'd like to log before breakfast."

With signatures in hand, Vique and his associate departed, bearing with them the cargo denied to the krows. Jakob entered Sven's workroom, savoring the scent of whiskey and cigars. Dr. Staley followed.

Jakob said, "Will there be an investigation?"

"I think I heard it was closed," said his superior. He breathed on the back of his artificial hand. Polishing the plastic skin against his opposite sleeve, he added, "If you meant of Sven's death, you know State won't waste time on a suicide."

Jakob's instinct was to break one of Sven's oak chairs over Clyde's head. He clenched his fists, shaking with the violence of the impulse. The tumbler Sven must have used to chase the pills was resting on a glass coaster, on top of the old desk. Concentrating on the tumbler helped Jakob cool his temper.

"You're sure it was suicide?"

The doctor polished his hand again. "Must have been. He was too smart for an accident."

"That he was," said Jakob.

The doctor's tone reminded him to be careful about what he said. Other blissmen in the office might pass in the hall at any time. Not all would share their grief.

Jakob took note of the lack of papers on Sven's desk. "No note," he said.

"Why would there be? It seems plain that Sven blamed himself for what happened to Aluel."

Only he didn't, Jakob was sure. Sven was too much of a philosopher to blame himself for the world's ills. His was a pure and noble spirit, untainted by self-doubt.

"We should be grateful, in a way," said the doctor. "He saved the office a mark on its good name."

As true as this probably was, the callous sentiment made Jakob grit his teeth. Sven's death had closed the book on the Teng-Garang saga. No doubt Flynn knew the fate of the number one suspect in the search for the conspirator. He had sanctified the office's reputation, and all they'd had to pay was the life of the best man Jakob had ever known.

A sudden weakness, such as he had felt in the hall, overcame him. He had to lean on the desk. His colleague was dead. Sven had been murdered, or murdered himself, for reasons Jakob knew but could not accept. The burden of conflicting thoughts threw Jakob off balance. Head spinning, he leaned more heavily on the desk.

The workroom was the largest single space in the office, larger than any room in the suite occupied by Dr. Staley. Dismissing the doctor's concern, Jakob composed himself enough to stand upright and pace the woven carpet in front of the desk. He imagined Sven gripping the tumbler as he dropped the hateful mind wipers into his mouth.

No! It was impossible. Sven must have been killed.

A potent argument against suicide sat on shelves built into the walls. Sven had been a collector. At home and at work, he surrounded himself with beloved artifacts of the World Before. Many of his pieces were valuable. Some would have been in a museum, if any such institution had existed in his lifetime. How could Sven have left it all behind?

Frowning, Jakob went to a shelf and scooped up a foot-high figurine made of jointed plastic. The woman it depicted was of bizarre proportions. She was dressed in a costume Sven always said belonged to a ballerina, whatever that was. Her flaxen hair scintillated in the sunlight streaming through the window.

Dr. Staley said, "You know, I always envied what he got away with. Out of context, the Studio would call that pornographic."

The context he meant was professional. Sven had kept quite a few trinkets the Studio would have censured if they had not accepted his claim that they were useful in matchmaking.

Jakob replaced the doll, leaving it beside other toys that had belonged to now dead children. He turned his attention to Sven's media collection. Several high shelves held ancient hardcover books, most of them printed after 1990, when acid-free paper became the norm in the publishing industry.

Margaret Atwood's *Alias Grace* cozied up to Michael Crichton's *Timeline* at one end of the top shelf. The next shelf down held a line of J. K. Rowling novels with gaps between volumes like missing teeth. Below that were novels by men with names like Follett, Grisham, Hubbard, Bradbury, and King. How many had Sven gotten around to reading? Their influence had made him different from common men, whose access to works depicting women interacting with men in daily life was carefully restricted.

Below the hardbacks was a few feet of paperbacks, and next to the paperbacks, a yard and a half of vinyl records. Sven had always been protective of his vinyl. He would reprimand anyone who made a grab for a record without asking—even Jakob. When sliding the sacred platters from their sleeves, he always wore gloves. On the first night Jakob had spent shut away with Sven in the workroom, he had watched him clean every speck of dust from disc one of *The White Album* with a brush. They had listened to the curious music for hours, sitting and drinking in companionable silence, until Jakob fell asleep.

Past the row of records was a short run of compact discs, followed by several long cardboard boxes. These contained comic books by the hundreds. Jakob lifted the top off a long box and slid out a copy of *Superman #75*, just to check that it was there. If Mr. Vique or his assistant had walked off with the issue, he would have been obliged to substitute one of many copies Sven had given him over the years. This proved unnecessary. He returned the cover to its place.

"Our friend was rather lost in the past," said Dr. Staley.

"You call him a friend?" said Jakob. He was thinking of how President Flynn used the word.

"Of course. Didn't you?"

Jakob didn't answer. His eyes fell on the filing cabinet that contained Sven's microfilm collection. An appointment book had been tossed on top. It lay open at the current date. A name and a time had been written in blue ink.

"Ching," Jakob read. "Ten thirty a.m. Doctor, does that mean anything to you?"

Clyde tapped his plastic fingers on the arm of the chair. "Ching sounds like a bastardized Chinese. Did he know any Chinese bastards?"

The quip sparked something in Jakob's mind. He flipped through the appointment book until he found what he wanted.

"The Emperor's Emporium. A junk shop in Chinatown. Ching might be the owner."

"Could be," said Clyde. "So what?"

"So, I have to go there."

"I don't see why."

Jakob hesitated. When the doctor had asked if Sven was his friend, he had balked at the label. The truth was, he lacked the vocabulary to express what Sven was to him. In his student days, there had been boys he had called "friends" due to their suffering together, or sharing common interests. Sven was so much more.

All through the early days of Jakob's career, Sven had been his mentor. When he advanced from his position as junior recorder to liaison to the Office of Justice, Sven had cheered. It had been Sven, in the end, who put in the recommendation that made Jakob a matchmaker.

Professionally, there was nothing he didn't owe Sven. When Jakob's young wife had died, Sven had been his comforter. No finer companion had there ever been. To call Sven a friend seemed an insult.

"I suppose someone should settle his accounts," Dr. Staley said. "If you want the job, fine. But ten thirty is impossible, unless you mean to reschedule Miss Chandigarh."

"Sin of Onan!" Jakob swore. "She slipped my mind."

"Unslip her then. She'll be downstairs any moment."

Jakob wracked his brain. The desire to follow up on Sven's business was overwhelming. He was sure he would be able to think of nothing until he found out what appointment Sven had at the Emperor's Emporium. Though the visit might be nothing out of the ordinary, the fact of Sven's absence made it seem vital. On the other hand, he couldn't put off meeting a potential centerpiece for the next installment of *Good Breeding*. Nothing was more important to the Studio, those blood-soaked gods of the municipality who had minutes ago announced their pleasure with the latest sacrifice.

"Will she be coming by limo?"

"Expect so. What say you bring her up to my workroom? I'd love to observe."

Jakob was sure he would. Thinking of how he could get out of exposing the young woman to Clyde's drooling suggested a way to solve all his problems at a stroke.

"Sorry. I'd rather have our first encounter one-on-one."

"Of course." The doctor could have insisted on being a nuisance. Glancing at their surroundings, he had the decency to let Jakob have his way. "You know your business, after all. I'll have security bring Miss Chandigarh to you."

"No need," said Jakob. "I'll meet her downstairs."

"Whatever for, boy?"

In for a penny, thought Jakob. "I think I can handle Sven's business and take care of Miss Chandigarh at once."

Dr. Staley considered for a moment. "As you like." He gave a wry smile. "Careful, dear boy. I'm told this one's nice."

"I'm up on my annies, Doctor," said Jakob. Indeed, he had started that very morning with a boosted cocktail of anaphrodisiacs.

"They work below the belt," said the older man. "Watch out she doesn't hit you higher."

Chapter Four: The Grand Tour

The vehicle that brought Kutri to Gas Company Tower was an armored Cadillac Escalade that had been converted into a stretch limo at the height of some distant, vastly wealthier age. It had electronic switches to roll down the windows, and air conditioning that could cool different parts of the vehicle to different temperatures. Kutri had never known such luxury.

The director of the Hindustan Bliss Center, Hermann "Papa" Paquette, had taken her for rides in his patchwork sedan, but its windows were hand-cranked and its vents only circulated warm air. When the limo pulled in front of the building Kutri had been told contained the matchmaker she was to meet, she considered asking the driver if she could please wait in cool comfort a minute longer. When a voice over the intercom said, "Stay where you are," she was happy to comply.

Several books had made the Pacific crossing in her luggage. She had taken the precaution of transferring a few to her straw handbag. Stooping forward, she drew out a collection of Ralph Waldo Emerson essays and a Punjabi edition of Amrita's *Pinjar*. She had read both often enough that she could open to any page and recite with perfect accuracy without looking down. This game had preserved her sanity during the long, hot days of summer back home. Since setting foot on American soil, life had been so exciting she hadn't needed to play.

Even now, she only glanced at the treasured volumes before lifting a square of cardboard from inside *Pinjar*'s front cover. The square was black and faded, with a hinge along the edge. Kutri sat up straight, holding the square level with her chin before parting its two halves. Papa Paquette's face smiled at her from the photograph within.

The driver had assured her that neither he nor her bodyguard, who was sitting up front with the driver, could hear anything she said unless she first toggled an intercom switch. Still, she kept her voice down as she said, "Did you like how I handled Mr. Simmons, Papa?"

The picture said nothing.

"He was a gentleman, compared to some. Few men would have accepted my *no* with such weak protest. He barely threatened me. He didn't beg. Do you think his restraint was natural, or is the poor man gelded? Auntie Bakshi told me old men are less ruled by their impulses, but I remember how your gray beard scratched my neck very well."

Her throat closed. Before she returned the photo to the poet's care, she touched the nail of her little finger to the image of the director's right eye. How much pressure would she have to apply to gouge it out? She'd asked herself this question many times, not always with the photo in mind. As brave as being half a world from home made her feel, she decided to leave the picture intact, as an aid to memory. Later there would be time to forget. For now, Papa Paquette's face was fuel for her ambition.

The reverie it had put her in was interrupted by a tap on the window. Kutri quickly hid the photograph. A dim shape appeared on the other side of the tinted glass.

"Yes?" she said.

The door opened and Kutri found herself at a construction site. Men were assembling some sort of structure out of metal pipes. No, she corrected herself, they were disassembling the structure. The men carrying bundles of pipes were moving away from the wooden planks that formed a foundation. Before she had time to register more, a man stepped from behind the door, immediately commanding her attention.

He said, "Miss Chandigarh?"

She would have been annoyed if he were not so handsome. The strong jaw, high cheekbones, and hazel eyes were captivating. His hair barely touched his collar and framed his face with waves the color of rosewood. She had seen attractive men on television, but this one bore more resemblance to a storybook prince than any man she had met in real life.

He slipped past her without looking. When he was in the facing seat, across the limo's open floor, he set his briefcase down and fastened his safety belt. Kutri's bodyguard, a barrel-chested man with deep-set eyes and midnight skin, came in through the driver side door to sit beside the newcomer. The bodyguard wore black combat boots, blue jeans, and a white turtleneck under a tan sports jacket. The handsome man's blue suit was stiff and formal by comparison. It wasn't until she saw the badge of office on his blazer that she guessed his identity.

"You're the matchmaker," she said.

"Yes," he said. At last, he looked up at her. His eyes widened. He blinked, stammered, "Y-yes. I . . . hope you won't mind a change in plans."

She had crossed an ocean to meet this man. "Not at all," she said.

"Excuse my manners," he said, smiling and stunning her anew. "I'm Jakob Freeman—your matchmaker, as you guessed, from the Office of Bliss."

"I'm Kutri. I know the paperwork said Chandigarh, but that is not my name. I will answer to it if you insist, but I prefer Kutri."

"That's fine. Kutri is . . . nice. Please, call me Jakob."

"I will. It is good to meet you, Jakob."

They shook hands. His hand felt cool, even through her glove.

Jakob said, "I apologize for being abrupt. It's been an unusual morning. The Studio held a public event on our doorstep. Then, a colleague of mine . . . was unwell. I volunteered to run an errand for him. I thought, well, we would have gotten around to a tour. Why not do it today?"

Kutri was delighted. "Why not, indeed? I have dreamed of seeing Los Angeles for many years."

"And how do you find it thus far?"

"Stark. Yes, it has a kind of beauty."

"Well, you're at least half right. I guess broken walls can be beautiful, so long as you don't have to live on the other side." He leaned in to work her intercom button, drawing a hard gaze from the bodyguard. Unperturbed, he gave the driver instructions.

Kutri said, "How exciting," and they were off.

Once the limo was up to speed, they opened the windows to watch the crumbled masonry fly by. Not much in the way of reconstruction had been done in the fifty years of the New System, but then Kutri supposed that the resources needed—men and machinery and expertise—were not readily available.

"Nine-and-a-half-million people lived in Los Angeles County at the end of the twenty-first century," said Jakob. "Here at the end of the twenty-second, we're brushing up against a hundred and thirty thousand. You would think that would be enough to stack one brick on top of another, but as you can see, not much of that goes on."

"The problem is not population?" said Kutri.

"No," said Jakob. "In some cases, it's motivation. It's hard to move men to restore a world they've only seen under a coat of dust, especially when day-to-day life is struggle enough. And we lost so many of the dreamers and doers—the people who knew how to build things. Most builders work for the Studio—the government, I should say."

"That was almost a poem," said Kutri.

"Was it?"

He gestured at a wall of rubble—broken bricks and sagging timber, fallen signs that had once held neon lights, and mounds of barely identifiable debris. "I've lived my whole life in LA and found nothing to write poems about. Have you heard of Grauman's Theatre? That's it on your left."

Kutri followed his pointing finger to a recess between two squat buildings. The peak of a roof covered in what might have been green tile projected slightly above an ash heap. Someone had dragged a ferocious-looking iron mask through the ashes, then abandoned it on the broken sidewalk. The walls to either side were coated in clinging mold. The scent of urine was thick in the warm air.

Minutes later, the limo arrived on the border of a cleared patch of land that Jakob said had once been a park. The local homeless had turned it into a tent city. Surveying the torn canvas tents and the abundant cardboard made Kutri wonder, "Don't these men have anywhere to go?"

"Of course," said Jakob. "A housing crisis is impossible in a city the size of LA. But the Studio owns the land. They let the worthy live where they want. These men are flawed. Psychologically, I mean. They don't want to work and they refuse help and medication. Some are criminals who should be locked up. The Studio is always sending hatchetmen to clear them out, but they always drift back, in time."

He had used an unfamiliar term. "What are hatchetmen?"

He seemed surprised that she didn't know. "Perhaps you call them something else," he suggested. "Police? Enforcers? They're like soldiers, only they don't fight Toscavites or the A-Nationalists. They punish the good-for-nothing and generally carry out the will of the Studio."

Kutri addressed herself to the limo's other passenger. "Are you a hatchetman?" she asked the bodyguard.

"No, ma'am. I'm SSO."

"State Security Operative," said Jakob. "They perform a similar function, but their salaries are paid by the Office of State."

Kutri sat back, considering. "We have an Armed Order Service in my homeland. These hatchetmen of yours, are they loyal to the people?"

Jakob seemed confused. Kutri tried clarifying her question.

"I mean, do they serve at the behest of the citizens, or of someone else?"

"Ah," said Jakob. "It's like I told you. The Studio pays the hatchetmen. State pays the SSOs."

That seemed an odd arrangement. It meant there might be times in which the two forces would be at odds. There seemed no cause to belabor the point, so Kutri let it drop. At length, the limo arrived in Chinatown. Judging from the frown Jakob gave his watch, the scenic route had eaten up more time than he had intended. He hopped from the limo as soon as the driver activated the intercom and said, "This is close as we can get," and went striding away without telling Kutri whether to join or stay behind.

She would have taken either as a suggestion, not a rule. She was her own woman and would soon be one of the most prominent in town. Leaving the limo behind, she followed Jakob along a path bordered by a garbage wall. The bodyguard stayed close behind.

Soon, Kutri began to catch glimpses of men staring out of doorways and the few intact glass windows. The buildings here were derelicts, as broken down as any Jakob had pointed out so far in the city. Here and there, wooden beams propped up the walls. Nearly all the standing infrastructure appeared on the verge of collapse. How anyone lived in such conditions, Kutri didn't know, but the farther along she walked, the more she saw people watching her pass.

One boy made so bold as to take a few steps in her direction. He extended his hand as though he meant to touch the fringe of her sari. The bodyguard growled in the back of his throat. The boy blinked like a sleepwalker and ran back to the shadows.

Two blocks later, the bodyguard called a halt. "Hold on," he said. "How far are we going?"

Jakob turned, startled. He seemed to have thought he was alone. "You—uh, what's your name, guard?"

"Mondt."

Jakob consulted a sheet of paper. "One more block, Mondt, then right a block on Ord. Does that sound okay?"

The bodyguard, Mr. Mondt, gave the slightest of nods.

To Kutri, Jakob said, "Sorry, I got distracted thinking about the errand. I didn't mean to drag you on this stretch. There's not much to see."

"On the contrary," she said. "I find it fascinating to see how people live."

"Fascinating," he echoed, glancing about at the broken neighborhood. "Not the word I would use."

Some minutes later, they descended a hill between an intact four-story building and an expanse of disintegrated concrete loosely contained in a rusted fence. A hand-painted sign hung on the wall next to a metal door. The door stood partly open. Depicted on the sign was a three-legged black bird against the backdrop of a yellow sun. To the right of these images was a column of Chinese characters. Below the characters, a legend below spelled out their meaning in English:

"The Emperor's Emporium. All welcome. Come in."

Before Jakob passed through the door, Kutri saw him square his shoulders as if he expected trouble. She would have liked to ask why. He moved so quickly, she didn't have the chance.

The interior of the shop brought to mind a sepia photograph she had once seen of a traditional Indian bazaar. So far as she knew, nothing like it now existed in her country. She was pleased to find it thriving in the distant land. Though thriving was perhaps a strong word.

The place was dusty, though not dirty. Tables ran the length of the front and side walls stacked with every manner of mechanized junk. The middle of the shop was taken up by a hodgepodge of shelves and tables displaying cracked screens, keyboards with missing letters, and long-tailed computer mice with the ends tied together and hung like bundles of spices. Further in, a set of audio speakers rested atop a rusted washing machine that someone had strung with blinking lights. A pile of electric torches occupied the middle of one aisle, while another was home to a dozen spools of red-and-white cable. The wreck of some wheeled device equipped with a push bar was ringed by an assortment of garden implements, all polished to a high shine.

Deconstructed engines, a stack of what Kutri thought were car batteries, and similar odds and ends whose purpose she could not begin to guess littered the remaining space. Kutri had never seen so much World Before junk collected in one place. Hanging from the ceiling were chains and extension cords and an assortment of tires, a seemingly endless fireman's hose, and a more diverse collection of bicycle frames than she had known existed. The only thing the Emperor's Emporium lacked was customers. Aside from Jakob, herself, and Mondt, only one other person was in the place—a young man in a white T-shirt who stood behind a service counter that ran the width of the room at the rear of the emporium. As soon as he saw them, he disappeared through a curtain at the back.

Jakob glanced at Kutri before leading the way through the jumble to the counter. As they were passing between an upright piano and a graffitied highway sign, he called out, "Mr. Ching? Anyone? Is anyone here?"

A voice behind the curtain said, "Coming!"

Seconds later, the curtain was pulled aside, revealing a middle-aged man. He seemed out of place in the chaos, with his slicked-back hair and neat, straight-collared jacket, but when he bowed, a jangle of metal keys on a key ring marked him as the custodian of this mélange of mechanisms. When he straightened, the man beheld Kutri.

"A woman!" he said. "A flesh-and-blood woman."

"Hello," said Kutri.

"Hello. Hello! Oh, you're welcome here, Ma. Anything you need from Jimmy, Jimmy will give you. Anything you like in the shop, take it. No need to ask."

Mondt clicked his tongue and set a fist the size of a softball on the countertop. Jimmy didn't notice.

Jakob said, "Are you Ching?"

"Yeah. Jun Ching. Friends call me Jimmy." He gestured to acknowledge Jakob, while keeping his eyes on Kutri. "And you're my friend. Best friend I ever had, if you brought the ma to me."

Kutri said, "I am not a mother yet."

"Close enough," said Jimmy. "My own ma's dead. Sis too. After them, I haven't seen a ma in years. To me, Ma, you're every mother who's ever been." He glanced at Jakob's blazer. "Blissman, eh? Cool. Is there going to be a camera crew? My shop's perfect for TV."

"Sorry," said Jakob. "No camera. Miss Chandigarh—"

"Kutri," she said, extending a hand across the counter. Mondt stepped forward, allowing Jimmy to touch her glove for a second, no more.

"Such an honor, Kutri Ma," Jimmy said, and touched the hand that had brushed hers to his chest.

"Miss Kutri is a candidate for *Good Breeding*," said Jakob, "but we're not here on official business. I'm doing a favor for someone, a man I think you know. I expect he calls you Jimmy." He produced a card and slid it across the countertop. Reluctantly, Jimmy left off beaming at Kutri to study the card.

"Sven? Sure. Sven, my good friend. He's in here twice a week. Sven a Blissman too? We don't talk about work, only the merchandise. Are you here to pick up his order?"

For an instant, Jakob seemed unsure, but he said, "Yes. Will you get it for me?"

"Anything for a friend of Sven's," said Jimmy. "Even if you didn't bring the ma, I'd help. But thank Buddha-bà you did."

He disappeared behind the curtain, the unseen keys jingling like bells. "I know it's here. Hey, Mitsuru! We've got customers. Guests. Go be nice." There was an indistinct mumble. "Go on. I'll be there in a second."

The curtain parted. A young man emerged. From his white T-shirt, Kutri recognized him as the person who had been behind the counter when they entered. Close inspection showed he was younger than she had thought. A tall child, really, barely an adolescent.

It was Mondt who said, "Shouldn't you be in school, kid?"

"Work-study program." The answer was delivered in a soft, lilting contralto. The youth's eyes, lovely and dark, with remarkable lashes, were trained on the floor.

"Your name is Mitsuru?" said Kutri. "I'm Kutri. Nice to meet you."

Mitsuru glanced up briefly and said, "Nice to meet you," then looked away again.

Unexpectedly, Jakob said, "I know you. Where have I seen you before?" A strange huskiness had come into his voice, as if the sight of the youth disturbed him.

"Excuse me," said Mitsuru. He backed through the curtain, almost bumping into Jimmy, who was on his way out.

"Careful. You see that, Kutri Ma? Your visit is karmaphala for the time I give boys like that. They're trouble, but with the right training, who knows?"

He set a package on the countertop—a perfect cube, somewhat wider and deeper than Kutri's palm. The brown paper wrapping, tied neatly with string, reminded her of a song from a movie she had seen in her childhood about people who sang a lot and lived in an impossibly large house in a place so beautiful it could never have been real.

To Jakob, Jimmy said, "Here you go. Give that to Sven and you'll be doing me a favor. I'll be fixing old radios all day. Don't think I'm running you off, though. Stay as long as you like. Especially not you, Kutri Ma. Stay my whole life!"

"I don't owe you anything?" said Jakob.

"No way. I'm thinking about wiping Sven's tab!"

"Thank you. Then we'll be getting back. It was good to meet you, Jimmy. I'm glad Sven has a friend like you."

Jimmy smiled. "Sure. I'll tell him you said so, next time he's in. You come back anytime. We've got everything here, all kinds of treasure. And brains, too. Anything you want to know about old junk or new, Jimmy can teach. Remember Jimmy, your good friend, okay?"

The return trip to the limo was more exhausting than the trip away had been. Kutri supposed this was because she was no longer impelled by curiosity. When they were finally sitting comfortably, Jakob and Kutri on one bench seat, Mondt watching them both from the other, Jakob said they should postpone their first in-depth interview for the next day.

"The other candidates are being processed by Justice," he said. "There's no rush. I'd like to give my superior, Dr. Staley, an initial report. Perhaps we can meet for breakfast tomorrow?"

"I would like that," said Kutri, meaning it more than she wanted to show. As the limo pulled away from the sidewalk, she checked her makeup using a compact she kept in the straw bag. Her forehead was somewhat shiny. She dabbed it with a cloth, then applied powder.

Jakob sat up sharply.

"What is it?" said Kutri.

He leaned against the seat back but held himself too rigidly to appear relaxed. "Nothing. I remembered where I saw Mitsuru, that's all."

"I'm happy for you. I get frustrated when I cannot call an important matter to mind."

"I'm not sure it's important, but it is strange. I saw that boy in the wedding party, on the night of the disaster. He was dressed as an apprentice geisha."

There was a keenness in Jakob's face that brought the first interlocutor's warning to her mind. She had passed the day in wonder at the unexpected attraction she felt to Jakob Freeman. Had she failed to read the signs of danger? It was possible.

Certainly it was unusual that he had changed their plans, taking her on a tour instead of conducting an interview. He had exposed her to more danger than staying in, though she was grateful for the trip. She had enjoyed it thoroughly, and hoped for experiences like it in the future. For the moment, she would leave the phone in her bag.

Perhaps Jakob was confused. "Are you sure it was Mitsuru?" she asked. "He said he was on work release. Isn't shop boy an odd choice for someone training in a lucrative profession?"

"I'm sure it was him," said Jakob. He balanced the package Jimmy had given him on his hand and tugged at the string.

"Won't your friend mind?"

"No. He won't."

The object Jakob lifted out of the box had clearly been manufactured. Still, it reminded Kutri of the stuffed dolls she had made for herself as a girl. This doll depicted some sort of animal. She couldn't tell what kind. When she asked to see it up close, Jakob passed it to her without comment.

The animal was four-limbed, plump, and cartoonish. It had been anthropomorphized to the point of wearing breeches, sandals, and an Asian rice hat and clutching a stick of bamboo in its hand. The contrast between the thing's large belly and menacing posture was enough to make her chuckle, though she was unsure what it was meant to be.

"Funny," she said. "It looks like a bear, but who ever heard of a black-and-white bear?"

Jakob didn't answer. He stared out the window in silence, all the way back to Bliss headquarters.

Chapter Five: Dancing the Web

When his paperwork was done for the night, Jakob's legs refused to take him home. He crossed Pershing Square and stood at the entrance to the subway for a full minute before he continued on, crossing streets and turning corners he had rarely seen before, let alone visited.

It was dangerous for a man to walk alone in the city. Thieves and rapists were everywhere. His jacket with its emblazoned badge offered some protection, but only against criminals who valued their continued existence. Those were in short supply. Despite his own will to live, Jakob's thoughts harried him as the streets filled with hopeless men, off work and looking for trouble.

Suicidal was the last word he would have used to describe Sven Thomson. At least, before Sunday's disaster. After the attack on Aluel and the brutal slaying of Kirimi Teng, all bets were off. Jakob hadn't spoken with Sven during the two-day office sabbatical. It was their tradition to forget work existed for those few days they managed to stay away. Given the circumstances, Jakob had been glad to give his colleagues their space.

He had not been the only blissman to land a kick on Kirimi, though Sven's example showed that a violent response was not inevitable. Had the savagery he had seen sent Sven into a depressive spiral? Jakob roamed the streets, searching blindly for answers where none could be found.

The copper sky had dulled to brown, and a rosy glow was on the horizon. Jakob found himself in front of a pub he had visited on a couple of occasions. Dr. Staley had once treated all the matchmakers to one night at Derby Flat's. Sven had induced Jakob to return once more, though it was a gloomier place than he should have favored. Watching the patrons hunch over their beers through the window, Jakob decided it was perfectly gloomy enough for him now.

He thumbed the door lever. Two men passed close behind. He didn't know if they had been following him or were only passing the same way, but the fact they'd come so close without him noticing was a good argument he was right to take shelter. He saw no faces he remembered in the joint, but the desolate air was familiar.

He did remember the bartender. The pot-bellied man had a thick beard and a tattooed chest. An orb of pale blue ink could be seen peeking out from behind banks of black clouds on a strip of skin above his apron. Jakob had no idea what the rest of the image looked like. He didn't dare to ask.

The last time they had been there, Sven had told the bartender that if he shared the masterpiece in full, Sven would give him a photo of their latest candidate in trade. The offer had scandalized Jakob, but it turned out there was no danger of Sven's having to make good. It was a joke at Derby's that no matter what the customers tried, the scene behind the apron remained a mystery. No one had seen it in full but the artist and the bartender himself.

Jakob signaled to the bartender. "Excuse me."

"A minute, pal," said the bartender.

Business was brisk. Jakob supposed this was a consequence of the good mood President Flynn's announcement had induced in the city. He had heard more than one blissman say he planned to hit the hot spots. Some men down the bar toasted each other and slugged down drinks. They were on a vacation from worry. The injustice of his own burdens tried Jakob's patience. He rapped his knuckles on the bar.

The bartender turned his way. "I said a minute— Hey, I remember you." He set down the glass he was holding in front of a barfly and strolled along to Jakob. "Sven's friend. He coming in later?"

"He isn't," said Jakob. "Sorry. Three fingers of SI, please. Neat."

The bartender winked. He fetched a glass and a bottle of standard issue rye from under the bar. "Shame Sven can't make it. Looking like a fun night."

A puckered scar ran from the bartender's missing right ear to the corner of his mouth. Jakob stared at the ruined flesh as the bartender turned to serve someone else. He knew what it meant: In his younger days, this man had exposed himself where a woman might see him. A sliced ear was the textbook sentence.

Jakob took a swig of his rye. It tasted like a burnt wick. Ignoring the burn in his throat, he drained the glass and tapped for a second.

"With you after this," the bartender said. He was arranging drinks on a tray.

The toy panda Jakob had collected from Jimmy Ching was in his jacket pocket. As he waited for the refill, he set it on the bar. Sven had probably cleared a space on his shelf before he died. There seemed little point in putting the panda there now, when the movers would be in to pack the collection away. Jakob sat ruminating on what he would do with the figurine until the bartender returned.

"How about leaving the bottle?" said Jakob.

"If you're good for it."

Jakob shoved up the sleeve of his jacket and unbuttoned his cuff. The thin, golden half-ring that had marked his wrist since his wedding day was exposed. Higher up the forearm was the genobrand that encoded his personal identity. The bartender held up a scanner, ready to flash a red light at the genobrand and tap Jakob's credit. When he saw the red x-marks tattooed on the half-ring, he set the scanner aside.

"Never mind. On the house. Sorry for your loss."

Jakob said, "Thank you," and accepted the bottle. He had learned not to argue with men who gave handouts to widowers. Far be it from him to tell them his pain was his own. It was not to be shared. The memories he had of his marriage were so cloudy, any man who sympathized probably knew as much about his grief as Jakob himself. "Cheers," he said, before draining the glass and filling it again.

"Maybe SI's not the best idea. How about a switch to beer? Something that'll get you sick before it rots you out."

"I'm good," said Jakob, swirling the glass. "Don't you have other customers?"

"Yeah," said the bartender. "I do."

As he moved away, a cheer went up from the tables. Jakob turned to see the cause of excitement. Two men were standing in the doorway. One, a burly fellow in a turtleneck and sports jacket like that of Kutri's bodyguard Mondt, wore a deep frown. The other man, flashy in a red suit tailored to within an inch of its life, blew kisses to the crowd. He had wavy, gleaming black hair worn collar length, and a neatly trimmed beard and mustache, reminding Jakob of a matador. He was so popular, nobody appeared to mind being pushed aside by the man's bodyguard as the pair blazed a trail to the bar.

Seeing the guy was headed for the seat beside him, Jakob tossed a peanut to get the bartender's attention. "Who is that?"

The bartender smirked, or perhaps the expression was a grin. With half of his mouth frozen in a perpetual upturn, it was hard to tell. "You boys ought to know your own. That's Nat Martinez."

Jakob set down his glass. The whiskey had done its work. Otherwise, he would have recognized the former star of *Good Breeding*. It had been six years since the match groom was in the spotlight. Jakob had been justice liaison back then, so they had never met in person, but Sven had called him in on a matter concerning the future Mrs. Martinez. Jakob's own wife had been in her last decline then, so he suspected Sven had meant to distract him from the hell that life had become. Sven denied that, of course, saying that he merely needed a second opinion on something.

So Jakob had left his wife's side for the first time in weeks. In Sven's workroom, he had met Belen Costa, as she was known at the time, and listened to her tell her story.

Belen was Argentinian, a trained dancer. She had strolled to the center of Sven's carpet as gracefully as if she were crossing a ballroom. Her taffeta gown was coal black, trimmed with red roses. An elaborate get-up for an interview, but Belen explained it was the same gown she had been wearing on her first day in Los Angeles, when she appeared before First Interlocutor Alec Simmons of the Office of Justice. She fell silent after that.

"Tell Mr. Freeman what Mr. Simmons asked you to do, Belen," Sven had said.

Belen nodded. "He said to me, 'Take off your clothes.'"

This was dreadful, a scandal.

"He wanted you to undress," said Sven.

"Yes."

Jakob was shocked. "Did you?"

Belen held her palm to her forehead. "I was afraid. I thought he would send me home."

The outcome she feared was unlikely. Though the Office of Justice had the right to refuse any foreign import, women included, the Studio wouldn't have allowed even a man like Simmons to interfere. Belen had suspected this but had not known for sure. Speaking out about his conduct was an act of bravery such as Jakob had rarely seen before or since.

Sven had asked, "Did the first interlocutor touch you?"

"No. He looked at me. He made a circle, like this." She circled the carpet, doing an impression of a masculine leer that froze Jakob's blood.

"He told me, 'Hold your hands above your head. Turn.' The room was cold. It made goose flesh on my skin. He spoke about this. He said it proved the women of my country are not hot blooded, as men think. He took a pen from his pocket. He did this"—she flicked her wrist—"and dotted my breast with ink. That is what he did. Is it enough?"

Jakob was unsure what she was asking. Sven said, "The first interlocutor is a powerful man, Belen. What do you think, Mr. Freeman? Did he abuse his power?"

"Yes," Jakob was sure. "A flagrant abuse."

"You will have him removed?" said Belen.

Sven had looked at her sadly. Jakob had hung his head. Even years later, the memory stung. The only thing more shameful than what the first interlocutor had done was their powerlessness against him. A written complaint to the Studio; was that all Belen's suffering had been worth? Jakob had acted coolly to Simmons, even obstructed a few of his minor enterprises. He had always felt guilty about not doing more.

"That for me, guy?" said the man standing in front of him.

Jakob looked at Martinez, saw the ex-star was pointing at his bottle. "Might as well be. I don't have the stomach." He scooped up Sven's panda and made to stand.

"What's the rush, guy? My name's Nat. What's yours?"

"Sorry," said Jakob.

"Funny name."

"I mean, I was just leaving."

Nat said, "I smell bad or something? Hey, Lucas, I smell bad to you?"

The bodyguard was standing a few feet away, trying to blend in with the wood paneling on the wall. "No, Mr. Martinez," he said. "You smell fine."

"Hear that?" said Nat. "Lucas says I don't smell, and he's very sensitive. Why do you want to go, guy?"

Jakob gave him a tight smile. "It's nothing to do with you. Something on my mind."

"I know the feeling. Happens to me all the time. Only thing you can do, in my experience, is talk it out."

"Sorry. I'm not in the mood."

Jakob's patience with strangers was done for the day. He rose and took two steps before Nat tapped his shoulder.

"Hold on, guy. I know you. Where from? Don't leave without telling me. It'll haunt me forever."

That was a feeling Jakob knew. "I'm with Bliss," he said. "Jakob Freeman."

"Freeman. Yeah, I remember. On the news. Sad story. Came out about the time Len and I were on our honeymoon. You were the blissman who got married, but your wife . . . A real shame. GS2 did a week of special coverage."

The impulse to leave was still strong with Jakob, but his will was overcome by Nat's charm. "It was GS4," he said, sliding back onto his stool.

"Right, GS4. They're all about the human interest angle. Always Len's favorite."

It occurred to Jakob that not all husbands were so comfortable expressing their wives' opinions. He never had been himself. If Nat was sincere, it reflected well on the marriage.

"How is Mrs. Martinez?" he said.

"She's the best. Thanks for asking. She remembers you, I'm sure. When we saw your story, she told me you met."

Jakob glanced away. If Mrs. Martinez had told her husband about the meeting, he was either a man of little feeling or skilled at not letting emotions show. Probably she had kept the details to herself.

The bartender dropped by long enough to take Nat's order of a dry white wine. When he was gone, Nat said, "Hey, tell me. What was that you put in your pocket a minute ago? It made me think of somebody else I used to know."

The possibility that Nat had looked upon the glory of Sven's collection made it impossible for Jakob to refuse the request. He displayed the panda and was rewarded by a vigorous nod from Nat.

"There it is. I was right. You know Thomson, yeah? *Mi hermano*. He loved stuff like that."

Jakob opened his mouth to ask if Nat had seen Sven since his star turn, but before he could get a word out, one of the drunks at the far end of the bar knocked another drunk to the floor. The fallen man came up cursing. He pulled a knife and stabbed upward, narrowly missing the other man. The bartender dropped the wine glass he had been polishing and shouted to a waiter as he seized a wooden baseball bat from a rack over the bar. Patrons who had been drinking at tables made a ring around the combatants, jostling for position and shouting bets. The bodyguard, Lucas, pulled Nat Martinez from his seat.

"There's a back way out," said Nat. "Come with us."

Jakob didn't object. Stuffing the panda in his pocket, he followed Nat and Lucas through an abandoned rec area featuring a three-legged pool table in the middle of the floor. A half-dozen arcade cabinets were arranged around the walls, some with darkened TV screens and built-in control sticks still intact. None of the cabinets worked, of course. Jakob had never heard anyone claim to have played one of the dead machines. He headed for a metal door beside a cabinet on which faded green letters spelled out the word *Galaga*. The door was marked "Emergency Exit Only—Alarm Will Sound," but when Lucas pushed, the only noise was the groan of hinges.

The alley outside was dark. Nat stepped close so Jakob could see his eyes. "You believe that, *vato*? *Hombres* be crazy these days." He laughed. "Makes you feel alive, you know?"

Jakob felt dizzy, but he had to admit, he was exhilarated. "I guess so."

"You know what?" said Nat. "I was wrong, back there. You don't need to talk about your problems. What you need is action. I see it now, *hermano*. Action is what you need. Ever watch 'em dance the Widow's Web?"

Jakob had never heard the words strung together in that order. "No. What is—"

"You'll love it, guy. And you're in luck. There's bouts every couple months and, wouldn't you know it? Tonight's the night. Come on. We're going. Don't say no. It's just what you need to get your mind off your troubles."

Between his spinning head and Nat's personality, Jakob saw there was no point arguing.

"If you say so."

"I do, guy, I do. This way. Car's around the corner. Don't worry about a thing. I promise you, after tonight, you'll see the world in a whole new light."

***

The drive took less than an hour, much less than Jakob would have expected if he had known how far they were going from everything he knew. The lights of Culver City disappeared over the crest of a hill as Lucas drove Nat's sedan into a valley lit by headlights and barrel fires. The landscape was a mix of sandy flatland and terraced slopes. Aside from the sand and the rusted fences that seemed to exist only to frame pampas grass, the most distinct feature Jakob could see were the abandoned oil pumps that looked like giant metal birds stuck in the middle of pecking holes in the ground.

Nat had insisted Jakob ride in the front seat, while he rode in back. As they bumped over a lower hill, he pointed over Jakob's shoulder at a level patch where vehicles could be seen weaving in and out of each other's paths on a stretch of hardpack. They seemed unconcerned about coming within inches of collision.

Unlike Nat's electric vehicle, every pickup, sedan, and SUV on the patch was spewing smoke from its tailpipe. Spotlights set on the sides of surrounding hills highlighted the smoke of many colors. One rebuilt muscle car spun donuts while wreathing itself in crimson vapor. A tri-wheel roadster drove around the perimeter of the patch, marking a misty boundary in peach.

"Is that where we're going?" asked Jakob, wondering how many of the close calls he observed were real and how many were a product of his buzzed imagination.

"Just a sideshow," said Nat. "Most of those posers don't even do their own bodywork."

Lucas took a left turn and guided the sedan through several curves and up a hill. When they came in sight of what Nat had actually brought Jakob to see, pointing was unnecessary. The immense metal structure that stood in the middle of the stony plateau was unmistakably the center of something, though Jakob still couldn't say what. He'd had no idea that the radiation shield over the city extended this far. Everyone knew the outlands were irradiated; surely they were at least at the fringes of that blighted area.

Nat handed him a pair of folding binoculars. They looked like antiques, something Sven would have liked for his collection. Nat worked the catch for Jakob and showed him how to focus. With the benefit of magnification, he made out a collection of gangways arranged in two vertical stacks. The materials appeared to have been scavenged from derelict fire escapes. Bits of railing, grated bridges designed for short spans, along with retractable ladders had been braced together to form a pair of four-story monstrosities that should have collapsed under their own weight, to say nothing of the weight of the men swarming over them like fleas over a corpse.

Nat called them, "Viewing stands. After the bout tonight they'll pull the pins and knock 'em down, so they look like junk."

"They look like junk now," said Jakob.

"What's that talk, guy? The best engineers in LA put the Web together. They're paid good money by the filthiest bookies. What you're looking at is the beating heart of black market entertainment."

"So it's illegal."

"Legal is what you can get away with, my friend."

Like the vehicle show, the grandstands and grounds were illuminated by mounted spotlight beams. Jakob saw a pair of tread-driven mobile cranes situated to the left and right of the space between stands. The telescoping booms had been extended to a length of more than a hundred feet, so that even canted at a forty-five degree angle, they towered above the stands. From the ends of each boom, a cable had been run out. To Jakob's amazement, a man could be seen swinging at the end of each cable. Backlit and moving fast, the bodies appeared as black blurs.

As Jakob watched, speechless, one man orbited his boom as the crane operator guided it through a dip and turn. The other man brandished a long pole topped by a vicious-looking hook. He tilted at the orbiting man, swinging like a pendulum, and snagged a leg of his opponent. The hook drew blood, but after tumbling end over end, the injured man managed to right himself. He caught hold of the cable, hefted his own hook, and swung back around.

The sedan dipped downhill at that moment, and Jakob, shocked by the plunge, dropped the binoculars in his lap. He said, "What are they doing? Do they want to kill each other?"

"Nah," said Nat. "They're Web riders. Nobody wants 'em to die. Not other riders, not the crowd, not even the bookies. They want action, like me and you. Action takes risk. What do you figure a man's life is worth these days? Less than those guys are getting paid, I'll tell you that."

Lucas parked the car under a thick-bodied palm tree, near a host of other vehicles. By the time they reached the stands, one of the Web riders was dangling at the end of his line. His hook hung from a short chain attached to his belt, and blood was oozing from a gash in his leg. Jakob could only tell the rider was alive by the jerky motion of one upraised hand.

The other rider was quite lively. He stood on top of a shiny metal dome, roughly fifteen feet in diameter, that capped a slim, thirty-foot tower situated in the square formed by the stands and cranes. The dome sat atop a wheel that extended beyond its base and rotated slowly beneath it. The Web rider's cable trailed behind him, its weight threatening to pull him off his perch. To combat this, he had anchored his pole to the encircling wheel. He had to shift his weight constantly as the wheel turned, which made him appear to be dancing.

From one side of the stands, the audience was roaring encouragement. From the other side, they were hooting loud boos. Over a public address system, a crackly voice bellowed a count. "Eight! Nine! Ten!"

An air horn sounded. The standing rider pumped a fist before dropping from the dome.

The amplified voice said, "That's it, boyos! That's change. Lo Ang takes the bout for Hard Line, putting the Sleazy Riders down by two in the series. Kole and Dutch better get their rest in the reset. If they go down again, that's game! Now, if you'll excuse me, folks, your friend Dusty Dog needs to settle a wager. Who was it told me that Sleazy was due? You're dead to me, boyo. To the rest of you, love and peace until the next bout!"

"Sounds like we missed a live one," said Nat. "Don't worry, reset only takes a few minutes."

Even as he spoke, the cable supporting the dangling man slackened. He plummeted ten feet to be caught by a crowd of supporters assembled below.

"I've never seen anything like this," said Jakob.

"There *is* nothing like it, guy. You afraid of heights?"

He didn't wait for Jakob's answer but grabbed his sleeve and drew him after Lucas. They went up the clanging stairs to the second level. Every man they passed was in motion, some hopping up and down, some bouncing in place on the bowing, creaking metal. A frenzied human mass hustled up and down steps and scurried over gangways, clearly used to unsteady footing.

Nearly all the spectators wore overalls. Stitched insignia identified them as ditch diggers and sewer scrubbers, though the smell made it obvious who did what. In the fists of nearly every man were stacks of plastic chits. Jakob assumed they had something to do with the betting.

The crowd was a good deal rougher than anything Nat, as a married man, should have been around, yet he slapped backs and traded jokes like he knew everyone there. On the way to the fourth floor, he even paused to place a bet with a pockmarked bookie. Jakob clung to the railing as stepped up to the stand's top floor. He could feel the grating sag underfoot as he stood next to Nat, watching the regulars jostle elbows without a care.

From where he stood, he could see both cranes, now emptied of their cargo, as well as the narrow tower with its dome and now stationary wheel. Nat drew his attention to a cluster of men standing beside the crane to their left. In the middle of the knot of bodies was a stocky youth with green hair. Assistants were strapping him into a harness while he tipped a bottle to his lips. Another man, presumably one of Green Hair's entourage, was rallying the audience on Jakob's side of the stands by shaking a hook in the air.

Nat said, "The guy with the green thatch is Kole Kash. He rides the line for black market cred. I can get behind that. Here, take the specs again." He handed Jakob the binoculars. "Look that way. There's the krow-bait we hate."

Jakob scanned the field. In the shadow of the right-hand crane, a bald man had just finished getting into harness.

"That's Dutch. He rides for Hard Line. His partner, Lo Ang, won the last bout. Now he has to drive crane. Get it? There he is, walking up."

The man Jakob had seen dancing on the dome approached Dutch. They stood for a moment before touching their foreheads together. Lo Ang screamed into Dutch's face. Dutch screamed into Lo Ang's. The screams were covered by the noise from the stands, but seeing two men pressed so close together was uncomfortable enough to make Jakob's skin crawl. He watched Lo Ang pass his hook to Dutch, who seized it, kissed it, then turned his head and spat. The crowd in the opposite stand began to chant.

"Dutch! Dutch! Dutch!"

Nat and the men around Jakob booed.

"You didn't pick sides at random, then?" said Jakob.

Nat said, "I never do. This is Sleazy side. We cheer the Sleazy Riders. Ain't that right, *hombres?*"

Several bystanders cheered in agreement.

"Yeah. So, the way it works is, one guy rides the line while the other drives. The rider has to dance the dome, one foot on for ten seconds, no help from the line. When he does, that's a match. Three out of five wins the game.

"You just saw Hot Rod, Kole's partner, get hauled to the side. He won't be back. That means Kole gets a backup driver for this match. There. That's him, the kid with a hook. Don't worry. I've seen him drive. He's good. Sleazy's down, but not out."

Nat couldn't have looked more determined if he had been about to strap on a harness himself. There had been moments Sven had that same determination, usually after one of his brilliant lectures about life in the World Before.

Jakob asked, "How did you become a fan?"

In a low voice, Nat said, "Between me and you, I like Sleazy fine, but I mostly want to see Hard Line go down."

"You have something against them?"

The determined expression departed, replaced by something harder. "Dutch and Lo Ang used to be hatchetmen, back before Flynn made cutbacks. You've probably never seen one of those mothercutters without his helmet. That's what they look like. Dead ugly. Good for scrap. Even though they got cut, they brag about being goons for the Little Angel. Hired 'cause of good blood. Ha! To hear them talk, every chromehead is groom material. You believe that? That they only keep their helmets on so the public won't see how pretty they are and make the Studio put on a hundred public weddings a year instead of six.

"What do you think, Mr. Blissman? Look at those two and tell me. How much pure blood are the races missing by not putting those *malparidos* out to stud?"

His request was simple enough for a blissman with a trained eye. Through the binoculars, Jakob examined Lo Ang as he was climbing into the crane's cab. His skin was pale. He had the high, broad cheekbones of a Fin or Chinese, but his bald head made it impossible to tell if he had been born blond or brunette.

The other man, Dutch, had a more typical complexion, light brown with red undertones. He might have been some breed of Pacific Islander, but more likely his blood was the usual blend. A mongrel mix flowed in the veins of most men, including Jakob's. It was nothing to get excited about. What made him different—what had granted him a wife—was his extreme privilege of working for the Studio in the capacity he did.

He folded the binoculars. "I see possibilities, but nothing remarkable. This is the first I've heard of hatchetmen being special genetically."

"That's because it's blankshot. Those guys talk and talk, but they don't say nothing. Some *bravos*, yeah? They get knocked in the gutter, they brag about the fall."

A particularly strong wind made the stand buck. Jakob braced, then said, "What gutter are you talking about?"

Nat said, "La-La Land is a gutter, guy. Didn't you know? You and me and everybody, we're all in it. Those idiots are in it. They only talk like they're above us. That's why we hate 'em, guy." He lowered his voice further. "And their old bosses too, eh?"

Jakob glanced around. If anyone had heard the treasonous talk, they gave no sign. He considered asking, "What did the Studio do to you?" They had made Nat a celebrity, married him to a beautiful woman, and paid him to keep her pregnant. What could they have done, after all that, to turn his love into hate?

Jakob felt a weird mixture of confusion and admiration. Any man who could talk this way about the Studio, which most men discussed in the same glowing terms usually reserved for the Big Dad in the Sky, was a man to be taken seriously. How close had he been with Sven? No word of complaint had ever passed his colleague's lips, so far as Jakob could remember. Had he missed something—some hidden, revolutionary current, for all those years?

Before any of these thoughts had formed into words, a horn signaled the start of the next match. The random assortment of electrically powered megaphones bolted to the grated metal gave a crackle.

The voice of the announcer, Dusty Dog, said, "We on?"

Nat pointed to a booth, where a man with a tide of gray beard washing over his belly sat speaking into a microphone.

"Remember, boyos, if Kole don't dance this time, Sleazy is benched until we loop the bracket. After last raid, who knows when that'll be?"

Elbowing Jakob, Nat said, "If somebody shouts 'raid,' we run, okay?"

Dusty Dog continued. "I hear Hot Rod's leg swole up so bad, it looks like it's got a baby in there. It'll be tough to pay the doctor without that winner's purse. What do you think, boyos? Can Kole Kash keep hope alive for the Sleazy fans, or is Hard Line gonna send 'em to La Brea on a tar pit tour? We'll find out in five . . . four . . ."

The two combatants rose into the air. As their cables retracted, they hugged their hooks to their chests. The audience joined Dusty Dog in the countdown.

At *three*, the booms of the cranes rotated ninety degrees in opposite directions.

At *two*, the booms rotated back, sending the riders, Kole and Dutch, hurtling through the air.

At *one*, the opposing hooks collided, striking sparks. Kole lost his grip on the hook, but it didn't fall far before rebounding back on the chain. Kole caught the hook, hefted it, and held it high, ready to strike back at Dutch.

The cranes swung the riders around for a second pass. This time, they flew more slowly, but in a wider arc. An instant before the hooks clashed, Dutch's crane let out line, dropping him below Kole. Hauling on cable, Dutch inverted himself so that he hung head down. He tried to snag the wheel, but Kole's driver let out line while pivoting his boom.

Kole swept close to Dutch, swinging his hook, and snagged Dutch's cable even as Dutch hooked the wheel. Dutch had barely planted a foot on the dome when he was hauled away. He twisted in midair, swinging the hook with fury. He caught the collar of Kole's coverall. The audience cheered as the sharp point of the hook slashed through the fabric.

Jakob's heart raced, certain the Sleazy Rider must have been badly wounded.

"Oh!" said Dusty Dog. "Bad cut. Kole's lucky he's still got his harness."

Again, the booms pivoted. This time Kole was carried in a nearly vertical ascent. Dutch's driver made a slight adjustment, sending the ex-hatchetman back to the wheel. Dutch tried to hook the wheel, but missed. The hook hit the dome and rang it like a gong.

"Time for supper!" said Dusty Dog. There was laughter on the Sleazy side.

Kole's driver swung the boom one way, then the other. He appeared to be floundering, unsure what to do. The crowd shouted advice. At last, the crane swung Kole in a tight arc, but too late. Kole's hook missed Dutch by a mile. Before Kole reached the end of his swing, Dutch caught the wheel and hauled himself onto the gleaming dome.

The Sleazy Rider fans moaned, but before Dutch caught his balance, Kole loosed the chain from his belt and hurled the hook like a javelin. It slammed into the back of Dutch's knee. Dutch flapped his arms, like he expected to fly, and slipped from the dome.

But he was still anchored. Instead of shaking the hook off the wheel so he could make a new pass, he clung to the chain, letting the wheel carry him in a circle as his driver played out cable. Hand over hand, he climbed the chain, then the hook. Kole sailed by, helpless without his own hook, which had fallen and been claimed by his crew below.

Dutch reached the wheel. He got his chest onto it, then, with a mighty swing of his legs, and threw himself up. He danced on the dome, shaking the hook. His cable trailed behind him, visibly slack.

"He's on," said Dusty Dog. His tone made it clear he had bet poorly again. "That's one, folks. Two."

To his complete surprise, Jakob heard himself shout, "No!"

Exactly when he had started caring about the contest, he couldn't say. The visceral appeal was obvious, but like Nat, he didn't care so much about seeing Kole rise as Dutch fall. The hatchetman had to go down, he had to be humiliated. Since the moment his wife's eyes closed for the final time, Jakob had wanted nothing so much.

"It's not over," said Nat. He pointed to Kole, whose trajectory was taking him down and away from the crane.

Below, one of his crew—a man so tall and broad he could have been another Lucas or Mondt—cast the hook at Kole. It flew so fast and clanked so thunderously, it might as well have been a lightning bolt. Kole caught it. Yes! He caught the bolt and let it glide through his hands until he was holding the hook high above his head.

As Kole passed the lowest point of his arc, the driver hauled in line. Kole flew upward like a dart and shot past the lip of the wheel. As he did, he brought his hook down in a devastating blow to Dutch's back. Off balance now, the weight of his cable toppled him. A solid kick from Kole Kash knocked him from the dome.

"Astonishing save by Kole!" said Dusty Dog. "I haven't seen a smash like that since the finals of '06. Or was it '07?"

Kole dangled for a moment before the crane driver swung him gently to the dome.

But Hard Line wasn't giving up; Lo Ang dipped his boom while hauling in cable, making Dutch spin as he arced at Kole. The rider was too stunned to do anything but act as dead weight. Kole dodged him easily and began to dance on the dome.

"One," counted Jakob. The crowd joined in for the *two* and *three*.

Lo Ang brought Dutch around, this time aimed at Kole's shins. Instead of dodging, Kole ducked, keeping one foot on the dome. Dutch missed him again.

"Four," counted Jakob. "Five. Six."

As Dutch bobbed and swung, Kole defended himself with his hook. Dutch was struck and deflected. Blood flew from somewhere, splashing the crowd as they counted. "Seven. Eight. Nine!"

The crane lurched. The lump that was Dutch jolted, pitched, and yawed in response to his partner's desperate driving. The puppet body, trailing its hook, flew at Kole for one last try. Lo Ang didn't seem to care what happened to the man whose forehead his had met earlier in a gesture of solidarity. He swung Dutch like a wrecking ball. With nowhere to go, Kole hunkered down, covering his head with his forearms. Dutch crashed against him as the crowd counted, "Ten!"

The air horn sounded. Kole flew from his perch, but no matter. He had won!

Dusty Dog bellowed, "He did it, by Dad! Sleazy Riders stay alive!"

No joy was ever greater, no victory more pure. Jakob hugged Nat, kissed him on both cheeks, pumped a fist, and shook the railing. The men around him, strangers he would have walked in a ditch to avoid rather than meet on the street, clapped him on the back and shook him by the hand.

"What did I tell you?" said Nat, shouting over the racket. "This is what you needed, right here."

"Did you see that hit?" said Jakob. "That was—I mean, what an ending! I, uh, hope they weren't hurt."

"Sure they were hurt," Nat told him. "If we're lucky, Dutch'll have a broke back. That ride was prime, guy, prime."

Jakob watched as helpers on the ground scurried to take Dutch and Kole off their lines. Kole had lost his wind, but he waved to the crowd to make up for his silence. Dutch was moving enough to show he was alive, but not much more.

A memory of Kirimi Teng's smashed body flashed before Jakob's eyes. He swallowed acid and crushed the handrail, more aware than ever of the creaking from the bouncing tower.

"You hear that?" said Nat. "C'mon."

For an instant, Jakob thought he meant the creaking, but other sounds were coming from below. There were roaring engines, a siren howl. Nat pulled Jakob along behind Lucas, who bashed a hole for them in the crowd. At the first set of stairs, Jakob had a moment to glance over the railing at a half-dozen vehicles zipping across the plateau, flashing their lights as the sirens droned.

"Raid's coming," said Nat. "Good signal, huh?"

Before they reached ground level, the Widow's Web spotlights cut out. The darkness was daunting, though incomplete. The bobbing lights of warning vehicles helped them find the swollen palm tree, where Lucas had parked the car.

"Will they use the COP?" said Jakob.

Nat held the door for his guest. "If we let 'em get too close."

Lucas put the pedal down to keep that from happening. Soon the glimpses of crane, dome, and stands that Jakob was able to catch in the bobbing lights were no more. The Widow's Web was out of sight.

When they had put enough distance in for Lucas to slow down, Nat turned to Jakob and said, "You remember my wife, *hermano*?"

"I . . . Yes."

"Great. We're having folks over Friday night. Seven o'clock, Arcadia Arms, conapt sixty-one. Come as you are. You want I should send the car?"

The night had become dreamlike. Jakob had to blink himself awake to answer. "No. No, thank you. But, what's going to happen?"

"Huh? Oh, dinner. You know."

"No, I meant, with the raid. What will happen to . . . everything?"

"What do you think? The Studio don't care about the black market, really. They only send their goons so they can let off steam. The chromeheads will wreck the stands. They'll move the cranes somewhere. Give it a month, we'll get it rebuilt."

"What about the men?"

"What about 'em? You think it's hard finding guys to fill the stands? Those riders put their lives on the line. Whoever don't get out will get his knees busted. Same ol' thing. They'll be back, most of 'em. The rest that don't make it, who needs 'em, you know?"

The binoculars were in the blazer's left pocket, opposite the panda figurine, which was in the right. Jakob tried to hand the binoculars to Nat, but he said, "Keep 'em. You coming Friday at seven, or what?"

The spectacle Jakob had just witnessed was like nothing he thought could exist in LA. If an illegal, underground sports industry, regularly torn to pieces by the Studio and built back from scraps, existed in Nat's world, he wanted to know what else was there, but feared finding out at the same time. What had Sven known of this hidden world? A novel thought struck him. What would Kutri think of it all?

He could never tell her, of course. His duty was to guide her, not confide in her, and anyway, what was she to him? A pleasant enough girl, and a beauty. Such a beauty. That angel face, skin brown as the clear sky. She smelled of cinnamon, and her cheek would be warm silk if he touched it with the back of his hand. Jimmy Ching was right. With those breasts, those hips, she was every Ma there had ever been.

"Hey," said Nat. "You with me, guy?"

Jakob said, "Yes. Sorry. What was the question?"

"Friday night," said Nat. He chuckled. "You coming, or what?"

Still unsure what to answer, Jakob sat back. He slid the binoculars away, taking the moment to steady his nerves. "All right," he said. "I won't say no."

"Good," said Nat. "I mean, I want you to say what you want, but one step at a time, yeah?"

Forty minutes later, Jakob stood in front of the security gate at Union Station. He waved to Nat as Lucas drove away. A familiar sequence of concrete corridors later, he collapsed, fully clothed, on the cot in the windowless bunker where he slept. Early Thursday morning, while it was still dark, he awoke.

Thoughts were racing in his head. How well had Sven known Nat Martinez? How well had Nat Martinez known Sven? It seemed everyone was a secret friend of his absent colleague. If Kutri had been a local, instead of coming from overseas, he was sure she could have told him secrets about the man he thought he knew better than anyone on earth.

She was a beauty, that one. Sven had been beautiful too, in his own way. What had Jakob ever done to deserve such beauty in his life? Nothing. He had never done anything to deserve beauty, yet beauty had come. Sven had done everything, and been rewarded in death. There was no justice in LA. What had Nat called the city?

A gutter. How right he had been.

Sven had deserved better than life in the gutter. Jakob could do nothing about that now. Perhaps he could do something for the girl, Kutri, instead. She seemed like she deserved better, at least. Her worth might be skin deep, but so what? She happened to be the only person whose life he could influence to good or ill.

He would show her truth, as he was starting to understand it. Sven had always said teaching somebody was the best way to learn. He would teach her LA was a gutter, learning along the way what that meant to him. Maybe together, he and Kutri could figure out where to go from there.

He got up, cleaned his teeth, and hung up his clothes. Hours of darkness were left before dawn. Back on the cot, he meditated on silken skin, amber eyes, and breasts and hips that formed an hourglass with the waist between. His body relaxed quickly. His mind, not so much. It took minutes of tossing and turning and a second, more furious session of deep thought before he was able to sleep.

Chapter Six: Angel Town

Kutri sat at a broad pedestal table in a room made of glass. There were two couples dining at the tables, each a bride and groom from a previous season of *Good Breeding*. She recognized the former chemical engineer Antoine Huxley and his wife, Janessa, who years ago had made news by carrying to term the first twin girls in a century. The other couple, Quinn and Karan Politis, were even more famous, being the oldest star couple still of breeding age. An immaculate beauty whose skin never showed a wrinkle, Karan's face appeared on screens all over the world. In LA, Kutri had seen her image on billboards only slightly less often than the image of the Studio president, Gerard Flynn.

A crowd had gathered to watch Kutri and the celebrities in their fishbowl. Through the glass walls, Kutri saw men wearing rags standing cheek-to-jowl with office workers in jackets and ties. Surely they had more pressing business than watching people chew, but they evidently didn't think so. For Kutri's part, she wasn't sure she would be able to take a bite under scrutiny, even if Jakob kept his promise to join her for breakfast. So far, even the grapefruit juice her waiter had poured for her felt too intimate. She hadn't touched it, despite the waiter's assurance it was a delicacy not to be missed.

Aside from the eyes outside the fishbowl, sets of eyes within also made her nervous. The presence of a man with a shoulder-mounted video camera was bad enough. But what really set her teeth on edge were the surveillance cameras set high on the glass walls. They were small, far smaller than any camera she had ever seen, and they glowed with a faint light.

Kutri was far from certain she would have noticed the cameras on an ordinary wall, where she might have assumed they were ornaments, or bubbles in the paint. The thought that hidden cameras might have watched her since she set foot in LA unnerved her. Last night, she had sprawled on top of the covers in the oversized bed she had been assigned as a candidate, reading *Pindar* in the nude. She had thought about Jakob while in the nude as well, imagining his hands stroking her skin in places she was used to feeling Papa Paquette's callouses. Though when she thought of Jakob, her mind conjured liberties Papa had never dared to take. He treasured his own life too much, so he only touched and imagined.

She was daydreaming of Jakob when the hiss of a sliding door announced his arrival. The blue blazer he had on was identical to the one he had worn on their first meeting, but she preferred the tan trousers he had substituted for yesterday's charcoal. How handsome he looked, though perhaps a bit tired. Mondt, who nodded to acknowledge Jakob's wave, seemed twice as alert, though dour as ever.

On three sides of the sheltered eating space, a line of helmeted hatchetmen was maintaining a two-meter perimeter. The fourth side of the space was a solid opaque wall. It belonged to the restaurant catering their meal. A hatchetman was posted by the door to the restaurant. He approached Jakob carrying an opaque plastic cube a little larger than his palm.

"Hold still," Kutri heard the hatchetman say. "I'll exclude you from the circuit." He touched the cube to the base of Jakob's skull. "There you go."

Jakob did not offer thanks but hurried to the table as the hatchetman returned to his post. The men on the other side of the glass raised their voices, the glass transmitting their shouts as a low hum. If there were words in the shouting, they were lost. Gestures carried the men's meaning.

Men raised their fists and tugged their cuffs, buffing the wrist and forearm. Other men groped the fronts of their overalls. Some simply pointed between their legs. The only men who did not tug, grope, or point were missing an arm or an ear, or in a few cases, a leg. She had seen a few like them peering out of the shadows, yesterday. How strange to see so many whose work was of the greatest danger.

After a few seconds of rude motions, the hatchetmen took action. Kutri saw one pressing a button on the box attached to his chest. The crowd seized with a shared spasm. Kutri knew about the Civil Obedience

Protocol but had never seen it in action. She recoiled at the grimaces, the frozen agony that spoke of inescapable pain. After a brief jolt, the crowd was released, much to Kutri's relief.

Jakob seated himself across the table. "I'm sorry you had to see that."

"I pity them," said Kutri. There seemed nothing else to say on the subject, so she changed it. "I'm glad you came."

"We had an appointment."

"We did. You didn't have to keep it. I'm not used to men who keep promises."

"I make a point of it. Still, if I hadn't come, it's not like you'd be eating alone."

Shrugging to stop a chill, Kutri tilted her head toward the crowd. "Their attention is flattering, but it is not very appetizing."

"You'll have to get used to it," said Jakob, sounding more like the matchmakers she had seen on television than he had before then. "There will be crowds from now until the Presentation Ball. If you're picked as match bride, it will only get worse."

He took a moment to wave at their dining companions, first the Huxleys, then the Politises. The women and their husbands waved back.

"Janessa and Karan could tell you what it's like. Maybe you'll get a chance to talk to them. From the moment you leave your apartment to the moment you go back inside, you're going to be watched. If no one made that clear to you, I'm sorry. The Office of Justice doesn't enforce ISBA as they should. If they did, what you should expect would have been made clear."

"Excuse me," she said, "what is ISBA?"

"The International Standard for Bliss Administration. Your Bliss Center was a signatory or they wouldn't have been eligible to offer you as a candidate. Clearly, though, they didn't train you for this level of scrutiny. Don't worry. I'm here for you now."

A thrill of pleasure ran through Kutri at his words, bringing with it the memory of last night on her bed. She said, "I'm so happy you are."

He smiled, then raised an eyebrow. "You haven't touched your grapefruit juice."

She gave a toss of her hair. "Oh, I will. I'm feeling quite hungry."

"Despite the company?"

"I would say, because of the company."

They kept a companionable silence for a minute after that, until a waiter—the same man who had brought the juice—entered the glass room from the restaurant wall. Behind the lanky, tuxedoed man came three rolling carts, each propelled by a small boy dressed in white overalls and a chef's hat.

A gasp went up from the crowd that was loud enough to hear as a hiss. Kutri herself gasped at the sight of three flesh-and-blood children, in this city of grown men. She would have thought it a vision. If any of the children had been a girl, she would have thought it a miracle. The absurd idea, combined with her joy at seeing the little ones, made her laugh out loud.

The waiter came straight to Kutri and Jakob's table. He clapped his hands. With the discipline of soldiers, the boys stopped their carts. At a second clap from the waiter, they tossed their hats in the air and began dashing around the table, whooping like a troop of macaques. The waiter clapped a third time. The boy with the darkest complexion ran off to join the Huxleys. The remaining two, both with wavy hair like Karan Politis, ran and grabbed a hand each of their famous mother.

All three boys hopped and cheered, partially in obedience to their script, Kutri was sure, and partially in genuine excitement. They didn't often get to come out before a crowd. Thinking back through past seasons, Kutri could think of only a few episodes that featured children. She listened to the muffled clapping of the crowd and marveled at how quickly they had forgotten their pain. Certainly, children were a blessing, even if they were all boys.

The families filed out under the watchful gaze of the shoulder camera and its mounted supports. Janessa Huxley and Karan Politis each gave Kutri an empathetic expression before passing through the restaurant door. She blinked back tears, moved by their concern toward her. What a joy it would be to join their circle permanently, first as match bride of *Good Breeding*, then as a veteran star.

The applause died down. The waiter, who had not twitched a muscle since his last clap, uncovered plates on the first two rolling carts. He set a plate in front of Kutri and handed another to Jakob. The third cart held water and a steaming container of coffee, as well as a decanter that smelled distinctly of jasmine tea. When the waiter asked his preference, Jakob waved him away and poured himself a glass of the grapefruit juice from the pitcher on the table.

He raised his glass. Kutri raised her own. They clinked and sipped. Immediately, Kutri regretted the action. The juice was as sour as pickled lemon. It took every ounce of her reserve not to spit on the carpet that had been placed over the concrete slab beneath the fishbowl room. Setting her teeth, she fixed her grin and forced herself to swallow. The horrible stuff stung all the way down.

Jakob held his smile through a countdown from the cameraman. At one, he said, "You can relax. They've cut away to another candidate."

"That was awful," said Kutri.

"What? I'm sure the children were happy to be here."

"Not them. I meant the drink. The waiter said it was grapefruit. It is like no grape I have ever tasted."

Jakob laughed, spilling some of his own juice. "Dad Above, I'm sorry. Fruit of any kind is hard to come by on this side of the Pacific. We practically drink vinegar. I'm sure you're used to something sweeter." The sound of his laugh—warm, free, and calming—was wonderful, even though it had come at her expense.

She laughed too, and said, "Much," sucking in cool air to cool her tongue.

"Do excuse me," he said. A moment later, he raised a hand to stifle a yawn. "Oh, dear. Excuse me again."

"Did you have a long night?"

"Yes. You could say that."

Did you dream about me? she wanted to ask. What she actually said was, "Is something on your mind?"

He patted a pocket of his emblazoned jacket. There was a lump there, on the right side. "You, mostly. Your match. I'll be reading up on the candidates for your match groom, today. All excellent gentleman, I'm sure, but I wish . . ." He grimaced and didn't say what he wished. "The actual selection is out of my hands, you see. I can only advise my colleagues. And here I'm the one who's supposed to get to know you, to shepherd you—in a way, to teach you the ways of the world."

Kutri stuck a fork into her poached egg. "You think I don't know what the world is? No, please, don't answer. I'm very happy to learn, happy to have you as teacher. Especially today, my first real day under scrutiny. Already, I feel the weight of expectation."

"May I advise you on that?"

"Of course you may."

"My advice is, enjoy yourself. This is your day in the sun."

Her outfit for the day was a simple minidress of opalescent blue. It had a businesslike cut that encouraged her to think seriously rather than playfully.

She said, "Will you be honest with me?"

"Yes. We have to trust each other."

"I feel that way too. After our trip yesterday, I decided you are the sort of man I can trust. Tell me, in truth. Can I make it to the top?"

He seemed genuinely surprised. "You have to ask? Miss Kutri, you're an excellent candidate. One of the best I've ever seen. I will be deeply surprised if you are not named match bride next week."

"You're so confident?"

"I am. Consider what you have going for you. You're attractive, obviously. I know the other candidates will be the best our trading partners can offer, but even sitting in a room with the divine Mrs. Politis, you shine like a diamond among pearls."

Kutri's cheeks went hot. "I can't compare. Thank you."

"You can compare. And you do, favorably. So, you're attractive, first. Second, you're intelligent. You've only ever seen *Good Breeding* as it's edited for TV, so I'd excuse you for doubting, but trust me, brains really do make the difference. The seven women we hope to acknowledge as candidates have all been vetted for intelligence. You score very well in that category, I assure you. Do you recall the season six years ago, when Janessa Huxley was chosen?"

She had watched every season, either live or in reruns.

"It's a not-too-distant memory."

"Janessa was the sole survivor of the first batch of candidates. We had to delay the program a full two weeks to find her competition. She was too brilliant, compared to that first batch, to raise any sense of honest competition. After Janessa, we raised the IQ requirement for all the candidates. At least in that regard, the partners do pay attention to ISBA standards. These days, they know better than to send any girl who is not the brightest spark of light."

"Flattery," she said.

"Not at all. Your intelligence sets you above most women I have seen come through the doors at Bliss HQ. That, and your physical qualities, make you almost impossible to beat. With your third advantage, well . . ."

She waited for him to finish. When he didn't, she said, "You see? You do overestimate my intelligence. What is my third advantage? I cannot imagine."

"Why, your Punjabi heritage, naturally. It really is quite rare. Quite precious, if I may say so."

She dropped her fork. Jakob's tone was different, but his choice of words were almost identical to the first interlocutor's. Suddenly, her appetite was gone.

"Did I say something wrong?" asked Jakob.

"Not at all. How could you? Tell me, how are relations between Bliss and the other offices? You mentioned the Office of Justice, how they will not keep this ISBA. Apart from that frustration, do you get along?"

A shadow touched his expression, but only for a moment. He said, "There's jealousy, from time to time. We all feel the other offices could work harder. Uh, with the exception of State." He nodded to Mondt, who was still standing close to the sliding doors. "Mostly, we all keep to ourselves."

"There are personal conflicts?"

"Some. Is there a particular conflict you're worried about?"

"No," Kutri said firmly. She had no intention of telling Jakob about what had happened with Simmons. "One hears rumors. You know how it goes."

"I thought I did," said Jakob. He slipped a hand into a pocket and scanned the heads of the men in the crowd. "I used to think conflict was a symptom of fatigue. We're dragging the world back to its feet by the lapels. Of course there are personal conflicts. It can't be helped."

She let the matter drop. Her teachers at the Center had said much about dragging the world to its feet, though they did not use quite the same terms. The impoverished masses had caused terrible trouble through the history of the World Before. The troubles had become more pressing in the Atomic Age. Weapons of mass destruction had been hoarded all over the globe, and the fall that made the world need a dragging happened when Jimmy Ching's nation, China, was blasted off the map.

Some claimed the Slow Plague had started in that land and spread out. The other nations took revenge, and as a result, much of Asia and Europe, and eventually the Americas, were now home to radioactive dust storms. Mutations occurred. Many men and women died. The men who survived were immune to Slow Plague. Not so, the women.

Nine out of ten women who survived the bombs sickened and died. Nine out of ten daughters thereafter died in the womb. The women Kutri had known were exceptions, rare females with the plague immunity that was common in the male. Behind her back, always in whispers, she had heard men say the arrangement was not all bad. There was no question of what to do with a prize so rare. It had to be locked up, protected, secure. The future depended on dragging the world to its feet, while women were kept where they belonged, on their backs.

Finally giving up on her appetite, Kutri set her fork aside. Jakob didn't see, because he was staring at his hands. Unless she had missed it, he had eaten nothing. Did these office types eat? Perhaps they subsisted on vitabars, tossed down the throat between meetings.

She said, "Tell me, is our schedule full for the day, or will you have time to show me more sights?"

He brightened considerably. "You're in a sightseeing mood? I think something can be arranged. You first appointment after breakfast is with your health trainer. I'll be in a staff meeting that won't last too long. After that, we're scheduled to conduct an interview—me asking questions, you answering. There's no reason to sit still while we chat. How does one o'clock sound?"

His smile slipped, slightly, as he made the proposal, suggesting he was pinning it on for her sake. As grim as her thoughts had been a moment before, this made her more eager to accept.

Chapter Seven: The Sights

Since the so-called Miss Chandigarh had now made a public appearance, the Studio required her security detail to grow. Counting Mondt, her protection was now to consist of no fewer than three state security operatives at all times. The two newcomers, who like Mondt wore jeans, turtlenecks, and suit jackets, sat opposite Kutri and Jakob in the limo. Mondt sat up front with the driver.

On their previous journey, Kutri had found Mondt's straight-faced stare intimidating, but the leers Tolson and DeGarre gave her were much worse. Neither man seemed to be able to look at her without running his tongue over his teeth, making a noticeable bulge behind the lip. Or the men would narrow one eye as they widened the other, approximating a wink. Kutri wouldn't have wanted to meet either man in an alley alone. They were as dangerous to her as any stranger off the street, she expected. This estimation set Mondt in a good light.

The Escalade left Gas Company Towers five minutes after one o'clock. The streets were crowded with late lunch foot traffic, but when they reached Highway 101, no people or cars were to be seen. Jakob confided that he wished he could show her the ruins of Dodger Stadium, but Chavez Ravine was overrun with wild dogs. There were wild men, he said, in other places, that prevented them from visiting. Kutri didn't mind.

She was fascinated by each overgrown neighborhood they passed. Pressing her nose to the glass, she marveled at the gargantuan palm trees that defined patches of land that had once held businesses and homes. She pointed to deer stalking the fringes of the urban jungle. The dogs Jakob had mentioned appeared to be everywhere, competing for scraps with the rats. Once, she spotted a solitary hawk gliding low in the coppery sky.

"The animals handle the fallout better than we do," Jakob explained. "The scientists say it's a mutation of some sort. Where we're going, we'll be out of the city's mag-shielding. Mondt has his weather radio. If he says, 'Get to cover,' make for the car."

"Where are we going, exactly?" she said.

Briefly, Jakob appeared troubled. "I thought you should see the famous sign." He tried a smile. It failed.

"Are you unwell? I don't want you to tire yourself out."

"I'll be fine." He took a deep breath. This time, the smile stuck. "Don't worry. Really. The view I'll show you can't be beat."

They drew level with Lake Hollywood and the vast, muddy swampland around it. At Mulholland Drive, Jakob instructed the driver to exit. The lack of traffic was good, as the road was obstructed in several places by decades-old abandoned vehicles. Maneuvering the limo around these obstacles would have been impossible with anyone else on the road. When Jakob spotted the ruin of a sign through an ivy curtain, he told the driver to stop.

"That's where we want to go. It looks rough, but trust me. I've been here before."

Beyond the sign was a parking lot. Tremors and neglect had rippled its pavement. The driver wasn't willing to risk the tires so he parked on the road and the group hiked in, Jakob in the lead, followed by Kutri, Mondt, and the other SSOs.

"I should have brought a machete," said Jakob, trying to shove through a wall of brush.

"Has it changed much since you were last here?"

"Not that much. It was bad back then. I had help. Do you mind, Mondt?"

The bodyguard motioned Tolson to take his place, then stepped to Jakob's side. Together, they opened a hole. It took some daring exploration on Jakob's part to circumvent the worst of the scrub, but ten minutes later they reached their destination: a circular viewing platform made of mortared stone.

Atop a nearby hill, a derelict building half stood and half leaned. Whatever view it had once commanded had been obscured when the roof fell in. Jakob pointed at the wreck.

"There's an example of what we call the So-Cal Trinity. Earthquake, looters, and time are the best wrecking ball. But that's not what we're here to see." He produced a pair of compact binoculars from a pocket. "Try these. They were a gift from a friend. You might have to play with the wheel for focus."

"Play," said Kutri. She was confused. "How should I play?"

He stood behind her, covering her hand with his own, and raised the binoculars so she could see. Mondt stepped closer, eyeing Jakob warily.

"Like this," said Jakob. "Turn the wheel until it looks clear."

She moved with the wheel, enjoying his closeness. At length, a set of tall, white letters emerged from the blur on the other end of the valley. She had seen pictures of the letters before, so knew about what to expect. The sign, after all, was the first image anyone conjured when they heard the name of the hills they were standing on, or the lake they had passed. There was, however, something special about seeing them in person.

She read the letters out loud. "L-I-T . . . T-L-E . . . A-N-G-E-L. Very nice. I remember there was talk of vandalism. You would never know."

"Look at the end of the first E," said Jakob. "See what's hanging there?"

"A rope."

"There was a vandal at the end, not long ago. He was not much more than a skeleton, once the vultures and crows got through with him."

Kutri tipped the binoculars and almost let them drop when she saw a mound of ragged clothing, poked through with bone, lying at the base of the E.

"They let them dangle a few days. Depends on how hungry the vultures are. Once the body is picked clean, they bring in a sharpshooter to blast the neck. Bang, snap, crash." His voice was a flat monotone.

Kutri felt sick. "Are you telling me the Studio murders people for vandalizing the sign?"

"There was only one vandal. The others were guilty of various crimes. And the Studio doesn't murder. When they kill, it's a legal execution."

"I didn't know—" Words stuck in her throat. "I didn't know they had that power. We don't execute people in the Punjab."

"You don't?" Jakob seemed puzzled. Accepting the binoculars she passed back, he shrugged. "They own the city. They do what they want."

Kutri peeked over her shoulder to verify Tolson and DeGarre were out of earshot. Mondt had stepped back once Jakob had moved to stand beside her. He was close enough to hear, but though she had known him only a day, his quiet competence assured her he cared about nothing but keeping her safe.

"Forgive me," she said to Jakob, "but is it wise to speak this?"

Jakob sat on the stone wall, pressing a hand to his jacket. "It's the world we live in. Some men live in the hills. The rest are in the gutter. Some are judged worthy; others fall."

"'Some shall be pardoned, and some punished,'" she said, quoting the Prince from *Romeo and Juliet*.

It struck Kutri suddenly, forcefully, that Jakob was in crisis. That was clear. She wished she could say something to bring him comfort, but had no idea what, so she went on, "I meant authority, before. I didn't know the Studio had the authority to kill people. Isn't it your Office of State that enforces the law?"

"What do you say, Mondt?" asked Jakob. "Do you enforce the law?"

"I'm a bodyguard."

"Of course you are. I'm sorry, Kutri. State has nothing to do with law enforcement. It was organized as a defense force. Military, you see? Not police. The Office of Justice used to operate the police force, but that was before 'Studio President' and 'Mayor of Los Angeles' came to mean the same thing. There are no police now, only hatchetmen. For that matter, there aren't really laws for police to enforce. The Studio says, 'Jump,' the officers ask how high. That's how it goes in the gutter."

He appeared deflated, as if the urge to lie down was winning over his obvious distrust of municipal injustice. Kutri thanked God for ennui, even as she prayed his inertia kept them both safe.

"Shall we go back to the car?" she suggested.

Jakob pressed his hands to his forehead. "I'm such an idiot. Forgive me. I didn't mean to spoil your tour. Never mind me. Please, take a moment, look around."

He held out the binoculars, which she took and returned to her eyes. She didn't want to see anything but the inside of the limo, but frightened for his mental state, she scanned the valley for something to comment on before she renewed her plea to go.

On their side of the 101 was only wilderness. She wouldn't have been surprised to see a mountain lion. But across the highway, on the far shore of Lake Hollywood were thirty-odd identical buildings shaped like small airplane hangars.

"What is that? The village, there."

She handed Jakob the binoculars.

After sighting through the binoculars, he said, "Not a village. The locals call it Lakeside Estate. Mondt, is the weather holding?"

The bodyguard adjusted a dial on his palm-sized radio. There was a hiss of static. Mondt said, "All clear."

That was enough for Jakob. "We can go, if you like. Get a look up close."

"I—yes. I would like that."

She told herself, later, that she should have insisted on ending the outing. His mood was a danger to him—possibly to her as well. She could see it but was so baffled as to what had caused the shift, she contented herself with getting on the move. As they returned to the limo, she thought about Simmons, his admonition to call if Jakob showed "unorthodox behavior."

If she had been inclined to trust Simmons, she might have excused herself to make the call. But she didn't trust him, at all. She trusted Jakob, on a deeper level than she could let show. And, to an extent, she sympathized with the sentiments he expressed. His revolutionary turn stirred passions she had learned about in books but never experienced in person. How thrilling it must be to be a man, to walk about free and unseen, all along having such thoughts in your head!

Before entering the limo, she asked Mondt to switch places with Tolson. Now with two men she trusted in her sight, she felt as comfortable as she could on the bumpy ride down Mulholland to the 101. They had to put the swampland behind them before they reached an accessible exit, then track back alongside roads until they found the swamp again.

Where the driver stopped the car, the rows of hangar-like buildings ranged to the right, concealed by trees. But, looking down the embankment below the road, Kutri saw several men in overalls with black-and-white stripes laboring along the muddy shoreline perhaps forty or fifty feet distant. Because the window limited the sight lines Kutri could get with the binoculars, she asked to have it rolled down.

Mondt checked with the driver, knowing that they might have to make a quick getaway if danger arose. Once the driver assured Mondt he was on guard, the bodyguard gave the order for him to roll the window down.

Framed in the window, Kutri saw a worker whose strength belied his obviously advanced age. He had chalky hair and sunken eyes that he kept lowered to the ground as he trudged along, pushing a wheelbarrow full of thick, brown mud. One of his arms was a prosthetic ending in a metal pincers that gripped one handle of the wheelbarrow. The other was a natural hand.

Sweeping the binoculars toward the fringe of the embankment, Kutri saw two men carrying a load of stones in a sling. Each was missing an arm, but on opposites sides, so they were able to work together efficiently. Another man sat cross-legged at the bottom of the embankment, scooping handfuls of muck into a bucket. Where his eyes and nose should have been was a jagged pucker of stitched flesh.

She swept the binoculars farther and saw an observation tower, three meters high, between where the men worked and the buildings. A guard occupied the tower. Though he wore a shiny foil A-Rad suit instead of black trousers and tunic, he was clearly a hatchetman. The chrome, featureless helmet was unmistakable.

"What happened to all these men?" Kutri asked. "Why are they guarded?"

Jakob explained, "The Studio doesn't execute every criminal. That would be wasteful. If a man is caught stealing something they care about, they cut off his hand. If he says something they don't like, there goes his tongue. There are various punishments, most involving surgery, for different crimes. Any crime against a woman is worth an arm or a leg."

"Crime against a woman?" said Kutri. "How is that possible?"

The idea was preposterous, on many levels. At the Hindustan Bliss Center, many things had been done to her against her will. She would never have thought to call them crimes, only liberties to be punished by Papa Paquette. None of Papa's own liberties were ever punished, of course. The same went for the other girls. Women in LA were so carefully guarded, Kutri was amazed to think any crime could occur.

Jakob said, "Every inmate has a story. Some of them were servants or drivers for wealthy families. Some tradesmen deal directly with wives. A month ago, there was this jeweler who was allowed to touch the hands of his clients, to measure fingers for rings. This man became obsessed. He bit a woman's knuckle. Before the bodyguard could restrain him, he chewed straight through."

"God have mercy. He is here?"

"No. That was a bad example, sorry. He was put down. But something like his story played out for every man missing an arm or a leg."

"Really, every one?"

When he answered, she could hear the grimace in his voice. "Must be. The Studio doesn't make mistakes."

A man with an artificial leg hobbled into Kutri's magnified view. He was carrying a load of tools. As Kutri focused on him, his foot slipped in the mud. The tools fell into the mire. The hatchetman on the watchtower began shouting at once for the man to get up. When he didn't respond, the hatchetman punched a button on his chest-mounted box. The fallen man and all the workers nearby jolted in paralyzed agony. Even at this distance, Jakob went rigid, as did the SSOs.

Thankfully, the effect was brief. Having delivered his shock, the hatchetman descended to ground level. He flicked out a baton and shouted again for the man to rise. Instead of giving him time, he lashed the fallen worker across the back. For a moment, the hatchetman appeared content. Then he saw the limo. As if he felt the need to perform, he lifted the baton to strike again.

"Stop!" cried Kutri, her voice shrill in her ears.

The guard turned, his gaze moving up the gentle slope. "Who's there?" he demanded, and took a step toward the car.

Mondt caught her shoulder, hauling her back from the window even as it rolled up, presumably under the driver's control. Before anyone could protest, Jakob slipped out of the back seat and around the back of the vehicle to address the guard down the hill.

"Leave that man alone!" he called out. "He's had enough."

DeGarre slammed the door Jakob had left open. Kutri saw the hatchetman stomp up to Jakob, tapping the baton lightly against the knee of his A-Rad suit. Jakob stood his ground. The helmeted man gestured at the limo. Jakob raised his hands. Behind the hatchetman, the man with the leg prostheses got to his feet. The hatchetman must have heard him, because he reached for one of his horrible buttons. Jakob lunged and seized his wrist. The hatchetman pivoted and felled Jakob with the crack of the baton to his forehead.

At eleven years old, Kutri had seen the building that housed the old Center dormitory leveled in a landslide. Jakob's collapse felt more devastating than that.

Mondt leapt from the limo and made his way to the rear. "Mothercuttin' orphan," he said. "Don't you know a blissman when you see one?"

Tolson stepped out of the front seat to watch the confrontation, though he kept his distance. Kutri's impulse was to slip out of the still open rear door and run to Jakob's side. DeGarre seemed to read her intention; he gripped her arm, hard enough to hurt.

The hatchetman reached for his buzz box.

"No need," said Mondt. "Give me my man and we'll go."

"This area is restricted," said the hatchetman.

"We took a wrong turn."

The hatchetman hesitated. Kutri couldn't see Mondt's face, and of course she couldn't see the hatchetman's, but from their posture she guessed they were taking each other's measure. The hatchetman glanced around, probably wondering what would happen if any of his charges escaped while he was distracted.

"Get him yourself," he said, and backed away.

Waving Tolson back, Mondt ran to Jakob and pulled him up by the arm. Jakob leaned on him all the way back to the limo. Kutri moved next to DeGarre so Mondt and Jakob could sit side by side.

"Floor it," said Mondt.

The limo lurched. They were away.

"How is he?" Kutri asked with a tremor in her voice. The stream of blood from above Jakob's eyebrow was thick and fast.

"Conscious," said Jakob, speaking for himself.

Kutri said, "You're bleeding."

"Head wounds always look worse than they are."

"And do men always act more foolishly than they should? You could have been killed."

"You were the one who shouted." Jakob bobbed his head at Mondt. "I owe you one."

Eyeing the blood on his jeans, the bodyguard said, "I'll send you the cleaning bill."

As they put Lakeside Estate farther behind, DeGarre produced a first aid kit from under the seat. As Kutri watched Mondt apply a bandage, she thought again of the miraculous cellular device Simmons had provided. Perhaps it would be a good idea to call. Even if Simmons put Jakob out of a job, at least he would be out of harm's way.

Or would he? She really didn't know what Simmons wanted or how far he would go to get it, so she chose to refrain. The phone was in her bag, and there it would remain. She reserved the right to change her mind if Jakob's head proved as hard as the baton had made it sound.

Chapter Eight: Gaps in a Ruin

Half the wall was missing, also a portion of the floor above. Jakob watched krows flit past the gap against the copper sky, imagining that at any moment, one might scoop him out of his hospital bed and carry him away. Would he cry for help? Would he struggle? There didn't seem to be a point.

He was sure the only reason he was alive, while Sven was dead, was the minor inconvenience his death would cause the Studio. They didn't value him personally, but he was an experienced cog in their bureaucratic machine. It would be marginally more difficult to replace than the man waxing the floor outside his hospital room. Killing him would cause a staffing problem. That was the only reason the Studio kept him, or any of the thousands of cogs like him, alive.

He had lived with his mortality since the age of eight. On a morning that seemed like any other, apart from an uncharacteristic quiet from some staff members at the Pasadena Polytechnic Institute, Jakob's student class had been summoned to the parade ground for an assembly. They had expected a lecture, or to be forced to compete in a group sport, a round-robin tournament of street hockey, maybe, or every-boy-for-himself murder ball. Instead, they had found the whole school lined up on the trampled dirt plain.

They were there to witness an execution. The fourth-grade English teacher was a stooped troll of a man who had never been popular with the students, not that any of the teachers were. Despite their indifference, every student gasped when a krow swooped down to clamp its talons around the teacher's shoulders. Even the hardest boys were horrified when the krow locked its forked tail between the teacher's legs and lifted him into the air before jolting his body with current.

The man's face spasmed. His head began to smoke. His last word was a tortured, "Uck!" Long before the current was switched off, the teacher was dead. His arms flapped like banners as the krow bore him away.

Jakob never knew exactly what sin the teacher had committed. Most of the rest of his student days were spent trying to avoid conversations about the men killed for various crimes. Until Sven's murder, he had been somewhat successful in imagining his willful ignorance was a defense. So long as he knew nothing of Studio abuses, he could never protest, so they could have no reason to silence his insignificant voice. That he did know—that everyone knew—about the rot at the heart of the system, was beside the point. So long as he kept his head down, it couldn't be fitted for a noose.

Or so he had thought. Sven's death had shown he was dangling by a thread that could be snapped at any moment, for reasons he might never know. He might be scooped up by a krow on the way to work. Or he might be bludgeoned to death by a hatchetman. It soured his stomach to see the krows hovering so close, as if they knew his every thought and were making plans to get him in the end. He tried clenching his eyes against them but kept getting scared they'd swoop when he wasn't looking. So he opened his eyes, and like every other time he had done this in life, the krows were always there.

Sven wouldn't have been thinking of his own life at a time like this. He would have been thinking about justice, or revenge. The Studio had murdered Sven, a man worth ten of Jakob, if not a hundred. They had murdered many such men. He should have been outraged. He should have plotted his own, righteous murders, his own revolution. Instead he lay in the hospital bed quaking with terror for his life. He felt the ache in his head and imagined what men like the men who danced the Widow's Web would have done in his place. The last hit to Kole Kash, and the brave way we he took it, answered the question.

What did Kutri think of him? He pictured her standing at the bedside, shaking her head and calling him a fool. That vision, delightful though it was, could never come true. She would not be allowed to set foot in the hospital. No one quite believed that any woman was truly immune to the Slow Plague. They were kept at a distance, and especially out of places like these, out of fear a concentration of viruses would overcome resistance.

Was there anything men did for any reason other than fear? Once, Jakob was fairly sure, he'd married for love. After a course of Aremoden, the drug that took memory, love went away.

As soon as Jakob had been handed over to the orderlies, Mondt and the other SSOs had spirited Kutri away. Her concern over his injury was touching. It was also puzzling. She was lovely, but so young. Their relationship was strictly professional. She should have seen him only for what he was—a cog.

What does she see?

One of the few memories the drugs left him of married life was wondering how different his relationship to his wife was to other relationships with women he would never experience. Was Kutri's concern like that of a sister? A vanishingly small number of men could tell him what that concern was like.

Even in the outlands and farmlands, where it was rumored the birth of a daughter could go unnoticed, it was rare for a girl to stay at home longer than a few years. The bounty on "found girls" was large. Some parents who neglected the law might keep their daughters at home, where they might act out the role of sister, or cousin, or neighborhood friend for a short time. But they would always be found. And punished! Their crime was awful, a theft from humanity, or so he had been taught, first at school and then at Bliss.

A painful throb in the temple pulled him out of his thoughts. He called for the orderly, a refrigerator of a man who had given him a sedative yesterday. When the orderly didn't come at once, Jakob called again. This time, instead of the orderly, a man of middle height with slick-backed hair entered the room, patting the air as if to say, "Quiet down." Jakob recognized Gar Eglund, the personal toady to Dr. Staley.

Ignoring Jakob's groan, Gar sidled to the bed and dumped a stack of green-and-white papers on his chest. Gar said, "Approval for Dupain, Tien, Wimmer." Despite his headache, Jakob recognized the names of the three bride candidates. Jakob and Gar had nothing in common but their mutual dislike, which at least inspired Gar to keep chit-chat to a minimum. "There are notes on personalities, the usual wink and nod. Staley suggests you skip to the signature. Here's a pen."

Painfully, Jakob shoved himself to a sitting position. He lifted the top page, only to find the entire green-and-white stack was one long, continuous feed. The seal of the Office of Justice was printed in the lower right corner of the first page. Minor feed errors had caused the sword-and-gavel motif to repeat lower and lower down on every page after that, so that half the seal for page ten bled onto page eleven.

Jakob flipped to the bottom of the stack, expecting to find a break in the middle of a passage that would require a reprint. The generator of the report had anticipated the problem, however, and printed several blank pages at the end. Normally, he would have skipped straight back to the page with a blank for his signature, but it occurred to him that he could use this chance to test his footing.

How did the office feel about the breach in protocol he had made by hauling Kutri to a prison camp, where he had assaulted a guard? If there was one thing Gar Eglund was good for, it was gossip. It was common knowledge at the office that if you had a secret you wanted exposed, you told it to Gar. If you wanted to know secrets, or simply opinions, there were ways to ask.

Jakob said, "I'll take my time, thanks. We want everything to be in order."

Gar scoffed. "Why wouldn't it be? But suit yourself. I can't stay. Sign it when you're done. Tomorrow, drop it in Staley's box."

"Tomorrow is Saturday, Gar."

"I know. Oh, I know. You don't expect the rest of us to wait for you while you malinger in bed? There's work to be done. You've already put us behind by taking the candidate to that . . . place. There were hatchetmen at HQ, a Studio rep. I mean, what possessed you, Freeman? What possessed you? Don't answer, I'm not asking."

"I've been trying to figure it out," Jakob confessed. "Help me, Gar. What are people around the office saying?"

"They're saying you had a nervous breakdown. I spoke up for you, of course. You've been reckless as a dog in heat since your friend died. But I get that, I do."

"What do you get, Gar?"

The greasy head bobbed from side to side. "Oh, don't be coy, Freeman. Everyone knows what you and Thomson were to each other. All this"—he made a vague gesture at the bed and waggled his fingers at Jakob's stitches—"it all makes sense. You've lost someone important to you. I understand that. If anything ever happened to my Staley, I don't want to think what I'd be like. Horrible. Throw yourself into your work. That's my advice. Leave the hatchetmen alone, of course, and don't go like Sven.

"You know, they say the pills are painless, but I think it must be awful to lose yourself like that. I mean, imagine if you forgot what you were doing halfway to the end. But never mind. You've had bad luck, Freeman. That's the point. Lousy luck, really, when you think you lost your wife and poor Sven, too. But cheer up, cheer up. Somebody else is bound to come along."

The urge to strangle the sleek weasel burned in Jakob. He did his best to douse his anger, telling himself it was only Gar's way, but if not for the ache in his head, he probably would have killed the little man.

Crooking a finger at Gar to draw him close, he said, "Are you up on your annies, Gar?"

"Aren't we all?"

Jakob balled a fist and feinted a punch. The target was Gar's crotch.

"Here's a booster," said Jakob.

It was an old playground jest. Gar knew it, evidently. He hopped away, covering his soft parts like a soccer goalie.

"No! Oh, very mature. I'll go, if you don't want sympathy. You only had to say so."

Gar eyeballed the candidate report, which had fallen from Jakob's chest to lie accordioned on the floor.

"Don't worry," said Jakob. "Staley will get his signature."

Gar's dignity returned. "See that he does." He spun on his heel and left.

Jakob lay stunned for a minute, wondering what was wrong with his brain. Gar had been only slightly more offensive than usual. Jakob had imagined throttling him often but had never come close to following through. Sven's death was too much. It had driven him mad. He had no idea how to get back under control.

Desperate for any distraction, he retrieved the continuous feed pages from the floor. In a few places the pages had split at the perforation, but he soon got them in order. He flipped to the first page, the only page that was properly aligned.

The report was written in a heavily technical legalese that soon lulled him into a trance. Only two key phrases in the voluminous report stood out. Both had to do, not with Kutri but with another bride candidate. She was a slender beauty from Indochina by the name of Cuc Tien.

"Potential race savior," read one of the phrases.

The other phrase read, "Lacks robust allure."

There, in summary, was the positive and the negative of Kutri's only real competition. The implication of the report as a whole was that Kutri and Cuc were the odds-on favorites for next Thursday's Presentation Ball. Both were race saviors, but unlike Miss Tien, Kutri had robustness to spare. It was as impossible to overstate the importance of the first quality to mankind in general as it was impossible to overstate the appeal of the second quality to individual men. The Studio and the Office of Bliss understood both these points.

The public had been fed the idea for decades that the future of the human species depended on repopulating the individual race lines, science to the contrary be damned. Scientists had never been as powerful a group as politicians and statesmen. Or at least they had not been as motivated to seek power. The politicians set the agenda, and every successful bride candidate had to push it. Kutri and Cuc did that admirably, in about equal measure.

Still, sex sold in the New Society just as it had done in the World Before, according to Sven's media collection. The story Jakob had told Kutri about Janessa Huxley's exceptional intelligence was true, but she hadn't made it as a match bride thanks only to her brainy edge. Janessa had, and had in abundance, the same quality possessed by Karan Politis and all the match brides that came before and after her, including Aluel Garang. She was the sort of woman who evoked a biological response in the most annied-up of men. Jakob had not seen Cuc Tien, but he was able to read between the lines. She was appealing. She had to be to have gotten so far, but other candidates surpassed her in sex appeal. Kutri was certainly one of them. Indeed, she had evoked a stronger response in Jakob than any he could remember. Though he couldn't be certain, he was fairly sure he hadn't felt such a strong attraction to his late wife.

Suddenly, he was impatient to be out of bed. He shouted for the orderly again, but not to ask for drugs. When the refrigerator came stomping down the corridor, Jakob demanded his clothes and release papers. The orderly shrugged. Why should he object? After changing Jakob's bandage, he returned his suit and went to scrounge up paperwork for the patient.

By this time, the sun was setting. Jakob spent the minutes he had to wait for the orderly watching men in overalls trudge home from a long day digging ditches or cleaning sewers. Where would they go for the night's entertainment? He smiled as visions of bar fights danced in his head.

Sometime after six o'clock, Jakob boarded the hospital's sole working elevator. The doors slid shut before him and a bell dinged. He rode downward, to freedom. When he stepped out on the ground floor, he found himself in the dark. The orderly had warned him this might happen. The power was fickle, at best. After giving his eyes a moment to adjust, he followed a pale glow in the distance to a hole in the hospital lobby large enough that a truck could drive through. A decade ago, one actually had. It was a truck belonging to the Mother's Men, a group the Studio called terrorists. They had driven the four-axle dump truck loaded with gravel at high speed, over the curb outside Good Samaritan, which was what Municipal Hospital was named at the time. The truck slammed into the lobby at full speed. Casualties, according to an edition of the *Los Angeles Times* archived by Sven, numbered six, including a Studio executive who had been on the way out after a highly publicized surgery, plus his bodyguards, a junior executive, and two bystanders.

Studio news accounts differed from the *Times*, saying thirty-two people, including doctors, patients, and children, had died. The driver escaped, per the *Times*. The Studio said he was shot dead at the scene. Among the few details both sources agreed on was the one anyone could see: the truck had left a huge hole. It remained as a reminder.

As Jakob stepped into the lamplight slanting through the lobby's breach, he was surprised to see he wasn't alone. A young man in a pale yellow jacket, a cap tilted over his eyes, was resting against a naked I-beam. He straightened at Jakob's approach. After carefully surveying who was coming, he bowed.

"Mr. Freeman?"

The voice was familiar, but Jakob couldn't place it. "I am Matchmaker of Bliss Freeman," he said, inserting the affiliation so he wouldn't get rolled as a nobody.

"Please come with me," said the young man.

"I'm sorry," said Jakob. The youth looked too skinny to threaten anyone, but he was always cautious of strangers. "I have to get somewhere."

He meant home, but the youth said, "Yessir. There's just time. Mrs. Martinez will start dinner at seven."

"Mrs. Martinez?" said Jakob.

A headache answered his attempt to search his memory. Finally, he managed to dredge up the invitation extended by Nat. He had dismissed it from his mind, mostly due to the strange eagerness of his new friend. Now he burned to renew the acquaintance.

"I forgot," he said. "You're a friend of Nat's?"

"I'm the driver."

"What happened to Lucas?"

"He's guarding Mr. Martinez."

"Aren't you a bit young? Do you even have a license?"

"I'm a professional." The driver drew himself up, tugging the cap down so it still hid his face.

"And you work for Nat Martinez."

"I-I've been waiting for you. Are you ready? We have to hurry if you want to be on time."

"Waiting," said Jakob. "How did you know I was here?"

The driver shrugged. "I go where I'm told, Mr. Freeman."

"Of course you do. Right. And you're right about the time, too. Where's the car?"

"Down the block. I'll bring it up."

"I'll be here."

The youth hesitated. He was afraid, perhaps, that Jakob would break his word.

"I'll be here," Jakob repeated.

This got a smile from the driver and a lift of the head that tipped back the cap's brim. At the first clear sight of his face, Jakob's eyes felt as if they'd bulged out of his head. He had to bite his tongue to keep from blurting out, "Mitsuru?"

Jimmy Ching's shop boy, whom he had seen at the wedding in the guise of a geisha, certainly got around. Whatever his reasons, he obviously didn't want to acknowledge they had met before. Was that cunning, shyness, or something else? Jakob could think of no reason for Mitsuru to be afraid of him.

Watching the youth hurdle a chunk of twisted ex-lobby, Jakob decided against a confrontation. He could always ask Nat about Mitsuru. Surely the invitation to dinner doubled as a promise to take him into confidence. Nat would pull him away from other guests to renew their heretical conversation, he was sure. All Jakob had to do to find explanations for all the recent mysterious events was follow Mitsuru out of the lobby. He did so, wondering as he tramped over heaped debris if the fatal tracks of the Mother's Men's dump truck were somewhere underfoot.

Chapter Nine: The Instruction of Kutri

Cameras clicked and snapped beyond the protective plexiglass that shielded Kutri from the press conference audience and the press, their LED flashes like tiny novas exploding into being before winking out.

So much light, she thought. *So many dying stars.*

Dazed, she turned her back on the glass. She resisted the urge to look up at a monitor, where she would see her own face, but instead, hurried away from the stage through a curtain to a metal door, which Tolson held open for her.

Or was it DeGarre? With her eyes still reacting to the flash photography, she was uncertain.

After she blinked, her first clear sight in minutes was of her bodyguard, Mondt. He was standing by a mini fridge in the spacious but sparsely furnished backstage area, spooning ice cream out of a carton. He put the carton on top of the mini fridge when he saw her. She motioned for him to pick it up.

Before the press conference that had just ended, a man in a paisley waistcoat with a bandana covering his nose and mouth had twirled her hair into something that resembled a beehive. She pointed at the chair he was standing behind now and asked, "Can you please take this down? The weight is—" She finished the thought by holding her neck.

The stylist nodded and waved her to the chair. When Kutri was seated, Mondt came to her, jabbing his spoon in the ice cream so it stuck straight up.

"I'm surprised a man as healthy as you eats ice cream, Mr. Mondt," Kutri said.

The ice cream was strawberry. Levering a pink-speckled mound into his mouth, Mondt said, "I didn't get big on vitabars." He paused, swallowed. "You looked good out there."

"I'm flattered," she said. It was her turn to ruminate. This was their third or fourth conversation of the day. She was sure he knew the subject foremost in her mind. "Is there any news?"

He took another bite, nursed it, and said, "I hear Tien's cute. Not much of a chest, though."

"You're not paid to tease, Mr. Mondt. I wasn't asking about my . . . competition."

"I'm not paid to talk, either. But no, there's no news on the walking wounded."

Kutri wished she could turn away, but the stylist was holding a fistful of hair, keeping her firmly in place. She drew a steadying breath. "I would like to visit him. You can take me."

"That's the difference between me and Freeman. He could take you where he wants. I go where I'm told."

"Yes, but he is the one I wish to see. If I tell you I would like to see my handler—" She lifted her chin, bringing a snort of protest from the stylist.

"Not how it works," said Mondt. He glanced at Tolson—it was definitely Tolson—but the SSO was too busy hunting in the mini fridge to notice. Between appointments, appearances, and photo shoots, the day had been endless. Kutri suspected the men were as tired as she was, though not nearly so anxious.

"You're surely not afraid of what Tolson would say if we went a little out of bounds," she said.

"Not afraid," said Mondt. "I'm sympathetic. Client goes somewhere she shouldn't, it's a hassle."

The stylist coughed. Kutri faced front while he took down the pins in her hair.

For fully a minute, Mondt ate ice cream while Kutri tried to put Jakob out of her mind. Jakob was so frightful with the blood from his forehead masking his face . . . No, she could not think of that. She tried speculating on the stylist's bandana instead. Was it a fashion choice, an imitation of the ubiquitous expression from the Slow Plague's early days, or was the wearer like the man she had seen at the Lakeside facility, the one with a surgical divot in his face?

Mondt asked, out of nowhere, "How old are you?"

Kutri was genuinely surprised. She made sure to sound jovial when she answered, "How dare you? I believe I'm being insulted."

"Back in school," said Mondt, "I took a class on childcare. We all had to, even mutts like me who had no chance of passing on the genes. The teacher had this doll he made us hold. It was heavy, like a real kid. Brown skin, cute cheeks. The first time I saw you, I thought, 'There's that doll, all grown up.' So tell me, doll. You old enough to have been alive back then?"

With a flourish, the stylist released the last clip holding Kutri's hair. With nothing to attach it to the plastic cone that had given it shape, the former beehive collapsed in a shaggy cascade.

"God be praised," said Kutri. She scowled at her bodyguard. "If you must know, Mr. Mondt, I am seventeen."

"Sack to that," Mondt said. "This turtleneck is seventeen. It used to be beige before the color wore out. Seventeen. If you're seventeen, I'm seventy-five."

It was a ridiculous hyperbole. Only characters in books lived so long. "Congratulations on your three-fourths centenary." When he sniffed, she added, "I might be seventeen. How would you know?"

He spooned more ice cream and gave her room to leave the seat. Once she had thanked the stylist, they departed the converted warehouse that had been the setting for the photo shoot. The junior blissman who had directed her in Jakob's absence showed her to the parking lot, where the limo was waiting.

Two sides of the lot were enclosed by brick walls. A third side was blocked by rubble. Their way out was a wall with a sturdy gate, watched over by a hatchetman. When the limo arrived, the gate attendant had been alone. Now, he stood talking with two men whose bulk and clothes made it plain that they, like Kutri's trio of followers, were in the bodyguard trade.

The limo had its hood up. The driver glanced up from poking around and said, "You have a visitor," when she approached.

"Who is it?" she said.

He gestured, in lieu of an answer, in the direction of the back seat. If Kutri read him right, he preferred not to say. She waited for Mondt to go to the window and make a cup of his hands so he could peeking through the tinted glass. When he saw who was inside, he took a step back and gestured for Kutri to open the door herself. Once she was inside, Mondt shut her door behind her, leaving her to speak privately with the first interlocutor of the Office of Justice.

She internally shuddered, remembering how the last time they'd met, he had asked her to remove her clothing. Today, he was dressed all in white. Aside from the color, the suit was so like the gray one he had worn on their first meeting, she actually wondered if it had been bleached. His face was a similar shade of pallor. Had something given Alec Simmons a fright? She had heard a rumor that the citizens of LA were wrong to trust their fifth-floor mag-shielding. It didn't, for a fact, protect them from fallout, said the rumor. Maybe radiation had blasted the color from Simmons's suit. It was a cruel thought, but it amused. She showed the amusement by twitching her lips.

"I'm pleased to see you too," said Simmons, straight-faced. "Though I'm not happy I had to seek you out. What constitutes unorthodox behavior, in your mind?"

Kutri decided hauteur was the best defense. "This . . . visit comes to mind, First Interlocutor. Perhaps having me watched."

"Of course I had you watched. You represent hope, opportunity, a considerable investment."

"Your investment, or the Studio's?"

"We have all made sacrifices."

Kutri fetched the phone from the straw bag. "You want this back, I suppose."

"Not at all. What I want is to know why you haven't put it to use."

She ignored this question to ask one of her own. "Who has been telling you stories, Mr. Simmons?"

He grinned. "There are too many to count. Miss Chandigarh, you're mistaken if you think I take an interest in every young lady who visits my workroom. It's like as I told you. You're special. If you come into danger, you have to reach out. Why didn't you?"

She returned the phone to the bag as she thought of what to say. "Because," she came up with at last, "the danger was not to me."

"That's untrue, and you know it. You weren't hurt, thank Dad, but you were in danger. What was Freeman up to? He had a nerve, taking you into a restricted zone."

"I asked to see it. And we didn't know it was restricted."

"You mean, *you* didn't know. Freeman took advantage of your innocence, Kutri. At the first chance he got, I might add. You're blessed to have me as an ally, more than you know. Who knows what Freeman would have tried next? Never mind; it's not too late. Only say the word, and I will have him replaced."

"You will not," she said firmly. The thought of being barred from seeing Jakob was suddenly more terrifying than all the fears she had had for his health. She pictured his guileless, handsome face. The idea of being kept apart from him made her more sick than she had felt when his head was gushing blood.

"I insist," said the first interlocutor. "My dear, you must be protected. Say the word—to me, to that replacement in the blue blazer I see talking to your driver—and Jakob Freeman will never put you in harm's way again."

The prospect was almost too awful for clear thought, but she managed to cling to the lifeline he had extended. She expected he had extended it against his will.

"Without my 'word' as you call it, you can do nothing. Is that not so?"

He cleared his throat. "The situation is as I told you before. The offices are independent. I can only interfere at your request."

"Then you will not. I will make no such request."

Simmons scooted to the edge of his seat, frustration sweating from every pore. "But you must. You simply must!" He flailed his arms as much as space would allow, spittle flying as he spoke.

There was more than he was admitting behind the insistence, clearly. Kutri had guessed as much, but since he was a petty man, she had thought his dislike of Jakob was petty as well. Now, she saw she was wrong. The first interlocutor hated the man about whom she was coming to feel quite the opposite.

Still, there was something more to the emotion he let show. Frustration that she was not reacting to Jakob's unorthodox behavior as he'd expected, yes, but was that fear? Torell, the toadying assistant, had said Simmons could elevate the lowliest of men and bring down the highest. A man like that would have no need to ask her permission to do anything, unless he was afraid of judgment from above. He would want to avoid acting on his own if the action he chose might bring a higher power's anger on himself.

Ah.

"You're afraid of someone," she said. "I wonder who it is."

He didn't deny her statement or offer to satisfy her curiosity, but merely slid back in his seat again.

"Is it the other offices you fear or the Studio? Perhaps it is both."

He made no answer, but beads of sweat were forming on his forehead. His pale face had turned so red, she was amazed they did not boil away at once.

She pressed him. "You keep saying I'm special. Forgive me. I find it hard to believe you're deeply concerned over the future of my race. It's your own future that concerns you. To whom am I special, First Interlocutor? Not you, personally. Do you fear upsetting someone who thinks of me in that way?"

A revelation struck her with such force, it nearly robbed her of speech. Doing her best not to stammer, she said, "It is the Studio who says I am special, isn't it? They have selected me, in advance, as match bride. Of course! I've always thought the voting was for show. The Studio has decided to present me, without a single vote cast. You show yourself in a panic, tonight, because you fear your vendetta against Jakob will get in their way."

"Ah!" said Simmons. "So it's 'Jakob' now, is it?"

He was too shrewd to believe the slip meant nothing, so Kutri decided not to pretend. "What if it is? You asked me to speak against him. For reasons of my own, I refuse. You have no real reason to speak against us, Mr. Simmons. So please, leave us be. Jakob is a capable matchmaker, and I need nothing from you. Leave us alone. Enjoy your peace. Isn't that the best course for everyone? Leave Jakob and me out of your schemes and we can all live our lives in peace and security."

Slowly, Simmons relaxed. He was no longer agitated, but his calm expression troubled her more than his thrashing at the air had done a minute ago.

"Be careful," he said. "You recall when I praised your intelligence? A man like me doesn't jump at shadows. There's nothing in the world I fear without reason, Miss Chandigarh. Peace. Pah! What peace? I will give you one last chance, Kutri. Think carefully. This will be your final chance to avoid danger. You think you know Jakob Freeman. Fool. He doesn't know himself. For your own safety, tell me to have him removed."

She answered simply, "No."

The first interlocutor shut his eyes. When they flicked open, he appeared to be looking through her. He slid toward the passenger-side rear door and left the limo.

Without turning back, he said, "Remember, Miss Chandigarh. It was your choice." He slammed the door.

Chapter Ten: Down from Above

Moments after his arrival at the Arcadia Arms, Jakob saw Mitsuru's haste had not been without reason. No guests were waiting in the curtained parlor that greeted him when a resplendently dressed Lucas opened the door. Lively chatter could be heard from the adjoining dining room.

Lucas said, "This way."

"One second," said Jakob.

Mitsuru had spoken little on their ride from the hospital. As Jakob turned to say goodbye, he saw the youth had already scurried halfway to the elevator. He considered raising his voice, decided not to, and let that mystery escape.

Truly, Belen Martinez set a splendid table. Arranged on the vast mahogany surface in the middle of the narrow dining room were ten perfect place settings. Each included a china dinner plate with gold edges, a matching salad bowl and bread plate, and a champagne flute bubbling with golden liquid. Like all else that could do so, the silverware gleamed with a high shine.

Nine people sat at the table when Jakob entered. No food had yet been served. Lucas conducted Jakob to the table's foot, opposite Nat's position at the head. A span of fifteen feet separated the ends, but the acoustics were so good, Jakob could clearly hear the scrape of Nat's chair as he pushed back from the table before rising.

"Hey," said Nat. "Glad you could make it, guy!"

The former match groom had slick hair, a dark suit, and a bright tie. He had an even brighter tie pin. Though Jakob wouldn't have cared to explain the reference, he was reminded of a character from a movie Sven had once shown him. The film was terribly violent and more than slightly vulgar. Its depiction of women involving themselves in men's daily affairs would have consigned it to a pornographic theater, which in this case would have been partially justified. What Jakob remembered most about the film was the way the men conducted business.

They were gangsters, Sven had explained—criminals. They made their fortunes by exploiting weakness in others, especially people in positions of power. Yet they still took time to care for their appearances, sharpening their looks like a butcher sharpens knives. Nat's fine grooming would have fit right into their company.

"Thanks for having me," said Jakob. "You didn't have to wait for me."

"We didn't," said Nat. "You're right on time. Everybody ready?" He clapped his hands. "Soup's on!"

A cheer went up from the other guests. Aside from Nat and Belen, Jakob knew one couple and had seen three individuals on TV. The man sitting on Nat's right, across from Belen, was a stranger, but next to him and opposite were the Huxleys, last seen at Thursday's breakfast. Seated next to Antoine Huxley and opposite, beside Janessa Huxley, were an older couple, Sil and Mella Banquo. Like the Martinezes and the Huxleys, they were *Good Breeding* alums, though their day in the spotlight had ended much earlier.

At a Presentation Ball nearly thirty years ago that Jakob had watched in reruns, Mella had exited the ballroom when another woman was named match bride. A moment before she passed through the door, one of the candidate grooms, who turned out to be Sil, broke away to offer his arm. The defection caused a minor scandal, which made for good TV. In the subsequent history of the program, events like that had happened a few more times, but never with the same freshness the Banquos had brought.

To Mella's left and Jakob's right was a woman called Mrs. Bette. She was one of the few widows Jakob could remember ever having been in the public eye. Still a beauty in her silver-haired maturity, she had taken her turn as one of the first match brides nearly twenty years before Jakob's birth. Mr. Bette had been a Studio executive before their marriage. Unlike most who would follow, he was allowed to return to his work as a married man. Coverage of the funeral, which Jakob thought had been about twelve years prior, was carried on all general stations. At the time of his death, Bette had been serving as the strong right hand of President Schuyler, the predecessor of President Flynn.

Sitting mere feet away from Mrs. Bette gave Jakob a funny feeling. He couldn't see the tragic figure from a vanished age without twitching his thumb, as if by punching a button on a remote control, he could switch to a different channel.

Across from Mrs. Bette sat another stranger. The man leaned close and said, "There's real Maine lobster tonight."

If true, this was an impressive boast. Flying in live lobster meant passing over the North Pole. The irradiated Middle American airspace would allow nothing less. Such an extravagance would strain even Nat's bank account. As a married man, Jakob had lived off a Studio stipend before the death of his wife. He vaguely remembered living comfortably, but not eating lobster off fine china in his own home. For a man who said the Studio made LA a gutter, Nat didn't mind taking their money.

Had he been honest with Jakob on the night they met? When they watched the wire dance together, Nat had talked like a revolutionary. Was it all an act, or worse, a trap? There were whispers the Studio employed men to ferret out malcontents. It had been Sven, now that Jakob thought about it, who had told him to watch his back. The Studio had murdered Sven. Had they also sent Nat to sniff out anyone who would challenge the suicide story?

A door connecting the dining room to the kitchen opened and a server entered. The covered tray he was carrying wafted steam from the edges: an aroma of boiled lobster and melted butter. Unmistakable, though Jakob had only smelled it a few times. Even the Presentation Ball couldn't spring for lobster every season. It was not his favorite smell—too subtle and too like the sea—but he did appreciate what it represented: Nat's generosity with this friends.

As the server set down his tray, Lucas began orbiting the table. He refreshed the guests' champagne, skipping Jakob, who had yet to touch his. As the SSO completed his circuit, the server continued to pass in and out of the kitchen door. He set so many trays on the long table, it was soon packed.

Nat raised a glass. "Salud!"

"Salud," said his guests. Most drank deep, though Mrs. Bette only swirled her champagne flute before setting it down.

Jakob sipped from his. The spirit wasn't new to him, but he hadn't tasted it in years. He didn't know how it would affect him. For a few tantalizing seconds, he let the sparkling liquid tingle across his tongue. It slipped down his throat, making no difference he could notice, so he sipped some more.

"I'm glad you all could make it," Nat said. "Seriously, everybody, even Joule." He gestured at the man who had predicted the lobster. "I forgot what you said to make me mad last time. Don't repeat it, okay?"

Joule, or Mr. Joule, whichever it was, saluted. "Keep the booze flowing, Nat, and I'll keep quiet."

"It's a deal," said Nat. "Now, folks, I need to be serious. Don't worry, I can't keep it up long."

"That's not what I hear from Belen," said Janessa. Whoops and laughter echoed around the table.

"Hey, okay. Okay, serious now. The one thing I got to do right tonight is introduce our guests of honor. We've got two VIPs here, you believe it? Sorry if the rest thought you were special, but these guys are the real deal."

He paused for chuckles. Joule sloshed some of his champagne. Lucas mopped the spill with a napkin and topped off his glass.

"Who are these luminaries?" said Nat. "Who could be such swell guys that they got me using words like 'luminaries'? The first I'm gonna talk about, because he's sitting close to me, is this guy here." He touched the shoulder of the man on his right, the other stranger to Jakob, aside from Joule. "Everybody got champagne left? Lucas, fill Mella's glass. She's a lousy lush."

"A great lay, though," said Sil Banquo.

Following more laughter, Nat said, "Sil, we'll take your word. Look, everybody. I'm about to make a toast here. To our first guest of honor, Mr. S*ss* Verder. Salud!"

Jakob blinked. If he hadn't been in a mentally excited state, he would have thought his ears were playing tricks on him, but as alert as he was, he was sure Nat had hissed instead of saying the stranger's first name. No one else at the table seemed to have noticed. Not wanting to attract attention, Jakob said, "Salud!" a fraction of a second behind the other guests.

"This guy is something else," Nat went on. "He's going places, I tell you. Verder, tell 'em your news."

Verder straightened his tie. "Well, since you asked. Ladies and gentlemen, you're looking at the new head of Central European Acquisitions. It's a decentish jump up the ladder."

"A decentish jump, he says." Nat stepped up behind his guest and squeezed his shoulder. "It's a rocket to the top! For any of you who don't know, that's a senior position. We've got a hoity-toity Studio executive here." He led a round of applause. "You believe this guy? So humble."

Leaving Verder to grin and nod, Nat turned his attention to Jakob. Entertaining a Studio executive at his table proved Nat was two-faced in his loyalties. But which face was true? Jakob considered trying to sneak out, complaining of a headache, but he saw it was far too late. All eyes were on him. He'd be lucky if he got out of the next few minutes without giving a speech. He hid his confusion by returning Nat's smile. His best defense, at the moment, was being agreeable. Charming, if he could manage it.

Nat said, "Now, this other guy, he's a different kind of wonderful. Everybody, meet Jakob Freeman, my new best friend from the LA Office of Bliss."

There were welcomes and applause. Joule said, "Pleased, so pleased to meet you."

"I ran into this guy Wednesday," said Nat. "Let me set the scene. There I was at the, uh, the vegetable stand. Yeah, that's right. I was at the vegetable stand downtown, buying fresh broccoli for my loving wife. What a guy I am, right? Not every husband goes shopping after dark, but nothing's too good for my Len. Anyway, this guy comes up. He's after carrots. Ain't that right, Jakob?"

Nat walked around behind Jakob and gripped the top of his chair. Jakob could see his eye, with a twinkle in it as usual.

"I thought to myself, 'There's a guy I want to meet. He cares about his eyesight.' You get me? He's getting his vitamin C. C is from carrots, right? Anyway, it ought to be. Whatever. I say, 'Hey, guy. Come over to the juice bar. I'll buy you a smoothie.'"

It was clear from the amused faces that no one was fooled by the story. They were delighted to go along, but not without teasing.

Antoine Huxley said, "I didn't figure you for a broccoli man, Nat."

Nat made a show of looking hurt. "I didn't say it was for me. Where do you *parásitos* think you're getting your meal tonight, eh? A man invites his friends over, he expects them to believe his lousy stories. You look here." He leaned over Jakob, pointing at his emblazoned badge. "What do you think this is? Then I noticed he was a blissman. You like the story now?"

"Hear, hear," said Janessa. She was joined by Mrs. Bette and Joule. Laughter ran around the room. Nat touched Jakob's shoulder.

"To my best friend," he said. "Mr. Jakob Freeman. Salud!" He had left his champagne flute at the other end of the table so could only mime taking a drink, but everybody else joined in all the same.

On the return to his end of the table, something appeared to catch Nat's eye. He said to Lucas, "Hey, guy. My friend needs a bread plate. What do I pay you for, eh?"

Lucas got a laugh with, "Something else," but Jakob was too distracted to join in. He was studying the setting in front of him. It had been exactly like everyone else's a moment ago. The lack of a bread plate seemed impossible. Had Nat pulled some kind of trick?

Jakob looked up, expecting to see Nat's back. Instead, his host was already seated at the table's head. Lucas set out a bread plate to complete Jakob's setting. Where had it come from? There were no cabinets in the dining room, no table stacked with dishes. Lucas was breathing normally, so he hadn't dashed from the room and back in half a second.

Fear made Jakob shiver. He felt like he'd been dipped in ice water. Pushing away from the table, he started to get up. A hand touched his own.

It was Mrs. Bette's hand. The thin lips didn't smile. "Don't go, dear," said the old woman. "You'll miss the show."

Before Jakob could say anything in reply, Nat clapped his hands, as he had done previously. The server came back in the room, leaned over the table, and whisked the cover off the central, steaming tray. The lobster was gleaming red and large enough to scissor a woman's breast in a claw. It looked like it weighed twenty pounds. The other guests applauded. The waiter whisked off the cover from another tray, revealing another titanic lobster.

"Glorious," said Nat's friend Joule.

"You like it?" said Nat. "Have some." He winked and, all at once, one of the lobsters disappeared. It was replaced by a collection of segmented parts—one of the lobster's claws, plus the torso and tail. The missing claw was lying on the plate in front of Joule.

There had been no transition. The lobster had been in one place, then it was in another. The waiter had changed position as well. Instead of standing behind Mrs. Bette, with a tray cover in each hand, he stood behind the Huxleys, close to the kitchen door, holding a knife. The blade was erect and moist at the tip. It had been anointed, presumably, with lobster juices.

"Hey, Jakob," said Nat. "You want some lobster? Plenty to go around."

Jakob felt as though his head had been cut off his body, stuffed with cotton, and stitched to his neck.

"What's going on?" he said.

"I'm serving lobster, guy. You want some?"

"How did you do that?" asked Jakob. He checked the faces of his fellow guests. They were all turned his direction, except Janessa and Verder, who were looking, respectively, at Nat and the segments of red, steamy lobster. Verder was licking his lips.

Nat said, "It cost a bit. But don't mind that. Eat up." He winked and the massive tail of the segmented lobster was on Jakob's plate. "*Bon appétit*, as the Frenchies say."

Jakob spun away from the table. He had no idea what was happening. Was it the head injury making him black out, or had Nat slipped something in his champagne? The cause wasn't important so long as he could get out of the dining room and the apartment of the man who said he was his best friend but must surely be an enemy.

Belen Martinez said, "Please, Jakob. Don't go."

During the interview about the first interlocutor's outrages, her voice had been sincere and tremulous. Now the tremble was gone. Only sincerity remained.

"You're under no threat," she said. "Look."

She gestured at his place setting, and Jakob, impelled by the warmth in her tone, did as instructed. No lobster tail was to be seen. Where it had been was a hatchetman's helmet. A jagged crack had broken through the chrome surface, showing him the dark insides. All along the fringes of the crack was a smear of rust brown that could have been paint or mud but was almost certainly blood.

Nat said, "You waited too long, guy. It's not juicy no more. What do you think of the dish?"

The other diners had shifted in their seats. Nat and Belen and Antoine and the Banquos and Joule and Mrs. Bette were all intensely interested in Jakob's answer. Janessa and Verder were hanging their heads. They appeared to be unconscious. Jakob glanced at the server. He was asleep on his feet. Lucas was very awake. He stood opposite the waiter, coolly detached. In his hand, he held a squarish device with buttons and a knob.

"Seriously, guy," said Nat. "You want what we're serving or not?"

Ignoring the complicating factor of Janessa's sex, Jakob made an educated guess about how the tricks had been done. "You have a buzz box."

"Something like it," said Nat, beaming. "Lucas, show the man."

Lucas extended the device, holding it just out of Jakob's reach. It had a homemade appearance, but the configuration of buttons and dials were familiar. He had seen much the same on a hatchetman's chest plate.

"What is this?" said Jakob. He did not ask Lucas, but Nat.

"I'll tell you, guy. Why don't we get comfortable first?"

Suddenly, they were in the living room. Jakob had his feet up in an armchair placed kitty-corner to the gas fireplace. Sil and Mella Banquo occupied two broad, lily-white chairs that formed one side of a triangle with the matching sofa. Belen Martinez sat on the sofa. Her legs were crossed in a way that split her skirt halfway to her thigh. Nat sat next to Belen. Mrs. Bette was in front of the fireplace, standing with her hands over flames that had not been lit when Jakob had passed through the room. Behind Mrs. Bette, Antoine Huxley and the mysterious Joule stood on a balcony Jakob hadn't known was there, since the sliding doors that now stood open had been hidden behind the curtain.

The living room's most striking feature had also been obscured from Jakob previously. With the curtains drawn and tied back, a wall of glass, seamless except for the balcony opening, was unveiled. After dropping his footrest with the lever, Jakob rose and walked to the window. Los Angeles, in all its World Before glory, spread out at his feet. He opened the door to the balcony, where the modern city, with its derelict buildings and streets barricaded with trash, could be seen from a four-story height. He reentered, marveling at the ancient bird's-eye view visible only from the inside.

"It's good, eh?" said Nat.

Jakob brushed his fingers over the glass that was not a window but some kind of advanced screen. In his whole life, he had never stood on a mountaintop or flown in a plane. The observation point on Mulholland offered the only comparable view. This made that seem like peeking over a fence. Black, white, and silver skyscrapers towered above matchbox low-rises, set off by orderly, crisscrossing boulevards of downtown. It was all unspeakably majestic, as was the pin-prick stars and streaking comets of headlights that gave a vibrancy to the city from so long ago.

"Breathtaking," said Jakob.

"Glad you think so," said Nat. "It's from the view from the seventy-third floor, about two hundred years ago. The vid was in the old security office. The tech to play it is from a shop in Chinatown."

"Jimmy Ching's shop?"

"Could have been. It could have been. Let's chat some more before we throw out names. You asked me a question. 'What is this?' I'll tell you, right now."

The illusory cityscape gave Jakob vertigo. He turned his back on the false window. Nausea made him remember his fear at the dinner table. Finding out he had been frozen by a knockoff buzz box didn't ease his mind one bit.

"I'd rather you didn't," he said. "Whatever game you're playing at, I don't want a part."

"Are you sure?" said Nat. "You know I can stop you. I won't, though. It's like I told you, guy. I want you to say what you want. I want you to do what you want, too."

Jakob was his way to the door. He stopped. "What does that do for you?"

"I'm a fan of free will. It also happens you and I have a lot in common. A lot of what you want would be okay by me, you know?"

He sounded so arrogant, so sure of himself, Jakob couldn't help but yell, "You don't know what I want!"

"Don't I? You want Lucas to quit messing with your head. Fine. Lucas, cut my friend Jakob out of the circuit. You want to get a handle on that anger of yours. It's new and it's scary. It keeps you up at night. You didn't know you had it in you until you helped stomp Kirimi to death on Sunday. What, did you think you were the only one who noticed? A lot of guys— But enough of that. Just remember it's not me who made you angry. Not us, I should say. Tell me, guy, who are you really angry at?"

A chill went through Jakob, followed by a flush. He felt savage, like he wanted to tear chunks of meat from another man's flesh. But Nat was right. The anger was not aimed at anyone in the room. To the extent it had a direction at all, its target was . . .

"Let me guess," said Nat. "The Studio. Maybe the offices. The folks in charge, like President Flynn. You're angry at the motherless sons who made your friend drink mind wipers until there was no mind to wipe. I'm right, yeah? I don't blame you. Believe me, we're all mad about that."

Without leaving the fire, Mrs. Bette said, "I'm furious."

Jakob crossed to the middle of the room. "What does Sven's death have to do with your tricks? What did Lucas do to me, anyway, induce a seizure?"

"Nothing that dangerous," said Mr. Banquo. "Just a jolt to the hypothalamus."

"It was terrible," said Jakob.

"Our enemies are terrible," said Belen.

With the grace Jakob remembered from her television appearances, Belen rose and went to him. Taking his hand in hers, she drew him to the dining room. Janessa Huxley was drooling, lightly, from the corner of her mouth. Verder and the waiter were not quite as relaxed, just totally insensible.

The bloodied wreck of a helmet remained at the foot of the table. Belen lifted it from the plate and carried it with her on their return to the living room.

"Please sit," she said.

When Jakob had taken her place on the couch, he accepted the helmet. It never occurred to him to refuse anything she directed.

"That belonged to the man who raped me," Belen told him. "One of the men. It was years before the breeding program. Year after year. Do you know what a woman is, Jakob, in the world of men? She is a grave to be desecrated, a grave to be robbed. Men hate us because we remind you of a better world. That world is dead. Women are its graves. Of course men dig us up. You so lust for its corpse."

The crack in the helmet had a distinct bulge in the middle. Turning to Nat, Jakob said, "You killed him with an ax?"

"My husband?" said Belen. She stroked Nat's cheek. "He's too gentle. I killed him. A hatchet for the hatchetman. It took work to hunt him down. Sil is very clever."

Mr. Banquo was blushing when Jakob looked his way. "You helped?"

"In the hunt," said Belen. "Not the killing." She pointed from herself, to Mella Banquo, to Mrs. Bette. "We do the killing."

Jakob's impulse was to throw the helmet across the room. He passed it to Nat, instead. "You're telling me you're some kind of vigilante group?"

"We're the judges of men," said Belen.

"We're freedom fighters," said Mrs. Bette. "Revolutionaries."

Jakob got to his feet. An overwhelming urge had seized him to put distance between himself and the women. Since Belen was in front and the older women on either side, he moved to the balcony.

"You make it sound like there's a war going on."

"There is," said Mrs. Bette. She faced him but kept one hand extended over the fire, as if only her will could draw it from the wood.

"The Studio wouldn't allow it," said Jakob. "At the first sign of violence, they'd crush you."

"They try," said Nat. He rotated the helmet and spat into the gap. "What we do means more than our lives." He set the helmet on the floor and stepped on the crest. "We've all got reasons. Antoine, tell him yours."

Until now, Mrs. Huxley's husband had been staring mutely at the dead streets of modern LA. He turned and passed through the sliding doors without a backward glance at Nat's alluring, long-gone view.

"You'll have to bear with me, Jakob," he said. "I'm going to start at the beginning. In all the pregnancies that end in a live male birth, the Studio doesn't wait to have an infant in hand before they start the Carter-Schnee protocol. Every man is expected to fall in line with the New Society from birth. They don't leave that to chance."

Jakob said, "Protocol? I have an implant, of course."

"The implant is only part of the protocol. You know, I was a Studio chemist, back in my bachelor days? Men with my abilities come to know Carter-Schnee not as an implant, but in its full form. It's a system, a protocol for enforcing civil obedience. My department was responsible for making the first link in the chain. Psychoactive compounds have to be precisely engineered, especially if they're to be administered in the womb."

Jakob was appalled. "You manufactured a compound to be given to the unborn?"

"I did. It's an injection. One of many given to pregnant women. Not just those souls in the Care Houses. Your mother, my mother. My wife."

Jakob could remember his mother as a sort of human spider, at the center of a web of fluid sacs. She had been confined to bed for most of his years at home, either dying of cancer, fighting to give him a brother, or both. In his mind's eye, he imagined a needle being slipped into her arm. Or did it go straight into the belly? With no idea what the compound looked like, he pictured it as a viscid yellow fluid, oozing from a hypodermic like clotted pus.

"What did this compound do?"

"What *does* it do, you mean," said Antoine "What I'm telling you is still going on. It affects development. There are certain proteins it dissolves to prevent parts of the brain from forming naturally. Impulse control is retarded in Carter-Schnee embryos. Do you understand? You and I and all the men born under the Studio's thumb are lacking the hardware we need for impulse control. That's the brilliance of Carter-Schnee, really. What the chemical destroys, the implant replaces. At baseline, a functional implant allows for normal, human impulse control. For the Studio, it comes with the bonus of being able to induce pain, paralysis, unconsciousness, and death. They burn our brains and exchange what we lost for a cattle prod."

The idea that chemicals were involved in enabling the Studio's obedience control was new to Jakob, but not surprising. Discovering that the hated implant compensated for something the Studio had taken from him was enough to make him want to scream. He gripped the handrail of the balcony, considered hurling himself over.

"The implant takes time to reset," said Antoine. "When you were frozen, on Sunday, you were under the effect too long. It was like that for every man present. When the freeze was switched off, your implants guttered. I'd say you acted like animals, only animals have some control."

The memory made Jakob legitimately ill. He ran to the balcony and vomited champagne, which was all he had in his stomach, four stories to the rubbish heap of a street. When he had recovered as best he could, he came inside to where Antoine stood waiting.

"You said the compound is given to men in the womb. And the implants are for men."

"That's right."

"So what's happening with your wife? It looks like she's in the same state as Verder and the waiter. How can a buzz box have any effect on a woman?"

Antoine looked away. Jakob got the impression he would have punched a fist through Nat's expensive screen. "When she was in the womb, the doctors made a mistake. They misread a scan, thought she was male. They treated her like a male. The compound—the same compound I produced for years before I knew her—did to her what it was made to do, up here." He tapped his head. "By the time she was born, the doctors had no choice. They had to implant her or watch her thrash herself to death, so they implanted the mothercutting blankshots."

Joule, hands shoved deep into his pockets, spoke up. "I was one of those blankshots, not that I take offense. Would you have guessed I was so old? These hands were good with a scalpel, back before they started to shake. Janessa wasn't the first miss-scan, or the last. Her marrying Antoine was particularly unlucky for any of us who wanted to keep our mistakes secret.

"There are signs a medical man, or a chemist who knows what to look for, is bound to notice, in a Carter-Schnee patient. When Antoine discovered what had happened to Janessa, he had Sil on his side by then, plus Nat and other friends. They offered me a chance at redemption. I never ask what would have happened if I refused. That's how I joined the family. A chemist and a doctor in one fell swoop! What a coup for the revolution, if only the price was not so high."

"It was not a revolution at once," said Belen. "Not until Nat and I met Antoine and learned of Janessa's suffering. And she does suffer, by the way. Mood swings, depression—all of a destructive sort. My husband is a marvel. He sought help on their behalf. In the end, he found Sil and Mella, who are both so clever with devices like the implant. And then, before we met Dr. Joule, we met . . . someone else."

Nat took a position between his wife and Jakob. "It's all about impulse control, guy. Belen told me about the hatchetman, the one with the helmet. She told me about all the men. I wanted to know, were they glitching, was something wrong with their implants? Sil and Mella said, 'No.' It's free will, guy. These *malparidos* are choosing to do what they do. We know because we checked. We got ahold of some implants and we checked.

"Can you believe that, guy? There were men who could control themselves, but still they hurt my Belen. It made me crazy. I wanted justice. I didn't know how to get it, so I went to the only guy with power who I knew we could trust. It was his brains, his brilliance that made us what we are."

"Who was he?" said Jakob. His mind had raced ahead to solve the puzzle, but he needed someone else to say the solution out loud.

"Sven," said Nat. "My blissman friend."

"He was the best of us," said Mrs. Bette.

Antoine said, "The very best."

Belen and the rest agreed.

Mrs. Bette said, "I knew him first, long ago. You can take it from me, Jakob, that Sven Thomson was more devoted to the cause of freedom than everyone you see assembled here tonight."

"He was our heart," said Belen. "The heart of *La Vie*."

"That's what we call ourselves." This was Joule. "The Life. *La Vie*." He pointed to the wraparound screen, with its vision of a lively LA, then to the balcony above the same city's corpse.

"We were angry," said Mella Banquo. "Sven taught us to focus our anger. He taught us to dream and to act on our dreams."

"He was a leader, that guy," said Nat. "Not to mention, our inside man."

Holding an arm out to Belen, Jakob let her conduct him to the sofa.

"You're saying that Sven, the man who has been my colleague—my friend—for years, was murdered because he was the leader of your revolutionary group?"

Mrs. Bette sank onto the sofa next to him and took his fingers in her hand.

"We're saying the New Society is our enemy, and as soon as God or Dad or whoever's out there gets behind us, we mean to tear it down and build something better in its place. Sven had a plan for that. He had a plan for everything. On Sunday, his plan failed. Kirimi Teng was supposed to announce our revolution on live TV. We had a way to follow up, but we never got the chance, because something happened to Kirimi. Maybe he changed his mind. Maybe he was never the man we thought he was. I don't know. The point is, the plan failed and Sven was killed. Someone must have betrayed us. Are you following me so far?"

Jakob answered honestly. "I'm trying. Kirimi was one of you?"

She nodded. "Sven recruited him and trained him to carry out his part. The monster he became was the opposite of what he should have become, but that's water under the bridge. He betrayed us and died. Sven was killed. But the plan, Jakob. The plan was brilliant, and it can still work."

"It can? You said it failed."

"There was a contingency. Sven planned for everything, even his own end. If Kirimi had done as he promised, he would have denounced the Studio, proclaimed revolution, and set every Los Angelino free with a wave of his hand. Sil has a device, you see, that can deactivate every obedience circuit in the city."

"You do?" said Jakob, staring at the man in astonishment.

Sil Banquo bowed his head modestly. "It's something we whipped up."

Mrs. Bette went on. "It would have been glorious. You saw what happened when two hundred men had their implants glitch. Imagine what every man in this city would do if their implants were switched off."

Visions of blood on swimming pool glass swam in Jakob's head. "They'd kill each other."

"Nah," said Nat. "Maybe. But not 'cause of us. We wouldn't glitch the implants, only block the circuits. The guys on the street, they'd know who to hit. How many hatchetmen do you figure are in LA?"

"Something like six hundred."

"Peanuts, against an army. They would have been kicked to the curb in an hour, them and all the Verders and Flynns. Imagine that, *hombre*! I'm telling you, Sven's speech—written by him, spoken by Kirimi—would set your blood on fire. After we set the men free, they'll torch the Studio and scatter the ashes. The whole rotten system will be done and dusted in one night."

He was speaking in the future tense. "You still think it can happen. You haven't told me how."

"It's like Rachel said." Nat gestured at Mrs. Bette. "Sven was our man inside. His contingency plan, one of many, is to use somebody else in his place."

"Me?" said Jakob. It was obvious from the way they were all staring at him that he was the somebody. "Why me?"

"You're an intelligent and capable man," said Belen. She returned to the sofa, replacing Rachel Bette, and sat so close he could feel the warmth of her thigh. "And you have a powerful motive. You loved Sven."

He couldn't deny it, not to her. "Dad help me, he was my world. When they were taking him away, I saw him. It was like I was dead myself. Or like I had slipped into another life, someone else's life, where I wasn't myself. How could Sven be gone and I'm still here?"

"You've grieved before," said Belen.

"For my wife, yes. I think I loved her, too. When she died, I double-dosed my Aremoden. It erased . . . everything. How we met, all our time together—gone. I've forgotten her name. All I can remember truly is her death. Why would it leave that, of all my memory? I thought of taking Aremoden after Sven, but I couldn't take enough unless I joined him."

He couldn't go on. A wave of regret carried him to the floor. He knelt in front of the couch, sobbing with his face in his hands.

Belen stroked his back. After a minute, she said, "This love is why you must help us, Jakob. You can now be the match for the flame Sven wished to set."

Though he felt like he weighed a thousand pounds, Jakob got off the floor and studied the band of quiet revolutionaries.

"What would I have to do?"

Nat said, "Don't worry about the details. Not tonight. Tonight, all we need to know is if you can keep a secret. If not, Artur's got some pills in his pocket. Say the word, and you can wake up at home with a headache, wondering why you taste puke. That's not how we want it, guy, but it's your choice."

"I'll keep the secret," said Jakob. The idea of using Aremoden again had become repugnant.

"Bless you, Jakob," said Belen. "Sleep here tonight, please. Lucas will show you to the guest room. Tomorrow, when you are rested, we'll discuss what you will do for *La Vie*."

Chapter Eleven: The First Promise

Streetlights outside her window made a glare on the TV screen. Kutri drew the curtains. At first glance, she had been impressed by the Bakelite walls and stainless steel countertops of her apartment, but had soon come to regard these features as cold, even hostile. The apartment felt warmer in the dark, almost homey. Besides, having the curtains open left her exposed. She had seen the mirror effect of the window glass from outside and couldn't help but imagine someone watching her through binoculars, shaped perhaps like those Jakob had shared at the lookout, and equipped with special lenses to let them see . . . everything.

Fenced in by dark fabric, she let the lilac robe that was her only garment puddle on the carpet. A rerun of *Good Breeding* was flickering in the background. In its dancing light, she made slow, naked pirouettes in the space between the TV and leather couch. She had no formal training as a dancer, but back at the Center, she had pored over pictures of ballerinas in books. When there was no one to see her, she liked to combine grace and abandon in her exercise, which her imitations of the women's postures certainly did.

She was too wound up to sleep. Earlier, Mondt had made a trip to the Municipal Hospital. He had delivered a troubling report back to her. Jakob was gone. He had checked himself out. After hearing this news, Kutri had tossed and turned in bed. After an hour or so, she had heard laughter and the clack of high heels from the hallway outside. With an ear to the apartment door, she had listened for clues as to which of her fellow candidates was making the racket.

Did the heels belong to Elise Dupain, the Parisian Amazon who was said to be taller than any woman in the history of the program? Or were they worn by Cuc Tien, the Indochinese beauty? Either or both might be resident in the apartment complex. Kutri had no way to know. An escort had shown her to her door, then locked her in, every night since her first in LA. She had seen no other girls, only heard them through the door.

She hadn't dared to call out. The women were strangers, and competitors at that, despite the fact they were the only persons on earth in a position to understand each other's mental stress. Even if Kutri had called out, the heavy door would have blurred her call into the laughter that was too loud, too boisterous to come from someone who could truly relate to how she felt. Had the other candidates been told to show themselves to Alec Simmons? She was sure they had. But none had been given a priceless gift, asked to betray her matchmaker, and gone on to be torn between attraction to that man and the need to protect her destiny.

Exercise improved Kutri's mood but slightly. A hot shower improved it slightly more. Wrapping her damp hair in a towel and her goose bumps in a blanket, Kutri settled on the couch to watch a marathon of *Good Breeding* highlights. Some of the segments dated back twenty-five years or more, but every one was a classic. With the insight the first interlocutor had given her into how the world worked, the shows were now more educational than ever before.

One of her favorite segments featured a short girl with curly hair and dimpled cheeks. If the darling had appeared in a Sears catalog, such as those kept at the Hindustan Bliss Center's library, her outfit would have been a floor-length skirt or a matronly robe. Her figure was too womanly for the editors of that modest publication to dress in swimwear. She was called Mella and was a great favorite to be match bride, in her time.

According to clips added to the rerun, the man on the street adored little Mella, calling her "sweet" and "cute" and complimenting the way she filled a sweater. The cameras loved her, focusing on her smile and the sway of her hips as she made her entrance to the Presentation Ball. Her gown, in Kutri's opinion, was a cut above that of the other candidates. The material had a sheen, and the tawny color lent the favorite's skin a healthy glow. The neckline, which could have been properly called a rib line, it cut so low, did a wonderful job of highlighting her assets.

Yet, she had lost. Another woman, slender and tall, had been presented on stage as the season's match bride. When this happened, the camera operator, in obvious surprise, spun away to Mella for several seconds before focusing on the victor. Mella's smile never faltered. It never even twitched. In testament to her worth as a candidate, she kept her place on stage, beaming with those charming dimples as the girl who had won the top spot hopped up and down with excitement.

There had been some compensation for Mella. When she left the ballroom, it was on the arm of one of the candidate grooms, a man she had presumably only met that night. They eventually married, Kutri remembered. A romantic outcome, but one that failed to make up for the injustice done when Mella was shoved aside. In the past, Kutri had told herself it was possible the Studio audience, who phoned or texted in their votes from communication kiosks, had done the shoving. Now that she knew better, she sympathized with Mella more deeply.

As the reruns flickered by, she wondered how she could ever have believed anyone but the Studio chose the match bride. Racial purity, a pretty face, and hips that were built to give birth always triumphed over other considerations that might have charmed a crowd but made no difference to the camera. The match bride was a type. A diverse type, to be sure—a type so broad it encompassed Aluel Garang, Karan Politis, and Kutri herself, women whose last common ancestor was millennia in the past—but a type, all the same.

The match brides were peaks on a chart of exceptional women, destined to be what they were by an accident of birth. How unfair! Just when Kutri had reconciled herself to having the public judge her qualities, she found out the competition itself was an illusion. She was no more in control of her fate now than she had been when her father intentionally "lost" her in that market. Suspecting as much had been irritating. Being convinced was intolerable. She cast her blanket at the TV, stomped to pick it up when it fell short, and sat naked on the floor, too frustrated in her anger to do anything productive.

The marathon night ended with highlights of the so-called "Golden Season," the one that saw the ascendancy of Karan Politis. Unlike in so many of the segments Kutri had watched, there was no waffling of the perfect match bride's lead from beginning to end. Karan came on strong in early polls and never flagged. Yet strangely, she wasn't the most perfect fit for the "type" in her season. Other women were darker, or lighter, and several had heritage more rare than the Mediterranean middle Karan represented.

What must Karan have done to stay on top? Picturing the nod the idol had given her Thursday morning at breakfast, Kutri wondered if there wasn't something sad in Karan's expression. It was impossible to say, from her new perspective, how much pity had been there and how much she was painting on with her imagination.

When the last clip of Karan's season started, Kutri fetched the TV remote. The Politis wedding had been the cornerstone of her self-education. She had watched it hundreds of times, aping Karan's movements. With her eyes closed, she could turn and wave and quiver her lip just like Karan. She could cry on command in perfect sync with the recording. That particular performance was the last thing she wanted to practice at the moment. She was about to switch the TV off when a face in the crowd caught her eye. The camera moved away quickly, making her wish she had a way to pause the picture. She had read once of a device called a DVR that could perform such a miracle. Without the aid of that device, she could only scramble close to the TV on bare knees as the cameraman moved through his prescribed motions.

Had she been mistaken? No. There was the sleeve of familiar blue. The camera panned; she saw what she knew she would: Jakob, in his early twenties, with hair somewhat darker than at present and skin glowing with youth, stood near the back of the wedding party. He appeared happy, deliriously so. And he wasn't alone. His arm was wrapped around the waist of a woman. Lovely, slim, fragile above all, she reminded Kutri of a porcelain vase. A lover would be careful not to crush her. He'd kiss her with eyes open to be sure she didn't shatter. She was a fallen flower petal, doomed either to dry up or to wilt. And Jakob held her tenderly, crooking his elbow to ward away stumblers who might crush her with a touch.

Kutri touched her own hip in the place Jakob was touching the woman's. She arched her back and lifted her head as the woman turned to treat Jakob to a kiss. Jakob stooped, so she wouldn't have to strain. As he lost himself in the moment, Kutri dragged her fingernails over her naked thighs. When the camera moved away, leaving Jakob to shelter his love, she scratched and scratched again, until welts rose on her brown skin.

She might have done more damage if not for the phone. It lay on the countertop in the kitchen, still in her bag. The ringing was so sudden, it startled her. Despite the distance, it sounded absurdly loud. The ringtone was an upbeat guitar riff, layered with a backbeat that dissolved into electronic warble. Simmons had played it for her, so she knew at once what the sound meant. He was calling her. She leapt to her feet.

By all the names of God, what should I say?

She pulled the phone from the bag but did not stab the "Answer" bubble at once. Flashing and vibrating as it strummed its chords, the phone was riotous with electric life. Simmons had entered the initials "FIJ" in her contacts, to indicate himself. They were not on display. That meant the caller was someone else. Someone unknown.

She dared to answer. "Hello?"

There was a hum on the other end, then a voice she didn't recognize said, "Hello, meat."

She didn't like the voice, or the greeting. "Who is this, please?"

The caller smacked his lips. "Manners! Lovely. I enjoy pretty speech. Never mind who I am, meat. What you should ask is, what do I want? You're watching TV. What station?"

"How do you know—"

"What station?" he said. "Never mind. Flip to GS1."

She thought of ending the call. Could he see her? The notion was terrifying. She had felt so exposed with the blinds open, but what if she was being watched while they were drawn, how could she ever hide? She held the phone at arm's length, searching the walls for any sign of a mounted camera such as she had seen in the cube of glass.

"Meat," the caller said. "Flip over."

"I don't know what you're asking or why I should listen."

"You will. Change the station, now, to General Station One."

It was an easy request to grant, and it gave her an excuse to cover herself with the blanket. GS1 was a few clicks of the remote away. When Kutri brought it up, she nearly dropped the phone.

Over the shoulder of an anchorman was a picture of Cuc Tien. The Indochinese candidate lay face up on the pavement. Her arms were splayed to either side of her body and her pelvis tilted so that one leg crossed the other. At the best of times, the form-fitting dress, which was the color of pearls, would barely have covered her from neck to mid-thigh. It had been rent down the middle, leaving her fully exposed.

There was nothing pleasant about the sight. Where Cuc's belly should have been was a gaping red wound. It looked like someone had stuck a knife in her navel, carved an X, and turned back the flaps. Coils of purple intestine were uncovered. They draped her breasts and her pubic mound. Cuc Tien was dead, very dead. Pints of her blood made pools on the ground. The black bodies of flies crowded the obscene loops of gut.

"Dainty, isn't she?" said the man on Kutri's phone. "Very sweet, but tiny. Hardly an appetizer."

Kutri wanted to switch off the TV, but her hand felt cramped. It refused to work the remote.

"Do you see what's missing, meat? Scrap of kidney, slab of liver. It's nothing she couldn't have lived without."

"You killed her."

"She had it coming, with her mouth. I let her breathe as long as possible, but oh, how she shouted! You know who I am now, meat. You know what I am. Do you understand why you should talk to me?"

"I—" Kutri swallowed. "What is it you want?"

"Good. Glad you asked. I have a message for you. You were rude to a friend of mine and the message is, well, bad things happen to rude girls. If you don't want them to happen to you, I need you to make me a promise."

On TV, the image of Cuc Tien was briefly replaced by the head and shoulders of Karan Politis. For the first time Kutri could remember, Karan appeared to have skimped on her makeup on the way to the interview booth. The anchorman asked her to comment on the night's atrocity.

Blinking as a spotlight caught her eye, Karan said, "It's unimaginable. To think of this tragedy, so soon after the Garang Disaster—"

The caller said, "Will you make a promise, meat?"

The sight of Karan awakened Kutri's boldness. "You know my name, yes? Use it, or use nothing. What would I promise?"

He was quiet a moment. "Don't be like that. I did you a favor, showing you what can happen. All I ask in return is to do what you're told. Promise you'll make a call to my friend. He said you'd know what call. And he said not today. Wait for Monday, when you see your *other* friend at the office. He's dangerous, that one, unorthodox. Get him alone—a minute's long enough—then make the call. Tell my friend what he wants to hear. It's simple, mea— Ah. It's simple. Do you understand?"

She did, but she had questions. "Why does he despise Jakob?"

"None of my business. None of yours. We live to serve, you and me. Do what you're told and you'll go on living. On Monday, get him alone. Give him something to remember, if you like. That's none of my business either. Just be sure you call my friend when you're through. That's all. Someone else will handle things from there."

"And if I refuse, you'll do to me what you did to Cuc Tien?"

He whistled. "Something like it, maybe. You're a juicier piece of meat. You'd bleed more, struggle. I like a struggle."

Kutri had the sense to hold her hand over the phone as she whimpered. She said, "You're bluffing. The Studio wants me for match bride."

"Do they? You'd be a good one. Maybe I am bluffing. Maybe you're the Blessed Holy High of Dad Himself in Heaven. Only you, though. Not your friend. He's on his way out. If not one way, the other. My way, meat. I've seen the boy insides, too. Like girl, but gummier. I held the beating heart of a boy once, in this very hand. Do as you're told, Miss Chandigarh. If not for your sake, for his. Are we clear?"

The anchorman on TV had moved on from the murder. A video of a forest fire in the outlands was being shown on the screen, but with such a vivid picture to show, Kutri was sure the discussion would return to Cuc Tien. Her splayed corpse would no doubt appear as often as the still the stations had been using of Aluel's savaged face. More often, perhaps. In her mind, she saw Jakob lying in Cuc's posture. Instead of a surgical X exposing his guts, his chest had been laid open, the ribs spread to show lungs but no heart.

She hugged the blanket. "I'll do it."

"What's that, please? Speak up."

"I'll make the call."

"Thought you might. Good. Monday, remember. A minute alone, then the call."

"And you'll leave Jakob alone?"

"I'd like to, meat, but I'm hired help. My orders are to get a promise, not give one. Do your part and hope for the best is my advice."

He hung up. An impulse to smash the phone seized Kutri. She set it aside instead. She spent the rest of the early morning touring the apartment, eyeing every bulge in the wallpaper with suspicion. Were there cameras trained on her at all times? Now that she had had the thought, it refused to leave her mind. It seemed obvious, too, that secret microphones would be in place, so she kept her silence as she plotted how not to betray Jakob.

She would warn him, secretly, give him time to flee. But how to do that when her privacy was so unsure? If only there were someone who could advise her, someone who knew about technology, about cameras and microphones and other such devices, new and old.

With a thrill that stopped her pacing, she remembered there was. If Jimmy Ching was half so clever as he boasted, he would have a way to secure her conversation with Jakob. All she had to do was convey her request to him without giving away the plan. She shuffled her feet on the carpet. The sound reminded her of waves sloshing against the hull of the *Scotus*.

She was tossed on a wave now, but not altogether lost at sea. Her fitness consultant was due at noon. That was plenty of time to plan out what she would do on Monday. The right stratagem would be simple, but it would have to be clever, if she wanted Jakob Freeman to live.

Chapter Twelve: The Burning World

On Monday morning, there was extra security at Bliss HQ. Jakob entered between two dour SSOs and stood for a moment, scanning the lobby. The large, mostly empty space, with its granite flooring and extra-wide TV screens built into the stucco walls, was host to eight SSOs in olive uniforms and black berets. Turning as one man, they watched officials and clerks pass through the security checkpoint that, on most days, was manned by a single operative. No scheduled event accounted for the change. Jakob asked the SSO scanning genobrands if the office was to receive special guests. The man gave no answer, only waved him on.

In the elevator, he met a clerk whose downcast eyes reminded him of his younger self. An SSO had installed himself at the back of the elevator. Jakob considered asking why the assignment was necessary, when such a heavy contingent was checking credentials, but the SSO looked grumpy, as though he was waiting for an excuse to fight. Jakob had slept fitfully over the weekend, so he was probably being paranoid. After everything he'd learned at Nat's, it was hard not to be.

La Vie's plan was simple and bold. It was also insane. Jakob had spent Saturday and Sunday being shown weapons, schematics, and maps of LA. With Lucas as driver, Nat had taken him to parts of the city he had never dreamed existed. Secret hideaways in buildings whose entries appeared blocked, underground passages between barricaded streets, and invisible fortresses in urban camouflage all really existed. They were not the myths he had heard whispered by drunks in bars or on the streets.

It made him wonder about other things he had been taught and told.

There was even a refugee camp, built partly in and partly under MacArthur Park, that was home to thousands of La Vie sympathizers. These were the heart of La Vie's would-be army, though most knew little about the organization itself. Some didn't know there was an organization. It was enough that they hated the New Society that had pushed them to the fringes, stomped on their rights, and taken pounds of flesh every time they dared to step out of line.

All weekend, Nat had treated Jakob like a son about to join the family business. Jakob had seen a few such fathers in old movies Sven had shown him. They were all much older than the sons, which wasn't true of him and Nat, but the enthusiasm Nat showed was still the same. The biggest shock to Jakob's system had come when he met a man he had known for some time.

Vic Carmen was broad and bald, with curious eyes and a firm handshake. "You're one of them," Jakob had said.

The man he knew as an actor who made his living playing *Good Breeding*'s chief of bliss had nodded grimly.

"Can't believe they got Sven," he had said.

Nat had given Jakob a wink.

"We get around, guy. You stick with me and see."

So Jakob had. Surprise followed surprise. By Sunday evening, when he was dropped off at home, Jakob had stopped conceiving La Vie as a group of privileged wannabe suicides in an upstairs apartment. They were a cross-cultural army, as diverse as they were well connected. If he could convince himself of their sanity, it would be easy enough to believe they could change the world . . . or at least whatever part of it the Studio actually controlled.

The clerk got off on the second floor. Jakob got off on the third. He paused to consider the options he confronted each workday. He could go left, to the lounge where his colleagues started their mornings over a drink they called coffee, though no part of a plant was used in the brew. He could go straight along the bright hall that led to the suite of rooms where Dr. Staley worked. Or, he could go right, along the dimmer hall that would take him past Sven's workroom and to his own. The compass of his instinct pointed right. He resisted, thinking there might be a piece of news his peers would relate that could explain why they were overrun with State brutes.

With Sven gone, he had no true friends left in HQ, but he did at least expect his workmates to be civil. Making conversation would be tiresome, however, and he was already tired enough.

"The New Society's a cancer, guy," Nat had told him on Saturday. He had been leaning over the railing of his balcony, letting his weight tilt him at the ground before catching himself, a game Jakob didn't dare to play. "We have to cut it out before we get on with life."

Jakob saw his point, but cutting wasn't the metaphor his mind kept conjuring. He kept picturing LA on fire. When the riot Nat had in mind razed the Studio and every other institution to the ground, some fires were bound to break out. Would they be able to stop the burning once it started?

Sven's workroom was dark, but Jakob could see by the light from the hall that the shelves had been stripped out. The absence of the collection— the toys, music, books, and especially the movies—left an ache in his chest. Staring through the doorway of the eviscerated room was like staring into Sven's grave. Not that he had one. The body would have been cremated days ago.

Jakob crossed the workroom, swaying, and punched the button that retracted the shutters. Light spilled in. He looked out at the view that Sven had liked to say was the dullest in LA. On most days, Jakob agreed. Only a postage stamp of skyline could be seen between crumbling buildings. But today, Jakob saw a wave of fire splashing over the city, consuming everything it touched. He shook his head and the vision was gone, but the fear it woke remained.

A cough alerted him to Mondt's presence. The bodyguard was standing at the door, looking like he disapproved of . . . well, everything, really. As Jakob opened his mouth to ask what he wanted, Kutri scooted past. She practically ran into Jakob's arms, only stopping when he took a step back, warning her with his expression. Her outfit was a taupe dress with buttons of gold. It hugged her waist and shrink-wrapped her breasts and hips. He left off picturing Armageddon for a minute.

"Hello. What are you doing here?"

"I've been waiting down the hall. A clerk said you would be here. I know I'm early."

That was an understatement. Their next scheduled appointment was that afternoon. Jakob needed the time to scrutinize the list of candidate grooms he had neglected in favor of touring the secret corridors of La Vie's LA.

"You are," he said.

Kutri searched his face. When she found his stitches, her eyes narrowed.

"I heard you left the hospital. That is all I heard."

Flushed with guilt, he turned to face the window. "I'm sorry. I should have sent a message."

"It would have eased my mind."

He forced himself to turn toward her again. This time, it was Kutri who glanced away. She examined the wall, where the outline of the shelves could be traced in dark paint and dry glue.

He said, "A friend of mine had this workroom. It was the same friend I did a favor for, at Ching's. I believe I told you he was ill. I'm sorry. That wasn't quite true. He died."

Exactly why he had to tell her now, he couldn't have said. It seemed like he had too many secrets. This was one he didn't have to keep.

"Oh, Jakob. I'm sorry," she said. With widening eyes, she took his free hand in both of her own.

He let the squeeze go on for a trifle too long, then took his hand back and turned away. "Sven used to keep the most amazing keepsakes, all treasures from the World Before."

For three nights, he had slept with Sven's final acquisition, the panda figurine, beside him on the pillow. Now he drew it from his pocket and offered it to her.

"I thought I'd put this where it belongs," he said. "But as you can see, there's no such place, now that the movers have gone. I think you would have liked this place. I wish I had shown you before the collection was packed up."

She pinched the panda between thumb and forefinger, lifting it for a closer examination.

"That would have been nice," she said. "But I think you are wrong about the bear. It does have a place. In fact, I came to ask if we can go back. To Jimmy Ching's, I mean."

He was surprised. Last Wednesday seemed so long ago, he had a hard time calling the face of Sven's other friend to mind. Ching had something to do with Mitsuru, too. Jakob had put that mystery out of his mind.

He said, "A return trip to Chinatown. I'm sorry. My work—"

"Mind the tailoring," said a voice from the hall. "Clearly, you boys don't know who I am."

Jakob hurried to the door. In the hall, Tolson and DeGarre were patting down Dr. Staley, who didn't seem to mind.

"It's all right, gentlemen. Let him through."

Beaming first at Jakob, then at Kutri, the senior blissman entered the workroom. He didn't mine its denuded state, presumably because he had given the order to have it cleaned. Jakob wondered if Clyde Staley had searched Sven's things before sending them to the basement, or if he had skipped all that and only pinched the scotch.

"Miss Chandigarh! We meet at last." Dr. Staley extended a hand. Kutri put her hand out automatically, but before their palms touched, she recoiled. Chuckling, Clyde wiggled the fingers of his prosthetic limb. "Forgive me. You figured on flesh, not polymer. How naughty not to warn you. May I?"

He extended the hand again. This time, Kutri allowed herself to be touched. Cradling her fingers in his mechanical grip, Dr. Staley pursed his lips. He kissed the air over the hand, as was, just barely, proper.

"There," he said. "That didn't hurt."

"I'm sorry," said Kutri.

"Think nothing of it, dear."

Jakob said, "Kutri, this is my superior, Dr. Clyde Staley. You'll find his plastic parts are harmless. It's the rest you have to worry about."

"Harsh," said Clyde, smiling. "Don't listen to gossip, young lady. Some of it isn't even true."

As if to emphasize his protest, the fingers of his artificial hand clanked together like the jaws of a bear trap.

"Ah! That's not supposed to happen," said Clyde. "I'm overdue for maintenance."

He removed his jacket and rolled up the shirt sleeve. When a foot of forearm was exposed, he thumbed a depression and tilted open a hidden panel. A lever the length of a fingernail was exposed. He made an adjustment that seemed minuscule to Jakob, but it caused the fingers of the hand to droop like flower petals.

"The problem is, you can't get the parts," said Clyde. He tweaked the lever's angle. The fingers snapped into shape. "I ask you, Miss Chandigarh. Did you ever see the like?" Bending his elbow ninety degrees, he made the arm revolve like a fan blade.

"My name is Kutri," said Kutri.

"Delighted."

Jakob said, "Doctor, is there something you want?"

"Oh, no. No." He stopped the rotation of the forearm and began to smooth the sleeve. "I heard the lady was in and thought I'd introduce myself. You know I wouldn't dream of interfering with *official* business, Jakob. If your *affairs* need to be conducted *in private*, do tell me and I'll go."

The emphasis on *official*, *affairs*, and *in private* got his point across. Thursday's irregularities had cost Jakob a measure of trust. He was not going to be left on his own with the candidate. Even the tidy band of bodyguards was not enough. Had someone warned the Office of Bliss to leash their dog? Caution was out of character for Clyde.

"You're welcome to stay, of course," said Jakob. "Before you came in, Kutri was asking about a trip to Chinatown."

If he had been studying her less intently, he would have missed the despair that flashed across her face. Her plans clearly hinged on having him, or possibly Jimmy, to herself. What was she up to? For her sake, it would be better that he kept his distance. The doctor's intrusion might be a blessing in disguise.

"A wonderful idea," said Clyde. "Have you eaten, darling?"

"No," said Kutri. "Not yet."

"Excellent. My second favorite club is in Chinatown. It's kitty-corner to the old library. Didn't I hear that you enjoy books, Kutri? You can see where hundreds are buried from there. The club admits only the most distinguished gentlemen, but a member in good standing can bring guests. You must accompany me to breakfast. And you too, Jakob. We'll find some bananas for your apes in the hall. The silent fellow in the corner can chew on a rock." The silent fellow was Mondt, who looked like he could do exactly that. "What do you say to that plan?"

Kutri gave a slight bow. Her tone was stiff when she said, "It sounds lovely."

Jakob raised an eyebrow. "Doctor, is your club a proper place for a young lady?"

"There are no boys swinging on the chandeliers, if that's what you mean."

"I don't want to impose," said Kutri.

Jakob was delighted she had picked up his reluctance. But Clyde said, "Not at all. Most days I'm swamped with work, but as it happens, I've read all the reports on my desk. There is one more I'm expecting, but until it comes in, I've nothing more to do but entertain you."

Effectively silenced, Jakob could tell that Kutri plainly wished to refuse but couldn't see how. She said, "How wonderful," and left it at that.

Bowing, Clyde waved at the door. "After you."

Kutri dipped a curtsy and exited in front of Mondt.

"A moment, Doctor," Jakob said before his senior could follow. "I appreciate what you're trying to do."

"Do you?" said Clyde. "Maybe above the waist, dear boy. Lower down, you're furious."

"Nothing's going on down there."

The doctor touched a finger of his natural hand to Jakob's stitches. When he pulled the finger away, there was a smear of blood on the tip.

"My, my," he said. "So much trouble over a girl who does nothing for you *down there*. Indulge me, Jakob. It's my own reputation I'm guarding. To lose one matchmaker may be regarded as a misfortune. To lose two would be carelessness."

Leaving Jakob to stew, he went into the hall.

Chapter Thirteen: The Price We Pay

Though her nerves were piano wires and her plans in splinters on the floor, Kutri's determination was undiminished. At her first sight of Jakob in three days, she had wanted to collapse in his arms and smother him with kisses. She was sure he would have kissed her back if she had tried. The sight of the stitches below his hairline had made her hang back. She was used to hiding her feelings. From a young age, she had been warned of the corrosive effect of too much passion. It was better to act discreetly than to behave foolishly and be found out, even when the situation was desperate. If she shouted a warning to Jakob, it might mean his death.

As she noticed the garbage mounds through the limo's windows, the threats of her murderous caller returned to her. She struggled to breathe slowly, calmly, quietly. With subtle movements of her head, she checked the lining of the window glass. She could see nothing that resembled a lens or a microphone. But what did that prove? She had a phone in her straw bag that would have appeared miraculous to the men in the limo. If such a technical marvel could be concealed, why not an invisible camera to monitor her every move?

"A terrible thing, what happened to Miss Tien," said Dr. Staley. He was sitting in the seat opposite, beside Jakob and DeGarre. Tolson was up front, as usual. The third bodyguard, Mondt, was in the seat next to Kutri.

"Terrible," Kutri agreed.

Jakob appeared confused. Was it possible he had missed the news about the murder? Cuc Tien's picture, as Kutri had predicted, was ubiquitous on General Stations. Jakob could not have failed to commit it to memory, unless he'd avoided TV all weekend.

On the off chance, she said, "Her killer is certainly a devil."

Jakob's mouth gaped, confirming Kutri's guess. He hadn't known Cuc was dead. Was the injury to his head worse than he was letting on? Perhaps he had slept all Saturday and Sunday, only waking this morning to stumble into work. She would ask, when they were alone. If he struggled to keep upright, she couldn't expect him to escape to the outlands on his own. Perhaps Jimmy would know someone who could help.

The limo pulled up to a curb in front of the former Los Angeles Public Library, Chinatown Branch, on the corner of the intersection between North Hill Street and Ord Street. Kutri remembered picking her way to Ord with Jakob and Mondt. The Emperor's Emporium was mere blocks away, though she could see no direct route to it. Except for the way they had come, the streets were crowded with rubbish and rubble.

Under normal circumstances, she would have been excited to glimpse a library. Even this ruin, made shapeless by overgrown vines, would have thrilled her by virtue of its history. Someone had cleared away enough brush to reveal the sign, which was written in English and Chinese. Nearby, men in filthy overalls and tangled beards sat with their backs to the wall. Aside from providing a place to lean on, the library appeared to serve no purpose, but Kutri would have been happy to see it, if she was not so worried about Jakob.

Dr. Staley pointed to a building standing diagonally across from the library's wreck.

"There," he said. "My home away from home."

The building was an eyesore. Behind a low, lemon-colored wall, a metal framework rose around a brutalist cube that dwarfed every structure nearby. There were no windows in the upper stories, making it hard to judge how many floors the cube had—four at least, if not five or more. Kutri searched for an outcropping on the roof that might support a magnetic field generator, but could make nothing of the clusters of strange antennae.

The doctor and director of the Office of Bliss leapt from the limo, followed more slowly by Mondt, who came around to open Kutri's door. When Dr. Staley leaned in to take her hand, Mondt grunted, warning him away. As soon as she was on her feet, Kutri offered her hand to the doctor, trying to make up for her earlier reaction. Instead of grasping the hand, Dr. Staley brushed it with the back of his prosthesis. She shivered. He laughed. He turned to link elbows, using his natural arm.

Jakob stayed close as they crossed the street. He was certainly on edge. Not a bad idea, under the circumstances. If only Kutri could get him to Jimmy's, she was sure she could convince him to act on her warning. She was a persuasive woman. She had once talked Papa Paquette out of stabbing an orderly he had discovered in her room. Instead of stabbing the man, Papa had doubled the width of his smile, but she had still saved his life.

Stepping onto the curb in front of the blocky structure, Kutri searched for a name. The place displayed no sign on the outside, no text of any kind, only a heavy door with a doorman sitting in front on a three-legged stool.

"What do you call your club, Doctor?" she asked.

"The A & L," he said.

"This stands for something?" she said.

"It does."

Most of the storefronts on the other side of Ord Street were nailed shut with weathered boards. The single survivor caught Kutri's attention as the doctor conducted her the last few meters to the door. The store's window was painted black. A twist of neon over the door had the shape of a woman whose hair was the only body part on the same scale as her bottom and breasts. Like the A & L Club, no words indicated what sort of place the storefront was, but Kutri thought she could guess.

"You vouch for this neighborhood?" said Jakob. He had seen the neon too.

"Not at all," said Dr. Staley. "Only the club."

He smiled at the doorman. The tip of the man's blue cap revealed thick hair of slate gray.

Dr. Staley said, "Don't get up, Ven."

"Thanks, Staley," said the doorman. "I won't."

"We're informal here," explained the doctor. "No status. No titles. Puts us on even footing. Wouldn't you say so, Ven?"

"Very droll," Ven said, lifting his right leg and stamping it down, making a clank, as of metal. Ven twitched his pants leg to reveal a prosthesis. "Even footing, he says. At least you brought a guest."

"A special guest, Ven," said Dr. Staley.

"And the rest?"

"Her entourage."

Ven took the measure of Jakob, Mondt, and the SSOs.

"Door's open," he said.

And Clyde said, "Dad bless."

The door led to a short entrance hall with a hardwood floors and an odor of incense masking neglect. Music was playing at the end of the hall.

"Bliss," said Dr. Staley. "The other kind." He led the way to the next room, where the party stood blinking in surprise.

They were standing in a space quite different from what Kutri had expected from the outside. Instead of story stacked on story, the main body of the building was an open rotunda, rising fifty meters to a translucent dome. The glass of the dome was yellow, making the pale Dr. Staley appear jaundiced.

A ramp spiraled around the circular main wall, its weight supported by projecting beams. Paintings on the wall had once, no doubt, hung straight, but they now appeared crooked because the ramp approaching them tilted at odd angles. Scores of busts and vases were set on tilted stands. Here and there was a figure statue or an ancient tribal mask. The effect was of faded glamour mixed with danger, owing to the questionable footing.

In the center of the room stood an immense object that Kutri had to frown at for several seconds before recognizing it as a partial reconstruction of Shiva Nataraja, the dancing god in a ring of fire. The material making up Shiva and the ring, as well as the pedestal Shiva stood on and the dwarf he was crushing underfoot, had a glossy sheen where it wasn't covered in dust. So much dust had accumulated that motes drifted in a stream from Shiva's raised left leg, creating the illusion that the god himself was being blown away, atom by atom, on a breeze.

A nozzle was connected to the unfinished idol by strands of plastic. The crane arm holding the nozzle was jointed for horizontal and vertical motion. Somehow, the apparatus had summoned the idol into being, drawing it up from the floor like a conjurer pulling scarves from a sleeve. After conjuring five meters of pedestal, dwarf, ring, and god, the magic had evidently run out. Shiva's legs, body, and four arms were finished, but he lacked a head. Was it sacrilege, Kutri wondered, to sculpt an idol but leave it blind, deaf, and dumb?

Around Shiva's base, a circular bar had been constructed. Leather armchairs and fainting couches had been arranged in a wagon-wheel pattern, with the bar at its hub. Most of the seats were unoccupied, but every man who was present wore a suit jacket. Quite a few had emblazoned badges of office. Kutri didn't spot any blissmen, apart from Jakob and their host, but justicemen and statemen were present, plus others whose badges she didn't know by heart.

There were no SSOs or hatchetmen. If the patrons got rowdy, they had to police themselves. Not that a disturbance seemed likely. The members whose hair was not gray or white were bald. All sat hunched in their chairs, staring at console TVs mounted in frames created to look like tombstones. Kutri genuinely had never seen a more sallow, cadaverous lot.

Only one man at the bar noted her entrance. His gasp induced a wave of turned heads. A few men toppled sideways at the sight of a woman in their sanctum. Several huddled into their jackets as though they were naked underneath. Their embarrassment was curious and comical. Kutri turned a toe and planted a hand on her hip, posing as she did at press conferences.

"How funny your friends are, Doctor," she said. "You'd think they'd never seen a woman before."

Dr. Staley laughed out loud. "You hear that, you reedy orphans? As you were, as you were." He headed for a distant cluster of armchairs, drawing the so-called entourage with a wave of his hand.

They had advanced some meters when Kutri's straw bag began to play music. As the strums of guitar strings drifted, everyone halted, glancing around in search of the source.

"Excuse me," said Kutri. She clamped the straw bag to her side, terrified they would take it from her and find the phone. She couldn't admit the song was her ringtone, alerting her to the second call she had ever received. There was no telling what Jakob and the others would make of her possession of the phone, to say nothing of what the caller might say. Snagging the first lie that came to mind, Kutri explained, "It's an alarm. From home. It reminds me to exercise."

She stooped, hiding the bag, and reached inside. There was an icon that read "Decline" and another that said, "Decline with message." Kutri wished she knew what message would put off her caller, but she had no idea, so tapped Decline instead. Days of toying with the phone had taught her its basic functions. With a few deft motions, she activated silent mode. She breathed a sigh of relief.

Fixing a bright smile, she said, "I owe ten jumping jacks." She pinched the fabric of her dress as a punchline. It was clearly too tight for any exercise that didn't start with tearing it off.

"Perhaps another time," Dr. Staley said. "You should eat first, for energy." He clicked his heels and set off.

The clump of furniture to which the doctor led the group was populated by two men. One was very old and wore a tweed suit. The other man, younger, wore a tuxedo with cummerbund. Neither man was watching TV. The old man sat with a blanket on his lap, talking to the younger fellow as he gestured peevishly with his right hand. At first, Kutri thought his left hand was hidden in the blanket, but when she drew closer, she saw that the sleeve of the tweed jacket was rolled up and pinned to the tweed jacket. If the old man had a left hand, it was preserved somewhere in a glass jar. The sleeve was empty.

"Is something wrong?" said Dr. Staley.

"I— Are you teasing me?" she said.

He said, "I don't see how."

"You do. You're teasing me. Please, speak frankly. What is this place?"

"It's a club for distinguished gentlemen, just as I said. All the members here share a special distinction."

Jakob said, "What distinction is that?"

Before the doctor could answer, the tuxedoed man stepped forward. As he did, he turned, and Kutri saw that in place of a right arm, he had an empty drinks tray mounted to his shoulder. There was a sort of support rod connecting it to his waist.

"Hello, Ellis," said Dr. Staley. "Delighted to see you. Kutri and Jakob, here, will be joining us for breakfast. Before you take the orders, would you mind telling Kutri how long you have been with the A & L?"

"Four years, miss," said Ellis.

"And how long since . . ." The doctor tapped his own shoulder.

"Not much longer, Staley. You know I'm not one to sit on my hands."

"Quite right," said Dr. Staley. "And quite droll. Thank you, Ellis. Fetch a whiskey with the menu, would you? And see that the coffee is from a fresh pot."

Ellis nodded. "Of course." He turned to the old man. "If you don't mind, Jon."

"Don't worry about him," said Dr. Staley. "It's not as if he can throw you out."

"Droll indeed, Staley," said Ellis. "I'll see to the menu and drinks."

"Doctor," said Jakob as Ellis departed, "what are you up to?" From his tone and expression, he was clearly fighting to keep himself under control.

"Calm yourself, Jakob. Kutri, allow me to introduce the founder of our club. Jon is . . . Jon? Ha! Look at that. He's asleep."

The old man was, indeed, snoring gently. When Dr. Staley touched his sleeve—the one with an arm in it—he jolted upright and swore.

"Sin of Onan!"

"Manners, Jon," said Clyde. "It's Staley, your old chum. I've brought someone to meet you. A woman."

"A what? Speak up."

He was easily the oldest man Kutri had ever seen. His wispy hair was all white. Threads in the white beard might once have been ginger but now resembled stains. His forehead was the texture of tree bark, and his eyelids resembled stuffed sacks. The eyes were cloudy white and probably blind. There was so little flesh in the suit that if strings been tied to the joints, Kutri would have mistaken Jon for a marionette. The weak and phlegmy voice was complemented by a click of ill-fitting dentures.

"A woman, Jon," Dr. Staley said. "She's a real beauty. Have a look."

"You know I can't see, mothercutter. And I don't want to. I've escaped too many traps to walk back in."

"You mean you've gnawed your way out."

Jon made a noise in his chest. His, "Droll" was automatic. It contained no humor and even less good will.

"Thank you," said Clyde, nevertheless. "Now, Jon. Please invite my guests to sit."

"Are there chairs? Sit, then. Sit!"

Dr. Staley flopped in a chair. The others kept on their feet. Evidently, the absence of pillows shifting tipped off the grumbly ancient man.

"Sit," Jon said. "Or do you expect me to stand?"

He twitched aside the blanket. Where there should have been knees, knots showed over empty trouser legs. Kutri stifled a yelp of surprise. Dr. Staley laughed.

"Wonderful," he said. "You're a fine host, Jon. Do you understand now, Kutri? Do you know where you are? This is the A & L Club. As in Arm and Leg. It's the price we have to pay to get in. Jon is the founder, the first to celebrate our distinction. As you can see, he's paid more than most."

"Rot," said Jon. "What rot. Is there really a woman? Don't listen to him, gal, if you really are here."

"I am here," said Kutri, refusing to sound weak. "Why shouldn't I listen to Dr. Staley?"

"Because he's lying, that's why. Are you still on your feet? Come close. 'The price we pay,'" he said. "Shame on you, Staley. Sit close, woman. I'll tell you the truth. A & L's not arm and leg—"

"It's Auber and Lucerne," said Jakob. His expression had gone from angry to disgusted. He sat on the couch to the left of the founder and added, "Correct?"

"Yes," said Jon. "Who are you?"

Dr. Staley answered. "One of my minions, Jon. Clever, but orthodoxically ableist."

Kutri glanced at the doctor, then sat down next to Jakob. The intensity of his stare at the old man was worrying. Were they about to have another violent episode? If she could have seen a way to leave the club and go straight to Jimmy's, she would have taken it. With everyone engaged, there was no way.

She said, "Excuse me. What is Auber and Lucerne?"

"Who are they, you mean," said Jakob. "They're the subjects of a pair of famous cases heard in Los Angeles Superior Court. Franz Auber sued for the right to dissolve his marriage. This was over half a century ago, before Mayor Brass put civil administration in the hands of the Studio. Further back, before the Slow Plague forced a change, couples who were unhappy were allowed to split at will. By Auber's time, of course, that was against the law. A man can't just leave his wife; it's monstrous. Before Auber and Lucerne, any man who tried would be locked up and medicated. They'd make him do what a husband should do. Franz Auber wanted to put his wife away so he could marry someone else."

Kutri was puzzled. "Where would he have put her?"

"A . . . turn of phrase," Jakob explained, though she could tell by his hesitation that the answer wasn't truthful. "It means to abandon her financially. You've heard of divorce?"

"I've read such a thing once existed," she said. "But wouldn't she simply find a new husband?"

"She didn't want a new husband," said Jon. "So, she fought back. Auber lost his case and was imprisoned. Hanged himself. After his death, a woman named Maria Lucerne filed suit against the city for wrongful death. She wanted to blame the courts for creating a situation in which two women lost their mate. She was a young widow, you see, and when she lost her husband, she took Auber as a lover. They wanted to marry, and when he died, he left her pregnant."

Jon spoke more firmly, clearly fond of telling the story. "A woman's power is in her belly," he told Kutri. "The justices didn't want a bastard dropped on their doorstep. Auber had been rich, one of their own. According to rumor, his own wife was barren, or frigid, which is worse. Maria Lucerne was better in every way. The court should have annulled the marriage and let them wed. As compensation, they did it posthumously and named the boy as heir to Auber's fortune.

"There were protests, naturally," Dr. Staley interjected. "If a dead man's marriage can be broken, why not a living man's, said the lawyers."

Jon scoffed. "They meant it as a warning but accidentally hit the nail on the head. When the city passed a strong anti-divorce law, it was struck down immediately in court. In the end, sanity triumphed. It doesn't matter if wives are rarer than left-handed guitars. A man has a right to get rid of one." At the end of this speech, Jon's dentures clashed, sounding like the bang of a judge's gavel.

"The city didn't agree, of course," said Dr. Staley.

Jon made a sound remarkably like a snorting bull.

"As a compromise," said Jakob, "divorce was allowed, but at a high fee. To divorce his wife, a man has to lose a limb."

Dr. Staley said, "An arm or a leg."

"True, but not what the club's name means," added Jon.

Jakob was wringing his hands. "This is a club of divorcees. I didn't know, Doctor, that you qualified."

"It was long ago," said Dr. Staley.

Kutri mulled over the information. No matter how she tried to think of it, the men with missing parts seemed to her like fiends from a folk tale, a roomful of Rumpelstiltskins brought to life.

"You sacrificed an arm to free yourself from marriage?" she said. "And you, Mister Jon. You sacrificed an arm and both legs?"

"One for each mistake," said the withered blind man. He stroked his beard with his remaining hand.

"I should not have thought one man could marry more than once."

In spite of the cloudiness, Jon's eyes took on a faraway expression. "The devils kept coming."

"What I meant was, I would not have thought a man could divorce and divorce again."

"A powerful man can," said Jakob. There was the same edge in his voice she had first heard at the lookout, then again at the lake. "I know who you are, Jon. Kutri, may I introduce ex-President Jon Schuyler, former head of Little Angel Studio. He used to appear on GS1 from time to time. As I recall, he was always seated. When Flynn took his place, I was struck by his energy. I now see it was an unfair comparison."

Ellis cleared his throat. He had returned and was standing at the fringe of the cluster of seats, holding a folded piece of cardboard. Silently, he passed Kutri the menu. A glass for Dr. Staley was balanced on the shoulder tray, along with a bucket of ice and a carafe of amber liquid.

"In my day," said Jon, "it was indecent for those who built the New Society to walk among ordinary men."

Jakob shook his head. "As if you had a choice."

Dr. Staley took the glass from Ellis, who clinked in a few pieces of ice, but even this did not distract the ex-president.

"You think I'm less of a man for putting away my grasping wife?" he shouted at Jakob.

"You put away three wives."

The old man snorted. "One was a grasper, two was a gold-digger, three was an ice cube."

Kutri tried to hand Jakob the menu. When he ignored her offer, she said, "Put them away where?" She didn't expect an answer, but wanted only to draw Jakob's attention. At the moment, he was digging his fingernails into the upholstery of the couch as if to anchor himself to it so he wouldn't bolt and run.

Jon answered, "In the lap of luxury. Men like me have no need to resort to the Houses of Care. We're not like other men."

He jutted his chin in the vague direction of Ellis. The waiter, or whatever he was, hung his head, as if studying the floor.

Kutri was at a loss for words. All the first interlocutor had said, and all she had imagined, about the prisons for perpetually pregnant women, came back to her and she closed her mouth. Had the quiet Ellis really sentenced his wife to such a place? Between the servant and master, she would have guessed President Schuyler was the most despicable, but at least the women he abandoned had liberty.

A chime interrupted her thoughts. The sound was not coming from her straw bag this time, but from the bar, where the men were already looking.

Ellis said, "How annoying. Excuse me. I should see if the call is for Jon."

Of course, the club was wired with a landline. Nothing strange there. Kutri got to her feet, eager to capitalize on the interruption.

"I should like to go," she said. "Jakob, will you take me?"

For an instant, his eyes appeared as glazed as Jon's. They cleared, and he said, "Yes. At once."

"Miss Chandigarh?"

The summons came from the bar, from the bartender, in fact.

"Miss Chandigarh?"

She would have been equally annoyed if the man had used her proper name, and anyway he was too far away to hear, but habit made her say, "That is not my name."

Dr. Staley said, "My dear, I believe you have a call."

It was a fair guess. The bartender was holding the corded receiver.

"I suppose I should get that," said Kutri, even as Jakob said, "Who knows you're here?"

Kutri said, "It's nothing, I'm sure. A photo appointment. Word must have gone back." She collected her bag, and as calmly as she could manage, took a step in Ellis's direction.

"Uh, this way, miss," Ellis said.

Mr. Mondt stepped to her side, while Tolson and DeGarre formed up behind. Ellis preceded them to the bar, glancing back from time to time to make sure he was being followed. Every time he did, he looked more ashamed at the recent revelation of his sin.

The trail he blazed was somewhat winding. After several detours around clustered club members, Kutri worked out he was blocking her from seeing what they were watching on TV.

"Will you stop weaving?" she said.

"Our members value privacy," was his answer, and would say no more.

At last, they reached the bar. The bartender had both his arms, but no legs. He sat in a harness, attached by ropes to a system of pulleys. With his weight suspended, he was able to drag himself around the circular bar like a seal dragging itself with its flippers along the shore. Not wasting time repeating his summons, he passed her the ancient plastic phone receiver at once.

She hesitated, fearing she knew the voice she would hear on the line. Covering the receiver, she glanced around. Ellis and the bartender caught the hint and gave her space. Tolson and DeGarre turned their backs. Mondt folded his arms.

Kutri said into the phone, "Hello?"

"You're late, meat," said the caller.

"We never set a time."

"We set a place, though. You were there earlier. Now you're not."

"You said you couldn't see me."

"I know where you are. You can't run. You can't hide. Neither can your friend."

How did he know her location? Someone in the club might have called, but it seemed a great coincidence that a stranger in this place should turn out to be allied with her enemy. Perhaps the ally was someone closer. Tolson or DeGarre might be her Judas. Dr. Staley seemed born for the role. But none of them had been out of sight since she had left the workroom. Was the limo driver her enemy, or was she being watched by technology, as she suspected?

She said, "I need time."

"Why? I showed you what I can do. If the first lesson didn't smarten you up, I don't know what will."

Cuc's murder had been a brutal sort of lesson. Kutri had gotten the point. She believed the caller could find her, or Jakob, anywhere in the city. Her only hope was Jimmy Ching. If she could get to him, if he could somehow secure her conversation with Jakob, there was a chance they could both escape. She had neither hope nor desire to escape on her own.

"You shouldn't rush me. You want a result. Why lose it by impatience? Give me until noon. That's all. Wait until noon. You'll get what you want."

The caller hesitated. A good sign.

"You think sun in the eye will make me blink, meat? Think again."

"You lose nothing by a few hours. I can't get away. I can't hide, as you said. I'm hungry. I'm tired. Give me time to eat and rest. Time to say goodbye."

It cost her no effort to put fear in her voice. She was deeply afraid—first, for Jakob and second, for the life she imagined living at his side. The loss of her old dream, that of coming to power as a match bride made the dream of life with him more precious. She had lived so long for the approval of *Good Breeding*'s audience that she had forgotten why she ever expected it to make her happy. Her new dream was better. If she could be left to love Jakob in peace, she was happy to leave approval behind.

"Noon," said the caller. "Not ten after, not 12:01. Got it? When the big hand meets the little one, the deal is done."

"I understand. Thank you. Noon on the dot."

"This won't happen again, meat. No more talk. No more time. Noon or nothing. No more chances. The end."

He hung up.

Kutri placed the handset in its cradle. Mondt was staring at her. If he wanted an explanation, he would have a long wait. Her time was fleeting. By the angle of the sun through the dome, it was already past ten. She had to leave this place and these despicable men who preferred losing limbs to living with the women they married as soon as she possibly could. But how?

The members valued privacy, Ellis had said. It was time to find out why. As swiftly as the tight dress allowed, she made a dash for the nearest cluster of odd-limbed men. Mondt grabbed for her arm but missed. She made a mental note to thank him. She was sure he could have caught her if he'd wanted.

Plunging between armchairs, she said, "Good morning, gentlemen. What's on?"

The program on TV was not the news. Kutri could barely make out a young woman's gasp over the rattle of mechanical limbs as members scrambled from their seats.

The woman on TV said, "I won't hurt you."

Kutri corrected herself. She wasn't a woman, but a girl. On screen, forest animals took cover in a hollow log, while birds huddled together in a nest.

The girl said, "Please don't run away. I won't hurt you. I'm awfully sorry."

Kutri had expected nudity, outrage, shocking abuse. What she saw was a cartoon girl in a canary skirt and a navy bodice with puffed sleeves. The cape she had on was scarlet within, royal blue without, a scarlet bow in her hair. Her butter cream skin was only slightly less pale than her gleaming white teeth. When she blinked, Kutri saw eyelids made dark with mascara.

"What is this?" said Kutri.

The contrast to her expectations left her utterly confused. As the girl was being prompted by tweeting birds to sing her troubles away, she attempted to read the faces of the men who'd quit the circle. They were crouching nearby, watching her and the TV from behind their chairs.

"Disgusting," said Kutri. It came out flatly, but the men cringed all the same. "How dare you?" she said, warming to the pretense of scandal.

On TV, the girl warbled a melody in imitation of the birds. Kutri bit a knuckle to keep from laughing.

"For shaaame," she said, stretching out the vowel.

She shoved the TV. The console flopped on its back. The glass didn't break, and no sparks shot to heaven, but the thump was satisfying. Kutri fancied she heard a scream from the girl, but it was probably a high note. Turning to waggle a finger at the club members, she saw Jakob running her way. Mondt shouldered aside a gawker as easily as if he were made of paper, and loomed over her protectively.

"We. Are. Leaving," said Kutri. "I can't stand to be around these *perverts* a moment longer!"

In her mind she was already dodging through the alleys of Chinatown. At this rate, she and Jakob could go on the run with an hour to spare. With Jimmy's help, they could be out of the city before her caller knew what was happening.

Her dreams of celebrity didn't matter anymore. What mattered was being with Jakob. She would make him leave the ruins of LA with her and never look back.

Chapter Fourteen: Historical Interest

"I could strangle Clyde," said Jakob. "I really could."

"Don't talk that way," Kutri told him. "Anyway, it doesn't matter."

They were walking along a dingy street on the edge of Chinatown. Jakob was in the lead. When she had stormed out of the A & L Club, he had run to catch her, but once he agreed to take her back to Jimmy Ching's, she had slowed her pace. It was Jakob, now, who had to be reminded not to rush. Every few minutes, Mondt mumbled as much, in monosyllables. Jakob's patience never lasted long. His mind was on fire, his nerves too tense to take ordinary steps.

Even knowing Dr. Clyde Staley's personality, Jakob had never imagined he could stoop so low. Divorcees and pornography piped by closed-circuit from the theater across the street! The very thought made Jakob stop in his tracks, trembling as he clenched his fists.

"Calm down, please," said Kutri. Her tone was urgent.

"I-I'm angry for you. That place—"

"It was nothing. The men there, what they did to their wives, was horrible. But to spend their time as they do, watching cartoons as they wait for death. I pity them, sincerely. Don't you?"

There was no pity in Jakob. Quite the opposite. He couldn't express how much he would like to bring down the strange, headless statue on top of the A & L Club members. He wanted to burn them, to feel the heat of flames as skin melted off their bones. How had he lived so long in this sweating corpse of a city without picturing it ablaze? Now he saw tinder everywhere except in the cool eyes of Kutri.

"Let's go," said Mondt.

"What?" said Jakob, glancing around. Mondt stood over Kutri like a firebreak, ready to stop a wall of flame from sweeping down.

"Let's go," he repeated.

"If we could, please," said Kutri. "I'm eager to see Jimmy again."

She did look eager, even anxious. Shoving thoughts of burning aside, Jakob continued on, leading Kutri, Mondt, Tolson, and DeGarre. A direct route from the A & L Club to the Emperor's Emporium would have been only four blocks. Unfortunately, direct routes were impossible in this part of the city. Chinatown was more of a wasteland than the banking district or Mission Junction, where Jakob had his sleeping cell. For reasons buried deep in decadent culture, the residents of Mission Junction respected the ancient, abandoned rail tracks that crisscrossed their ground. They refused to heap trash on the tracks. Unique among LA neighborhoods, they carried their trash out, dumping it in Chinatown, Little Tokyo, and the derelict campus of the University of Southern California Hospital, all of which made those places more junk-choked than they might have otherwise been.

Navigating the maze of garbage did nothing to improve Jakob's mood. He began to imagine the trash piles burning to ash as the men who watched from doorways were reduced to cinders. He didn't know the watchers. Part of him remembered they were men like himself—not the monsters who ran the Studio, but ordinary citizens who would rise up against the monsters. Still, when he saw them staring Kutri up and down, it was hard not to picture them as skeletons charring from the heat.

Rounding the corner onto Ord Street, Jakob came face to hair with Mitsuru. The young man was leaning against the wall of the Emperor's Emporium. He was dressed in jeans and a T-shirt, an outfit Jakob associated with the 1950s, thanks to the education from Sven. Except that Mitsuru's jeans were partly dark blue and partly faded, as though they had been worn on a wading expedition through a toxic swamp.

The colors of the shirt were crisp and clean in contrast. A man's face was printed on the front of the T. The face had a calm expression and was framed by a rectangle of red, white, and blue that brought out the contours of his forehead and cheeks. Below the face was a word printed in tall block letters. H-O-P-E. Hope. Even worn ironically, it was hopelessly out of date.

"Mitsuru?" said Kutri.

The youth left the wall to bow. "Hello. You've come to see Uncle?"

"He's not your uncle," said Jakob. There was nothing Han in Mitsuru, though now that Jakob saw him in the light, he was sure there was not more than 60 percent Yamato either. The rest of Mitsuru's DNA was the usual catch-as-catch-can blend.

The young man seemed like he would have preferred to be anywhere else. "It is what I call him. Will you go in?"

"Yes," said Jakob. He would have liked to ask what Mitsuru was really doing at the shop. Could he have been following Jakob and only just now run ahead, or was their meeting truly a coincidence? He couldn't ask in front of everyone else. Annoyed at the crowding, he rounded on Tolson and DeGarre. Knowing Mondt would refuse the command, he told them, "Watch the door."

Tolson and DeGarre swapped glances but didn't object. Jakob motioned Kutri and Mondt ahead of him.

Kutri told Mitsuru, "It's nice to see you again," as she entered the shop.

Mondt entered next. As Jakob passed Mitsuru, he saw curiosity fight with shyness on the youth's face. Mitsuru wanted to say something, or wanted Jakob to say something. The repressed wanting was familiar to Jakob, though he had no clear memory of ever seeing it before. For a moment, he thought Mitsuru might be something more to him than a human shadow. His chameleon changes made it possible they had crossed paths before the wedding, and not long ago, considering Mitsuru's age. Yet the momentary impulse of Jakob's troubled imagination insisted he had known the youth a lifetime ago.

Shrugging off the feeling, Jakob gave Mitsuru a nod and passed through the door. Kutri was his concern now, not the kid who might be a spy for Nat, or some unknown enemy, or who might just have a knack for turning up. After passing through the door, Kutri had stopped inside the shop. She stood watching him with her hands folded, a reflective pose.

She said, "Was that strange for you?"

He said, "Was what strange?"

"Meeting Mitsuru. The last time we were here, you said you had seen him at the wedding."

"Yeah. I'm over that. You meet people all the time in LA."

"Isn't he rather young to be on his own?"

"How do you know he's on his own?"

"If his uncle is not his uncle . . ."

"I'm sure he's fine. We were all young once."

She searched his eyes, then let the subject drop. Clearly, she had more on her mind as well.

She said, "Can you believe the change in this place?"

It took Jakob a moment to see what she was talking about. There was music playing, vibrating guitar strings undercutting a voice thick as old coffee grounds, singing gibberish:

Oh ye-ah! Can you see th-a-hem?
Ow down a borsch, yeah,
But da doh wabe.
I see dem,
Rou da runway, yeah
An I know an I know an I know
I don wanna shay.

The music was new, but the tables strewn around were still piled with junk. Shells of gutted appliances were still scattered here and there. Tires still hung from the ceiling. But now that Kutri mentioned it, Jakob saw fewer tables than there had been before.

Several tables had been bunched in the center of the shop. Some of the shelves had been pushed to the walls to widen the aisles, though the floor was still too crowded for easy walking. There was more method to the layout than had been clear on the first visit—mechanical oddities stacked together in one section, household objects stacked in another. In addition, racks of clothing were now part of the clutter, along with several new bookcases.

Kutri noticed the books. "You see?" she said. "It's wonderful."

"Right," Jakob said, her excitement bringing a smile despite the stress of the day. "Don't wait on me. Go on."

She returned the smile before bounding to the book corner. Mondt went in pursuit. What a beautiful, simple life she led. With nothing to worry her but books and clothes, she could have her head in the clouds even while her boots stayed in the gutter. How great it was that she could walk around blindfolded, smiling and laughing at the garbage city, while Jakob dreamed of burning it down. He wished he could be so innocent, so carefree, so unburdened.

As had been the case on their last visit, no customers were in the shop beside themselves. This time there was also no one behind the counter. Mitsuru was outside. Jimmy Ching had yet to put in an appearance. As Kutri flipped through a hardback, Jakob strolled among the shelves. He picked up a gray plastic object from a line of similar objects and turned it over in his hands, wondering what it could have been.

The thing was roughly square, as wide as his hand, and inscribed with a band of notches, like railroad tracks, along one side. At the top of the band was an indented grip, suggesting the block was meant to be shoved into or tugged out of some recess. A label had been stuck to the center of the object's flat face. Time had dulled its color, erased whatever text might have been there. All that remained was the faded cartoon figure of a man. He wore blue overalls and white gloves. He had a huge mustache and animal ears sprouting from a red cap.

Ah. A game cartridge, then. The World Before had been a strange place, but people then knew how to have fun. As Jakob returned the cartridge to the shelf, the sound of jangling keys announced the entrance of Jimmy Ching. He emerged from the curtain behind the counter and winked at Jakob knowingly.

Right. Well, it made sense that Ching, friend of Sven, was in on the secrets of La Vie. Jakob had forgotten to ask Nat about the shop and its owner, but Sven's frequent visits would have made it the perfect front for passing messages across social and economic borders. Plans might have been hidden in the sleeves of Sven's records or sandwiched between the pages of his comic books. It thrilled Jakob to imagine the clandestine exchanges, even as it saddened him to think that some of the interests Sven pretended to have might have been only a ruse.

"Kutri Ma," said Ching. "You're back. Welcome! Welcome to your silent friend, and welcome to the friend of Sven." He lowered his head. "I heard about my friend. Kutri Ma, you take no pills?"

Kutri closed her book, holding her place with a finger. "Only vitamins."

"Good. No pills for you3 too, Sven's friend. Only annies, eh? Now, forgive me—tell me your name. Also the name of your quiet friend."

"Jakob Freeman," said Jakob. "That's Mr. Mondt."

Ching bowed, low and slow. The import of his warning, the implied sympathy and their desire for revenge, were not lost on Jakob.

Kutri said, "You've redecorated."

"I have," said Ching. "What do you think, my friends?"

"The visibility's better," said Mondt.

"Is it?" said Ching. "Oh, yes. This is important. I watch, all the time, who comes in my door."

Kutri beamed, as if she couldn't hear a bit of the tension in this talk. She said, "It's wonderful."

Ching replied, "I was inspired by your visit, Kutri Ma. Too much clutter, I said, not enough books. When Kutri Ma comes back, she must see what treasures I have found. Thank Buddha-bà you have come back Now, please, you will never leave?"

"I'm flattered. Jakob, can we stay forever? Don't answer. To refuse would put a strain on your friendship with Jimmy. I do want you to be friends."

They spoke like this for a short time, enjoying the lightness of the company. No one mentioned Sven again, or the Garang wedding, or the murder of Cuc Tien. On the trip to the club, Jakob had been too distracted to give this last bombshell the thought it deserved. Now that he did, he recognized how frightened Kutri must have been when she heard of the murder. It was remarkable she'd been able to come out in public. Dad bless Mondt for giving her the confidence. Dad curse him, Jakob, for giving no comfort at all. Guilt doused his visions of burning LA, briefly, and replaced them with the urge to get Kutri someplace safe before the end.

"It's been a long morning," he said, breaking up the conversation. "Sorry, Kutri, but we should get going soon. It's going to be a busy day."

"You're right," said Kutri. "We must get down to business. Jimmy, Jakob has something for you. The very piece we came to collect last week, in fact. It's become homeless, or rather, it has nowhere else it belongs."

Jakob felt in his pocket and found the panda figurine was missing. Back in Sven's workroom, Kutri had taken it from him to examine. Dr. Staley's arrival had distracted him from taking it back.

Seeing his distress, Kutri said, "I have it in my handbag. Mr. Mondt, would you fetch my bag, please? Large for what it is, a straw bag, colorful. I know men don't notice. I set it near the door, I think. Jakob, perhaps you could help him look?"

Jakob set to the task at once, compelled as much by loyalty to Sven as to Kutri. Mondt refused to go far, but when Kutri suggested she might have left the bag at the book rack, which was close, he went to search. The colorful straw handbag was sitting on a low shelf near the door. Jakob caught it up, cried, "Eureka!" and carried it to the counter, where Kutri was showing Ching a passage in a book. As Mondt rejoined the party, Kutri shut the book and clutched it to her heart.

"Thank you, Jakob. Thank both of you. How silly I am." She opened the bag and drew out the panda. "This belongs here, Jimmy. It belonged to your friend, Sven. I think you should have it back. Jakob agrees."

"That's right," said Jakob. "There's nowhere else for it." Seeing the chunk of plastic was more of a relief than he would have imagined it could be. "Please, take it, Mr. Ching. Sell it, or keep it for yourself. Whatever you think is right."

Ching kept his hands away from the figurine. "Something will be done," he said. They passed a moment in silence. "This is kind of you. I think . . . Yes. There is something I would like to show you, Jakob. And you, Kutri Ma. Will you come with me to the stock room? It's not far, only through the curtain and down the elevator. That part of the shop I only show my very best friends."

Mondt cleared his throat.

"Friends like Mr. Mondt," said Ching. "Will you all come?"

Jakob had no firm objection. The underground shelters he'd visited with Nat were all safe and maintained. He assumed Ching's stock room would be the same. Very likely it served a dual purpose, as a storage space for knickknacks and a bolt hole for revolutionaries. He might as well check the accommodations. In a few days, when it was time for the liberated men of LA to riot, he would want options.

"Thank you," he said. "For a minute. We can't stay long."

"I promise," said Ching, "you will be glad you came."

Chapter Fifteen: For the Life of the World

The elevator was cramped, hardly big enough to accommodate four riders, especially when one was as wide Mondt. Kutri squirmed next to Jakob, giving him a quiet smile. Jakob spent the rest of the ride staring at a control panel that held seven buttons and a red switch. The switch was slotted between the words "E. STOP" and "RESET" and was currently flipped to the reset side.

Before the door dinged, Jimmy Ching said, "You know, this elevator is one of few places I can't get TV reception? I tried mounting a TV in the corner, to impress visitors. No good. No waves can get in here, as none can get out."

"How annoying," said Kutri, a moment before the doors opened.

Mr. Ching swept out and disappeared in the dark. After a brief wait, a click sounded and Ching appeared again, holding the chain of a hanging light.

"Welcome to the Emperor's Emporium's Emporium. Here you will not find the emperor, but many gifts that are fit for one."

They were in a room that would serve well as a hideaway. The walls and the floor were made of concrete. The concrete ceiling was braced with beams of corrugated metal. Ducts, vents, and several loud boxes were sucking in and blowing out air. The room was dry and cool, not to say cold. The air the boxes conditioned smelled pleasantly clean. Though the chamber had no decorations to speak of, it had a sort of aura that made it feel like what it was, a secret treasure vault where few would ever go.

Chests, dressers, and wardrobes were everywhere. Tables and chairs and a dozen articles of furniture Jakob couldn't identify were covered by sheets and stacked with boxes. A few crates were wrapped in brown paper, like packages on a dock, ready to be shipped somewhere. A draft from the blowing machines made the sheets wave and the paper crinkle. If a ghost had leapt out of the sturdy wooden cabinet Ching revealed by whisking away a sheet, Jakob would have been only slightly surprised.

No ghost did leap out. Raising a hand for patience, Ching searched for a key on the key ring that had previously been heard but not seen. With at least a hundred keys to search through, it seemed a miracle when Ching found the one he wanted in a few seconds. He fitted the key to the cabinet's lock. Display lights flickered as he spread the doors on their hinges.

The objects under the lights were among the most precious Jakob had ever seen. He marched straight past Kutri, open mouthed, and said, "This is amazing. Sven spoke of this place, but I thought he was joking. It couldn't be real."

There were a hundred items in the cabinet, each as rare as dinosaur bones. Video games and gaming consoles shared space with record albums, compact discs, and art books. There were cardboard crowns for the Burger King, a stair-step display of mobile phones, and three shelves devoted to board games, all still in their boxes. Sven had coveted a copy of the game of Life, though he admitted it sounded grander than it played. Three copies sat on top of a stack of slim green boxes marked Tripoley, next to a taller stack of Monopoly variations.

Some game boxes promised adventures to exotic islands or legendary Camelot, several showed players building railroads, and a number had wild box art and foreign text. The top shelf of the cabinet was filled with the smaller boxes of card games. Jakob had heard of Magic: The Gathering, and Pokémon, plus the traditional hearts and wizard. He thought Sven had whispered the names Shadowrun and Android, but he couldn't remember the details of how they were supposed to play.

Near the middle of a cabinet was a jumble of stuffed animals with heart-shaped tags in their ears—monkeys, dogs, bears, and pigs. Ching sifted through the pile of creatures and pulled out something from underneath. It had a black-and-silver handle with a short rod of translucent yellow plastic fixed to the end. Ching flicked the handle and the rod telescoped, extending like the baton of a hatchetman. Behind Jakob, Kutri gasped, though the toy was too flimsy to pose a threat.

Ching said, "Forgive me. You're in no danger, Kutri Ma."

"I'm sure," she said. "I heard Mr. Mondt stiffen, that's all. I was afraid for you."

Ching said, "Mr. Mondt is a very good friend."

The stock room had double the floor space of the shop upstairs. With help from his jangling keys, Jimmy Ching showed off cabinet after cabinet, treasure after treasure. By the time he brought his guests to a broad, sheeted case in a shadowy corner, Jakob felt dazzled by all he had seen.

"Why hide this away, Mr. Ching?" he asked. "Why not offer these things for sale?"

"Nothing is hidden," said the shopkeeper. "All awaits the right buyer. This case, for example. It holds a special collection. Of no interest to most. To the right man, very interesting, indeed. My friend Mondt may like what he sees. Before I show you, let me repeat, there is no danger. I'm a collector. I supply collectors. What you will see is not dangerous. I keep it for historical interest."

He whisked off the sheet and unlocked the case. The doors were of glass, so Jakob and the others got a preview. The case held guns of all sorts. A pair of machine pistols with long magazines, like some Sven had, were called Uzis when they popped up in a film and were mounted in the middle of the case, their barrels tilted down to form a V. Other pistols, rifles, shotguns, et cetera, were hanging on pegs with the barrels pointing left, as if Ching expected to outfit an army of right-handed soldiers who would be in a hurry.

Kutri stepped to the case. She touched an Uzi, showing more interest than Jakob felt. He was repelled. There was no "historic interest" for him, nor did he trust that was why Ching kept the weapons. This was an arsenal, or part of one. It was a detail of La Vie's master plan Nat had failed to mention. Why Ching had chosen to reveal it now was unclear to Jakob. Only later did he work out that it had been Mondt's interest Ching meant to catch.

"Here is my favorite piece," said Ching. He put his hand on a blocky pistol. As he lifted it, Mondt stirred to motion. His large, powerful body eclipsed Kutri's small one. In a movement so swift it might as well been teleportation, his hand dipped in his jacket and drew out a gun.

"Whoa, steady!" said Jakob.

Kutri said, "No, Mondt."

Ching stood frozen. The pistol was in his hand but he was not pointing anywhere in particular. Mondt's weapon, a sleek, compact piece that somehow managed to look comically small and terrifying at the same time, was aimed directly at Ching's heart.

Kutri said, "He was only showing me. Put that away, please, Mondt. Jimmy, you've gone too far."

Ching seemed to forgot he was holding the pistol. "I . . . Why would you—"

"Put it down," said Mondt.

Ching stammered something in a different language, presumably his own. He was still not aiming the pistol. Kutri was frightened but also somewhat annoyed.

She said, "Don't do anything foolish, either of you. Jakob, come with me." She came out from behind Mondt to close her fingers around his forearm. "Mondt, Jimmy, I'm leaving. No one can threaten me if I'm not here."

Mondt said, "Get back behind me, Miss."

Kutri shook her head. "Don't hurt him, Mr. Mondt. Jimmy, don't be foolish. Jakob is taking me to the elevator, where I'll be safe."

With desperate strength, she tugged Jakob's arm. He let himself be tugged. When the doors to the elevator opened, she practically tackled him, rushing him inside. He started to object. She held up a hand. The instant the doors were shut, she leapt on him and covered his mouth with her own. She broke away to slap the emergency stop when the elevator began to rise.

"That fool," she said.

Before Jakob could say anything, her arms were around his neck. She kissed him deeply but efficiently, like a swimmer taking air between strokes. His resistance lasted all of a second. Kissing her back was like floating, or falling. He guessed he wouldn't know until he whacked the ceiling, or the floor. Numb to everything else, he kissed her lips, her cheeks, and the bridge of her nose. When she drew away, he broke out in laughter. Tears were in his eyes, making her look blurry, but he had never seen anything so beautiful in all his life.

She said, "You have to run. Alec Simmons wants you denounced. He had Cuc killed as a message. Are you listening? You have to flee to the outlands. Jimmy will help. I'll come to you later, I promise. I love you. Run!"

She made a slap at the switch, but he caught her hand before she could start the elevator again.

"I love you too," he said, "but I don't understand. What does Alec Simmons have to do with us?"

"Nothing, if you leave the city."

"I can't do that."

"You must. For your life, you must go."

"I can't, seriously. I'm part of something, Kutri, something you don't know about. It's also about life. Not just my life. Your life, the life of the city, maybe the life of the world. I have to be here for the Presentation Ball. I have to stand with you when you're made match bride."

She backed away, withdrawing as far as the elevator allowed. It seemed a long way, after they'd been so close.

"How do you know I'll be made match bride?"

He laughed. "You have to be. You're perfect. The viewers would have to be insane not to vote for you."

The brief downturn of her lips went away. She threw her arms around him and kissed him fiercely.

When she stopped again, she said, "Please, Jakob. You must go. He'll kill you."

"Simmons? I know him. It's not his style."

"He's hired a man. A killer. The man who called me at the club."

She produced a device from her handbag. It took Jakob a moment to recognize it as a mobile phone. Had she stolen it from the stock room? No. None of the phones in Ching's display had been that nice. So far as he'd been able to tell, none were powered either. Miracle of miracles, when Kutri tilted her phone to give him a better look, the thing actually glowed.

She said, "He called on Saturday, then again at the club. He knows where I am at all times."

"Who does?"

"My caller. The first interlocutor's hired man."

"Did-did Simmons give you the phone?"

"Yes. He wants me to call him, to say you have behaved badly."

"You should do that." The response escaped Jakob's mouth before he had time to think it through, but even as he spoke, he knew he was right.

"Never," said Kutri.

"Trust me. Call him, Kutri. Tell him what he wants to hear. Say you'll denounce me, just not at once. Say you'll do it in public, on Thursday night."

"I will not do it."

"Do you love me?"

"Yes. Yes, by God, I do."

"Then call Alec Simmons. Tell him you're going to denounce me on live TV, in front of a global audience, at the Presentation Ball. He'll go for it. How could he not? Nothing could be more humiliating. So call him. Tell him . . ." He drew breath, groping for inspiration. "Tell him I rejected you.

broke your heart. If there's one thing Simmons understands, it's petty revenge."

"You've gone mad."

"Ever heard of a lover who isn't crazy? Trust me, love." He held her, kissing her once more, for as long as he dared.

Chapter Sixteen: Circle and Wave

For a day and a night, Kutri had quiet, though no peace. The last words of Alec Simmons kept echoing in her head.

"All will be as you say."

It had been a sobering end to their discussion. Simmons had gone from smug, to confused, to angry as she set up Jakob's plan. After minutes of pretending the terror she felt was actually anger, she had finally convinced him of her hatred for the man she loved. In a painful moment, she had heard the disbelief in his voice turn to delight as he accepted the lies she told against Jakob.

"I offered him everything. My body. My soul. I said he was my God, to command as he wished. How dare he refuse me!"

They were despicable lies. If she had heard them from any lips but her own, she would have struck out in anger. She kept away from mirrors for the rest of the day. It was the only way to stop herself from smashing her reflection.

"He came with you into the elevator?" Simmons had asked.

"He did. I unpinned my sari, offered myself. He seized me by the wrists. There was hunger in his eyes, as I wanted there to be. But when I gave no resistance, he pushed me away."

It was at this point in the story that she had stopped wanting to laugh scornfully and started wanting to wring her own neck. She could count on one hand the men who had been as kind to her as Jakob. She had loved exactly two such people, the first a sad-eyed boy at the Center who had died on his fourteenth birthday, the second the man she was telling Simmons was a monster.

"He called me a whore. He raised his fist as if he would hit me, the coward. I believe he must have violence. Without it, he is impotent. When I wouldn't fight, he cursed me and struck the wall. When I think what I offered . . ."

The more she despised her lies, the more delight Alec Simmons took in them. The voice that had been so cold as he propositioned her in the workroom and threatened her in the limo thawed first in wonder, then amusement. By the end of their call, he was thoroughly won over.

"You hate him as I do. Excellent. I'll take your report to the Studio."

"No! Not yet. What sort of revenge is a private denunciation? Jakob Freeman must pay for refusing me. And for crossing you, Alec."

It was the first time she had used his first name. She put warmth in the syllables, making them breathless. They were allies, in his mind. All the better if he thought they could be more.

"You have another plan?"

"The same plan, a better time. I will denounce him in public, on television, at the Presentation Ball. What could be more humiliating?"

The first interlocutor saw the appeal, she was sure. At first, he said nothing in response.

"Imagine it, Alec. Imagine his face. How will he feel? We will crush him, together. We will destroy him. Imagine the triumph."

"I . . . I am imagining."

"It will cost nothing. Two days. And you're a patient man, Alec. You've waited how long? Only two more days and you will have your revenge complete."

"It's not that simple."

"You think it's simple for me? When he thrust me away, I wished him to suffer. I had the pin of my sari in hand. If I were not patient, Alec, I would have stabbed him in the eye. Wait until Thursday. Call off your hired man. The revenge will be sweeter if we . . . come to it . . . together."

Her pauses were deliberate. They had their intended effect. She could practically hear Simmons chewing his lip. At last, he cleared his throat.

"We'll do it. Yes. Consider it done. All will be as you say."

And so she had made a deal with the devil. Lying to Mondt about the elevator had seemed nothing after that.

Would Simmons keep his word? As Kutri waited for an answer, the hours dragged by. With agonizing slowness, Monday ended and Tuesday began. When the sun came up on Tuesday morning, Kutri was in the kitchen, leaning against the counter and keeping an eye on the fateful phone. She kept imagining the pieces in the chess game she had to play with Simmons moving on their own in ways she could not see, even as she willed them to keep their places on the board.

Kutri, as queen, was safe behind the lines. Jakob and Mondt, her faithful knights, stood flanking her, nearby. Jakob seemed determined to expose himself to danger, but at least the threat from Simmons, whom she thought of as a bishop, was not as immediate as it had been. The most important result of her strategy so far was the movement of her mysterious caller, the enemy knight, away from Jakob. Naturally, she would have liked to have him off the board, but that was a goal for the late game, not the middle.

The unknown that concerned her the most was the identity of the kings. On her side, Jakob had mentioned a "something" he was involved in that was "about life." During their minutes in the elevator, he had made it clear he would do the will of this something, but refused to say more.

The opposing king was even more elusive. Murdering Cuc Tien, even by proxy, had been too reckless a move for Simmons to undertake. Even if her caller had acted independently, the fact the investigation had gone nowhere was proof of a conspiracy she suspected was too broad and too high for Simmons to have orchestrated on his own. All day Tuesday she wondered who ruled the enemy bishop.

Jakob kept away, busying himself, she supposed, with the inspection of her candidate grooms. Kutri went to meetings with her nutritionist, her fitness trainer, and various costumers. Everywhere she went, men and cameras watched, leering and undressing her mentally, as they always did. She longed for the day to end, and had to remind herself to be patient at least five times a minute, if not more.

Late Tuesday night, the phone rang. She answered at once. From the other end came a sigh. Her caller said, "I'm disappointed, meat."

She said, "You'll do nothing until you are told. Your employer and I agree."

There was a smash and a crash of something breaking. The voice that answered her strained on the edge of madness. "That guy? Sweetheart, he can't tell me what to do." He hung up.

It was Wednesday when she saw Jakob again. The Wilshire Beverly Hilton, where the Presentation Ball was to take place, had not been on either of their tours, but she had seen it so often on TV, she felt she ought to know every inch. Pulling up in front gave her an odd sense that she had been wearing blinders all her life. The hotel was more than the few square meters of tree-lined drive and the picturesque fountain near where the red carpet was rolled out. It was looming and dirty, like all of LA.

Most of the trees were artificial. This she knew. What was invisible on TV was the dilapidated state of the balconies above the hotel's third floor. Cracked and sagging and filthy with mold, they looked as if they would collapse any moment, crushing the photogenic balconies of the lower stories. Also missing from the TV images was the security wall that enclosed the hotel. The trash piled outside the wall reached almost to the top, so this was clearly a necessary feature. It simply happened to be one the Studio wished not to show.

They also preferred not to show the sky. Within the confines of the Wilshire Garden walls, Kutri found herself studying what appeared to be a roof of clear glass. But from close up, she could see it was painted in gradients of a color somewhere between the ancient blue of legend and the dull copper that hung over the city. The contrast with the true sky was striking. The fake, however, was only halfway between the legendary baby blue—that had appeared, in truth, somewhat after the Slow Plague began and people were no longer free to drive everywhere in their pollution machines—and the present orange, a remnant of the wars.

The Studio had thought of everything. They cared nothing about the filth and squalor in the streets but made sure to polish the wallet-sized chunks of real estate they would show on screen to a high shine. On every side, down, and up, the calculated gleam was enough to make her forget the grime on the other side. Or, almost enough.

"Did you sleep well?" Jakob asked as he approached.

Her heart thumped so hard, she felt her rib cage move.

She said, "I was . . . somewhat cold."

"Sorry. We'll have to do something about that. And I'm sorry I haven't checked on you. Arranging matters, you know. The suitors, the parade. It's taken all my time."

"A shame," she said, "that so much work had to fall on you."

"To be honest, I volunteered. After the other day, I wanted to keep myself busy. Anything to avoid Dr. Staley."

So, they weren't keeping all their thoughts to themselves. She said, "You're too hard on the doctor. I find him amusing."

"Many do," he said.

They exchanged half smiles. Kutri made a point of rolling her eyes at the nearest camera, in case the first interlocutor was watching. There were several cameras visible, each with a crew. All were under the authority of the director, a stout man with a beard who was at that moment gesticulating at her fellow candidate, the Parisian giantess Elise Dupain. Elise had her entourage of State Security Operatives and a matchmaker dressed in the familiar Bliss blue. Makeup and hair experts stood impatiently at the fringes of her circle while the director made a scene.

"What are they fighting about?" Kutri asked Jakob.

"Eh?" He was not looking at Elise but at the line of black-clad hatchetmen against the far wall. "Oh. Who knows? Mr. Housris, the director, is famously exacting. Some would call him fussy."

"Some. Not you."

"Not me, no. I never have an ill word to say about anyone."

The other bridal candidates arrived individually, each with her entourage. Each also had her own air. Some appeared arrogant, like the sky-high Elise. Some were quietly confident, like Kutri herself. Pania Maniapoto, a small, dusky Oceanian who came naked to the waist, hugged herself shyly until a roving photographer called out her name. On cue, little Pania fluffed her hair, puckered her lips, and arched her back, graciously bobbing her painted breasts.

In all, there were six candidates and six entourages. Remarkably, even in such a crowd, Cuc Tien's absence was felt. The women posed and primped and gave radiant smiles. But the sadness hung behind their smiles like a funeral. Worse than the sadness was the fear. The day was warm, with no hint of chill, but Kutri felt as though icy fingers were sliding up her spine.

A young man close to Mr. Housris yelled, "Places, people! Press and security, stand clear. Matchmakers and candidates, come to center. Thank you!"

After sparing a glance at Mr. Mondt, who nodded, Kutri stepped forward with Jakob. The rest of those summoned stepped with them, encircling the director and his aide. In contrast to the young man's clarity, the director spoke in a muddled rush at a volume barely above a whisper.

"Here is what you'll do. In two minutes your bubble limos will arrive—one for each of you. There are two platforms on each limo—one in the rear bed, the other over the cab. Both are protected by bulletproof domes. You'll board the lower platform with your matchmakers, then step up to the top platform by yourselves. Your platforms are round and they rotate." Mr. Mondt gave a quick smile or grimace. "Your clothes dressers put you in flats for a reason, ladies. Your job is to look perfect and not fall, which is why there's a clear plastic T-brace for you to lean against. You stand, you wave"—he demonstrated—"and you let the platform turn you around so everyone can see you. The skin you're showing now is *all* you will show. Got it? Tops that are on, stay on. Skirts split at the knee will stay at the knee. This means you, Ms. Legs-to-the-Mag-Shield."

Glowering, Elise straightened her miniskirt. She had reduced the garment to minimal length. Tugging it to maximum gave her thighs a whole five extra centimeters of coverage.

"Don't glare at me, buttercup," said the director. "This is not a peep show. Don't worry, ladies. Whatever goodies you have, you'll get to show before the voting. The parade is a preview. Always leave them wanting more."

He went on to advise the blissmen to stand directly behind their bride candidate close to her platform, facing front, with back straight, chin up, and gaze in the middle distance. He assigned each candidate a riding order as they filed out of the garden to board the limos.

As the director had indicated, each car had been stripped down to its substructure behind the front seat and a flatbed platform affixed to the frame. The bride candidate's rotating stage was built atop the car's low cab, roughly a foot higher than the matchmaker's rear platform. Over all was a bulletproof bubble.

Kutri hesitated only minutely before she followed the director's instructions, allowing Jakob to help her onto the flatbed, then leaving him to mount her small, circular stage. The floor was wood and more slippery than she'd expected. She wondered if the other candidates had the same trouble or if her dresser had sabotaged her deliberately by choosing shoes with slick soles. Why, she wondered, could they not have covered the platform with a rubberized mat or a piece of carpet? Even with the T-bar—which was essentially two plastic dowels about two inches thick—she had to brace herself to stay upright as the limo lurched into motion.

Kutri and Jakob were in the third bubble car of the parade. No sooner had the illusory grandeur of the Hilton slipped behind them, when the fourth limo, with Elise Dupain rotating on its top platform, attempted to pass. The driver of Kutri's car cut the wheel, moving to block his colleague. Kutri would have been thrown off her feet if not for the T-bar brace and Jakob's quick move up the steps behind her to offer his arm. Kutri realized that, though she was on a higher stage, Jakob's head was nearly level with her own; he was that tall, and she was that petite.

A symphony of honking sounded from the lead vehicle—an open-top roadster carrying Mr. Housris. Through a megaphone, he shouted, "Stop that! Stay in line." His voice was barely loud enough to make out.

Kutri could only laugh. Once she caught her balance, she went back to waving. Perfection, however, proved elusive. Every time the car took a turn or hit uneven pavement, she slipped sideways and had to lean heavily on the brace. This parade was hardly a graceful way of showing off the potential match brides. Anxiety made everything seem ridiculous, and she giggled until she was dizzy, grabbing Jakob's arm or shoulder.

"Stop that," he told her, half-heartedly. "You don't need to do that."

"Stop what?" she said with faux innocence.

"We can't touch."

"We can. We just did."

"Men are watching."

She pretended to be scandalized. "They are? Oh, dear. Where are their hands?"

Spectators lined both sides of Wilshire Boulevard—not so many as Kutri had seen on TV, though now that she was here, she realized that a large audience would have been impossible. On TV, the Preview Parade appeared to have half the city's population in attendance. The trick, it turned out, was using the right camera angles while audience members moved around. Men in suits or overalls or filthy T-shirts cheered as the bubble limos passed, then, when the cameras moved on, half of the audience scurried to fill in gaps farther up the road.

This was part of the reason the parade moved at walking speed. *Patience*, Kutri told herself. She concentrated on waving to the crowd and on the hatchetmen spaced at intervals along the route.

"There's something I've been meaning to ask you," said Jakob. "At the shop, the other day, you showed something to Jimmy Ching. I think it was a passage from a book."

"It was."

"Do you mind if I ask what passage?"

He had left her room to refuse, in case the information was sensitive. She considered for a moment and decided it wasn't.

Still waving and rotating, she said, "I don't mind. It was from *1984*, by George Orwell. Do you know it?"

"Slightly."

"The passage is one I have always found interesting. It concerns Mr. O'Brien, a friend of the hero, Mr. Smith. He switches off a telescreen; that's a television, in his world. Smith is surprised. 'You can turn it off!' says Smith. O'Brien says, 'Yes. We can turn it off. We have that privilege.' Strange, isn't it? To think it a privilege simply to turn off the TV?"

Jakob agreed it was strange. The implication—that Smith was amazed O'Brien could turn off a device that was designed not simply to be watched but that also watched *him*—was probably not lost on her lover. He simply knew better not to make a comment where they might be heard. It was possible he had missed the point, though, so Kutri made a mental note to clue him in once they were safely somewhere else—the outland.

She could picture the scene. She would step onto the porch of their rustic cabin as he rose from his rocking chair. He would be holding the novel in the crook of one arm while a child slept in the other. The baby would have his eyes and her nose, or vice versa. She would be happy with either.

She knew about the A-Rad Wall, of course, and the belief of those living in LA that a wind out of the east would make it necessary to breathe through masks, but there was no such wall around New Delhi and no fear of westerly breezes here. But she had sometimes wondered, didn't LA's food supply come from somewhere outside the wall? She had started to ask several times but thought it might be considered rude. Whatever the truth was, on the future day she told her husband, Jakob, the secrets of Orwell's book, the air would be clean. She would enjoy the blue sky and wonder when the next rain would come. Parched ground would give up no produce! How hard their lives would be, and how perfect. The sacrifices they would make would be as nothing next to the joy they made together.

At the intersection of Wilshire Boulevard and South Santa Monica Boulevard, the fourth bullet car in line tried again to pass. This time, it had more room to maneuver. The fourth car's driver steered wide to the left. When Kutri's driver moved to block him, the fourth swung hard to the right, stabbing his car's nose into the space Kutri's limo had left. Her driver swung the tail around with the swiftness of a headman's ax. Following a crunch and a lurch to the side, the limo came to a sudden halt. Kutri flew forward and collided with the transparent wall of her protective bubble.

She tumbled to the platform, head hurting. As she pushed up onto her elbows, a wave of dizziness hit. The platform continued to turn, making focusing difficult, but as it carried her around, she saw Jakob lying crumpled on his platform, eyes wide and staring, jaw clenched. His limbs jerked stiffly, in rhythm, as though he were keeping time to inaudible music. As she tried to make sense of this, she realized she could feel a breeze.

Could the bulletproof glass have been breached? How?

Movement caught her eye. The glass was not broken; a hatchetman was holding the bubble dome's door open. He or another of the security force must have activated his crowd control device.

As Kutri tried to clear her head, the hatchetman lunged toward her, reaching for her arm. Though he did not appear especially tall or strong, he was able to drag her from the platform. His grip was not painful but was inescapable. The moment her feet touched the ground, she tried to jerk away. Uncoordinated and still a bit dizzy, she failed.

"Easy," said the hatchetman. "Do you know what a day I've had? And what a night! Won't do, meat. It won't do."

Even muffled by the helmet, she knew that voice. A wave of terror greater than she'd ever known washed over her. She tensed to wrench herself away. The hatchetman felt her intent and lifted a hand. With a flourish, he made a knife appear. Another and it vanished.

"Be smart, meat," he said.

She sagged. Motioning toward Jakob, she said, "You won't hurt him."

"If you say so," the killer said.

As he pulled her away, she cried out over her shoulder, "Don't follow me, Jakob! Leave it to the authorities, to Mondt."

She saw him panting now, struggling to answer, but the paralysis still had him in its grip.

"No worries," said her captor. "You'll see him again. If you're nice, all in one piece."

Kutri heard the director shouting orders. Several hatchetmen had begun jogging in their direction. The false hatchetman dragged her to a break between buildings and bolted with her down an alley. A car was waiting; a bullish man stood by to bundle her up and stuff her into the trunk.

Chapter Seventeen: The Second Promise

The manhunt for the kidnappers of Kutri Chandigarh was the biggest media spectacle the city had seen in years. Nothing in Jakob's memory could compare. The hatchetmen had been active for mere hours after the Teng-Garang attack, and only in the one location. After Kutri was snatched, hatchetmen flooded the streets of LA. From the moment of their appearance, it was clear they were there to stay.

The hatchetman army marched in lockstep, forming long, narrow columns between piles of debris. Hatchetmen entered every shop and every bar, turning out patrons and owners alike. They penetrated low-rent sleeping collectives and high-rise apartments of the privileged, showing a remarkable disinterest in bribery as they clomped their way to fifth penthouses all over the city.

No place was safe. And no man, either. The black boots of hatchetmen trampled citizens on every curb, showing no preference for either purebloods or mongs. They operated their buzz boxes freely, freezing men of all sorts in their tracks. Thousands of batons cracked thousands of kneecaps as Studio cameras broadcast the search.

Hardly anyone pretended a mere investigation was the Studio's motive. The men of LA were being trodden underfoot. The only question anyone asked was where so many hatchetmen had come from—more than anyone ever estimated or even imagined.

"Are they clones, do you think?" Dr. Staley asked Jakob. They were sitting together on granite floor of the Bliss HQ lobby. The screens in the walls showed scenes of hatchetman violence.

"Are *who* clones?" Jakob replied.

All of the Bliss employees had been herded to the lobby. They formed a pitiful knot of powerless men, about sixty in total, including the clerks.

"The new hatchetmen, Freeman. They might be clones."

Go away, Jakob wanted to say. *I can't stand you.* But what he said was, "I'm not sure what problem that would solve. Don't clones have mothers?"

"They grow in a test tube, I think," said Clyde.

"I find that . . . hard to believe."

"I suppose. But many true things about life here are hard to believe."

The scene of the abduction played forward and backward in Jakob's mind. It had never stopped playing since he'd witnessed Kutri being dragged down the street. She had been carried by her captor past the lip of an alley in the part of Beverly Hills known as the Triangle. Why it was called that was a mystery. Someone had told Jakob it was because people disappeared there, but he didn't see the connection between triangles and disappearances. Those were real enough; you heard about them on the news. But the missing person was never a woman, and no one had ever disappeared in broad daylight. There had also never been a crime committed by someone disguised as a hatchetman. The masquerade itself was punishable by death, but no one had ever gone up on a krow in hatchetman black.

Jakob was so tired. Straining against the Carter-Schnee paralysis had sapped all his energy. He could hardly sit up. Even keeping his eyes open was a chore, as hatchetman guards sneered at his colleagues and himself in passing.

"Doctor," he said, his voice barely above a whisper, "I have to get out. I have to find Kutri."

"Do you?" said Dr. Staley. "What's the point? If you do find her, Freeman, you won't like what you've found. She had spirit, spunk. She won't have given in without a fight. Imagine that lovely brown skin, dear boy, blooming a garden of purple bruises. You don't want to see that. All that abused flesh. The thumbprints, the scratches, the corkscrew welts along the inner thigh where they whipped apart her legs."

Jakob lunged at him, roaring, as adrenaline gave him a sudden flood of energy. He straddled the doctor, slamming the man's back against the floor. One slam was enough for the ever-watching hatchetmen. One of them slapped his chest device and Jakob flopped on his side, muscles rigid, body wracked with pain. Every blissman in HQ wore the same agonized expression, as they all suffered collectively under Carter-Schnee paralysis.

All except the doctor, that is. Aside from being winded by Jakob's attack, he was remarkably calm. Tilting his head, he winked at Jakob. As the paralyzed matchmaker watched, the doctor rolled on his stomach and pushed himself up.

"You never did know when you were beaten," said Clyde Staley as he dusted off his suit. Since his face was now out of view, Jakob could only assume he was the one being addressed. To someone else, presumably a hatchetman, Staley said, "Put that away. You can see I'm not like this riffraff."

What was happening? The doctor had an implant like other men, didn't he? Jakob had seen him stiffen in his seat at Aluel's wedding. When the paralysis snapped, Clyde had attacked Kirimi Teng just as the rest had done. And on other occasions, Jakob was sure he had seen the doctor under the influence of Carter-Schnee discipline.

"Clear a path, will you?" the doctor was saying. "I'd like to speak to President Flynn."

"Stay there," said a hatchetman. "Stay there and sit down."

Dr. Staley laughed. "I'm sorry. Do you think you're in charge? I'm off the circuit. All the circuits, including the one you just tried."

The hatchetman punched another button, then another.

"Yes, that one too. And that one," said Clyde. "What does that tell you? Hmm? That I'm no office drone. You can't order me to pull my pants down. I mean, you might try. Would you like me to pull my pants down? Never mind. My point is, President Gerry is a dear, dear friend. I'd like to speak to him immediately. You can raise him on that helmet thingy of yours. Or, no. I suppose you can't. You're not that important, not nearly important enough to get anywhere close to my friend. But I am. I'm important enough to have the sort of immunity from Carter-Schnee effects you've only ever seen in senior Studio executives. Isn't that right? Now come. Clear a path through these wretches. It gets depressing, you know, seeing men in this state. Clear a path and order me transport. You can drive me to the most senior man. And he can drive me to his most senior man. And so forth. I'll get to Flynn eventually."

He stepped over Jakob, not waiting for the path he demanded. From the scuff of his shoes, Jakob could tell when he paused to make a half turn.

"Oh," he said. "Bring that man too. Do you have an exclusion box?"

"No," said a hatchetman, different from the first one who had spoken.

"Shut up," said the hatchetman who thought he was in charge. "Don't listen to what he says. He's a nobody."

"If I'm a nobody, how am I standing here?"

Seconds ticked by. To distract himself from his agony, Jakob counted. He got to thirty-four.

The boss hatchetman said, "I'll call it in."

"Oh, do!" said Dr. Staley. "Only, do it outside. You don't want to stew these men in their juices too long. You know what can happen, eh? Take my assistant and me outside. Then make your call."

There was a moment of grumbling, but not a long one. A hatchetman lifted Jakob by the armpits and dragged him out to the sidewalk. He was set down, still frozen painfully and completely baffled by the turn of events.

The hatchetman who had carried him returned to the lobby. Another, whom he guessed was the bullied officer, approached with Dr. Staley next to him. He twisted a dial. "Control?"

"You know," said Dr. Staley, "I've changed my mind."

The doctor stepped in front of the hatchetman. Jakob saw the artificial hand dart out and clasp the black-clad testicles. From the utter stillness of the hatchetman, everyone plainly had reason to fear the mechanical grip.

"Twist that the other way," Dr. Staley said, "or I'll twist these any way I wish."

The hatchetman did what he was told, returning the communication dial to its original setting.

"I do want you to make a call, but for transportation only. Have a car, or whatever, park around the corner. We'll walk there. And switch off that obedience circuit. My men have had enough."

The hatchetman made a high-pitched noise that could have meant many things, but in this case meant *yes, sir*.

***

The transport was a minivan with sliding doors on either side. The vehicle had no back seats. Jakob rode shotgun, having heard the phrase in one of Sven's Westerns. Dr. Staley's agility at the steering wheel was another of the day's surprises.

When the Carter-Schnee fog had dissipated, Jakob said, "You're with La Vie."

"Who?" said Clyde. "You mean Sven's band of merry traitors? Absolutely not. I am acting out of the common motive of all mankind, my own self-interest. Flynn has staged a coup. He'll destroy the offices, if he doesn't take them over. Either way, we're out of a job. The way relics are treated these days, it seems prudent we find somewhere to hide."

"I don't want to hide, Staley."

"Oh, is it Staley now? Tell me what you want to do, dear heart."

"I have to find Kutri, and I need help. Can you take me to Sven's merry band?"

Clyde shook his head. "Consider my position. I'm no rebel. What advantage would I gain by putting myself at their mercy?"

It was a fair point. Clyde Staley's position in the office hierarchy was too high to call him a neutral party. Nat and the others would see him as an enemy, similar to how Jakob had seen him until mere minutes earlier.

"You don't have to put in an appearance. Just drop me off." They were somewhat north of Chinatown. "This isn't the way to your club. Where are we going?"

"An A & L safe house. Where we go to plan murder. It's a lovely spot. Sure you won't come? At times like these, it's good to have well-heeled friends. You don't qualify as a full member, but I think I can get you provisional status if I twist a few arms."

Jakob ignored the offer and the jest. "Was it well-heeled friends who got you off the obedience circuits?"

Smirking like a small boy, Clyde pushed back a section of his hair to reveal an inch-long scar behind his ear.

"No circuit can touch me. A simple procedure, as brain surgery goes. All the Studio high-ups get it eventually."

Jakob remembered Mr. Verder, the freshly minted executive at Nat's dinner party. It was lucky for La Vie he was fresh, though Jakob supposed his response to the buzz box had been tested before he was invited to the Martinez home.

"You had your implant altered," said Jakob.

Clyde Staley smoothed back his hair. "Killed it dead, all but the bits that keep me friendly. Stick with me, son, and I'll find someone to free you the same way."

His offer was generous, downright moving considering the contempt Jakob had had for the man. But Jakob answered, "No. Thank you, Staley, but I won't join your club. Not even as a mascot. I need to find my friends. Will you take me or do I have to walk?"

"Run, you mean. Until the chrome heads catch you and stomp you into the ground. We've avoided the patrols, thanks to my serpentine wit. On your own, you don't stand a chance."

"Still," said Jakob. He reached for the seat belt release.

Dr. Staley gave a sigh. "We're cut from different cloth, Jakob, but I don't want you dead. Are you sure? No. Forget I asked." Slowing the van, he leaned against the steering column, lacing his flesh and plastic fingers together. "Answer me this, instead. Is the girl worth it?"

What girl? he could have said, trying to play cool. The doctor would have seen straight through him.

"She is," he said.

Clyde became serious, something Jakob had never seen happen before. "I suppose you think you know me. But you were surprised to find I had a wife. Her name was Neva. Would it surprise you to know that I cared for her? I will deny it outside this vehicle, but between you and me, she was a wonderful woman. I was unworthy. We parted amicably. For her sake and mine, I had to pretend otherwise. I spend a good deal of time pretending. When you lost your wife and then Sven, I sympathized. I still do. Where do you want to go?"

"Try a left," said Jakob. After that, apart from directions, they traveled in silence.

***

The Barracks, as Nat called the place formerly known as Hollyhock House, stood on a hill that no doubt commanded a beautiful view in the Old Society days. Encroaching brush had made it now barely accessible. Jakob had to push through bracken by hand, since he lacked a machete. From the moment he waved goodbye to the departing doctor, it took him a dozen minutes to locate the hidden path to the house, and another ten to negotiate the switchbacks and false trails.

He stood peering up at a crumbling wall and a roof that was all but covered by creeping ivy. Had he been a fool not to go with Dr. Staley? He might have begged the well-heeled for help. But why would they care about him, about Kutri, about anyone but themselves? They were men who lived in relative splendor, while the rest of the world was a ruin. They would have turned him away or turned him in. For a moment, he imagined another destiny. The picture of himself with an artificial arm made him shudder.

The sheltered approach to the house was as dark and foreboding as a tunnel under a mountain. Jakob faced the somewhat cleaner-than-it-should-be door and knocked. No one came, so he knocked again. This time, the door creaked. Had it been unlocked all along? The carpet of crushed leaves from outside continued into the foyer. Certainly no one could have crept up to the door without Jakob's knowledge.

All at once, he was in the leaves, rolling in them, fighting. He was pinned by lean arms attached to a lithe body. Belen Martinez smiled at him. "Don't tell my husband we had a tumble."

There was a time when he would have enjoyed the flirtation, not to mention the press of her body on his. Now he was in a rush.

"Where's Nat?" he said.

Belen let him up. "The library. With Mella and Rachel."

"While you guard the door?"

The aged inventory Sil Banquo, who emerged from behind a wall that was equal parts ivy and vertical wooden slats, said, "They do the killing, remember?" He was carrying a rifle. Even without the light coating of dust, Jakob would have known it was an antique. "Good to see you, Jakob. What's it like out there?"

"Perhaps," said Belen, "he should tell us all at once."

The threesome entered the house for the short walk to the library. They crossed a gallery space with shattered windows that opened on an overgrown garden, and entered a hall. Withered ivy was everywhere, rustling crisply at every breeze that touched the walls and crunching underfoot. As they reached the library door, Nat leaned out then darted into the hall to embrace Jakob.

"You made it, guy! You made it. Come on in. We're making plans."

"I need a rescue," said Jakob. "I don't know where they've taken her, but I know who—"

"Wait," said Nat. "Come in. Crash. Try to talk sense."

The assembled La Vie members had apparently chosen the library because it was in better shape than the rest of the house. The tall windows still had their glass. Chance, or a sturdy door, had kept the ivy to a minimum. A hole in the roof let in a beam of light, but aside from that, the room was structurally sound.

Shelves lined the walls, and books lined the shelves. Some were in tatters but most were whole. If Kutri had been there, the sight would have taken her breath. In the middle of the room, Rachel Bette sat in the only chair; others had been made into kindling, stacked in the corner. Mella Banquo sat on the floor at the ancient widow's feet.

"Welcome, Jakob," said Mella.

Mrs. Bette said, "What's this about a rescue?"

"I know who took Kutri," he said. "We can find her, get her back."

"And why would we do that?" asked Mrs. Bette.

"You're crowding the door, guy," Nat said. He pushed past, pausing briefly to check Jakob over. "Hey, uh, maybe he's on to something, Rache.

We were talking about taking the offensive. We can give Los Angelinos their free will. Then what? The Studio's got everybody so scared, they want to hide in their beds. Some revolution that'd be. But if we had the girl—"

"Kutri," said Belen, from the hall.

"Are you watching the door, babe, or what?" said Nat. "Like I was saying, if we had Kutri, we'd have a chance. Flynn's extra thugs, wherever they come from, are in the street because of her. When she shows up again, maybe they'll stand down, at least a little."

This argument was alien to Jakob, but he leapt on it at once. "Of course they will. Kutri's the favorite for match bride. That's why you picked me, right? As her matchmaker, I'm sure to have an audience when I give Sven's speech."

Mrs. Bette held up a hand. "It wasn't the deciding factor in your choice, but I'll admit, it didn't hurt. Why bring it up now, when the plan is wrecked?"

"Because the man who rescues Kutri will have an audience too," said Jakob. "The eyes and ears of the world will be on him. If you want to get your message to the people, you need me to be that man."

She studied him for a long time. Her glare could have cracked stone.

When he could take it no longer, Jakob said, "I can do it. I can save her."

"Your competence is not the issue," Mrs. Bette said. "We were betrayed, Jakob. I thought, just maybe, you were the betrayer."

From the moment he had met Nat at Derby Flat's, the thought of betrayal had never crossed his mind. "How could I be? You were betrayed at the wedding before you brought me in."

"You might have been another betrayer. Or Sven might have whispered in his sleep."

"He didn't. I mean, I'm not. I didn't betray La Vie. I never will."

"I believe you. It doesn't solve the problem. *Someone* betrayed us. So long as that man lives and we don't know who he is, how can we take any action at all?"

The answer came to Jakob at once. "'Move fast and break things.' I heard that in a World Before film. Always liked how it sounded, never understood what it meant. Maybe until now."

With a hearty laugh, Bette's sphinxlike demeanor collapsed. "Thank you for that," she said. "You're a saint of a fool or a fool of a saint. I'll have to see more to say which. But I'm sorry, it still won't work." She looked grave again. "We have to at least know how far away the betrayer is."

Jakob didn't understand, and said so.

Nat said, "This kidnapping, guy. It proves Flynn is on to us, every step. It's like the traitor's one of us, this crew, or one of the rest you met at my place. We could walk out of here and right into a trap. That's what Rache thinks, anyway. I don't believe it."

"You're a fool too, Nat," said Bette. "Jakob, consider. Flynn knew about the plan. He knew you were going to make Sven's speech at the Presentation Ball. He knew we would unleash hell. Taking the girl was Flynn's idea. He did it to stop us."

"No," said Jakob. "That's wrong. It was the first interlocutor of justice, a man called Alec Simmons."

Nat snarled and pounded his fist into an open hand. "That *malparido*? I should have killed him up front. Forgive me for not killing him. When he touched Len, I should have. Now you pay the price."

Rachel Bette rose from her seat. She had the sort of presence that made Jakob want to do the opposite of whatever she did, as a sign of respect. He perched on a windowsill.

She said, "Thank you for your insight, Jakob. And forgive me, as well, but you don't know Flynn like we do. He's behind all the evil that infests LA. This kidnapping has his fingerprints. It has his stink. Others carried it out, but he gave the order. He hides behind others, as out of our reach as ever. His forces, greatly amplified, are in our streets. Our forces, the army we could use against his, are scattered. We're trapped like rats, waiting to be eaten by the snake in our nest."

Mella Banquo's gaze followed Mrs. Bette's to the floor. Nat studied Jakob. Jakob met Nat's gaze.

Jakob said, "Do you remember, any of you, what it was like to be a child? I remember fear, mostly. Fear and loss. Sven had a toy collection; it was one collection out of many. Such wonderful toys. If I had owned anything like them, as a child, I would have felt set apart. I wouldn't have shared my treasure. I was too afraid to share. Sven wasn't afraid. He was the bravest, most generous man I ever met. He gathered everything he could that was good in this world and shared it with me, never asking for anything back. I know, in some ways you knew him better than I did. Because you knew his dream. You knew he wanted to tear down this lonely world and put something better in its place. Would he have stayed trapped where we are, or would he have fought on, do you think?"

175

Before giving her answer, Rachel Bette rolled her eyes. "He was the biggest fool of all. Fine. Fine! We fight on. Flynn is untouchable. Tell me what you know about Simmons."

Jakob did, and when he was done, La Vie made a new plan. Jakob's heart barely had time to settle into its usual rhythm before the meeting was over and Mella Banquo was leading him to the second-floor terrace, where he could watch her flash a signal light. Nat came too, to get some air. On the terrace, they met Lucas. The bodyguard was leaning against the parapet, keeping lookout. He was unsurprised to see Jakob.

"You knew I was coming?" Jakob asked.

"Sure he did," said Nat. "He told me, and I sent Len to say, 'Hi.'"

They watched Mella tilt the ancient spotlight on its tripod. It had been lashed, haphazardly, to a dented car battery. A larger, more cumbersome apparatus stood nearby. Jakob remembered seeing something like it at the Emperor's Emporium. He thought it might be a gas-powered generator. He had another idea about what the device hooked up to it with wires might be. This device was black and vaguely box shaped. It was the size of a mini fridge and had switches and dials on its face that seemed familiar. A second set of wires ran from the device to the wall, where staples helped them climb past the awning, to the roof.

"A buzz box," said Jakob. "Giant-sized."

"Got it in one, guy," said Nat. "Sil's toy."

As they watched Mella switch the spotlight on and off, on and off, Jakob felt his legs weaken. He sank to the floor, too exhausted, physically and emotionally, to stay upright.

"Hey, *hombre*, you need a beer," suggested Nat.

"Not the best idea in my condition," said Jakob. He lowered his voice. "Promise me something."

"If I can, guy."

"Promise me you'll save her, even if it does nothing for the revolution."

"Eh? Sure. We'll save her, guy. You and me. I promise."

He looked sincere in the dull copper light, and even more so in the flickering, artificial flare that signaled to the next in the chain of revolutionary bolt holes.

Chapter Eighteen: White Lace

Two things were true about the face of Karan Politis. First, it was beautiful, even without makeup. Second, it meant death. Nothing was more clear to Kutri. From the moment her lovely, fatal idol entered, she knew.

The Belle Dame of *Good Breeding* seemed unaware of this truth. As she knelt in front of Kutri, setting a tray of finger sandwiches and grapefruit juice on the low table that was the room's sole piece of furniture, she gave a smile that was south of lighthearted but well north of commiserating. She expected her guest to enjoy dinner. Her optimism was touching, though naive.

Kutri had eaten no lunch, but these sandwiches were fresh. Judging by scent, they were a vegetarian recipe, all roughage and mint. But they were no more appealing to Kutri than the mince and mushroom contrivance Karan had brought on the same tray, hours earlier.

It was possible Karan was being deliberately obtuse. All Kutri had seen of the woman led her to believe she was intelligent and not cruel. She was trying to spare Kutri's feelings by pretending she was a guest who needed care, rather than a prisoner who longed for escape. The smile she wore was false, but kind. Or—and Kutri gasped when she thought this—she was a psychopath, a sinister black widow who enjoyed pampering her victims before the kill.

"My dear," said Karan, responding to the gasp, "are you well?"

She lowered herself to the plush red carpet, sitting on her knees across the table from Kutri. The walls of the room were floor-to-ceiling mirrors, so this had the effect of bringing her tousled hair, slender waist, and narrow back to eye level. Kutri stared at the reflection and at the concerned face of the woman she had dreamt of being like. A third possibility occurred to her, then—a third explanation for why Karan was playing the kind hostess, when it was clear she was about to witness Kutri's murder, if not commit it herself.

The idea was horrible. For the first time since she had been torn from Jakob at the bullet car, she allowed thick, salty tears to spill down her cheeks.

Karan lifted a napkin from the tray. "Don't cry," she said. "Well, do, if you like, but tell me why you're crying."

"I don't want you to die," said Kutri.

"Me?" said Karan. "What makes you think I'm dying?"

"You must be, or only I am, and you are my enemy. Do tell me which it is, please, so I may decide which is worse."

The star of the Golden Season placed her thumb beneath her chin and the tip of her pointer finger on her cheekbone, a pose of deep thought. It was exactly the same pose, in fact, that Kutri had seen on a billboard that was visible from the window of the workroom of Jakob's late friend. After a moment of thinking, Karan shook her head.

"I'm not your enemy," she said. "I can understand why you would think so, but I'm not. And we are not dying, truly. I'm not dying, and neither are you."

"Your being here says otherwise."

"Does it?"

In the light from the dome lamp overhead, Kutri could make out lines on the naked face. Karan's forehead had wrinkles, and her eyes had crow's feet. Age made her mortal but not ugly. Like any painting, her looks were more impressive when you could see the brushstrokes.

Kutri said, "Why would my kidnappers let me visit the most memorable woman on earth, if they thought I might live to escape?"

Karan smiled. "My dear, it's perfectly simple. We're visiting because I insisted. I visit whom I please, in my own home."

"This is your home?"

"Yes. This is my exercise room. I do stretches, mostly. Yoga. Do you exercise, dear?"

"I've fallen off lately, but I do what I can."

"Some women never exercise. They complain about their back pain and their neck pain, but they never do anything to make themselves strong. They don't exercise. They don't eat properly. I ask you, whose fault is their pain?"

Karan motioned meaningfully to the sandwiches. To please her, Kutri took one of the thin wedges in hand, though she did not bite. She had no appetite and was still afraid the food was poisoned.

Instead of eating, she said, "Why am I here, Karan?"

"I insisted on that, too. When I heard you would be moved, I insisted this is where you would stay. There was an argument. You can see, I won. Would you take a bite, please? I ask out of concern for your health."

Kutri ignored the request. "Moved? I was kidnapped. An entire parade and the crowd watching it go by was stunned by nerve shock so I could be dragged from my cage and stuffed in a trunk. Not to mention, the man doing the dragging is a murderer."

None of this information was news to Karan, apparently. She appeared momentarily downcast, then leveled her chin.

"It's all a game, I'm afraid. The best we pawns can do is stick together."

"I'm not a pawn. Nor should you be. We're worth more than pawns. More than queens! You say it's a game. I say, we're the players. We should stick together as women who know our own minds. Help me, Karan. You've been very kind. Now let me leave. There are friends I can turn to—"

Karan stopped her with a sharp gesture of the hand. "Don't speak of your friends. They—*we*—know what sort of friends you have. That matchmaker of yours, the shopkeeper. It's their fault our plans had to change, their fault you had to become my guest. Don't misunderstand. I was like you once. An idealist. Starstruck. I rested my faith in the glitz and glamour of Angel Town. To be the star of *Good Breeding* was my dream as a girl. When I achieved the dream, I grew up. You must grow up now, Kutri. Your disappearance has caused a great deal of upset. Very soon, you will be called on to play a new role."

Kutri tensed. At last, here was the explanation for why she was being kept around. "What role?"

"The same role you have been playing," said Karan. "The match bride."

The chess pieces in Kutri's mind rose off the board, each seeking a new place. The first interlocutor's scheme, the murder of Cuc Tien, the hints Jakob had given about the obligations that kept him from fleeing the city—they refused to form a pattern, though she did see portions of the whole. Karan Politis was a pawn, as she had said, despite Kutri's confidence that she could have done better for herself.

"You're working for the Studio," said Kutri.

"Hmm?" said Karan. "Well, technically. I live off their stipend."

"But the kidnapping," said Kutri. "It was done with their knowledge, their consent."

"Was it?" said Karan. "They are well-informed."

"You're not helping me."

"It's as you say, dear. You might escape." Karan winked at her own reflection.

Kutri was getting frustrated but could think of nothing else to do, so she plowed on. "What about the murder? The man who kidnapped me also killed Cuc Tien. Did the Studio know, or did these people you say you argued with do it, if they're not the same? Did *you* know?"

Pain crossed the face of the world's favorite wife and mother. "I had nothing to do with murder," she said. "I tried . . ."

Leaving her confession half finished, Karan rose to go. Kutri rose as well. Her mind was racing. There were enemies around her whose motives she'd never guessed. This woman, a woman who called other women weak for not exercising while seeming to surrender after every half-hearted fight, was about to leave Kutri without an ally.

"Wait, please," said Kutri. "If we stand together, we can be strong. We don't have to be pawns, Karan. We can beat the men at their game."

Backing away, Karan said, "I wish . . ."

"Yes?" said Kutri. "What do you wish?"

"I wish you would eat up, dear," said Karan, and kicked the door's footplate. There was an answering knock, followed by the sound of bolts drawing back.

I'm on my own, Kutri thought.

She said, "I would like to use the restroom."

"I'll see to it," said Karan, and left.

***

The minder who came to fetch Kutri was the same man she had seen in the alley. He had lifted her into the car trunk as if she'd weighed no more than a large pillow. After the ride, the chrome-helmeted kidnapper had tied on a blindfold, and this man, presumably, had carried her all the way to the mirror room, with hardly a grunt. He was tall and broad, with a heavy jaw and chest and fewer centimeters of neck than there were hairs on his bald head.

If Mr. Mondt had challenged this man to a fistfight, Kutri would bet her life on her quiet protector. She had no idea where Mondt was, however, and fancied her chances of winning a man-on-woman fight were somewhere between slim and none.

She asked the minder, "Would you please turn around?"

She was in the half bath. The minder was in front of her, watching her every move. Everything about the Politis apartment was lavish, from the carpeting to the chandeliers, but it was still rather cramped in this most private of spaces.

The minder stayed put. That was fine with Kutri. Her sari was loose enough that she could lift the back without losing her dignity. She eased her underpants to her ankles as she sat down. The minder saw the lacy garment and completely failed to move his eyes away. He stood watching the wisp of fabric ring round her ankles. His jaw moved like a man's might while he sucked a lemon drop.

Kutri asked, "Would you turn around if I gave you a gift?"

He didn't answer, but he did follow her hands as she slid the underpants over her slippers. They were white lace, frilly. She might have chosen something like them to wear on her honeymoon. All the clothes provided by the Studio were dainty.

She flexed the waistband, watching the minder move his jaw. When she twirled the waistband around her finger, he blew out a breath. Nothing visible was happening below the belt. Clearly, he was up on his annies. But he was still a man, with a man's curiosity. She twirled the panties once more and held them out.

His eyes riveted to the wisp of lace, the minder hesitated. He had been told to watch her closely, she was sure. But she was weak, only a woman. There was nothing she could do to get out of the windowless room. All this she said with a tilt of the chin. Her offer was generous. When would the minder get such a chance? He'd most likely never even seen a woman's undergarments before.

After a glance over his shoulder, he scooped the underpants into his meaty palm, grazing Kutri's wrist with his fingertips as a bonus. She managed not to shudder, but said, "I'm grateful." The minder turned his back.

The kidnapper, who was also her caller and Cuc Tien's murderer, had been clever. With the minder's help, he had stripped her of her pins. She had been forced to tie her sari in one of the few pinless fashions she knew. She had, in addition, tied her petticoat. Untying the petticoat was easy. She did it silently. Her slippers, too, came off without a sound. Standing on the toilet seat without making a clatter was tricky, but the sureness of bare feet helped. With the rolled petticoat knotted in her hands, she leapt at the minder's back.

He stumbled forward, trying to shout. She cinched the silk around his neck. A man with less muscle would have gone quiet. This one grunted like a blue bull in rut. Kutri twisted the petticoat while she attempted to cross her legs around the minder's middle. He was too thick. He caught her legs and swung her around. The fight nearly ended before it began.

At nine years old, Kutri had been taken from her family and sold at Chandigarh Women's Market. There had been days, even whole weeks, when no man used her for his pleasure—until her menses began at thirteen. Then Papa Paquette had her DNA tested so as best to decide her future. That test had revealed the purity of her lineage, and her life had changed. Suddenly, she was untouchable, protected by her racial purity, but that did not mean that men still did not try her. It was human nature, she supposed, to want what is forbidden, to be hungry for the danger it represents.

Papa was brutal in his protection of that purity, knowing well the chances it might raise his status in the world. She didn't know how many men Papa had killed whose lust for the forbidden had rendered them blind to the danger that was Kutri. She knew only that men had died.

One of those deaths had been at her hands. She'd discovered then what she knew now: the silken petticoat was a weapon. She clung to it firmly as she had done once before, and kicked off the minder's belly. Swinging around to his back, she dug her knees into his tailbone. Her forearms bulged and her sinews swelled as she hauled back on the horse. She made sounds like an angry cat—high-pitched, feral.

Her wrists twitched. Her muscles burned. She was thrashed against one wall, another. Nothing on earth could shake her, not when she had come so far. She gave up trying to be quiet and roared through the pain, letting instinct lull her into a strangler's trance. She felt the panic in the minder's body—the bunching of his muscles, the gasps for air. Life and death were in her grips. She had become four-armed Kali—goddess of life and death. She was wrath incarnate, writhing grimly on the minder's back, sweating as she rode him from the small bathroom into the hallway, and from there into the empty living room.

Finally, the minder fell flat on his face, lifting no hand to save himself. Kali's petite devotee held on for seconds more, squeezing with her thighs, extending her senses to detect movement or hear breathing. When the minder failed to so much as twitch, she untwisted the petticoat from his neck, keening and sobbing and wondering if the muscles in her arms would ever unclench.

She slipped from the man's back, slumped on his shoulder. Her gaze swept the room; a couch and a loveseat formed a white leather L. Tasteful chairs were arranged to face the couch and loveseat. There was no TV. Across the room from Kutri was the sliding glass door to the balcony. Karan stood in front of the door like a statue, partly hiding her pale skin behind curtains.

Kutri levered herself into a sitting position. "Karan," she said, "do you have a weapon? How far are we from Chinatown? When will the kidnapper be back?"

In the gaps between questions, she paused to let Karan answer, but Karan's features remained frozen. It was enough to make Kutri wonder if she had an implant, like Jakob's, that made her stand so rigid, so straight.

"I'm going," said Kutri. She had to pause to catch her breath. The body reeked, already, of escaped gas. "You can come with me. You can, Karan. Come stand with me. Be strong."

With an effort, Kutri rose. She extended a hand. Karan covered her mouth. Whether she meant to stop a scream or to block a blow, she clearly wanted none of what Kutri offered.

Suddenly, Kutri felt an urge. It was savage, insistent. It would not be denied.

She pointed down the hall. "My slippers. Fetch them!"

Karan jolted from her stupor. As she ran to obey, Kutri wrung out sweat from the petticoat. The garment reeked of drool too, with snot and a trickle of blood. She shook it and spread it like a shroud over the dead minder. She swabbed and neatened her sari as best she could. The minder had dropped his payment in the bathroom doorway. She scooped up the undergarment and dropped it in his hand.

Karan returned from the hall and lay the slippers at Kutri's feet. Her eyes were red, but she wasn't crying. Her lips trembled, as if from the cold. Her words were difficult to make out at first, but then Kutri clearly heard her say, "Don't. Kill. Please. Don't. Kill. Me."

Donning her slippers, Kutri said, "You don't want to be here when the other comes back."

"I have nowhere to go. I have nowhere—"

"I have somewhere to go," said Kutri. "Come with me."

Karan shook her head and kept shaking it, the movement becoming wild, uncontrollable. Kutri stepped forward and cupped the creased but beautiful cheek in her palm, trying to still the frantic motion. Karan jerked back and slapped the younger woman across the face. Kutri smiled and slapped her back. The idol fell, crumbling to her knees.

Rubbing at the welts Karan's fingernails had raised, Kutri let herself out.

Chapter Nineteen: The Other Freeman

Most of war is running. That was the lesson Jakob learned on his first day as a guerrilla fighter. He ran through streets made black with the smoke of burning garbage. He ran down alleyways where the crack of gunfire rolled a steady beat. He leapt over dust heaps and piles of trash and ran some more. He only ever stopped running when Mella, much tougher than she looked, paused to toss a hand grenade, or when Lucas darted off to scout ahead. Nat ran with Jakob, neither man letting the other get far behind.

Their first stop was a weapons cache. There were a dozen men there, plus three women as ready to kill for the cause as Mella, Belen, and Rachel. Only the women of La Vie could be soldiers, in the word's fullest, deadliest sense. The men served in support roles. Of the men, only the sentries and bodyguards went armed, and they would shoot to wound, if they had the skill.

"We give life," Mella said to the first woman she saw as the group entered the subway tunnel that housed the cache.

"And we take it," said the woman, completing the motto of La Vie Army.

Nat went to a man in overalls who looked, despite a tangled mass of hair, like he knew his way around.

"Any word on our wheels?" asked Nat.

They had abandoned the idea of driving Nat's limo or one of the other vehicles parked near the Bunker after Lucas mapped out a series of roadblocks from his watch post. The network was impassable by any car or light truck. Nat had told Mella to signal ahead for something with more muscle.

"You're out of luck in East Holl or Silver Lake," said the hairy man. "We passed on the message, but there may be nothing north of the Ten."

"You hear that, guy?" Nat said to Jakob. "Looks like we'll have to hoof it. How are you holding up?"

Jakob's lungs were smoldering. His calves clenched like fists. A pretty brown face was firmly in his mind when he said, "I can go on for eighty blocks, a hundred. What's the holdup?"

"All on me, *hombre*. You know how I love to talk."

They were away, again, in eight minutes. The plan was to beard the lion in his den. So far as Jakob knew, the lion was Alec Simmons. His den, in this time of crisis, would be the Hall of Justice, headquarters of the office that employed first, second, and third interlocutors, as well as hundreds of other bureaucrats whose jobs had nothing to do with law enforcement. Jakob had lived most of his adult life within a mile of the blocky gray building. It was bitterly ironic that his current location was a war zone away.

So he ran. Lucas had a knack for knowing when a hatchetman patrol was about to glance their way. When he ducked behind a low wall of trash, everyone ducked. There were six in the group when they left the cache: Jakob, Nat, Lucas, and Mella had been joined by two of the women.

For a woman her age, Mella was amazingly fit. Her skill with grenades suggested throwing them was all she did in her spare time. Still, she was no match for a younger man, fighting close. It was the women from the cache who carried loaded pistols and sharpened knives.

At the corner of Glendale and Temple, the newcomers insisted on fighting through a roadblock manned by six hatchetmen instead of going around. They had a point. The garbage walls were so high in this part of town that a detour west and south would have lengthened the trip by several blocks. With the sun going down, going north around the muddy lake bed of Echo Park was out of the question.

Mella lobbed a grenade that skipped off the roof of a bus shelter. It dropped in the middle of four of the hatchetmen standing in a cluster. The blast scattered them, blowing one to bits.

The younger women charged to the fray, pistols blazing. The hatchetmen had not expected to fight women. They stabbed at useless buzz boxes as sparks flew from their helmets and blood spurted from holes in their black uniforms. All six met their death within minutes.

When Jakob arrived at the scene, his guts gave a twist. One of the hatchetmen had a holster in his belt, a gun in the holster. Truly, the fight had been kill or be killed. Still, he found himself moving away from the dead men. With his face turned to the side, he searched the dull, amorphous heap of deceased hatchetmen for some object to interest him, preferring the rot of a century to any fresh corpse.

"Hey, guy, look at this," said Nat. He had removed a hatchetman's helmet and was holding it up. Mella and one of the other women were stripping a different hatchetman of his tunic.

Nat said, "There's enough without holes to put together some sets. Sound like a plan?"

The man he was squatting over was placid in death. His face was young, untroubled. Its yellowish-brown shade and nondescript features was the perfect example of what the blissmen called middle-muddle: a face that came from nowhere and everywhere. It had no particular ancestry, no visual claim on a homeland. The hatchetman could have been anyone's brother. He could have been Jakob's brother. For all Jakob knew, he was

"I know what you're thinking," said Nat. "This is war. See why we let the women do the killing? It ain't for their sake. Here. Time for a costume change." He proffered the helmet, nodding toward the tunic Mella held out to him.

It turned out Lucas was too large for a disguise, so Nat and Jakob made up a patrol of two, while their companions faded into the shadows along the way. A patrol of three watchmen hove into view, going in the opposite direction. Jakob felt the urge to dart into hiding, but Nat, as if reading his mind, simply said, "S'okay, *hombre*. They think we're *compadres*."

He raised his fist to helmet height in salute as the real hatchetmen passed by, and Jakob, quaking inside, echoed the movement. The patrol saluted back, never breaking stride. Jakob welcomed the surge of adrenaline that followed, and the greater sense of imperviousness that came with it as he and his companions continued their march.

***

The hatchetman at the Hall of Justice stood to attention. Something about Jakob's uniform, or about Nat's, commanded respect. Jakob decided it was the holstered gun, which Nat had claimed for himself. Everything else about their uniforms looked identical to Jakob, aside from the chip in his helmet's chrome.

He had expected his vision to be severely limited, but found this was not the case. There was a sort of lens on the inside of the chromed glass that skewed everything but gave a surprisingly broad field of view. The helmet was stuffy, hot, and uncomfortable, but it was functional. The same was true of the tunic and trousers, the boots, the belt, and the buzz box. Discomfort was part of a hatchetman's life, evidently, but they didn't let it get in the way of shoving other men around.

If the justicemen had been herded to the lobby of their HQ, like the blissmen, they had since been cleared out. Four hatchetmen were guarding the lobby, poorly. One passed under an arch of the portico to glance at the two new arrivals. He saluted, then went back under the arch to the window, which was practically opaque with grime. Nat shook his chromed head as if to say, "How 'bout that?" and led on to the elevator.

It was now Jakob's turn to take the lead. He had never been inside the first interlocutor's workroom, but he had been to the reception area on the fifth floor. He pressed the button and the elevator rose. A moment before the car dinged, he heard a loud bang and a man's cry. He ran from the elevator, evading the hand Nat reached out to snatch him back.

Around the corner, in reception, a figure in black was doing something to the neck of a man on his knees. As blood ran between the kneeling man's hands, the other man pulled the trigger of a revolver, exploding the head of a third man who had been standing behind a desk. Three desks in total were arranged in a semicircle at the far end of the room. Corridors extended from behind and to the side of each desk.

A yard from where Jakob stood, a body lay sprawled. A bullet hole showed the victim had been shot in the back. The kneeling man had been brought down in some way that was not immediately fatal but appeared it soon would be. Having completed two and a half murders in this room alone, the man in black swung the revolver Jakob's way.

Bang! Bang!

The man in black was on the floor. Nat stood at Jakob's elbow, holding his newly acquired gun. Jakob put a hand to his chest and found only a beating heart.

"That was close," said Nat. "Stupid too. Don't get out in front of the guy with the gun."

"I wasn't sure you'd use it," said Jakob. "Did you kill him? Is he dead?"

"Hope not," said Nat. "Rache'll have my head."

He hurried to where the killer lay sprawled and kicked away the revolver.

Jakob ran to kneel by the bleeding victim. He recognized the first interlocutor's receptionist but couldn't think of the man's name. The receptionist was holding his neck. Blood squelched between his fingers, a leak in a dam about to break. The guy tried to speak but blood gushed. A gash in his neck was a valley too deep to escape. Jakob could do nothing but step back, away from the puddling blood. Moving quickly, he checked the other victims. Both were dead.

The killer was lying a yard from the last man he had killed. His black clothes belonged to a hatchetman, but close up, they were obviously a bad fit. Stolen, most likely, and from more diminutive corpses than had outfitted Jakob and Nat. His helmet was off, which reminded Jakob of how much his scalp itched and how all the little aches and pains ping-ponged around in his skull. He wrenched off his helmet and set it aside.

"Happy . . . you made it," said the fallen man. His voice was soggy, owing to a sucking chest wound, but he kept his tone bright. "I like operating . . . with an audience."

Blood had splashed to cover his face. Otherwise, Jakob would have known him at once.

Nat removed his helmet and said, "Joule. Joule! Why'd you do it?"

"Come close and I'll tell you," said the surgeon. In saving Janessa Huxley's life, he had effectively given birth to La Vie. Sven had been the group's father, Rachel Bette its mother, but the screaming passage to life had been overseen by someone who killed without mercy while dressed like the man who had kidnapped Kutri.

Though, to be fair, it was a popular disguise.

Jakob said, "Don't. Don't do it."

Nat had made no move to come close to Joule and continued to make none. Something glinted in Joule's palm. He had an implanted blade, like the one that had scarred Aluel Garang.

Joule gave a laugh that turned into a cough. "Worth . . . a try."

"It's the end for you, guy. Come clean. What are you doing at Justice?"

The wound in Joule's chest gaped like a mouth. His cough became a gurgle. In the hand-to-hand fight with death, he was losing fast.

"Tidying . . . up."

Jakob stopped Nat's next question with a gesture. He said, "Were you at the parade?"

Joule nodded. "All the . . . pretty floats. I wanted . . . a souvenir."

"Where did you take Kutri?"

"To the—" Joule coughed. "To the top."

"Where, Joule? Where is she now?"

Nat put a hand on Jakob, holding him back. He said, "You're krowbait, Joule. Come clean."

"Come close," said Joule. "No?"

With the swipe of the palm, he cut his own throat. Jakob lunged, but it was too late. With a hiss of air and a spurt of blood, the surgeon's life ran out.

Nat seemed stunned. Much of the blood had splattered on him. Jakob took his arm.

"Get up," said Jakob. "Come on. Remember why we're here."

They skirted the body of the false revolutionary and ran down the middle corridor. At some point, Nat had picked up his helmet. It was under his arm when Jakob skidded, almost falling, into the first interlocutor's workroom.

Alec Simmons was sitting on the floor. His back was propped against the front of his desk. He had blood on his gray suit, a smear on the desk's gray metal. Blood was spilled on the gray floor too, but not a tenth as much as they had left in the reception room. Simmons was wounded, probably dying—and very angry.

"What happened?" he demanded. "I heard shots. Did you kill him?" The effort of shouting caused him to tilt to one side. He righted himself, keeping a firm hand over the place on the suit where blood was soaking through his suit coat.

"The killer is dead, if that's who you mean," said Jakob.

"Freeman?" said the first interlocutor. "That's you. I know your voice."

It was a long way from the workroom door to the desk. Still, Jakob felt sure Simmons should be able to see him. He crossed half the difference between them and froze. What he had taken for shadows over downcast eyes were pits where eyes should have been. A thin, red rivulet ran from each socket.

"He blinded you," said Jakob.

Simmons said, "Did you kill him?"

"No."

Simmons cleared his throat. "Of course not. How foolish to expect you to do something pleasing, here at the end."

Nat strode past Jakob, going one knee in front of Simmons.

"I killed him," he said. "Put two bullets in a guy I thought was my friend. You and I aren't friends. So tell me, are you dying enough or do you need a couple bullets too?"

In his haste to save Kutri, Nat's cause to hate Simmons had slipped Jakob's mind. He hurried forward. Nat calmed him with a look. The threat was leverage to get Simmons talking, no more.

Simmons said, "I'm dying, certainly." He sounded more annoyed at the question than the fact. "We're not friends, you say. Who are you?"

"Don't you know? Figures. Even if you could see, it wouldn't help. Anytime I was around, you didn't look at me. You only had eyes for Len."

The first interlocutor frowned for a moment, then said, "Ah. Len. Belen Costa, she was, now Martin? Martinez. And you're the husband, Nathaniel. I know you as well as I wish to. Tell me. There are no children, but I'm sure she's put on weight. Does her pelvis still make a sharp angle?" He pretended to rest his fingers on a thigh while his thumb hooked the bone.

Nat's hands went to Simmons's throat. He didn't squeeze, so Jakob didn't interfere. From Nat's face, he was clearly tempted but still in control.

"How 'bout you don't ask questions," said Nat. "Give answers, instead. Jakob, tell this"—he growled something in his own language that was so complex, it might have been an exorcism—"what we want to know."

"Let him breathe," said Jakob. He took Nat's place in front of the pale man. Since Simmons had no eyes, there was no reason to look him in the face, so Jakob focused instead on the edge of the desk. This was after a glance at his adversary's wound, imperfectly covered by a trembling hand. Jakob thought it was a stab to the heart. Cleaner than a gunshot but just as fatal, especially considering who had done the stabbing.

He said, "First Interlocutor . . . Alec. I was in the bullet car when Joule took Kutri. Do you know where she was taken?"

Simmons pursed his lips as if Jakob's question didn't deserve an answer. "It was a simple matter. She had the phone. She had only to denounce you. Do you know, if she had shown herself to me, like the others, I wouldn't have asked? So long as I got what I wanted, I was content to put off revenge. It was her pride, Freeman, that doomed you. I only focused my wrath on you because she left me wanting."

Images of Simmons ordering Kutri to strip played through Jakob's mind. He fought the urge to choke the first interlocutor himself, carrying out Nat's threat.

"I seconded a complaint about your conduct," said Jakob. "If you wanted a fit target for revenge, you should have picked yourself. I didn't make us enemies, Alec. You did. But I don't care about that now. All I care about is Kutri."

The eyeless face became grotesque. The expression was hard to read and painful to see. Hatred was there, certainly. Was there also disbelief?

"You think I hated you for the complaint?" Simmons paused. His face went placid. "I see. A good joke. They destroyed you, Freeman." He made a sound between laughter and a sob. "I didn't know they took so much. Pitiful. I could almost feel for your loss."

Tears formed in the sightless pits that used to house eyes. Thick and pink, they streamed from the inner corners and down the man's nose. They streamed over his lips and blew in a mist as Simmons spoke, reminding Jakob of the colored smoke from the cars in the wasteland past Culver City. The difference was, when Simmons smoked his last, no amount of fuel would get him started again.

"You have no idea," said Simmons. "Are you even the man I hated? Not if they took it all. You must think me petty, a man who punishes others for his own sins. But no. It wasn't me who sinned, or even you. It was the other Freeman."

Jakob shook his head as if the motion would help him make sense of what Simmons was saying. "The other . . . What are you talking about?"

"Aremoden. Ah! It's made you a shell of the man you were. It scooped out your memory and left you a shell. Do you remember her at all? My Yasuko?"

Pain sparked at the back of Jakob's head. It was so like a Carter-Schnee shock, he was surprised that his limbs didn't stiffen. The name, Yasuko, was familiar. He had no idea where he had heard it before, but there was no doubting he had. The syllables lashed at him, like the flails of an electric whip.

"She was my life, my love, my world," said Simmons. "She came to me when her husband threw her out—oh, not you. Not *him*, I should say, the other Freeman. She came to me. She would have stayed. I was kind to her. I cared for her, I kept her safe. The other Freeman came and took her. He exposed her to the evil she most feared. He might as well have killed her, have dripped the poison in her veins himself. Yasuko! My Yasuko. And for his sin, they wiped his mind. How tragic they didn't tell me. It could have saved so much fuss."

There was nothing Jakob could do except mouth the word that was so familiar and painful.

"Yasuko," he whispered. "Yasuko." Each time he said it, lashes of lightning stung his soul. "Yasuko. She was . . . my wife."

Simmons struck at him, swinging a palm with all his strength. Jakob accepted the tap to his cheek.

"Not yours," said Simmons. "*His*. The thief!"

Jakob pushed more words out of his mouth, wondering where they'd come from. "I forgot her, almost all of her. I only remember her death. It wasn't poison, Alec, but disease. Cancer. They tried to cut it out."

"Who tried?"

"A surgeon."

It was Nat who said, "Joule?"

Simmons repeated his sobbing laugh. "Does it matter? They're all the same. Every dog has a master." His voice was weakening.

Nat held him so he wouldn't slip sideways and said, "Who's yours, Simmons, eh? Are you going to tell me you're the big boss? Who sent Joule to tidy you up?"

The flaps that had been the first interlocutor's eyelids vibrated, as though they had tried to shut and gotten confused by the landscape.

"He should have been my dog," Simmons said. "Got him . . . as a favor . . . from a friend. The business should have stayed between us. A lateral transaction. Deal . . . between top . . . men."

Simmons was fading.

Jakob said, "Where's Kutri?"

Simmons said, "I don't know."

Jakob squeezed his shoulder. "Where could she be?"

The first interlocutor of justice cleared his throat. Then he sagged. Jakob thought he was gone. With a sudden, fierce strength, he threw himself forward, grasping Jakob's shirt with spasming hands.

"Mitsu!" said Simmons. "Flynn wants . . . Mitsu."

"Mitsu? You mean—"

"For your sins, Freeman, take care—" The next noise he made was a death rattle. He dropped to the gray floor and said no more.

Nat said, "Mitsu. Who's that?"

"He must have meant Mitsuru," said Jakob.

"Who's Mitsuru?"

"The-the young man I keep seeing around. Your driver."

"Lucas is my driver, guy."

Jakob studied Nat to make sure he wasn't joking.

"You sent him to fetch me, the night of the dinner party."

"I didn't send anybody, guy. I was glad you showed up."

"Mitsuru," said Jakob. "You must know. He kept appearing, wherever I went. I thought you put him on me, as a shadow."

"Sorry," said Nat. "Honest. I never heard of the guy."

Chapter Twenty: The Wild Man

Hatchetman patrols were everywhere, on every street. All had their horrible buttons and ugly batons. Some wore holstered guns. Kutri was sure that had not always been the case before she killed a man.

Had they found out so quickly? Certainly, they didn't need guns to manage men. They had their buttons for that. It was women who called them to use desperate measures. Females were the lethal sex.

Back in the elevator, after Jakob pushed her away, he had outlined the chaos his friends were hoping to bring to the city. There would be death and destruction, but in the end, change. The fury of the dispossessed would blaze like a fire through the city streets. The occupation by men in chrome helmets, that she had brought about, was like nothing Jakob had envisioned. She had ruined his plans by strangling her minder. Though, again, she was staggered to think word had gone around so quickly.

Where would Jakob be in these circumstances?

The answer was obvious. With his friends now, working out how to spark the cataclysm they wanted from this oppressive slow burn. Finding the rebels was her primary goal. Aside from Jakob himself, Jimmy Ching was the only person she knew who might be a member. His association with the mysterious group was an assumption on her part, but it was the only hope she had. Sadly, by her surroundings, she knew she was nowhere close to Chinatown.

The high-rise apartment was in a part of LA she had never visited, either with Jakob or on a photo shoot. The drive from the parade had seemed to take a long time, conceivably above an hour, though it was hard to tell time from a trunk. She had no way of knowing how far she was from any of the landmarks Jakob had pointed out on their trips. Nor could she call upon her education to help.

In her studies back home, her interest in geography had been mild. Now she cursed herself for not giving more attention to the subject. If she had known the value, she could have spent weeks cross-referencing atlases until she memorized every detail of LA's layout. It would have cost her far less effort than it was now going to cost her to find a familiar street, if she ever did find one.

I killed a man, she reminded herself. *Jimmy Ching would call this karmaphala.*

Karan's apartment had a view of an overpass, which seemed strangely far down from her. By counting flights of stairs, Kutri had determined Karan lived on the fifteenth floor. Evidently, she and Mr. Politis were unconcerned about radioactive fallout. She thought that odd. There was a near total absence of trash heaps in this part of the city, though the streets were still dusty, with many cracks in the pavement.

The floating T-frames of krows were likewise absent. Naturally, that would be the case. The rich and famous, who lived in this place, held themselves to a different standard than the rest of the city. Grim reminders of ultimate justice were for the valley. She recognized that she was on The Hill.

Once outside the apartment building, traveling south, she crossed the overpass. Then she took a vaguely westerly route, stepping carefully to avoid turning her ankle on loose pavement. Avoiding the patrols was difficult, but not impossible. Though they had surely been ordered to bring her in for murder, they mostly seemed interested in chasing any bystanders they came across into cover. When Kutri did see a patrol, she ran, taking turns at random, until the noise of their passage was far behind.

At least it was dark. The hatchetmen had lights clipped to their belts, which told her their position before she happened upon them. On one occasion, she rounded a corner and found herself facing the backs of a patrol who had paused to torment a vagrant. They stood in a circle, stomping the man as his curled body rocked back and forth. Kutri wished she could do something for him, but what? After despairing a few seconds, she snuck away.

In sprints and stops, she passed block after block, until at last she came to a patch of land that was different from the rest. Across a large, lightly rubbished parking lot, she saw a path between low, crumbled buildings and something like an overgrown park up the path. It would have been inaccessible, thanks to the fallen superstructure, if someone had not been kind enough to cut out a few beams and haul them away.

Scattered here and there among the debris were metal letters. Each was as tall as Kutri, and those she could see were mostly intact. Between the missing letters, and those completely covered by vines, she had more an impression than a recognition of what the sign had once said.

LO A GE S Z O

She read the letters three or four times before she guessed their meaning. Once she did, she passed them quickly, hurrying into the refuge she had found.

She was far from Jakob, possibly farther than before she'd started her run. She needed to pause, to consider her course. She needed rest. This place, the remains of a zoo that had once been famous, seemed as good a place to rest as any. No footprints showed in the dust of the parking lot, and the path, though well-worn, looked like it had been made by animals, not men. In her books, zoos were peaceful places. They were where the civilized protagonist might go to ponder a crisis. Wild nature was a benevolent presence, or at least an impartial one, in the books she had read.

Nature had taken over this zoo completely. Past the entrance, barely two walls stood together. To the path's left stretched a kingdom of long-leaved eucalyptus trees. They had clustered too thickly over the years, causing several to fall. The trunks broke through roofs and walls, leaving ruins.

To the right of the path was a swampy pool. The surface was scummed with floating plants, mostly algae, but here and there floated a patch of lilies that resembled scattered green dinner plates, some with lotus-shaped bowls atop them. Moonlight sifting through clouds lit the trees, but the floating plants gave their own light. The algae was a field of blue-green speckles, bobbing whenever it was stirred by the wind. The lilies wore splashes of color around their outlines, mostly blue green, but with here and there a bright line of white or a paler red.

The light show was fascinating. Kutri immediately forgot her exhaustion and stood enjoying the pond, trying to take it all in. A little past the swamp was wreckage of a flagpole. Its rusty, jagged peak resembled a finger jabbing at heaven. The rest of the pole, and whatever flags it had held, were buried beneath heaps of roots, vines, and leaves. She made her way to the mound and seated herself, the better to watch the swamp lights.

Though charmed by the surroundings, she was not so mesmerized as to ignore danger. A sharp, bitter tang to the air had something more in it than earth and rot. Sounds that might have been branches creaking, or might have been animal growls, issued from several directions at once. The shelters beasts had lived in were no more. Had they died out or gone into hiding? Given how many generations had come and gone, they might have mutated past the ten-to-one birthrate that applied equally to humans and wildlife. If some mutated alligator lumbered from the trees to devour Kutri, she would at least die with hope in her heart that mankind, too, might have a future.

Hearing a twang and a thud, she turned her head in the direction of the sound as the shaft of an arrow sprouted from the root-covered flagpole. She threw herself sideways. Back in the direction of the eucalyptus trees, she saw a wild man emerge from the shadows.

He fit roughly the picture she had always had of a loner in the outlands. These men were figures of romance, mythic and dark. Like ancient, wise tribesmen, they had a spiritual quality that elevated them above their modern counterparts. Competent self-sufficiency and a closeness to nature permitted them time to gaze at the heavens. Apart from hunger and thirst, both of which they could satisfy with a fistful of berries, they walked untroubled by any of the typical manly urges. Or so she had always thought.

This wild man was fondling himself. He wore tattered strips of leather as garments, so everything he did with his hands was achingly obvious. As she got to her feet, forgetting her caution in shock, he spat into his hand and began to apply the contents to his groin. The hand not being used for this purpose held a crude wooden bow. When she took a step back, he stopped massaging himself and drew an arrow from a quiver hanging from the strand of wire he used as a belt. There was a hatchet balancing the weight of the quiver on the belt's other side.

He said, "I didn't have to miss."

She said, "I thank you for missing."

Snorting, he shot an arrow into the ground at her feet.

"Please stop," she said. She meant the shooting mostly, but also anything else he had in mind.

The wild man only drew his string tighter. The arrow was aimed between Kutri's breasts. She lifted her shoulders, sure, in that tremulous moment, that her path had reached the end. Instead of piercing her, the wild man eased tension on the bow string, though the arrow did not dip.

"Come to me slow," he said. "And let me see your hands."

There was nothing in her hands, so she showed them without hesitation. She took one step, two. Did he mean to kill her or merely take from her what the rest always wanted? She wished she had a weapon, but she hadn't found her pins and had left the bloodied slip behind. As the wild man let the bow hang at his side, once again giving him a free hand, she remembered she was never weaponless.

Instead of walking toward him, she took a few graceful steps to the side. Rising on her toes, she lifted her arms and executed a twirl. The main knot that secured her sari was at the waist. She whipped her head quickly around as she turned, a little ballet move called "spotting," maintaining eye contact with the wild man, and touched the knot. His jaw slackened. From the blur of motion at his groin, he was clearly enjoying the performance.

She freed the knot with a tug. Fabric lifted as she twirled again, exposing her smooth back to the night air. Instead of letting the sari fall from her completely, she hugged it to her chest. Over her shoulder, she saw the wild man cringe and go into convulsions. She looked away as he made honking noises, like an animal, or like the minder she had killed.

At the last honk before a gasp, she spun to make a run at him. She was certain she could knock him down and have his bow out of his hands before he recovered. What happened then would depend on how he behaved. If he was at all typical of an outland man, she would have to amend her fantasy about going there with Jakob.

Before she could start her run, the wild man cringed again, this time without pleasure. He grunted, slapping a hand to the side of his head. A stone had hit him in the temple. Kutri saw it at his feet, pressing down the eucalyptus debris.

The wild man drew his bowstring, aiming first at Kutri, then into the darkness at his side. A hail of loose stones—pebbles and a few missiles of decent weight—rained down. A particularly large stone struck his knuckles. He lost his grip on the bow.

Now, Kutri ran straight at him. She would not miss her chance. Momentum, as much as intent, threw her into a tackle. She grabbed for the man's hatchet on the way down and had to grapple, not with him, but with a vine that snagged her wrist as she caught the weapon's handle. The wild man thumped to his side, and the hatchet came free from its loop. Kutri rolled up, shaking the bladed edge at the wild man. She was ready to fight, ready to kill, both him and stone hurler, if necessary. Anyone else who cared to try her could wait in line.

A slim figure appeared. The thrower of stones had been crouching in front of the wreck of a sign that partially hid the luminescent swamp life.

"Stay there. I'll get the bow," he said.

Actually, she wasn't sure about the *he* part. The voice was so reedy and light, it could easily have belonged to a woman. All Kutri could tell about her rescuer was the person's size. Only when the shadow moved did she recognized its shape. She held back from speaking the name, for the fear of the wild man, but she was more relieved than she could have said to see her rescuer was Mitsuru.

The wild man struggled to his knees, the move taking longer than it should have. Clearly, he had been hurt in the fall.

Mitsuru said, "Don't try anything. There used to be a concrete wall back there. It left me plenty of ammo."

"Please," said the wild man. "I'm as good as dead without the bow."

Lifting the weapon, Mitsuru said, "Come back for it later. For now, just go."

The wild man grumbled. Slowly, and not too steadily, he got to his feet. Mitsuru feinted at him, pretending he would lash the bow across his back.

"Mercy!" cried the wild man. He lurched away, leaping the tree roots, grunting in pain or frustration at every step.

Only when he was out of sight did the young man from Jimmy Ching's shop step into the moonlight. He dropped the bow and asked, "Are you hurt?"

Her nakedness seemed not to trouble him at all. As she wound the sari, she said, "No. He never touched me."

"Good," he said.

"How are you here, Mitsuru?"

"Later," he promised. "In the car."

"You have a car?" she said.

Of course he did.

***

The vehicle's interior was warm and a bit stuffy after the openness of the outdoors. Still, Kutri was happy to be sitting in comfort—kneeling, actually, as her shins were on the floorboards and her back pressed against the front of the seat. Mitsuru was also scrunched down in the floor space, on the driver side. They were waiting for the lights of a hatchetman patrol to disappear.

Rarely had she felt so tired, and never in a moment when it was impossible to sleep. The urgency of her thoughts would have kept her awake, on their own, without the adrenaline that had made her clutch the wild man's hatchet so tightly that her fingers ached.

They had progressed very little in what felt like a long time driving. Really, they drove in short bursts broken up by several long stretches of sitting, watching, and waiting. The car was an electric, with a sleek, low profile. The jet black exterior allowed it to move invisibly, as well as silently, through the dark city streets. But there were so many patrols, she wondered if they would ever reach their destination, wherever that should prove to be.

"Won't you tell me where we're going?" she asked, not for the first time.

"Somewhere safe," replied Mitsuru. "You have to trust me."

She fixed him with a glare, thought it was too dark for him to see. "Do I?"

He said nothing.

She said, "Is the car really yours? It's not, say, your uncle's?"

"He's got nothing to do with this," said Mitsuru.

"No? Then who does? If you want me to trust you, you have to return the favor."

It seemed, for a moment, that she had touched something in him. The silence thickened. She felt sure he was about to reveal something about his motives. Abruptly, he slid back into the driver's seat. The patrol was still present. She could see the lights.

"What are you doing?"

He twisted the knob that controlled the car's headlights. Cursing herself for relying on someone else to save her life, Kutri pushed up from her crouch and started to leave the car.

"Wait. Look," said Mitsuru.

Ahead, through the windscreen, she could see the patrol. A hatchetman standing in front of his fellows at the end of the alley, facing the car. He had a flashlight and was switching it on and off, completing a sequence.

"It's all right," said Mitsuru. "They're on our side."

Before Kutri could object, the car shot silently down the alley. They drove straight at the hatchetmen, who scattered, beams from the headlights bouncing off their chrome helmets. The car burst from the alley, skidded into a turn, and darted off down the street.

"If they're on our side, why did you just try to run them over?"

"I didn't. We just have to make the escape look real, in case someone is watching. They cannot simply let us go."

When they had gone a few blocks, Mitsuru said, "Are you going to use that?" He glanced at the hatchet, still clutched in Kutri's hands, to show what he meant.

Of course not, was the answer. She simply said, "No. But I do need you to explain. How can hatchetmen be on our side?"

He stopped the car at an intersection. There were no patrols about, so he drove on through.

"They work for my employer," he said.

"And who is that?"

She got no answer, only a guilty look. It was the guiltiest since Brutus, Judas, or Mir Jafar.

"Mitsuru," she said, "where are we going?"

"Trust me," he answered. "Only a little longer."

"You're not taking me to Jakob?"

"No. I wish I could." The youthful face, seen in flashes under lamplight, was achingly sincere. Changing tone as well as subject, Mitsuru said, "You asked how I found you. I was sent. Simple. My employer sent me."

"To the ruins of Los Angeles Zoo?"

"The apartment tower, where you should have been. The patrols made me late. I got there just in time to see you cross the overpass. If not for the patrols, I would have picked you up at once."

"If only they were all on our side."

"Yeah. If only."

Piles of trash began to appear on the side of the street, a sure sign they were getting back to the LA Kutri knew. Mitsuru steered down a side street to avoid another patrol. As they waited for it to pass, Kutri thought of a question that was neutral enough that he might not shy away from answering.

"There seem to be so many hatchetmen," she observed. "Where did they come from?"

"The houses," he said, his voice holding some of the disgust she felt on the topic.

"You mean the Houses of Care?"

He nodded. "No one knows how many there are. The Studio says a number on TV. Everyone believes it, but it's not half true."

"And the hatchetmen, the ones on 'our side,' come from there?"

"They were born in the houses. My employer, and the men he works with, took them from those places and trained them to be what they are."

She almost held back from asking the next question, but felt she needed to know.

"And are you, Mitsuru, one of the boys they rescued?"

"What? No. I'm nothing like them."

"Oh. I thought . . . It seemed personal to you."

"I hate the houses. They're everything that's wrong with this city. And there was a man I knew, he used to threaten—" He shook his head emphatically. "Never mind. Doesn't matter."

The patrol had moved on, though not by much. Mitsuru hunched over the wheel, showing the time for conversation was over, and put the car in drive. He drove slowly, carefully, keeping to the dark places. After a few more close calls, they came at last to an area of old houses that appeared mostly intact. Lights in the windows hinted some houses were inhabited, despite the rubbish on the opposite side of the street.

They parked in front of a house set atop a steep little hill and exited the car. Mitsuru drew Kutri to a set of concrete stairs set into the hill. His touch was quite soft for a young man. He showed her the entrance to an inclined tunnel covered by the ubiquitous vines. Once Mitsuru pulled these aside, Kutri was able to make her way up comfortably, if not quickly, as she still had to watch where she stepped.

At the top of the tunnel was the hint of a path around the quiet house. As they came around back, Mitsuru pointed down a short slope to the wreck of a patio. Positioned in the middle, in front of a pair of French doors that someone had nailed shut, a circular plate was set in the stone. It looked like a manhole cover, only with a handle and a hinge.

Mitsuru grasped the handle. It took him time to move the heavy thing, but once the cover was out of the way, Kutri saw a ladder leading down that emerged on a landing with a steel door.

After the pair climbed down, Mitsuru spoke to a grill in the door. "It's me."

There was a pause. Then, with a groan, the steel door opened. Light poured out, unbearably bright. Kutri had to shield her eyes, so the man inside saw her before she could make out his face.

He faked a gasp and said, "Darling!"

She blinked at Dr. Clyde Staley. All at once, she became acutely aware that she had left the wild man's hatchet in the car. The doctor had been civil enough to her, so far, but she wished she had something sharp to use against him, just in case. Her usual weapon, the one she had used to get the hatchet off its owner, was less effective against the Staleys of the world. He was a man who knew his own mind.

"I'm too bushed for a tumble," Staley said, "but if you're really desperate, I'll give you peck. Or a kiss on the cheek, if you prefer. Nothing to say? Well, don't stand there, my dear. Please, come in."

Chapter Twenty-One: Roll of the Dice

"I have to get out there," said Jakob, slamming the hard plastic case he had been holding down on the table. The case was an odd object, a rectangular shell in faded green that looked as if it used to fluoresce. The papers inside were held by a metal clip. He had slammed the case so hard, some of the papers jolted loose, but they didn't go anywhere, as the case was closed. "Send me out, Nat. I'll go alone. If there's a car to spare, I'll take it. If not, I'll walk."

Nat kept his place at the table, where he was examining a city map with bright ink marks to show La Vie assets.

"Where are you going to go, guy?" said Nat. "I've got people looking for our girl all over the city. They'll find something, some clue to where he took her—Joule, I mean."

Nat gritted his teeth. It was the first time either man had spoken the traitor's name since they left the Office of Justice. That had been hours ago. Since then, they had been shut away in an underground La Vie hideout that was formerly a subway line. A cave-in had cut off the branch from the main system some time in the recent past. The cave-in had been helped by dynamite.

Feeling his friend's discomfort, Jakob pushed away from the table. He shoved his chair against a filing cabinet that was the closest thing they had to a partition in the open, echoey room, and started to pace. More than two dozen La Vie loyalists were sheltering with him and Nat. At least half that many could be seen coming and going at any given time. None of the drop-ins were known to Jakob. Few stopped long enough to think about asking for a name.

Furious activity was happening on all levels of Sven's revolutionary engine. Runners made regular reports to Nat of battles fought in Culver City or Montebello, Compton or Eagle Rock. They carried messages away, too, to be flashed in code by spotlight, as Mella had done at the Barracks.

For most of the night, Jakob had been watching the frenzied, serialized activity of foot soldiers coming to speak to their general, then running to relay his orders. The operation was impressive, seeing so many men in overalls coordinate their activities with so many men in suits. Normally, the two groups had zero respect for each other, but as Nat had explained, the Studio kept a boot on every neck.

War is an equalizer, at least on the losing side. That was the second lesson Jakob learned on the subject, after the thing about most of war being running, and he thought about it long into the night.

At the center of chaos, Nat stood resolute. He kept his calm no matter what reports came in from the field, which made Jakob feel guilty about bothering him every twenty minutes, asking to be sent after Kutri. The requests were always denied, but Nat never made good on a threat to have Jakob bound and gagged, so he supposed he wasn't causing too much trouble. Maybe Nat wanted him to interrupt, to break up the tension. Little else was doing that.

The chair was uncomfortable, with a hard seat and creaking slats. Still it lured Jakob, until in time, he sat down and crossed his arms, pretending to be deep in thought, instead of about to nod off. How could he sleep while Kutri was anywhere but in his arms?

As the night wore on, a wrestling match between his body and mind broke out. Both were tense; both needed sleep. The match ended in a double fall. A hundred nightmares later, Jakob was startled awake by a loud groan from Nat.

The ex-groom and current general was on his feet. One hand rested on the table map. The other held a fist-sized object that was too dark for Jakob to make out. A messenger, this one a young woman, had just handed the object to Nat. Her hair hung straight down, because she was focused on the floor. Nat was looking down too. He slipped the object inside his tunic and thumped the table with a fist. The messenger jolted. As her head came up, Jakob recognized her as one of the women who had been part of their group when they wiped out the hatchetmen at the roadblock.

Jakob guessed at the message and said, "Lucas?"

Nat said, "No. Mella. She was leading a raid up on Radio Hill, east of the old stadium. The boys in black use it as a repeater station. Mella thought if she could take it, we could hack the broadcast. All the break points we had planned to hit are buttoned up."

Because of Joule, he didn't say.

That was another part of the surgeon's betrayal. La Vie had found out quickly that the weak points in the broadcast infrastructure had all been strengthened. This had happened sometime before the rollout of hatchetman patrols, and been discovered shortly after. At a stroke, years of recruiting, bribery, and intelligence gathering, all done to secure a list of "break points," as Nat called them, had been rendered useless.

Before the kidnapping, the plan had been for Jakob to give Sven's speech at the Presentation Ball, then for La Vie to hack the broadcast and show reruns as the city burned. Pulling off the hack was more important now, seeing as the Presentation Ball wasn't happening, at least on schedule. They had to gain control of broadcast infrastructure in order to get the speech out the first time.

Nat told the messenger, "Give me all the losses."

She ticked off three fingers. "Mrs. Banquo, Evie, and a young technician we added before the raid. Sorry. I don't know his name."

"Well, it wasn't Lucky," said Nat. "Sorry about Evie. I know you were close." He returned his attention to Jakob. "Hey, *hombre*. You still want to do a thing?"

The honest answer was *No*. Jakob preferred dozing in the chair to taking on a mission that distracted him from finding Kutri. Nothing in the messenger's report seemed to put the rescue higher on Nat's priority list. He considered shaking his head and walking off, finally making good on his threat to go alone. But Nat's face held him back. It was iron. All humor was gone. If Jakob had met him on the street looking like that, he would have run the other way. Under the circumstances they were in, he found the expression magnetic.

"Maybe," he said. "What do you have in mind?"

Nat shook a fist. The gesture didn't look angry, more like he was getting ready to throw dice. When he flicked the hand open, Jakob saw he had guessed right.

"Roll of the dice," said Nat. "Could go either way. What do you say?"

Jakob felt as though a great weight were pressing down from above, like he was at the bottom of the ocean, with thin currents tugging at his ankles. He could swim left or right, but the currents were too strong for him to swim back. If he chose the wrong direction, he would drown.

Right was chase after Kutri. Left was follow Nat. Both were journeys in the dark. But at least Nat had a map.

"I say I'll do it. For you."

"Not me, guy," said Nat. "For Mella, maybe. Or La Vie."

The messenger, and other strangers standing around, shouted, "La Vie!"

All Jakob could manage was a nod.

Nat said, "Here's the plan. There's a spot like the one that did for Mella, but better, and on enemy ground."

"It's all enemy ground," said Jakob.

"Sure," said Nat. "But some parts are worse than others. You know David and Goliath, guy? Lesson is, if you want to kill a giant, aim for the head. Come look at the map. Tell me, this giant we're killing, where would you say its head is?"

He wasn't pointing at anything in particular, only resting his fingers on the map. Jakob walked to his side of the table, lifted his hand, and set the index finger on the place Nat had to have known he would choose: Little Angel Studio, the filthy heart of darkness at the south end of Burbank.

"We can do it," said Nat. "We can bash our way in. Use their own tech to get you on air."

"Security," Jakob pointed out.

Nat shrugged. "It's never been worse than it is right now. Think: The boys in black are in the street. They're rolling jaywalkers, stomping drunks. They've always been jerks, but you ever seen it that bad? Me and Bette blamed Flynn for the surge, but I think now maybe we got it wrong. Looking up close, I'm sure it ain't Flynn calling the shots. He's lost control, at least of part of his army."

It was an alarming thought. "Even if that's true, he's not lost them all. Say Flynn's got a hold of a couple hundred. Could we handle that many?"

The smile, and all the humor behind it, returned to Nat's face. He laughed and picked up the edge of table. Walking sideways, he rotated it one-hundred-and-eighty degrees.

"Sure we can, guy. I'm telling you, we can." He nodded at the plastic case, which was now back in front of Jakob. "Hold on to that thing while I get a gang together, will ya? And make sure you bring it when we leave."

"I know the speech," said Jakob. He had been studying Sven's words carefully. Though they occupied only a page and a half of the paper in the case, he could easily see how they would set fire to the world.

Nat said, "You'll need the rest, too. They're codes. We'll go over all that in the car. For now, just give me a minute, okay?"

Jakob lifted the case.

**

The gentle rocking of the car was too much for Jakob. He was asleep in the passenger seat long before they reached the location of the rendezvous Nat had organized. Nat woke him by rapping on the case in his hands.

"Study that, guy," said Nat. "Get the first column down. I'll be back with the driver."

He was clearly excited. Jakob glanced out the windscreen and saw why. Lucas was standing in front of a circle of cars. His chin was up, his hands folded. Nat approached him and slapped an arm. Lucas nodded, mumbling something. Then, miracle of miracles, he actually smiled. With Nat in the lead and each man walking tall, they returned to the car.

"I'll get in the back," said Jakob.

Nat said, "No. Stay put. Study."

Lucas drove the rest of the night.

**

They made three more stops on the twisting route north-by-northwest. Vehicles were waiting at each stop. Some led, some followed, and some were dispersed to the four winds. By the time Nat's "gang" was complete, there were twenty-something transports in the attack caravan. At the head was one of La Vie's dearest assets, a genuine armored truck, military grade, with urban camouflage rendered useless by the headlights. The brave souls who had excavated the beast from a base at Los Alamitos had done a good job of preparing it for covert duty, but Nat wanted it to be seen. It would have been hard to miss, lights or no lights, with the two ten-foot radio antennas mounted in back.

"You got the third column down yet?" he asked from the back seat.

"Almost," said Jakob. "I take it we can't take the page with us?"

"Makes me nervous, guy. Think what the other side would do if they got our codes. There's a lighter in my pocket. Before we head out, I'm burning it all. Leave nothing behind. Not that anything could go wrong with my brilliant plan."

"Perish the thought."

Jakob had been given only vague hints about what the plan involved, but he trusted Nat. Anyway, after they had picked up Lucas, studying the codes had occupied all his attention. Each was a three- to four-digit number, with the digits standing for rapid flashes of a spotlight. To transmit the code "121," the sender would flash once, count a breath, flash twice, count a breath, and flash once again. The nearest partner in the spotlight network would relay the message until it reached the receiver.

Code 121 meant "Message begins." It was supposed to be followed by the receiver's code. There were many receiver codes, but Nat had told Jakob to learn just one, 2112, the code for the Barracks. In addition to 121 and 2112, he needed to know code 222, which meant "Message ends," and all the codes in column three. Each was a shorthand designation for how to destroy a way of life. Codes 313, 323, 333, 3113, 3223, and 3333 had been specially reserved. To the La Vie planners, the group headed by Nat and Mrs. Bette, they meant "Do something with the secret weapon," the long-range version of Sil Banquo's buzz box. What the *something* was varied by code. It could be, "Set the men of Los Angeles free from the obedience circuits so they can riot," or it could be, "Calm every man so he can focus on escape."

With the start, end, receiver, and reserved codes memorized, Jakob knew enough to inform the Barracks what action to take. This would be necessary only if he was the last living member of the attack force on Studio HQ, but Nat insisted he be prepared. The codes came with brief explanations to the right of the third column. There was only one code Jakob found mysterious.

He said, "What's code 3223? It says, 'Savage release.' What's that mean?"

Nat gave him a look that might have been troubled, though it was possible Jakob was misinterpreting interest as a moment of doubt. Real or imagined, the moment passed, and Nat was perfectly confident when he said, "Ah, you don't need that one, guy. It does what it says, but don't worry. Today's a thirty-one-thirteen kind of day."

The sun was coming up. Between fatigue, Nat's cheeriness, and the subtle glow on the horizon, Jakob decided to take the de facto general at his word. Code 3113 was the goal. Sven had given his life for 3113. It was the code that would deliver men from Studio bondage by disabling the obedience circuits. What the men of LA did with their freedom would be up to them, but if they were anything like Jakob, they would use the gift, and the exhilaration from Sven's speech, and burn the New Society to the ground.

"That all you needed?" said Nat. "You've got the speech and the codes down, otherwise?"

"Yeah. Got it." Jakob closed the cover of the plastic case. "Are we close?"

This time, Nat's face was confident from the start. "Real close."

Seconds later, they pulled off the highway and drove down a street that ran parallel to it for a short distance. The military vehicle in the lead took a turn, followed by a pair of suburban vehicles nearly as large as itself. The one on the left was bright yellow with the word "HUMMER" splashed in blocky yellow letters across the bumper. The vehicle on the right was a brawny white pickup with a covered bed.

Smaller cars and trucks trailed in the wake of the big boys, flashing their brake lights as they took the turn. Nat's car, driven by Lucas, pulled to a halt near the center of the pack.

"Last chance to back out," said Nat. It was impossible to tell if he was being serious.

Ahead, past the cars and the trucks and the powerful military lead, a three-lane road led over a gentle hill between long, flat buildings. An overpass near where Lucas parked had collapsed and been cleared away, leaving only a concrete support to Jakob's right. Far to the left, partially obscured by a dingy, corkscrew spiral of a building, was a black-and-yellow sign that read Little Angel City.

A spotlight was mounted on the fallen overpass support. Opposite the support stood a tower of newer construction. Four feet of machine-gun barrel were poking out of a slot in the tower. A good half of Nat's force were already positioned beyond where the gun was pointing, while Nat, Lucas, and Jakob sat directly in the line of fire.

Jakob said, "How are we not dead?"

"Part of the plan, guy," said Nat. "We turned the tables."

He leaned between the seats to point at the lead vehicle. It took a second for Jakob to realize he was pointing specifically at the twin antennas.

"They buzz us, we buzz them. Hatchet*man*. The clue's in the name."

Once he said it, it was obvious. Every man in the city had gone through the same brain surgery as an infant, including chrome heads. All were equipped with a Carter-Schnee implant. Sil Banquo, probably with the late Mella's help, had figured out how to get on their wavelength.

The tower was too dark for Jakob to see inside, but he could easily picture a hatchetman sitting frozen in his chair, one hand reaching for a trigger he'd be unable to squeeze until long after the target was gone.

Nat rolled down his window and shouted, "*Vive la résistance*! Let's go, go, go!"

The military vehicle sprang forward, dragging its companions in its wake. Bits of the caravan surged ahead of the car Jakob was in, but Lucas proved his worth as a driver by making up ground with a few quick maneuvers. They were soon back in the middle of the pack. This time, the pedal was to the metal.

Several more gun barrels could be seen poking out of the featureless gray buildings looming on either side of the street. As the caravan crested the hill, one got off a barrage. Shots sparked off the lead vehicle. Lucas dodged cars that slammed on their brakes, cursing the drivers.

The military vehicle increased its speed, outstripping the rest of the caravan and ignoring the bullets that pinged off its armor. The Hummer, on its left, had a tire blown out. It skidded sideways and crashed into concrete barrier.

Jakob watched for return fire from the vehicles, but there was none. The only muzzle flare, glimpsed briefly in the dawn light, came from a machine gun in the distance. After one outburst, it fell silent. Jakob puzzled over this for a moment before realizing what had happened. The gunner had been too far out for the antennas to freeze him with their buzz box–like signal. Now the armored vehicle had made up the difference.

It braked to a halt. Chasing the distant gunner had taken it past a turnoff and nearly run it out of road. Brake lights flashed as the rest of the caravan came to a halt. Nat got out. A few shouted orders later and the driver of the Hummer was out and getting medical attention. No time to change a tire. He and his passengers were bundled into other vehicles before the little cavalry moved on with the military vehicle and the pickup leading the way again.

The caravan followed a snake's trail of streets, gravel paths, and bone-rattling rumbles over bare ground. At last, it stopped at a tall fence that closed off a road. A wooden barrier stood in front of the fence. Though made of chain links, the fence itself had been rendered opaque by thick gray plastic tarps shot through with holes.

Jakob said, "Uh, Nat?" as the armored vehicle revved its engine.

"I know, guy," said Nat. "It's not much of a gate. But it will be."

The vehicle charged the barrier. Splinters exploded up and out. They were still raining down when the fence bowed, struck full force by the beast of a machine. Posts tilted and fell. A sizable chunk of fence flopped to the ground.

Lucas made a sound that might almost have been a laugh. Nat hopped from the car before Jakob could find the door handle. Moments later, Nat was standing beside Antoine Huxley, the driver of the armored vehicle, when Jakob ran up.

". . . know what hit 'em," Nat was saying. "You see that, guy? With guts like that, who needs luck? Hard part's over now. Want a last look at your speech?"

Jakob said, "I don't need it."

Nat laughed, slapped his shoulder, and went off carrying the plastic case and a lighter. Jakob shook hands with Antoine. They watched as a clean-up crew dragged splinters out of the street. At their back, past the fallen fence and an acre of scrub, pristine streets and perfect replicas of buildings from the World Before stretched as far as the eye could see.

Chapter Twenty-Two: The Red Carpet

The Wilshire Beverly Hilton was unchanged since Kutri's first visit. Still looming, still dirty, it presented the same few meters of attractive entryway as it had the day before. A man was sweeping the red carpet when Kutri was let out of the car by Staley himself.

"A moment, dear," he said. As Mitsuru came around from the driver's side, Staley gestured at the sweeper. "Take care of that, please. I have to see to the cameras."

A black sedan was pulling up to their car's bumper. It had followed from the hideout, carrying a full load. As the day was still new, this was the first chance Kutri had been able to see the driver in full light. His steel gray hair and blue cap were distinct, marking him as the doorman at the doctor's club. As he stepped from the car, his artificial leg gave a whine of complaint. Driving seemed an odd duty for such a man. She supposed Dr. Staley wasn't spoiled for choice.

The man in the passenger seat was a stranger to Kutri. From his bulk and outfit, he was clearly a bodyguard. The reminder made her miss Mondt, her own protector. The man sitting diagonally across from the bodyguard, behind the driver, was the server from the club, Ellis. Today, he was not wearing a drinks tray in place of his right arm and hand, but the strut that had supported the tray was there. It projected from his shoulder and waist, forming a triangular brace at the outer corner of which a cylinder as long as Jakob's forearm had been affixed.

Kutri watched as Staley directed the bodyguard to fetch a video camera from the trunk and attach it to the strut. There was fussing as the burly man labored to complete a task outside his training, wordlessly struggling. The sedan's final passenger kept an eye on Kutri. Kutri could see only part of his forehead from where she was standing, but an instinctual revulsion, combined with her reason, told her he could be none other than the former head of Little Angel Studio, Mr. Jon Schuyler.

The sweeper was out of sight when she turned her back on the sedan. Mitsuru was walking her way, keeping to the asphalt beside the red carpet. She motioned to him to speed up. They had not spoken privately since the hideout, and it seemed unlikely they would have another chance.

"How do you figure in this, Mitsuru?" she whispered as soon as he was in earshot.

He whispered back, "I work for Dr. Staley."

"Doing what, exactly? Don't say driving. You've done much more than drive."

"Everything I did was at the doctor's orders. Not that he liked it. He would have liked me to hide, but I wouldn't. The fight's more mine than it's his, anyway. I told him, if someone was going to watch you, you and"—his hesitation was accompanied by a look of pain—"and the matchmaker . . . I told him it would be me."

Kutri gave him a moment to fidget. Of course, the youth obliged.

She said, "You're reluctant to say Jakob's name. Why? Please, Mitsuru. Remember, I trusted you."

From the other car, Staley called out, "Aha! At long last. Miss Kutri, give us a smile."

Kutri obeyed, turning to the camera with a pleasant expression.

"Don't strain," said the doctor. "The lens cover is on. Stay where you are, please. We have technical checks and an intro to shoot. All before the rest of our guests arrive."

For a moment, she hoped she would be able to finish her talk with Mitsuru. This was quashed when Staley said, "What is that you're wearing, M?"

Mitsuru dusted a shoulder. The T-shirt he had on certainly caught the eye. The artwork on the front showed a gigantic gorilla straddling a pair of insanely tall, World Before towers. A cityscape was behind the gorilla, and several jet airplanes were diving out of the sky. The gorilla was crushing a plane as it looked at a woman held in its other hand. The expression it showed the woman was unreadable, because it was wearing a surgical mask, like so many masks Kutri had seen in pictures from history class. Everyone used to wear them, back in the early days of the Slow Plague.

"Go change, Campfire," said Staley.

"It's Camfeer, sir," said the bodyguard.

"Whatever. Watch Miss Kutri, and— My goodness! Ellis, find someone to do M's hair," said Staley.

"I can do it myself," said Mitsuru. Just as he finished, the first in a line of vehicles made the final turn of their approach.

"Ah!" said the doctor. "Our guests. Miss Kutri, back in the car, please. The rest of you, look sharp."

She knelt on the back seat, watching the vehicles arrive as the bodyguard took his place at the door. The first to pull up behind the ex-president's limo was a tall panel van. When the sliding door opened, Kutri saw a gleam of reflected light within. A hatchetman stepped from the van, followed by a troop of his fellows.

Dr. Staley fluffed the lapels of his blazer. He was, undoubtedly, the man in charge, but what did it mean, and what did he want from her? If she could have run away, she would have, but since she couldn't, she supposed she would discover Staley's plan in time. She sat down and said a prayer:

"Lord Vishnu, Thou the Preserver, if I cannot be with Jakob, please let him be somewhere safe."

Chapter Twenty-Three: Battle of the Backlot

L essons in urban warfare kept popping into Jakob's head.
You don't see the one that gets you.
That was a lesson he learned as a tight knot of La Vie fighters came around the side of a building to the sudden thunder of rifle fire. Those who died were calm or determined. None seemed surprised.

The other lesson, from the same incident, was *There's always someone you don't expect.*

The backpack with three-foot-tall antennas, carried by Antoine Huxley, froze the rank-and-file hatchetmen in their tracks. But a special squad of hatchetmen kept on fighting. These wore red helmets instead of chrome ones. Instead of chest units, they wore body armor. If the number of red hatchetmen had been anything like the number of chrome ones, the assault would have turned into a massacre only minutes after Antoine burst through the gate.

Thank Dad, there were fewer than fifteen of the red killers, by Jakob's estimate. They deployed in teams, often giving light opposition on one side of the La Vie force, while others of their number pressed in from the flank. In this way they slowed progress to the target, gradually divided the attackers into smaller groups, and whittled down what was left. There had been seventy men and women backing Nat at the start, but after forty minutes of fighting, fewer than twenty remained with Nat, Antoine, and Jakob.

It was impossible to say how many others had been killed, how many were fighting their own skirmishes. Lucas had been among the first diverted. He had disappeared down a side street of the immense Studio backlot many gunshots before Jakob's group turned onto a row of facades styled to look like a city from the World Before. Since then, nobody in their group had seen hide nor hair of the big guy, no matter how many times Nat asked.

Pressing his back to a plaster wall that was faux brick, Jakob tried to catch his breath. His foot was close to one of the dangerous trenches that had robbed them of their second biggest asset after the Banquo buzz box. Spikes could jab up from the trenches, set off by pressure plates that would let a man cross, but clunked as they stabbed the tires of anything heavier.

The pickup had been the first to go, followed by a couple of smaller vehicles, before Nat had made the decision to abandon the convoy altogether. Since then, La Vie and the red hatchetmen had been playing the human version of cat and mouse. Heavily armed though they were, nobody on the La Vie side was a cat.

"You know this one?" said Nat. He had run up from behind, and now took a place between Jakob at the corner of the flimsy imitation of a building. The machine pistol he used to gesture across the street resembled one of the Uzis from Jimmy Ching's collection.

Jakob said of the view, "It's familiar, but I'm not sure."

Fake store fronts lined the side of the street, giving them shelter, but on the side Nat was indicating, most of the block was dominated by a single long building made of faux cut stone and with a distinct narrow glass entryway.

"It was in *Captain America*," said Nat. "*Hobbs & Shaw*, too. You see those flicks? Oh, and *Dirty Harry*. Bank scene. The greatest. Clint shoots the car from the corner, and the guy coming out, then he walks over, you know? He's chewing his lunch and he says, 'You feeling lucky, punk?'"

Jakob said, automatically, "That's not the line."

"It's not?"

Jakob recited, without putting on a gravelly voice, as Nat had, "'You've got to ask yourself one question. Do I feel lucky? Well, do you, punk?'"

"Hey, that's good," said Nat. "I think you're right, guy. You must have watched that flick more than me."

"I never did. Sven had a book of popular misquotes."

"Course he did, guy. Funny, he was always playing stuff like that for us. Said it was training. What did he watch with you?"

Jakob could have answered that question in many ways. Some of the best nights of his life had been spent watching classics from Sven's film collection.

He said, "Period pieces, mostly. Light drama. Westerns."

"That's okay. So long as you got in some *Man with No Name*."

Someone gave a whistle from across the street. Nat whistled back. At the signal, a La Vie fighter poked the barrel of a gun out from behind a derelict car. When the gun persisted in not being shot, the man himself stepped out. He crept along the sidewalk about ten feet, turned, and raised a hand. He looked like he was about to wave the all-clear when a shot rang out. The man fell on his face, blood spurting from his chest.

Nat leapt from his hiding place, swearing, his Uzi spraying bullets. The rule about La Vie women doing the killing was evidently suspended, not that the rapid-fire pistol had a chance of avenging the dead man from a distance. Before Jakob knew what he was doing, he had taken hold of Nat's sleeve and was dragging him back to the building's shadow.

A second shot rang out. Jakob listened closely, but there were too many echoes to guess the sniper's location. At least he had saved Nat. Suddenly, another La Vie ally popped out from behind the same car as the dead man, which was parked in front of the building that had been a bank in *Dirty Harry*. The ally ran in a diagonal line across the street, firing a revolver from the hip. He got off a total of five shots before the sniper shot him down.

"There he is!" said Nat. He charged clear of the wall once more, this time spraying useless shots with slightly more focus. He yelled as he ran, and a half dozen La Vie fighters joined him, yelling as they darted from cover. They blasted away, firing pistols and rifles. No one knew exactly where to aim, but their numbers made up for the lack of precision.

Someone put a bullet in the sniper, or else the mob action broke his nerve. A rifle fell from a third-story window halfway down the block. The gun clacked on the pavement, drawing a whoop of celebration from Nat, even though it wasn't followed by a body.

All of the shooters cheered, except one woman. She took a knee, clutching her side. Antoine came out of hiding behind a blue box that Jakob remembered vaguely had something to do with the ancient postal service. The backpack with the buzz box antennas was Antoine's responsibility, so he had been right to hang back when Nat charged. He stooped beside the woman and held her shoulders, keeping her from falling over.

Her name was Grace. She happened to be the La Vie member who had brought news of Mella's death. Her husband was a justiceman, and in the reverse of Antoine's situation, he was unaware of her rebellious streak. Jakob had heard the story from Nat, back at the hideout. He had not spoken to Grace directly, so he wondered, as he knelt opposite Antoine, if he should introduce himself. She gave a tight smile that showed there was no need.

"What a time for Doc Joule to bail on us," said Antoine.

Jakob swallowed. He had no idea how much Antoine knew about the traitor. "Did you hear the reason he did?"

"No," said Antoine. "I'm sure he's got one. Just wish he was here, that's all."

Jakob was saved from further talk of the surgeon when Nat shouted, "Hey, Huxley! Get up here."

"We've got wounded," said Antoine. Under his breath, he added, "Friendly fire."

"Jones," said Nat. The La Vie member he had indicated ran back to take Antoine's place.

The group moved on. Inside of three minutes, they fell into an ambush. The target was close, so the fighters formed a wedge and pushed ahead. Jakob found himself at the back of a human shield with Nat and Antoine. Waving his Uzi, Nat tried to surge to the front. A fighter toppled into him, saving his life as the fighter himself was shot in the head.

The wedge broke. Fighters scattered, returning fire when they could. Mostly, they ran. A pair of men in overalls lifted Jakob off his feet. He was carried, facing away and heels bouncing off the pavement, around the corner and across the street. As the men reached a curb, one of the men holding Jakob was shot. The other stumbled, thrown off by the weight shift. He did his best to roll Jakob, instead of smashing his brains on the sidewalk.

As soon as Jakob could tell up from down, he got his feet underneath him. The falling man had tossed him into a field of artificial grass. While Jakob was seeking cover, Nat sped past, making such a racket with the Uzi that the red hatchetmen paid Jakob no attention. Even when the Uzi cleaned its clip and started choking, they kept out of his sight line, which gave Nat and Jakob both the second they needed to duck behind a tall, narrow plaque standing close to the front of the AstroTurf lawn.

Jakob had only a moment to glimpse the building in front of the plaque. A moment was all he needed. The place was their target, their chosen destination, and he knew the facade well, in movie form. It had played the part of a courthouse and a city hall in movies he had seen with Sven.

In *Back to the Future*, Jakob's favorite movie from the World Before, it had served as the centerpiece of the quaint 1950s town that the time-traveling hero knew as a larger, impersonal city. Sven had pointed out the symbolism, how the parking lot that replaced the courthouse grass in the hero's time represented the loss of innocence. Neither man had laughed at the irony. The filmmakers would live long enough to see innocence sicken in the Slow Plague, along with everything else.

The building was fronted by a set of wide steps. There were three pillars at the top and three doors behind the pillars. The door in the middle was large and ornate. The others were comparatively plain. This pattern was turned on its side for the windows. Decorative trim surrounded the windows on the first story, while the windows of the second story were austere. The windows of the third story were mere rectangles, slightly creepy in the way they stared down from above.

If there had been rooms behind the rectangles, they would have made excellent watch posts. But Jakob could see, by peeking around the plaque, that the illusion of World Before grandeur ended a yard behind the glass. A black wall of something like marble, laced with swirling, silver tracery, was visible behind every window. The flat roof of the two ends of the building, as well as the peaked roof above the pillars, appeared to slot into the black wall. Looking through the windows revealed this as a trick of the eye. The roofs simply ended where the wall began. The courthouse front was a disguise for the sleek black cube that was Little Angel's Broadcast Center.

It wasn't much of a disguise. The surface of the front wall rose high above the facade—so high it seemed the spotlights on its top were touching the clouds. In the center of the portion above the facade's peaked roof, the swirling silver trace work formed an image—more like a pictogram than a picture. Jakob had to squint to make out more than squiggly lines. When he did, he saw the image was of a woman, heavily pregnant. She had wide hips and six pendulous breasts. A pair of wings curled around from her back to point their tips at the gap between her thighs. The wings were meant to be made of feathers, he thought, but they looked like jags of rusted metal, pasted together to form the halves of a buzz saw.

The clock on the jutting portion of the building under the peaked roof was tiny compared to the image. In *Back to the Future*, a clock like it was destroyed by a bolt of lightning in a pivotal scene. To see it reduced to a minor feature in the mishmash of old and new made Jakob want to headbutt the architect. Did the Studio have to drain the life out of everything he loved?

Nat tossed away the Uzi. For a moment, as he saw the red hatchetmen helmets popping up all around the square, he seemed lost.

Recovering his smile, he said, "Sorry, Sundance. Looks like it's Australia for us."

For Nat's sake, Jakob tried to think of a quip, but before he could say he was Butch, a rattle of gunfire came from a connecting street. A knot of La Vie fighters charged out, dividing their fire between red hatchetmen in front of them and unseen targets behind. Lucas was leading the charge.

"That's it, Luc!" shouted Nat. "You show 'em what you're made of!" To Jakob, he added, "I ever tell you he used to ride the web?"

That was worth a smile. Nat winked and slipped a hand inside his hatchetman tunic. Whatever he found there, he kept it concealed.

"Is that a weapon?" said Jakob. "Got one for me?"

Nat only grinned. "*Ya estamos otra vez.* We're back again. Sorry, guy. You're too important. You need to get in there, get out on the air. Antoine can handle the tech stuff, or someone else can. It's got to be you who shows your face."

"Why? I'm nothing special."

"That's where you're wrong, guy. Len said I should tell you, but be fair, I didn't count on having to shoot our way in. All you need to know is, there's a history between you and Flynn. You forgot it. He didn't. When you show your face on the air, he'll think you remembered. He'll think it's why you joined up."

"Why does that matter?"

More gunfire announced a move by Antoine, who came running along the sidewalk, leading a squad of allies in a firefight with a red hatchetman posted on the steps. One of Antoine's antennas had been shortened by a foot. He had a gash on one cheek that showed where a bullet had done some trimming.

With a swift glance, Jakob took in what Antoine was doing, how it meshed with the chaos stirred by the surprise attack. Neither effort would be enough. The red hatchetmen were on their bellies in the fake grass, or in cover behind fake trees. They had briefly panicked, when Lucas charged, but were firing from the best positions in the square. They were going to win and Jakob was going to die, unless someone did something unexpected.

Nat said, "Stay alive, guy. Stay alive if you want answers."

And with that, Nathaniel Martinez, husband of *Good Breeding* match bride Belen Costa Martinez, darted from behind the plaque and ran toward the courthouse steps, yelling insults. His shoulder took a bullet before he got close, and Jakob thought his leg took another, but when Nat came to the low hedge that divided the grass from the sidewalk, in front of the steps, he hurdled it without breaking stride.

A red hatchetman came out from behind a pillar. His partner, the shooter who had been targeting Antoine's group, switched his aim to the general. Both fired. Nat dove. He sprawled across the lower steps, whipping his arm out of the tunic. Something dark flew out of his hand. Jakob thought it was what Grace had given him, the last gift from Mella.

There might have been a shout. It might have been in Jakob's head. It might have been, "Sven!" or it might have been, "Belen!"

The explosion was stunning. It smashed two of the pillars and blasted a crater in the fake courthouse steps. The red hatchetmen on the steps died instantly. Others, in the square, stopped shooting to cover their heads.

The unexpected had happened. Jakob wouldn't waste his chance. With ringing ears, he dodged from behind the plaque and charged the steps, praying all the way the Big Dad would make Nat's sacrifice mean something. At the steps, he looped the crater and passed between ruined pillars. He didn't check to see what was left of Nat, didn't find out if his veins held blood or liquid gold. Antoine and his group followed him up the steps, shooting targets across the square.

Then they were inside the Studio.

Chapter Twenty-Four: The Other Big Event

Unlike the rest of the famous hotel, the International Ballroom, with its multitiered seating and crystal chandeliers, was as impressive in person as it had seemed on TV. If not for the hatchetmen standing around, Kutri would have thought herself lost in a fantasy. Her dreams of the Presentation Ball looked so like what she was seeing in life, she felt dizzy. *Good Breeding* was a scripted contest, she knew, so no actual contest at all, and the Studio that put it on the airways was evil.

So why did being in a place of the Studio's power still give her goose bumps? She was practically giddy, as lightheaded as the little girl she had been the first time she had seen the beautiful ball on screen all those years ago.

What a fool she was, what a child. She had killed a man in a high-rise apartment. The man she loved was who-knew-where in a city gone mad. What right did she have to wear a pretty dress as cameramen scrambled to capture her best angle, while the other candidates stood twitching their creased garments as stylists buzzed around, applying steam with portable irons? She had no right at all. And yet, here she was.

Dr. Staley was also buzzing about, doling out smiles to candidates and frowns to technicians. He had assured everyone they would be seen by a huge audience, despite the broadcast of the Presentation Ball being moved to the morning, from its usual night slot. Also despite the chaos going on in LA. The chaos, according to Staley, would help. With hatchetmen using draconian tactics, ostensibly in an effort to locate Kutri's kidnapped self, what choice did men have but to stay indoors and watch the screens?

Mr. Schuyler, their patron, had connections that would ensure the broadcast went out on all the right stations. Kutri assumed this would be through an act of electronic piracy. If the other girls were worried about the legality of the act, they kept it to themselves. Kutri followed their example.

The ballroom was wonderful. The tables where guests would normally have been seated were all in place, so the view she had was exactly as she had seen in the many preview shots she always drooled over in the gap between seasons. There were dozens of tables, all set with fine china and champagne flutes, on tiers ascending from Kutri's position. The lowest tier, where four of the six bridal candidates, including herself, were assembled, hosted a wide, clear space for dancing, directly in front of the stage.

Some kind of plastic composite had been used to construct the stage floor. Its colors changed every season, so the shimmering blue, with streaks of pink and gold, was new and quite lovely. Two statues of naked female angels connected the floor to the ceiling on either side of the stage. Their wings and nipples were firmly erect. Around the stage's semicircular front, seven places had been marked out for the candidates, though, naturally, not all would be needed.

A name plate was fixed to the floor at every place, so it was easy to see what the Studio's plan had been when seven candidates were available, and when the Studio was running the show. Between the place marked for Kutri and the place for Viola Wimmer—the dimpled Swede in braided pigtails now chatting with her stylist at Kutri's side—the circle for Cuc Tien had been ringed with pink roses. The memorial was touching, though somewhat disheveled, as if the arranger had used his feet, or possibly a shovel, rather than careful hands.

In the middle of the stage, near the back, a curtain on a circular rod had been drawn around an eighth place. Kutri had never seen this done in a previous season. No one had approached the eighth place in the twenty minutes or so since she arrived. She had no idea what the curtain hid or what purpose the place served. Nor was there anyone to ask. Mitsuru had disappeared shortly after Staley started calling him "M." He had yet to reappear.

As if summoned to quash her curiosity, Staley straightened from a hunched conversation with a cameraman and said, "Ladies! Our technical troubles are resolved. Take your positions backstage."

Viola Wimmer and Pania Maniapoto hefted their skirts. They hurried to the side of the dance area, where an open doorway led backstage. Elise

Dupain, the tallest and surliest of the candidates, did not follow at once but took a moment to berate her hair stylist in French. In a frenzy of movement, the man freed the last of her hair curlers. She rolled her eyes, fluffed her bosom at the man, and traipsed back with the others. Thanks to her sky-high legs, she had to stoop to keep from striking her head on the door frame. Not wanting a confrontation, Kutri waited for the giantess before she, too, passed through the door.

Several screens hung on wheeled dollies in the backstage area. Most showed the ballroom. A few had been tuned to other channels. A man with a clipboard, who had earlier been introduced to the women as Gar, lined them up in front of the largest screen. He glowered at Kutri, who was to be the first to enter, and asked if she knew exactly what she must do.

"Certainly," she said, with a little curtsy.

"Don't bow to me, missy," said Gar. "Know your cues, do your part, and we can all get on with life."

Disbelief at the nearness of her dream crowded out all that should have been in Kutri's mind. Jakob, Simmons, her kidnapper, Karan Politis, and the minder; they all sped away. Only Mitsuru lingered, and only because she expected he would see her take the stage. The moment had come! Today was her dream. A rejected dream, to be sure, a dream she had replaced. But what could it hurt—letting the dream play out? She was still going to choose Jakob in the end.

On the screen, she watched Staley lift a microphone in his artificial hand. He said, "Ladies, however many of you there are, and gentlemen. What a break from the circus we have for you today. You've been glued to your sets, no doubt, watching the insanity unfold. You know ours is a planet in peril. Now, more than ever! The Municipality of Los Angeles, our precious hub of entertainment, has been overrun, horror of horrors. Civilization as we know it is on the brink of collapse. Our bold New Society—will it last? I know, folks, that it makes a nice change from the usual misery porn, but really, is this what we want?"

He strolled over to the central, circular curtain and picked at the fabric. As the camera zoomed in, he gave a confident smirk. A sudden twist of the lip turned into a sneer of outrage.

"Little Angel Studio has launched a military coup. It's shocking, I know. Giving us martial domination when what we want is erotic delectation. We want bust, not marching dust. We want skin, not bullets in. Boots on necks kill ratings in any sane Nielsen state. But when was the last time anything programmed by the Studio was sane?"

The fingers of his flesh hand took hold of the curtain. "You remember our last grand finale?" He started to move the curtain. A technician must have taken over from there, because the curtain kept rasping around the metal frame while Staley kept still.

When the curtain was compressed to a six-foot-wide backdrop, a woman was revealed. She sat so motionless in her chair that, for a moment, Kutri thought she was some kind of mannequin. Even when the woman eventually moved, Kutri allowed herself to think she was seeing an animatronic. But the play of muscles under the ebony skin was unmistakably human. The fantasy collapsed and Kutri had to accept that the woman revealed behind the curtain was the bride who had been killed on live television, Aluel Garang.

Her outfit was the same as she had worn the last time she appeared on TV. Her cream skirt was splashed with blood, along with the gold belt and the gold netting over her breasts. Blood had dried in the holes of the netting, so the ensemble was rather more modest than it had been at the wedding. Aluel was missing her neck bands, also the peak of her hair, but these were all minor details, hard to notice with her face . . . right there.

It consisted of a forehead, eyes, and half a nose. The flap of skin that covered Aluel's mouth and one nostril resembled putty. The surgeons had simply stretched it, laying it over the mouth and the portion of nose, before pinning it under her ear. Stitches along the jawline demonstrated that this was not quite what had happened, but the picture was close enough.

"Horror of horrors," Staley repeated. "This is not what we want at all. If we wanted butchery, we'd watch a butcher. No, I submit to you, ladies and gentlemen, that if this is what the Studio programs for our pleasure, we should find our pleasures elsewhere. Let's start today, shall we? Right here, right now, let's begin a new era. Or, you know what? Better yet, let's go back to what works. The grand old days, as they say. We had a Golden Age of innocence, once, programmed by our best, most trusted friends.

"What happened, hmm? The Studio wants you to believe that *we* changed, not it. That we wanted grit and murder on TV, instead of seven lovely ladies giving us their all each and every season, year in and year out. The truth is, the Studio couldn't keep up the hits. They flagged and faded and gave us grim instead of glorious. I mean," and here he gestured at Aluel, "what's that about?"

The curtain rasped back around, concealing Aluel's mangled glory. As the camera zoomed out to reveal the curtain and its frame, the whole apparatus being elevated on a portion of floor that was revealed as a wheeled platform, Gar waved his clipboard at Kutri.

"Get ready," he said.

On stage, Staley said, "I would like to introduce a man who gets it, folks, he really does. And he knows what must be done! First, though, how about a palate cleanser?"

Backstage, Aluel and her apparatus were abandoned between the pink curtain visible to the audience and a painted backdrop. Under Gar's direction, Kutri reached this corridor around the same time. She stood face-to-what-was-left-of-face with Aluel. Awed and appalled to be so close to the idol, at first she could only stare. Ashamed of herself, she dipped her head. Aluel stayed frozen, staring vaguely over Kutri's shoulder. Possibly, Aluel misunderstood the greeting as a refusal to see her clearly. In any case, she remained as she was.

The clipboard jabbed Kutri's ribs. "Go on," said Gar.

Music was playing. Something tinkled, like bells. Kutri thought she heard a sitar. Gar shoved her at the curtain. At her approach, the heavy fabric twitched aside. Kutri passed through, entering stage left as the gap in the middle of the curtain, through which Aluel had gone, closed.

At center stage, Staley was gasping. He said, "There she is, folks. The source of our recent panic, the center of dread. Ladies and gentlemen, I am proud to present Miss Kutri Chandigarh!"

There was nothing Kutri could do but cross the stage in the direction Gar was pointing. She thought of her favorite candidates from years gone by, trying to mirror their poise. Karan Politis was the gold standard in this, as she was in all things besides sisterly support, so it was her face Kutri pictured as she swished her peacock gown across the gold and pink striations.

Over the years, at least a fifth of her waking hours had been spent picturing this moment. It was over in three seconds. All she could think while it lasted was how she wished she could see herself.

Afterward, the moment left hardly a trace in her memory. There was only the conviction she had done it badly. Her high heels had clicked too loudly. Everyone had seen her stumble as she swirled past her name. Fame was fleeting, and she had bungled it at the beginning, on the very day she expected it would end.

The director of Bliss appeared not to have noticed the stumble. He beamed, though not quite at Kutri. Instead, Dr. Staley made eye contact with a camera was over her shoulder. From the place that had been chosen for her, Kutri could see the glass eye of another camera darkening and brightening as its operator adjusted its zoom. The mechanical indifference of the machine gave her a chill. She managed to suppress her shiver and freeze a pleasant expression.

Staley said, "It's a miracle, don't you agree? How did our leaders, the executives of Little Angel Studio, fail to find this little peach? Why did her rescue have to fall on the Offices of Bliss, State, Justice, Finance, and Records? I'll tell you. The rot starts up top. Did you know I was in school with our so-called president?

"Little Gerry Flynn, as we called him, was on his way in while yours truly was getting ready to graduate. I remember him tugging up his trousers as he tottered down the hall. It couldn't have been easy, going from room to room without a belt like that. He did get good grades, though. He'd have to. He was such a pet of the teachers, doing favors all the time. Who knew, back then, he would prove such a disappointment? I mean, some of us guessed. But we didn't know. There was one who knew, and knew very well, the sort of disaster Little Gerry would prove to be. Let us greet him now, this visionary, this masterful man whose insight, folks, may save us still."

The stage right of the curtain twitched. Ex-president Schuyler was rolled out. Ellis was pushing his wheelchair, with the help of an artificial arm. Instead of setting the brake and stepping aside, he continued standing behind the chair after making the delivery. He really had no choice. The arm was without a hand. It was attached to both the strut and the chair.

"Here he is," said Staley. "The man who never disappoints. Ask any of his wives, eh? He's a natural born leader, a man with decades of leadership experience. The divine Miss Kutri comes to us today, ladies and gentlemen, thanks to the leadership of this man. We have asked him to serve as our special guest tiebreaker in today's competition. More importantly, he's here as executive producer of our broadcast. I put it to you, why should not a man like him lead us through the season? We *need* leaders like Mr. Jon Schuyler. Much better him than a beltless limp sack like my old school chum, Gerry Flynn."

He went on to explain how Schuyler had overseen a dozen record seasons of *Good Breeding* before being forced into an illegal, unnecessary retirement by the Studio board. Here was a man who had led the New Society to its highest heights, who had been the architect of so much excellent TV, and he was treated so badly. It was shameful.

"Ladies and gentlemen," Staley said, "a round of applause for our great leader, Jon Schuyler. May his producer credits never end!"

Canned applause played over the public address system. Jon lifted his last remaining limb to give a royal wave. He had a confident smile that was a complement to Staley's resurgent smirk. Their performance had been rehearsed, clearly. It was plain they had been planning this moment far longer than Kutri had been in the city. Years longer, given what Mitsuru had told her about the extra hatchetmen. These men had embezzled children from the Los Angeles Houses of Care and raised them into young adulthood, assembling an army.

She thought back to her kidnapping, an affair carried out by a man dressed as a hatchetman. He was aided by another man, the man she'd killed, and a man she guessed, from his build, must have been an operative of the Office of State. Alec Simmons was a justiceman. And hadn't he said a friend from Records had aided in his acquisition of the phones?

They were all connected, these monsters, these men. Simmons was a bishop in the chess game. Her caller-kidnapper was a knight. Mitsuru was a knight as well, or rather the other bishop, as he stood close to the king and queen. That king and queen were the two aged men now gabbing on stage. It didn't matter which was which. What was important was that they viewed her as a pawn. That attitude alone was enough to ensure they were her enemies.

Staley stooped before the ex-president and asked, "Jon, would you say a few words before we bring in the rest of our candidates? Perhaps you'd like to opine on the failures of the current administration to protect its vulnerable citizens." He glanced meaningfully at Kutri, then at the flowers in Cuc Tien's place.

The wheelchair-bound ancient coughed, as if about to speak. Staley pulled the microphone away.

"Oh, forgive me, Jon. I forgot my manners. Before he answers, can someone please fetch a water for the president?"

The bland look on Jon's face was telling. This was part of the act. Letting the microphone hang at the end of his arm, Staley watched the curtain, waiting to be obeyed. The wait was so short it could not have been spontaneous. Mere seconds elapsed before Mitsuru emerged from behind the curtain with a glass in his hand.

He was wearing a kimono, but only light makeup. In full geisha regalia, he would have been hard to recognize. The clean demeanor, though feminine, was easy to see through.

Staley said, "Thank you, most excellent assistant." He grabbed the wrist of the hand holding the glass and pulled Mitsuru into a side hug. Turning to the camera, he introduced the youth. "This is M, dear friends. Been with me for years. Thank you again, M."

The moment Staley let go, Mitsuru hurried away. The exchange could not have been more awkward, but Staley seemed delighted with how it had gone. Instead of handing the glass to Schuyler, he tossed it away, over his shoulder. It smashed, with a tinkling splash, near the edge of the stage. Straightening up, he turned his back on the patriarch.

"Now, where were we?"

Chapter Twenty-Five: Past Time

Brothers of the City of Angels, hear!
We've been buried long enough.
Death pays the wages for sin, they say.
I tell you, the debt is long paid off.
It was paid by our fathers' fathers,
Or their fathers further back.
We, the living, must live free,
Apart from this living death,
This solitary hunger, in isolation,
Watching beauty behind a glass.

It is past time, brothers, to cast off
The chains long rusted, kept in remembrance
Of a heavy burden, not our own.
We must leave the World Before
In the soil, where it belongs.
Leave, too, the New Thing,
Put in its place by the slaves of death.
I call on you, this day,
To take up The Life,
To live and rejoice in hope.

Brothers! Never was freedom won by—

"**C**ut!" said Antoine Huxley.

It wasn't the first time he had said it, but the first time Jakob heard. He had been reciting, with passion, the eternal words of Sven Thomson, the light in darkness, La Vie in death.

A woman in scavenged, red hatchetman armor stood close to Jakob. A burly stateman stood at the door leading out to the hall. The door was partly opened, because after blowing its lock with some sort of explosive, the stateman said it wouldn't close fully again. Antoine stood at a console, his head obscuring one of the many screens attached to walls around the broadcast control room.

"Sorry," said Antoine. "You're not going out. There's interference. Not from the Studio. I could stop anything they put out from here. This is somebody else."

He stepped away from the console, which was identical to several others in the room, so far as Jakob could tell. There were no bodies draped over this one, no splashes of blood from the fight that had reduced the dozen fighters Antoine had rallied to four, counting the chemist and Jakob himself. Apart from lack of bodies and bodily fluids, there was nothing to show the console was special, yet from it Antoine was supposed to be in control of the Studio's entire network of repeaters and other devices that sent their programs around the globe.

Jakob stepped to the side, trying see past Antoine's head to what was on the blocked screen.

"Whoa," said Antoine. "Don't bother. Stay behind your mic. I'll put it up." With a touch of a button, he made other screens flicker to life.

The screens showed the stage of the Wilshire Hilton Ballroom. In front of the pink curtain, standing on a pink and gold floor, was a cluster of figures. Either there wasn't any sound or Antoine hadn't found the volume, and the shot was too wide for Jakob to recognize anybody in the cluster. But the woman who stood yards away in a flowing, peacock ballgown was the center of his world.

He said, "Is this live?"

The screens flashed white and flickered. The stateman at the door fired his pistol into the hall. He leaned against the door with his shoulder, shouting for the woman in armor. She ran and sat, sliding her back against the door. Her boots fought for traction.

"Is it live?" Jakob said.

"I don't know," said Antoine.

"I have to go to her."

"You've got a speech to give."

"What's the point if you can't get it out?"

Antoine set aside the buzz box backpack. It didn't do anything against any of the Studio types in the Broadcast Central. That was why so many were dead.

"We'll record it," said Antoine. "I'll flash a signal. There are codes you don't know. Somebody will cut this thing, then I'll get you on air."

Jakob warred with himself. He peered at Kutri, so small there on the screen. In his mind's eye, Sven's sunken face swam in front of her image, followed by a vision of Nat throwing Mella's gift.

He said, "Fine. Do it in one take."

"Just a sec," said Antoine. He punched buttons. "Ready. Three . . . two . . . one!"

"Brothers of the City of Angels—"

All over the control room, the screens flickered, then shone bright white. An attention signal blared. The assault force four covered their ears. On screen, the second most famous face in the world appeared. President Flynn was pale against the dark background, but the red in his cheeks made it clear he was furious.

"Freeman!" he said, almost a scream. Unlike the attention signal, his voice came not from the screens but straight through to people's cochleas via Jakob's implant. "I know you can hear me. I hope it hurts."

It did. Jakob could tell by the way the other men winced that they were hurting as well. The woman fighter looked confused, but she didn't forget her job. She pressed her back against the door harder than ever as someone outside shook it, trying to break in.

"I know what you want," said the president. "Your friend, on screen, made it clear. I don't know why you're here, instead of with him, and I don't care. Give me back what's mine, Freeman, and I'll make you a deal. Understand? Give back my— Give me back what's mine and you can have amnesty. If you don't, if you hurt someone you shouldn't, I'll make you suffer. I swear, I'll make you and every one of your rebel friends beg for death before it comes."

He waved a white leather glove, cueing the camera to zoom out. The background he had been standing against was the plaque in the courthouse square, the opposite side from where Nat had said his last words. The gunfight in the square was finished. A fresh squad of red hatchetmen stood around a knot of La Vie survivors. No one seemed to notice the dead scattered on the fake grass.

Lucas was at the front of the knot of survivors. Not one to waste time, Flynn went over and belted him in the jaw. The bodyguard hardly flinched, but he did bleed. His hands were behind his back, evidently cuffed, or Jakob was sure he would have snapped the president's neck. Instead, Lucas spat in Flynn's face.

The closest red hatchetman raised a weapon. Flynn held up a glove.

"Everything you've done so far can be fixed, Freeman. The property damage and the lost personnel? Trivial. Send a message to your lieutenant. Tell him not to do anything foolish. You and I will go by air. Once we make the exchange, you can walk away. You and all your friends. Take the women, if you like. Take whatever you want."

The screens went black. Jakob's implant went silent. Antoine and the other man turned toward him, expectation on their faces. Jakob spoke first.

"What does he want from me? Antoine, Nat said there was a history. I don't remember. After my wife died, I scrubbed most of our lives with Aremoden. Do you know what I did to Flynn, what I took from him? Tell me. I need to understand."

Antoine shook his head. "I'm sorry. I knew there was something Nat and Rachel were keeping back. I don't know the details. What do you think Flynn meant about a lieutenant?"

The screens gave an answer, though it took a moment for Jakob to understand what he was seeing. After a flicker, the silent scene of a Presentation Ball reappeared. The camera had moved on. It was no longer focused on the cluster of people but on one man, director of the Office of Bliss, Clyde Staley. He stood at center stage, talking into a microphone as Elise Dupain, the candidate with impressive legs, made an entrance from stage left.

"It's him," said Jakob. "*Clyde Staley* is the lieutenant."

"I know him," said Antoine. "The head of Bliss."

"My colleague," said Jakob. "Dr. Clyde Staley. Flynn thinks I'm in charge of the revolution, and he thinks Staley is one of us. Why? What's he doing?"

Antoine said, "You tell me. Is he holding something for you, something Flynn wants?"

Staley was applauding. He had finished his praise of Elise and was introducing the next candidate, Viola Wimmer. She entered and strutted toward her place before stopping. With pantomimed drama, Staley slapped the back of his hand to his forehead, pretending he had forgotten something important. He made apologetic gestures to the camera, which pivoted to show shards of glass in a puddle of water.

The picture snapped back to Staley in time to see him straighten and give a command. In too rapid an answer, a geisha approached from backstage, carrying a broom and towel. The appearance of Mitsuru gave Jakob a chill. Not that it should have been a surprise. The youth was everywhere.

Jakob told Antoine, "I don't know."

But he had a guess what President Flynn wanted. The dying words of Alec Simmons came back to him: *Flynn wants . . . Mitsu. For your sins, Freeman, take care . . .*

"I'm taking the deal," said Jakob. "How long can you give me before you flash a signal?"

The door gave at that moment. The stateman and the woman in armor were thrown back. Red hatchetmen charged in, weapons raised.

"Take me to Flynn," Jakob called to them. "No one dies, and this man stays where he is. No one bothers him, understand? I'm adding that to Flynn's deal."

Antoine stiffened, but he didn't object.

"Tell Flynn what I said," Jakob commanded.

"You can't trust him," said Antoine.

"I trust you," said Jakob. "Give me as long as you can."

A nod passed between the two men. That was all the time they had. President Flynn's voice broke in on their implants, accepting Jakob's terms. He marched off with the red hatchetmen.

Chapter Twenty-Six: The Villainess

Music, dancing, and sparkling lights failed to work their magic on what should have been Kutri's night. To be fair, it was near morning and her cheeks had long ago gone numb from pinning on a fake smile. Sweeping her back into the fantasy that was the Presentation Ball might have been possible, even with two candidates absent—one dead—and no Studio audience, if she had been less focused on was happening outside the ballroom walls.

Where was Jakob? Her conviction that Dr. Staley was her enemy filled her with fear for Jakob's well-being. The doctor had charmed her, initially, with his silly talk, but she was fully prepared now to believe him a wolf in sheep's clothing. That he was hard-hearted was no shock. Any man who could slice off bits of himself would not scruple to slice others who had slipped from his affection. He had played her, played Jakob, and played God-knew-how-many others, in a game whose purpose she could barely guess at.

She knew it had something to do with power. Specifically, the doctor wanted Schuyler in and Flynn out. He had raised an army of hatchetmen, partnered with Simmons and her kidnapper, and likely arranged for the assault on Aluel, all in an effort to bring about the substitution. Surely there were elements of improvisation in the doctor's plan, but what of it? The important fact was that he was her enemy, a callous manipulator who cared nothing for the casualties he left in his wake.

Her turn came to be on the dance floor. As she gave her hand to a clumsy suitor, she turned off her smile in favor of aloof boredom. The suitor didn't notice. He cared more about her breasts and the inches of torso her gown left exposed than he did her face. With a tug, he got her twirling. Based on how he moved, he had certainly never heard Mahia music in all his life. The upbeat tune was all flute pipes and cymbals, but he sloshed around to it like a drunk dancing to a fiddle.

By squinting, she may have found the guy passable as a Hindustani. In reality, though, she doubted he could have found her part of the world on a map. So much for the conscientious vetting of the Los Angeles Office of Bliss. This man, and the other suitors, might as well have been picked by lottery. They were all ugly idiots, none of whom she would have dreamt of making the father to her children. Or perhaps it was simply that none of them were Jakob Freeman.

The folk song ended. Something different began. A bass line like a rhythmic rubber ball, bouncy and insistent, pulsed with a scratchy, up-tempo backbeat. The ringing female voice told a tale at odds with the buoyant rhythm, the tale of a woman trying to be her own person in a male-dominated world. It was anthemic—half roar of exhaustion, half battle cry.

The lyric made Kutri wonder what perverse imp had prompted someone to select it, but also to ponder the reality the song dredged up for inspection. If women were the prize, the gems, the essential piece of a society, why was the world not theirs to control or at least partner in control? It made her wonder if there was any part of the world in which that partnership was practiced. She already knew that New Delhi's reality was different from LA's. What other realities might exist beyond the city's A-Rad Wall?

As the song played, Kutri danced away from her suitor. The other women and suitors took the floor for the final frolic. Each candidate had danced with all three suitors already, after which there had been a brief intermission to take phone-in votes. A medley from Cuc Tien's homeland had played during the break, then each candidate had danced with the two suitors who survived the voting while the eliminated man left.

Kutri remembered loving the dance portions from past seasons of *Good Breeding*. She had danced along at the Bliss Center until sweat stood out on her flesh. In person, the dancing was a chore. At least her exercise had prepared her to weather the storm. Viola and Pania, the least fit of her fellow candidates, stood clutching their sides as soon as the music stopped. Kutri was winded but stood upright.

She raised an eyebrow to Elise, hoping to share a moment. The giantess was barely out of breath. Instead of returning Kutri's glance, she sniffed. What a snob the woman was! In a normal season of *Good Breeding*, she would have been set up to make guest appearances as a villainous fitness instructor or some such. Spurned by an audience who preferred Kutri's exotic looks, she would be determined to get revenge for her loss. Alas, her scripted rise and fall would never happen.

"Wasn't that a blast?" said Staley from the stage. "That concludes the bouncy bounce portion, I'm afraid. Back when the Studio was running the show, they used to break in at this point to show you the news. I'm sure we've all seen the threads of society fray. What's the point in watching society unravel? Instead, let's bring M back, shall we? We'll have a show this time. Come out, M!"

Nothing convinced Kutri of Mitsuru's importance more than Staley's frequent excuses to get him on camera. Who was watching the youth so avidly? She feared for him almost as much as she feared for Jakob. She would take Mitsuru with her, she decided, as soon as she got a chance to get away.

The candidates left the dance floor. On the backstage screens, Kutri watched Mitsuru begin some sort of dance that involved twirling lights at the ends of short lengths of cord. As she watched, the stylists unwound the top of her gown and hauled the skirt portion from her hips. Stripped to brassiere and slip, she went to the washroom to sponge away sweat.

She met Elise along the way. They did not collide, but the tall woman rebounded as if they had. When Kutri opened her mouth to ask what she meant by it, Elise put a finger to her lips, giving a look more furtive than angry.

In a tone completely at odds with that look, she said loudly, "Why don't you watch where you go?"

A line of Staley's hatchetmen stood between the main screen and the washroom door. They should have been keeping an eye on all the candidates, but were clearly not. Elise nodded at the last in the line as Pania, who had approached the stylists once Kutri had departed, was stripped from her gown. The garment zipped in the front. As Kutri watched, a stylist pulled its top portion behind Pania's shoulders, exposing round, glistening breasts.

Even with their helmets on, it was clear where the hatchetmen were looking. For the moment, everyone but Pania was invisible. Elise's hand closed around Kutri's wrist, and her face was a plea for silence.

Letting herself be drawn along, Kutri ran with the giantess.

The backstage area held no end of corridors. More swiftly than Kutri would have thought possible, she and Elise left the ballroom behind. They were in a dark corner of the hotel, facing a window. Elise made a gesture toward it.

"Look," she said.

There was nothing remarkable about the view. A road led between overgrown piles of trash. Between two of the piles, a single large palm tree endured. Past this landmark, one could glimpse a few buildings of the city.

Kutri said, "What is it you wish me to see?"

Elise touched the glass, which was dusty on the outside but clean within. "There, in the middle distance. You see that spotlight?"

Her voice had softened. So had her accent. The arrogance that would have made her a good TV villainess was gone.

"Where?" said Kutri. "Oh, yes. I see it flashing."

"A signal," said Elise. "A warning. I counted the flashes. 'Ready,' it says. 'Wait. Ready 3223.'"

"What does that mean?"

"It means the men will fall quiet for a time. Then there will be danger."

"From the men?"

"The men with working implants, yes. They'll freeze for some minutes. When they are free again, they will be wild with violence. You remember the wedding of Aluel?"

Kutri shuddered. "How could I forget? But how do you know this, Elise?"

"The light is from my allies." The tall woman drew back her shoulders. "We are fighters for freedom. For life."

This last declaration drew a gasp from Kutri. "Do you know a man named Jimmy Ching? Or Jakob? Do you know Jakob Freeman?"

"Later," said Elise. "We must go, quickly."

Aside from Jakob, on the occasion when she had first seen him from the limo, Kutri had found nothing so alluring in all her life. Elise could lead her to safety. Between her, and Jimmy, and Kutri's own determination, she was sure she could be reunited with Jakob. They could escape, perhaps to the outlands, though not unarmed, and have children, a rocking chair—her new dream. The prospect was infinitely preferable to staying trapped in the lion's den.

She let temptation thrill through her for a moment, then said, "I can't. Not without Mitsuru, the one Dr. Staley calls M."

Elise rolled her eyes. Not all her attitude was an act. "He will be like the others. Frozen, then dangerous. We can't take a man."

Kutri was far from satisfied, but Elise seemed firm on the point. She said, "What about Pania, and Viola? Will you go back for them?"

"There's no time. I tell you, we must go."

"I'm sorry. I can't."

Elise glared at her intently. The glare became a stare and arrived at last at empathy. "Tell me, is there someone you love? No, don't say. I see it in you. You must go for your love's sake, if not your own."

I have killed a man, Kutri reminded herself. Aloud she said, "My love is why I can't go. I saw him take a blow for a stranger. Here, on the head. He wouldn't leave a friend."

"*Je suis une imbécile*," murmured Elise. "I'm a fool. Fine. We'll go back. With luck, we won't be missed. You warn this M. I'll warn the others. Be ready to flee at a moment's notice. At the latest, we must go when the paralysis hits."

"When will that be?"

Though no part of Kutri obscured the living skyscraper's vision, she craned her neck before answering, "This signal is a warning, as I said. The crisis will come, but when, who can say?"

"When it does, I'll be ready," said Kutri.

Elise sniffed as if in doubt.

***

The disappearance of half the bridal candidates did not go unnoticed. If a hatchetman had spotted Kutri and Elise returning, he might have asked questions. Gar, thankfully, was too frazzled to do anything but thump his clipboard.

"There you are," he hissed. "Go. Go!"

Kutri, who was a little cold in her slip and brassiere, was galloped through wardrobe. She was thrust into a billowy white skirt and had the bra swapped out for an earth-toned corset. A metal choker, gold plate with thin chains, was strapped around her neck. She found herself in the wings again, waiting to be hustled on stage.

The talent portion of the competition was in full swing. Pania's remaining suitors were trying to make her laugh, evidently. One man was down on a knee, belting out a confusing song about not having thrown up with his friends for too long. The other man was trying to juggle, of all things. He was failing badly.

Staley cued Pania with his eyes. She rose from her gilded chair and plucked the juggler's balls from the air. As she exited stage right, she tossed the balls over her shoulder.

"Doesn't she handle them skillfully?" suggested Staley, triggering the canned applause. "Get your votes in, pals and gals at home. Only one suitor will get to stand with the match bride today, though we'll have the rest back for funsies. Punch the buttons to put your favorites on top. While you're calling in, we'll bring out our next candidate. Once lost, now found, if she was water, we'd all love to be drowned. Put your hands together for Miss Kutri!"

There was more canned applause. Leaping forward to avoid Gar's clipboard, Kutri nearly tripped, but she caught her balance in time to enter gracefully. Staley was beaming. For an instant, she forgot he was a cold-hearted cobra, swaying to lure her to sleep before the strike. Before she could cross to him, something peculiar occurred that she would not understand for some minutes.

A second after her entrance, the pitch of the applause shifted to a low, regular thrum beneath the sharp claps. Staley surreptitiously glanced at the ceiling while Kutri herself stopped to determine what was happening. The clapping stopped. The thrumming continued, becoming louder and more insistent, settling into a low-pitched drone.

For a moment, the drone was all that could be heard. The moment was followed by a shout, and a blast. Gunshots, like a thousand of Mitsuru's pebbles clacking against the pavement all at once, sounded from outside. Staley slapped his natural right hand into the artificial left.

"Finally," he said. "The *real* show."

The camera crew and the candidates were all too frightened to take offense.

Chapter Twenty-Seven: Savage Release

In the middle of an intersection, near Jakob's old school, was an object called a helicopter. It was only an antique shell when he and the other schoolboys had found it on a fateful field day, but the crushed metal and yellowed glass of the dome had haunted Jakob's dreams ever since. Round and insectile, the misshapen lump had resembled none of the wrecks young Jakob was used to seeing scattered around. He had wondered what it could be. Later, when he found out it was not some kind of warped camper van but the remains of a functional aircraft, the shock left him stunned to the core.

It was Sven who showed him a propaganda film about a more angular version of the whirlybird. The craft had crashed in an urban war zone and the survivors had to fight for their lives. Jakob remembered little of the film's plot, but the image of a flying attack chopper soon joined his dreams of the childhood wreck. Both floated and dipped in the copper sky he conjured at night. By day, after he first saw the film, he spent several lunch hours studying the sky, past the mag-shielding and the upper stories of ruined buildings, trying to spot dark shapes propelling themselves with tilted blades or hovering ominously, like unburdened krows. Of course, he never saw any, since helicopters had gone as extinct as dinosaurs long before he was born.

So when President Flynn showed him to a helicopter, parked coincidentally in an intersection of backlot streets, Jakob had a hard time hiding his amazement. Some of his surprise showed through to the pilot, who narrowed his eyes. If Flynn noticed the flicker of fascination, he gave no sign. All the Studio president's attention was focused on achieving his goal, which he outlined to Jakob on their dreamlike ride.

By the time their helicopter, which was the last of five like it flying in an inverted wedge, reached Beverly Hills, Jakob had to sit on his hands to keep them from shaking. Nothing Flynn mumbled made sense, but his words had a way of stirring memories. Jakob had forgotten so much, it was troubling, but more troubling was the shape of what he had started to remember.

As he watched red hatchetmen from the leading helicopters drop on lines to the cracked pavement in front of the Hilton, Jakob felt a crazed impulse to cheer them on. They were not just soldiers of the enemy assaulting a hotel. They were echoes of his will invading the void where years of his life had been scrubbed away.

He turned to yell at Flynn. The whirring blades were so loud, this was the only way to be heard. "You'll really let me take Kutri?"

Since the president was speaking through a mic implanted in his jawbone, there was no need for him to raise his voice.

"Give me what I want and you can take the world," he said.

A light lit up on the pilot's console. The pilot listened to his headphones, then raised a thumb to the president. The president returned the gesture.

Blades slowing but still making too much noise for speech, the helicopter set down in a tornado of dust. Twin lines of red hatchetmen stood before the Hilton's entrance, forming a corridor. Flynn leapt from the helicopter and stomped past the dry fountain that cars had to skirt on their way to the entrance. The president didn't duck or lower his head, showing no awe of the helicopter. Though Jakob could see feet of space between his neck and the rotating blades, he hunched like an old man as he followed.

They stopped in the lobby. Red hatchetmen were stationed at all the exits, while one knelt on top of the desk, keeping watch. Bodies were strewn on the floor. Two of the dead were non-red hatchetmen. One was a bodyguard. Jakob thought of Mondt for the first time in hours.

A red hatchetman approached from the lobby's far end, dragging someone. The dragged man wore no helmet, though he was dressed in black. As he got closer, Jakob saw his outfit was a tuxedo. He also saw the man was missing an arm.

"Ellis?" he said.

The servant looked up. "Hello, sir."

The red hatchetman let go of Ellis, who got to his knees.

He said, "I have a message."

"No messages," said Flynn. "Get him out of here. If I get what I want, he lives. If not—" He made a cutting gesture across his own throat. At Flynn's signal, the man who had dragged Ellis in started to drag him out.

"That was more or less it," called Ellis. "That and a special knock. I'll do the knock myself."

When he was out of earshot, Jakob rounded on Flynn.

"Whatever happens," Jakob said, "you'll be careful about the women, right?"

"If I get what I want," said Flynn, "they'll be safe."

"And if you don't?"

"No promises." Flynn's mouth gave a twitch. He added, "*Every daughter's a gem.* You may think I'm lying, but I believe that. Always have."

"How can you say that," asked Jakob, "when you tried to make Kirimi Teng murder his bride?"

"You thought that was me?" said Flynn. He laughed. "We knew Teng's plan, of course. His speech would have been top-flight television. Think of the ratings! We would have given him a minute before we shut him down. A broken kneecap later and we could have had a debate cycle on News Two and Four. You know the lefties love Four. They're always talking about having a voice, how the press has to be free so opinions can get out. We test-screened what we guessed the speech would be. The numbers for the urban demographic would have been huge. So, of course we wanted Teng to go through with it. What went on air beat our projections by a long shot. What Teng did was ratings gold."

Struck breathless by this speech, Jakob had to pant to get his lungs going. "You—the Studio—you didn't program Teng to attack Aluel?"

"Course not. If we had known the ratings we could get, maybe we would have. I mean, my fault for hiring hacks, but my writers would never have come up with something that great."

The watchman on the desk said, "Mr. President."

From the far end of the lobby, to which Ellis had been dragged, a knot of chromeheads approached. They stopped ten feet from Flynn and stepped to either side. Dr. Staley and Kutri stood revealed.

"Jakob," said Kutri. She started forward, paused, saw no one was about to stop her, and ran the rest of the way.

He lifted her into his arms and kissed her, feeling her arms around his neck. Everyone else vanished from the room. For seconds that felt like minutes, they were the only two people in the world.

The first person who came back to Jakob's consciousness was not in the lobby. He was not even real anymore. An inch outside the circle of bliss that contained him and Kutri, Nat stepped out of an imaginary mist. His essence was solid, not like a ghost. Mella, who walked beside him, was slightly faded but still in color.

When Sven appeared, with a gray complexion, Jakob lost his hold on Kutri and set her down. The Sven of his conscience shimmered, nearly transparent. Before the specter faded away, he mouthed three words that almost broke Jakob: *I love you*. Taking Kutri by the arm, Jakob stood between President Flynn and Director of Bliss Staley.

"Murderers," he said. "Men have died in this fight. At least one woman has died. She was a good, courageous woman and a good man's wife. I want answers, now. The president tells me he didn't turn Kirimi Teng against his bride. Who did? And who killed Sven?"

Dr. Staley arched an eyebrow. "Sorry, is that a mystery? Teng turned Teng. Sven killed Sven."

"No," said Jakob. "Impossible."

Staley said, "It makes perfect sense to me. Kirimi was imbalanced. Sven too, in his way. He saw the fault in Kirimi, the twist in him that made him go bad. Shame on poor Sven for keeping it to himself. The results paved the way to his bitter end."

"I don't believe you," said Jakob. "Sven overlooked nothing. He certainly would never have let a dangerous flaw in Kirimi go unresolved. What twist are you talking about?"

The doctor sighed. "They called it misogyny, back in the day. A hatred of women. It was practically universal, when there were more women to hate. My friend, Gerry, knows something about it. He used to beat his wife."

Flynn said, "That's a lie."

"Is it? She said you beat her. She put up with the kinky stuff and the whoring, but she drew the line at jabs to the kidney. Life could have been sweet if you'd stopped at a smacked bottom, Ger! All it took was meeting a boy who was kind to her and, poof, she was out of your life."

"He stole her," said Flynn. "He stole my wife and my—"

"Yes," said Dr. Staley. "About that. Do you know, if not for the child, we never would have swayed Jon Schuyler to our side?"

From her place at Jakob's side, Kutri said, "What do you mean?"

"Ah," said Staley. "There's a tale. I've given you most of it. Sure you want the rest?"

The woman Jakob loved hesitated a moment, but at last she said, "Yes."

"Well, you know," he said, "your beau is a lucky mothercutter. Some men never find love. Jakob found it three times. Maybe Gerry, there, would say four."

She appeared puzzled, but not unconcerned. "I know he loved a woman, and a man."

"Oh, at least them," said the doctor. "The woman's the key. Jakob, do you know what *President* Gerry's after?"

He didn't answer. He couldn't bring himself to.

"Yasuko was the woman," Staley continued. "It was a delightful year, the year of the Golden Season. Bliss never had it so good. Jakob was a clerk then. I took him to meet our blushing match bride, Karan, because she thought he was pretty. Well, of course, I wanted to please Karan, but ultimately she only had eyes for the prize—Quinn Politis. Her best and closest friend, though, took a shine to our Jakob immediately and wasn't about to let her eight-month marriage to an abusive Studio exec get in the way."

Veins pulsed in Flynn's forehead. He opened his mouth, but before he could interrupt, Clyde Staley continued.

"The offices were closer back then. Alec Simmons was often about. He used to wear blue suits, before his gray phase. He liked Yasuko, wanted her. I've heard him say he had her, but I doubt he ever did. He's the sort to invent stories, especially when jealous. Yasuko's heart was Jakob's from the start. He was a gentle youth; she was married to an abuser."

Jakob, who had not even been able to remember his wife's name, went hot and cold in turns as images that were barely whispers informed him they were memories. From the corner of his eye, he saw Flynn open his mouth again to protest, but no sound emerged.

Staley merely cocked an eyebrow at the Studio exec and continued his story. "It was a whirlwind romance. Youth and foolishness led to an unfortunate closeup at the Presentation Ball that made their feelings more public than they should have been. That was awkward for the office, but when Sven and I heard Yasuko's charges against her husband, we decided to fight in her corner. A man can do what he wants to his wife in the New Society, so long as he doesn't threaten her ability to bear children. Since Gerry liked to punch below the belt, he had to go. We said as much to the president, as Jon was and will be again.

"Jon didn't care for Gerry, but he was loath to turn on him without good reason. That's what I meant about the child. If it had only been Ms.

Yasuko's life at risk, who knows? Jon might have let Gerry go. As it was, he agreed he couldn't. He judged his vice president of acquisitions guilty. Gerry's pleas went nowhere with him, though they did rally his friends. Their move to depose came too late to prevent sentence. It was handed down and carried out by the time the board took action. Surely, you've noticed the gloves."

All eyes were on Staley as he said this, so no one stopped Kutri from lunging at Flynn and snatching a glove from his hand. It was the left glove, and it came away with a hiss of Velcro. Underneath was a thumb, plus a middle finger and a pinky. Two articulated dummy fingers filled the extra spaces.

"Those are nifty," said the doctor. "You must give me the name of your prosthetist, Ger."

A red hatchetman reached for Kutri. Flynn stopped him with a glance.

"Enough," said the president. "I don't care about your slander, Staley. I'm here for what's mine. Give the command, Freeman. Do your part."

In a split second, Staley's face went from puzzled, to amused, to triumphant. He bowed to Jakob. "Oh yes, dear leader. Command me. Though, if I may ask, what did you ask of the devil's pussbag, here, in exchange?"

Caught off guard, Jakob could only glance from one man to the other. His mind played back Clyde Staley's tortured explanation as he tried to spot where Teng's attack, Sven's death, and his own memory wipe fit in Staley's scheme.

Staley had introduced Jakob to Yasuko, who was being abused by her husband, Flynn. They had fallen in love, in full view of Simmons, who was more than capable of dreaming up a relationship where there was none. Whatever had happened between Simmons and Yasuko, Flynn's wife and Jakob had gotten together, been indiscreet, and been sheltered from Flynn's wrath by Dr. Staley and Sven. President Schuyler had sided with the blissmen against Flynn, ordering fingers chopped off and the marriage annulled. Eventually, it had cost him the presidency.

Nothing in this tale, or the events that spun out of it, seemed real to Jakob, any more than it explained Kirimi or Sven's actions. Could they really, as the doctor said, have acted on their own? Had he?

"Who did *this* to me?" he asked Staley, pointing to his own head. "Who took my memories?"

"You did, my boy," said the doctor. "That part of your story is true. When Yasuko died, Flynn came after you. Your solution to the situation was the Aremoden protocol. After all, you couldn't restore to poor old

Gerry what you didn't even remember you had. Let alone where you had hidden it."

"What I had?" repeated Jakob, feeling as if he'd stepped into an alternate reality. He glanced at Flynn, and so witnessed the moment the older man finally grasped the import of the conversation.

His face red with enraged realization, Flynn growled, "Freeman's not in charge."

"Not of me," said Staley. "You thought you were fighting one war, didn't you, Gerry? Studio goons on one side, Sven Thomson's merry men and women on the other. But I told Jakob already, I don't hold with revolution. Sven's friends fight for freedom. I'm a more practical man. You can't fight two wars at once, Gerry. That's a sure way to defeat. So be practical. I have what you want. You have what I want. It's a big ask, I know, but would you please make me God and drop dead?"

Gun metal rattled on both sides.

"Wait," said Flynn, calling for calm with his abbreviated hand. "No one has to die today. Least of all, me. Bring her out, Staley, and you can walk away."

Staley said, "Why would I, when I'm winning?"

"She? She who?" asked Kutri.

"A moment, dear," said Staley. "We're nearly finished. Gerry?"

The president looked like his skin was about to tear and something inhuman break out from the inside. He gritted his teeth, clenched his fists, and stomped his feet. He did everything a kid having a tantrum would do but fall down and pound the floor.

At last, he said, "You'll regret this, Staley. I swear, I'll have you gelded. Fine. You want power for your puppet? Give me the paperwork. I'll sign. Jon Schuyler, acting president of Little Angel Studio and the Municipality of Los Angeles. Let him destroy this doomed revolution. It is real, eh? Not one of your tricks?"

"Very real," said Staley, "I assure you. I'm glad you see sense. And I do have paperwork, of course. I'll just add a bit, if you don't mind. Jakob may think ill of me, and dear Kutri too, but I wish them no ill. You will let them go, without a fuss, in addition to the terms I have written?"

Flynn shrugged. "What else could I do? You'll be in charge. These men"—he motioned toward the red hatchetmen—"are loyal to me. We'll leave as a group. What happens to your blissman and his woman is none of my business. I have to see her first, though, before we put ink on paper. You can't deny me that."

The doctor, beaming, gave a short bow. "Indeed I can't. Thanks for being reasonable, Ger. Kutri, time to answer your question."

He nodded to a hatchetman at the back of his escort. That man signaled someone down the hall. Kutri wrapped her arms around Jakob. They waited together, holding each other.

Standing on tiptoe to draw close to his ear, Kutri whispered, "I saw a signal sent by spotlight. 3223."

Barely remembering to keep his voice down, Jakob said back, "Where did you hear that?"

"You know what it means?"

"Yes," he said. "We have to get out of here."

Chapter Twenty-Eight: The Blessing

Ellis entered the lobby, leading a small squad of Clyde Staley's hatchetmen. When they broke formation, Mitsuru could be seen standing behind at the back, on his own. The geisha outfit was still pristine, despite the strenuous dancing the youth had done.

Jakob whispered to Kutri, "Are you sure the message was 3223?"

"Yes," she said, fearful of the sudden pallor of Jakob's face.

The men standing close to Mitsuru, though they were supposedly on the same side, were pointing their guns at him. Mitsuru didn't appear to notice. His eyes were on Jakob.

"Come to me, Mitsu," said President Flynn. When no one moved, he added, "Staley, make him come."

Staley said, "I'm not his jailer. I tried to be, but it didn't take." He shifted position, opening a path between Mitsuru and the president. Only Kutri and Jakob remained standing in that path.

Ellis raised the briefcase in his hand. "Papers, Staley."

"Hmm?" said the doctor. "Oh, excellent." He waved the server forward. "As I said, I'm not M's jailer, Gerry, but I'll put in a good word once you sign."

The president's face burned. "Give me a pen."

Ellis moved so calmly, Kutri could almost have forgotten the guns on both sides. She watched Ellis move past Flynn to the unmanned concierge's counter near the hotel's front doors, shaking the briefcase to show it contained what was needed. He placed the briefcase on the desk, opened it, and turned to hand Flynn a pen.

At the other end of the room, Mitsuru mumbled something.

Staley said, "What's that, M?"

Loudly, this time, Mitsuru said, "I'm not going with him, whatever you say."

Staley tilted his head and splayed his hands in a gentle plea. "Oh, be reasonable, M."

Emotion made Mitsuru's voice tremble. "I want to go with my father!"

Ignoring the guns, he launched himself the remaining distance to dive into Jakob's arms. Kutri could only stand aside and stare. Whatever she had expected Jakob might have that Gerard Flynn might want, this young person was not it.

Caught off guard and off balance, Jakob took Mitsuru by the shoulders and held him at arm's length. "You!" he said, as if meeting someone he had not seen for a long time.

Flynn spun on a heel. "*I'm* your father, Mitsu," he snarled.

"I want *him*," Mitsuru spat. "I hate you!"

"Now, M," said Staley. "Don't be nasty. Gerry, remember your temper. No need to chew through your lip."

Dawning joy spread across Jakob's face. Still holding Mitsuru by the shoulders, he said, "I remember now. You're Mitsu. Yasuko's daughter." And he hugged the girl to his chest.

Flynn said, furious, "Leave her, Freeman. She's nothing to you."

"You're nothing," said Mitsuru. "He took care of me. He loved Mom. You never did either of those things."

Dr. Staley tried to get the president's attention by tapping the paper on the desk. "Contract, Gerry. Affirms your retirement, gets Jon out of his. I've put in a clause that makes you guardian of a certain young runaway. The Studio took her from you when it took your fingers. Lucky for you, my office says she's great breeding stock. She needs a protector. Why not you? Sign and initial, it's all a done deal."

"I'll never be his," said the person in Jakob's arms.

"Come now, Gerry," said Staley. "What were you hoping for in this reunion? You'll have to build trust, but all things come in time. For now, sign."

In answer, Flynn snarled. He lifted the contract and, for a moment, paused like he would scrunch it up and throw it in Staley's face.

Kutri watched the wave of tension sweep through the ranks of the hatchetmen, red-helmeted and chrome alike. Had the president really expected Mitsuru's unconditional love in exchange for his power? If so, she thought him a fool. No one could command the heart—she knew that from experience now. Yet, many fools in history had started bloodbaths on the basis of their delusions of control.

Flynn slapped the contract down. His shoulders slumped. He clicked the pen.

Glancing from Mitsu to Jakob, Kutri said, "You can't let him—"

That was when the paralysis hit. Jakob went rigid and fell to the floor. The hatchetmen behind Kutri fell, as did Ellis and Dr. Staley. President Flynn and his red hatchetmen remained on their feet, along with Kutri, who wrapped protective arms around Mitsu.

The pen struck the tile with a loud clink of metal on stone. Flynn had dropped it, in surprise at this unexpected victory. Shooting daggers via his eyes at Kutri, he took a long stride toward her and ground out a single word: "Move!"

She had no pin in her hand, no hatchet, but she lashed out at him anyway. The slap echoed off the lobby walls.

"Witch!" said the president. "Hold her. No, hit her."

Two red hatchetmen caught hold of Kutri; one pried Mitsu away from her, the other held her fast, dealing her a fisted blow above her left eye. She fell to the granite floor, landing with her face close to Jakob's. Warm blood oozed over her eye and across her forehead.

Flynn was now grappling with Mitsu. From the fierceness of her kicks, the young woman had clearly trained to defend herself. She would have won a fair fight, but the same red hatchetmen who had grabbed Kutri pinned her arms. They hefted her between them as a third man caught her legs.

Kutri tried to stand. Though Jakob's face was frozen, his stare seemed to beg her to stop. A boot met Kutri's shoulder. She was spun around, away from Jakob, so that she faced the fallen doctor. It shocked her to discover that his face was not frozen.

Quickly, though carefully, Staley's lips shaped words: *Stay down.* He sealed the advice with a wink.

Behind Kutri, Flynn said, "Take her to the bird."

"Orphan maker," said Mitsu. "Let me go!"

The lobby doors hissed open. Staley framed the words *stay down* again. He did it so intensely, it was like a silent shout.

The door hissed shut. Mitsu's screams were cut off.

"When we're in the clear, kill them," said Flynn.

Out loud, Staley said, "Ellis."

The servant appeared. He had been hidden behind a screen of hatchetman in black. In less than a second, Ellis was up on one knee, his body turned so the hollow cylinder attached to his arm strut faced the president and his murder squad. A blaze erupted from the cylinder. For an instant, Kutri thought they were all going to burn to death, but the fire was a muzzle flash, not light from a flamethrower.

The rattle of gunshots was tremendous. It was impossible to tell if Ellis was doing all the firing or if the red hatchetmen were firing back. Only as bodies began to fall did the truth become clear. Red hatchetmen jolted, flinging their arms out, and toppled to the floor. One black-clad victim tripped over Jakob. Another fell between Kutri and Staley, rolling as stray shots found his carcass.

There were thumps and screams from every direction. From behind came the crackle of shattering glass. Finally, the machine-gun rattle was fully replaced by the moans of the dying.

Flynn's voice broke through the whine in Kutri's head. "Get off!" he shouted.

From the other side of a smokescreen, Ellis said, "I'm out, Staley."

Staley said, "That's enough." His tone was positively chipper. Rising to leap over the fallen red hatchetman, he extended a hand to Kutri. She took it, allowing the doctor to help her to her feet.

Next, he crouched beside Jakob. Staley held a plastic cube in his hand. It reminded Kutri of something she had seen before. After a moment, she remembered seeing a cube like it on her second day with Jakob. Was that only a week ago?

The doctor pressed the cube to the back of Jakob's neck. He twitched, slumped. Then, growling, he lunged for Staley's throat.

"Don't . . . be . . . an ingrate," Staley said as Jakob shook him.

Kutri took Jakob's arm, said, "Leave him. It's all right."

The rage seemed to fall from him like the dust from Shiva Nataraja. As she helped him up, he murmured, "Mitsu."

"Go," said Dr. Staley, handing him the cube. "Save her, if you can." As Jakob accepted the gift, he added, "Oh, and the A-Rad Wall? It's a lie."

Kutri puzzled over the remark, but Jakob was already drawing her away toward the broken entrance. Seeing Ellis in the ruined hotel lobby, Kutri called to him, "See that Elise Dupain makes it out."

"I will," Ellis said. For a man who should have been deaf in one ear, he heard well enough. "Good luck."

Jakob ran for the door, drawing Kutri after him. They skirted a pile of dead and wounded red hatchetmen that had fallen over President Flynn. His protectors had trapped him, leaving him to choke on their blood.

The last thing Kutri saw, as she and Jakob passed through the doors that had more glass missing than not, was Staley aiming a pistol at the president's head. Smiling, he directed a blessing at the departing pair.

"May Dad in the Sky keep you," he said. "Remember what I said about the Wall. Total rubbish."

"May Brahman grant," said Kutri, "that we never see you again."

They left the Wilshire Hilton's lobby, a perfect resting place for dreams.

Chapter Twenty-Nine: A Family of Rats

Outside was a scene from a World Before action movie. A helicopter hovered some feet off the ground. To the right of the fountain, one of the red hatchetmen who had taken Mitsu was waving his arms, while his partner kept hold of her. Neither man was watching the exit. Soldiers or not, they were fleeing for their lives.

A third red hatchetman was lying in the splinters of glass in the covered entryway. He had a bullet in his back; his helmet lay on the carpet. The gleaming red metal reflected dark red blood on bright red plush. Stooping, Jakob scavenged the man's pistol.

The weapon was heavy. After Jakob found the safety, he worked it with his thumb and pressed his shoulder to an entryway pillar, to stop himself shaking. Fear surged in him as he aimed at the red hatchetman farthest away from the stepdaughter he had forgotten. Now that he remembered her, she meant more to him than anything, with the possible exception of the woman at his side.

Kutri's small, strong hands wrapped his own, calming his trembling, adjusting his aim. He squeezed the trigger three times, and the red hatchetman dropped. The hatchetman's partner turned, unholstering his weapon. Mitsu seized his arm and aimed a sweeping kick at the back of his knees. Unbalanced, he head-butted the girl, his helmet colliding with her forehead. Jakob gave a wordless shout as Mitsu crumpled at the man's feet.

Four more shots rang out. Two grazed the helicopter's glass dome. Two struck the red hatchetman in the chest and belly. He collapsed, falling nearly atop Mitsu.

Through the cockpit glass, Jakob could see the pilot's wild-eyed assessment of his own danger. He clearly had the same Carter-Schnee immunity as the red hatchetmen, but his loyalty only extended so far. Watching bullets score the protective glass pushed him past loyalty's limits. Jakob saw him haul back on the helicopter's flight stick and the bird rose, buffeting everything and everyone below with a down blast. In seconds, the impossible craft cleared the Hilton's roof and soared away. Only when it was gone did it occur to Jakob that the other four helicopters must have buzzed out at the first sign of danger.

Before his hand had stopped throbbing from the kick of the gun, Jakob was at Mitsu's side. She was stunned but breathing. He lifted her, marveling at her lightness, and told her everything would be all right. With Kutri behind him, he ran along the drive, past the line of vehicles pulled up to the red carpet.

Despite Staley's blessing, Jakob didn't trust him to let them go. Likely he had expected Jakob to die, not actually rescue Mitsu. She could still serve as leverage with Flynn, after all . . . if Clyde Staley had let Flynn live. The Studio president was at the blissman's mercy, but he might refuse to sign the contract. What would Staley do then?

"Car," said Mitsu in a shaky voice that tore at Jakob's heart. A tug from Kutri brought him to a halt.

"That's right," she said. "He drove. I mean, she drove."

"Yeah," said Mitsu. "Let me down, Dad."

"You're hurt," said Jakob.

"I'm fine."

The set to her eyes, the stubborn pride was alien to the vague, windblown memory of a child who bounced on Yasuko's hip. So many years had gone, not that the Studio or the offices would have stood by while he tried to keep hold of the little girl.

He said, "I'm so sorry I left you."

Mitsu closed her eyes, resembling somewhat more that lost child, and said, "Me too."

He set her down. She took a moment to get her balance, then led the way to the first car in line. It unlocked at her touch. They got in and wheeled around the fountain. Mitsu became Mitsuru again, for the moment, focused and slightly surly. Kutri sat behind Mitsu, in the seat diagonal to Jakob, holding his hand.

They would have gone straight out the gate of the hotel's security wall but found it blocked. Parked in the middle of the two-lane gap was a stretch

SUV limo that belonged to the Los Angeles Office of Bliss. What was left of the gate was bent around the limo's grill.

"I knew he would come," said Kutri. She flung open her door and left the car.

Mr. Mondt, the bodyguard, was slumped on the steering wheel. He must have just rammed the gate, or been on the way to ram it, when Sil's machine had done its work.

Kutri held a hand out to Jakob as he joined her beside Mondt. "The cube from Dr. Staley, please."

"It might have been too long," said Jakob, remembering that night that seemed so long ago, when he had been part of a mob that kicked a man to death.

"Too long for what?" she said.

"The Carter-Schnee lockdown. If it lasts too long, it can drive a man mad. At the wedding, it made us kill Kirimi Teng. Just now, when Clyde released me— Well, you saw. I nearly strangled him. I felt so much rage, and that was after seconds in lockdown."

Kutri tilted her head and parted her lips. Jakob expected a protest. Instead, she kissed the stitches at his hairline where the Lake Hollywood hatchetman had done his work.

"After what Dr. Staley did to you and to the people you loved," she said, "your rage was real and deserved. It's not madness to save ourselves and the people we love. That is not at all like what happened with Kirimi Teng. Love isn't evil, Jakob. You're not evil." She hesitated then said, "I killed a man trying to escape. Trying to come to you. Was that evil? Am I?"

Again, she held out the hand.

He shook his head. "No and no," he murmured and reached into his pocket for the little cube. He was puzzled for a moment when he thought he felt something else in his pocket. He could have sworn he felt the panda figurine, but he had left it in the care of Jimmy Ching.

"We can't be sure he won't hurt you," said Jakob.

"I'm sure," said Kutri.

He gave her the cube but raised the pistol.

She said, "You won't need that."

"I have to be ready."

"For me, Jakob, please. Put it away."

He did. She touched the cube to the back of Mondt's neck. Huge hands took her wrists. Making a sound in his throat, Mondt tried to haul her into the cab. Jakob started forward, drawing the pistol.

"Don't," said Kutri. "Mondt, I'm safe. Unhand me, please."

He stopped pulling, stopped growling, and lay back trembling against the seat, still with a grip on her wrists.

"I'm safe, Mr. Mondt. I'm safe."

Mondt let her go. Jakob was relieved he didn't have to kill the big man . . . or try to.

***

That night, the city burned. Not all of it, not as much as the authors of the burning had wanted, but some. Most of those authors were dead. So far as Jakob knew, only one woman and two men of La Vie remained. One of the men might be broken. The other might be a prisoner, if he was still alive.

Mondt was even quieter than usual. He had insisted on driving, but after winning that fight, he had said barely two words. Perhaps, Jakob thought, he had only a finite number and had used them all up.

They drove to the abandoned lookout off Mulholland Drive to watch the city going through its death throes—or possibly its birth throes—sheltered in the back of the SUV as rioters passed by below.

"What did Clyde mean," Jakob asked Kutri, "when he said the A-Rad Wall was a lie?"

"I think," she said, "he meant there's no radiation for the wall to keep out."

Jakob felt, for a moment, like a man who'd been deposited on an alien world. "What? How's that possible?"

"Well, there's no wall like that around New Delhi or the village I was born in. Have you never wondered, if no one could live beyond the wall, where all your food came from?" She shrugged eloquently. "I wondered."

"That explains something Nat showed me when we first met," said Jakob, thinking of the sideshow. He shook his head. "So many layers of deceit. All to maintain control?"

"Isn't that what those men were all about?" asked Kutri. "Flynn, Schuyler, Dr. Staley? Control?"

"They control nothing now." The observation came in a rumbling growl from the long-silent Mondt. He turned in the driver's seat to look back at Jakob and Kutri. "Control is also a lie."

Through the hours they waited in the abandoned garden park, sheltering in the back of the SUV, Mondt kept watch. Eventually, though, the area around them grew dark and quiet, and they emerged to survey their surroundings. Now, Mondt stood at the back of their little group, refusing to take his eyes off Kutri, while Jakob showed Mitsu how to focus the binoculars. She didn't point the device at the ruined sign, as Kutri had done, but at the fires in the city. The Mulholland lookout offered excellent views of those, too.

"Will it spread?" asked Kutri, after Mitsu had watched for a while. "Will it consume every brick, all the rubbish, every mote of dust?"

"It's a shame," answered Jakob, "but probably not." He put an arm around her shoulders.

Despite his offer of comfort, she shivered. "I fear the loss of life."

Turning to study another part of the city, Mitsu said, "Men are rats."

Kutri shook her head. "That's cruel. In my summers at the Bliss Center, when new girls were bought in markets, I heard them called 'meat' and many other things. I decided, after that, not to call people names."

"I didn't mean to," said Mitsu. "Rats are smart. They know when to run for cover."

"Mitsu," said Kutri, "are you calling us rats?"

Jakob's daughter looked away from the holocaust to give a smile. "We should be so lucky. Yes. Let's be a gang of rats."

"Not a gang," said Jakob. It was too close to a mob . . . or a party of ill-fated revolutionaries.

"What should we be, then?" asked Kutri, leaning against him, her arms around his waist.

He made his smile an echo of the one Mitsu wore, and offered it to each of his companions. "A family. We'll be a family of rats."

They watched the city burn for another hour before they set off for the lands beyond the wall.

About the Author

Blake Rudman enjoyed a former, successful career in executive management, building his own companies from the ground up.

Success or not, Blake's heart has always been in the written word, and the myriad ideas he spent much of his spare time jotting down in notebooks, Post-Its, and scraps of paper whenever the inspiration hit him.

Now a breakout author of five noir thriller novels – all to be published in 2023 – Blake's destiny of becoming a writer of some renown is well under way.

When he's not working diligently on his next novel, Blake spends quality time with his family and tropical fish.

Follow Blake's blog at: https://blakerudman.com
Facebook: @BRudmanThriller
Instagram: @BRudmanThriller
Twitter: @BRudmanThriller

For all Blake's books, visit him at:
www.hellboundbookspublishing.com/authorpage_rudman.html

Blake Rudman Novels from HellBound Books:
Available in Kindle, paperback, hardcover, and audiobook.

The Gentleman's Choice

"Caught in a whirlwind of adverse publicity following a viewer's death, the streaming show, The Gentleman's Choice becomes the target for a sadistic killer – and it's up to PI Vanessa Young to put a stop to it before more young women are murdered."

A sleazy internet dating show blamed for a viewer's death, a host with a dark, secret past, and a killer with a sadistic grudge…

Someone is kidnapping and murdering previous contestants from the popular streaming show *The Gentleman's Choice* – a strictly-for-adults hybrid of *The Bachelor* and *Love Island*. Private Investigator, Vanessa Young, is hired by a victim's family to infiltrate the show as a contestant to expose and capture the killer.

Vanessa and the show's charismatic star, Cole Gianni, begin to fall romantically for each other, until Vanessa's plan goes terribly awry when they're drugged and taken to a remote location to take part in their captor's own brutal, ultimately fatal, version of *The Gentleman's Choice*.

With the clock ticking toward their fateful final night, Vanessa and Cole are forced into a battle of wills to survive their tormentor and escape with their lives before it's too late…

Dark Beauty

Tessa and Kristin Morgan are identical twins, exquisitely beautiful, and have the world at their perfectly pedicured feet; they are also profoundly different beneath their stunning facades.

Tessa is the laser-focused academic with her eyes firmly fixed upon a career in neurology, while Kristin exploits her striking looks and undeniable power over men to carve out a single-minded path to fame and fortune as a model and actress; an ambition she also holds for her sister.

But, on the night of the pair's debut as top-tier models, and with a high-profile movie role in the bag, tragedy strikes the twins in the form of a cruel acid attack by an unknown assailant. Thus, a gruesome chain of events begins - one that leaves a trail of blood, death, and devastation behind both Tessa and Kristin.

As Tessa fights to rebuild her life and uncover the truth behind the attack, she finds herself getting closer and closer to an uncomfortable truth about her sister and her search for the truth turns into a nightmare struggle to stay alive.

"As with *American Psycho*, Blake Rudman's *Goodbye Stranger* has a wealthy, successful man whose wonderful family life masks a much darker side. Throw in a once-trusting, increasingly suspicious wife, and the stage is set for twists and turns you'll never see coming!"

Danielle Harrington has the life many women envy: She's beautiful, rich, has two wonderful children, and is married to *the* Preston Harrington - the handsome, charismatic, retired quarterback who won two Super Bowls.

Unfortunately, something is very wrong with Preston. Having suffered more than his fair share of injuries and concussions, he becomes quiet, withdrawn, and distant. As Preston spends more time away from his family, Danielle begins suspect an affair without realizing her husband is involved in something much, much worse…

Following a series of tragic incidents and the return of an old nemesis from the past, things begin to spiral out of control for Danielle as Preston's dark side puts her and their children in terrible danger.

Redline

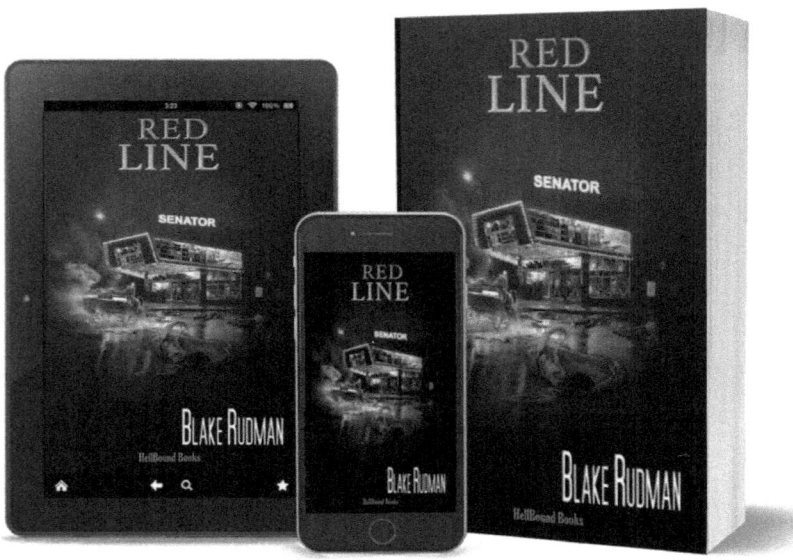

"If Lee Childs' Jack Reacher or Clive Cussler's Dirk Pitt tackled a terrorist scheme that utilized subliminal messaging to sow social and economic chaos on a global scale, it would look a lot like *Red Line*." Baltimore Police Detective Mitch Wilson wants a nice day out with his wife and son. Instead, they are all caught up in a catastrophic terrorist attack that has repercussions across the USA and triggers events that could alter the course of civilization.

Having lost everything, Mitch sets out to seek justice – and revenge and stumbles upon a global conspiracy.

On the other side of the world, renowned linguistic professor, Yasaman Karami, flees her native Iran for the freedom of the west; she holds one of the keys to defeating the terrorist organization.

Yasaman and Mitch's worlds collide as, alongside federal agents and allies, they race against the clock to hunt down the terrorist masterminds and prevent worldwide catastrophe.

Kutri

The Slow Plague, a gender-targeting infection with no cure, killed billions of women and girls worldwide and created a dystopian society in which the survivors are treated as highly valuable commodities.

Although their market value is high, women's rights decline as they become objects of avarice, awe, and worship – possessions to be owned or won in high-stakes games.

Kutri Chandigarh, a rare beauty, is shipped from her native India to Los Angeles, a shattered metropolis barricaded behind a radiation-proof wall. Within the city stronghold, a bleak, broken, male-led society is mesmerized by stupefying programs pumped out by Little Angel Studios: an endless parade of reality TV shows.

The studio's #1 hit is Good Breeding: a bevy of ethnically "pure" young women compete to marry a chosen suitor and produce a "perfect" family under the scrutiny of the public eye.

Kutri has dreamed of wining the competition since early childhood. But, when she arrives in LA and meets Jakob Freeman, her assigned matchmaker, the fantasy quickly turns sour and twists into a horrific nightmare extending far beyond Kutri and the man she chooses for herself.

As Kutri tries to escape the fate she once coveted, Jakob is swept up in events that threaten him body and soul and spark memories of a past he has so desperately tried to forget.

Follow Blake's blog at: https://blakerudman.com
Facebook: @BRudmanThriller
Instagram: @BRudmanThriller
Twitter: @BRudmanThriller

For all Blake's books, visit him at:
www.hellboundbookspublishing.com/authorpage_rudman.html

www.hellboundbookspublishing.com

Milton Keynes UK
Ingram Content Group UK Ltd.
UKHW050256080224
437310UK00006B/159/J